DARLING AT THE CAMPSITE

ALSO BY THE AUTHOR

Thank You, Goodnight: A Novel

A Beginner's Guide to Free Fall

DARLING AT THE CAMPSITE

A NOVEL

ANDY ABRAMOWITZ

LAKE UNION
PUBLISHING

This is a work of fiction. Names, characters, organizations, places, events, and incidents are either products of the author's imagination or are used fictitiously. Any resemblance to actual persons, living or dead, or actual events is purely coincidental.

Published by Lake Union Publishing, Seattle

www.apub.com

ISBN-13: 9781542020145
ISBN-10: 154202014X

Cover design by Kimberly Glyder

Printed in the United States of America

For Mom and Dad

Shipwrecks are *apropos* of nothing.

—*Stephen Crane*

PART ONE

EVERYBODY KNOWS THIS IS NOWHERE

CHAPTER 1

My brother was always gone, but it wasn't until he died that I started dreaming about him. The same dream too, with storms and boats and heartless bodies of water. The first of these dreams arrived the very night after I heard about the boating accident that ended his life. He came to my store, a long yellow kayak tucked under his arm, and tried to coax me onto the river.

"Come out with me," he said.

I would have followed him anywhere. I'd been waiting for an invitation like that since the day he moved away. But I was scared, for both of us.

"There's a monsoon out there," I told him. "You can't take a canoe onto the river."

Holden gave me that look I once knew so well, that mien of benevolent opposition, like he knew better—better than me, better than Mom—and it was a waste of everyone's time trying to convince us. "It's going to be fine, Ro."

"Stay here," I said. "With me."

"Meet me behind the house," he said, undaunted.

I'm frightened, Holden, is what I didn't say, praying I didn't need to, that he'd see it all over my face and that would be enough. "Come on, man. Don't go," I urged him.

But he pushed open the door, and the gathering winds stirred his hair like October leaves. He eyed the cloudbursts boldly and said, "There's never been a better time to fly."

I didn't know what he meant. *There's never been a better time to fly.* I suppose it didn't mean anything, since it was just a dream. But I woke up, pondered it, struggled to make sense of it for days after that. I needed it to mean something. But understanding can take its sweet time. Like my mother used to say, one must wait for the common sense of the morning. She was quoting someone—I want to say H. G. Wells? Dickens maybe? Patti Darling has always relished a good pithy invocation of some nineteenth-century wordsmith, preferably a native of the British Isles, death and Britishness imbuing them with brilliance and quotability. In my mother's presence, even the tamest activity could go south on a dime, and suddenly it's book club. I assume that's life with all English teachers. I used to want to be one, but not that kind.

I wish Holden had listened to me. But he stopped doing that a long time ago and became just someone else who walked away. And I got the message, from him and everyone else. I have learned the virtues of turning your back. And yet, fast asleep each night, I try to save my brother when the terror of his impending end stutters across my eyelids. But even the most surrealistic dreams do not, at heart, stray far from the truth: I never could've talked him out of that boat. The only way I could've done him any good would've been to follow him in.

Common sense is something morning never seems to deliver to my door. Dawns have broken left and right, and here I am, the shape of me still drooping over the counter of this record store that Daisy and I opened, the ink on our college diplomas barely dry, for the fiscally unsound reason that we enjoy listening to music. Liking music is not a business plan. A little common sense might've sorted that out.

Old City is twitching to life the way things do on early autumn days in northeastern towns. Launching Metaphysical Graffiti may have been a costly mistake, but at least we picked the right neighborhood to perpetrate it. Bistros, saloons, boutiques, consignment stores, socially conscious coffee shops, one-man whiskey distilleries—they all thrive on these streets. Except on our block. Here, the foot traffic is but a memory, discouraged by vacant storefronts and an apparently permanent array of dormant construction equipment that has obstructed the sidewalk for as long as we've been open. There's the sneakily off-brand pharmacy (Aid-Rite), the beer store with the intimidatingly posh-sounding name (Cold Beer To Go), and us. Small wonder we can afford the rent. There are those who euphemistically refer to our block as "historic," but not without a mild defensiveness that suggests wishful thinking. "Historic" is, I suppose, better than "deteriorating" or "often smelling of urine."

The front door jingles, and not only does an actual human being walk in, but it's not even Newman, our jelly-bellied mail carrier (no, that's not his real name, although I don't know that for a fact), or even Larry Levin, who owns the art gallery around the corner and who pops in a couple of times a week to see if I want to "partake" (his code for smoking weed). I usually decline, but I guess I accept often enough to keep him asking. Larry can get high whenever he wants because he's fifty-four with an ex-wife and a son at Penn State, so this is basically who Larry is and no one is expecting much to change. I'm thirty-three and poor, so if I pack a bowl before noon on a weekday, I'm "someone to stay away from," a "ne'er-do-well" to the older set. Doesn't mean I won't do it. It just means I won't do it all the time. And I'll feel bad about myself afterward.

Our customer draws my attention not merely because she is just that, a customer (an exotic-bird sighting around here), but also because she's cute. (When we do get a patron, it is generally a malnourished hipster or a slightly overnourished dad, neither a particularly attractive demographic.) Hers is a wholesome beauty, which is sort of my wheelhouse, being native to the Midwest. The siren's call of home: the dirty-blonde locks of a farmer's daughter, cheeks as smooth as a lake frozen over, the apple-green sweater clinging lovingly to her form under a lightweight jacket the color of oatmeal. You can just tell that everyone loves this girl. She's good to her grandma, this one.

Daisy is out on the floor QC'ing the alphabetical integrity of our inventory. As if we'll still be in business on that far-off day when someone gets interested enough in our goulash of CDs, vinyl, cassettes, books, pins, patches, and belt buckles to notice that a Pearl Jam disc was misfiled among the Js. Like Ms. Jam is some alt-country singer whose first name is Pearl.

The comely customer wades up to me, cocks her head, and bites her bottom lip. "You know, you really do have the most wonderful . . ."

Please say *eyes*, please say *eyes*.

". . . display of concert posters up on the wall."

"Mm. My favorite part of the store," I say. (I would've said that about the waste bucket in order to agree with her.) Then I make sure she sees the dreamy gaze I cast upon that wall, as if to imply that each poster bears a story I only partially remember, each tale taking place in a desert or in Rio and lasting an entire weekend. I have no such stories. The posters come from a warehouse in Cherry Hill.

The woman rolls out a red carpet of a smile, sweet yet kooky, and I didn't see kooky coming, not from her, and now I like her even more, but something drops inside me because I know women like this never like me. Many types of women don't like me. Daisy often opines that this is because I don't make it clear enough that I'm interested in being liked, and although that may be undercooked, cornball, *Dawson's Creek*–caliber advice, she does have a point. After all, I wonder how clear I made it back when we first met that I was very interested in being very liked by her.

The customer shops, Daisy organizes, and I withdraw behind the counter to kill a few minutes in my Facebook scroll, see what my "friends" are offering the world today, the folly and self-promotion, the humblebrags and straight-up conceited brags, the political grandstanding and the Sharing Without Borders. There will be a warped expectation that we should all "like" someone's father's stroke or a screenshot of a Peloton ranking or the rundown of a medical chart. ("Arthur's colonoscopy went fine, just a few polyps!") And there I go, liking them all despite myself, even offering comment on Arthur's small intestine. ("Glad the coast is clear!") This is the small way in which I register on the great conveyor belt of connectivity, reaching out to the world from behind the safe digital veil.

And of course there's the compulsory peek into the life of festivity, felicity, fulfillment, and fitness being lived by Margot Beckett, my original midwestern beauty. It's a yoga pic today. I almost don't look at it. Every day I almost don't look at it. There she is, in a ring of substantially identical blonde mommies, their well-attended figures hugged by Lycra, their palms pressed together in front of their chests, like it's, *Ready, ladies? Namaste on three!* Every time I wing past one of Margot's posts, I kick myself for accepting my ex-girlfriend's friend request. She sent it years ago, I accepted, then waited for the private message that never came. Like I'm not her first kiss, first sex, first stayed-up-all-night-to-catch-the-sunrise, first everything. The guy with whom she made all kinds of plans. The future father of her children. The man who, someday after we'd done it all, would either widow or bury her.

"So after all that, nothing?" Daisy is saying to me now.

I look up. "What nothing?"

"She bought nothing."

"Who?" I ask.

"Who? How many customers have we had? That girl you leered at so hard, she needs a pregnancy test."

I scan the room. Daisy and I are alone. "She must've left."

"Well, gee, Rowan, before she left, did she happen to put back the hundred bucks' worth of merchandise she was holding?"

I stare lamely back at Daisy. "She wouldn't."

"Wouldn't she?"

There must be some mistake. She was so into me. She'd found me alluringly musky and charcoal (having whiffed the brand-new deodorant flavor I'd painted onto my pits this morning). She'd already pictured me in her pillowy den, already smelled the Sunday morning bacon and maple pancakes I would fix for her on our kitchen island. She was finally going to be the one, the one who allowed me to move on.

"You got pantsed in your own store," Daisy says. "You're a sucker." It's more of a diagnosis than an insult.

"I fall for things," I muse.

"See, this is what I'm talking about," she says, and I don't know what she means, but nonetheless her point is well-taken.

"Have we ever had a theft before?" I wonder aloud.

"Not a thwarted one," Daisy says tightly. "And the record still stands."

CHAPTER 2

Elton is belting out "Levon" with grievous gusto, and no one's even listening. It's just me and *Madman across the Water*, a record I played to hell and back in tenth grade and put on this afternoon to see if I'm still sick of it, but I'm not really paying attention. I'm preoccupied with trying to help Rose, a total stranger in Massachusetts, whose girlfriend has the makings of a drinking problem and, lost for the right words with which to broach the delicate subject, is betting ten bucks that I can put those words in her mouth so that she can speak them.

Daisy breezes in from a late lunch and scoots onto the counter to check her email. Within seconds, she's hissing, groaning, and emitting other unhappy noises, which culminate in a succinct declaration I've heard from her before:

"I hate insurance."

"I know," I say.

"No. Like, seriously—hate."

"Yeah. I know."

It's monthly statement day. We go through this every month.

"Let me get this straight," she goes on. "I'm not allowed to legally drive a car unless I send State Farm a hundred and twenty bucks every single month to cover an accident that hasn't happened and may never happen. Isn't that the definition of *fascism*?"

"No, I think it's the definition of *insurance*," I reply.

As a general rule, accidents happen; more to the point, they happen to Daisy. All the time. She dents her Mazda with such frequency that it would not surprise me to learn that State Farm has a stand-alone Daisy Pham Division with a half dozen designated adjusters who do nothing but manage Daisy-related claims all day long. I assume the outrage of the moment is due to yet another premium hike thanks to some recent vehicular dustup, another black mark on a driving record that isn't so much spotty as it is outright lawless.

My partner rages on, progressively likening insurance premiums to income tax, the draft, and inevitably, McCarthyism, and I lend her one ear while the rest of me wonders what to recommend to Rose, my customer who needs to carefully suggest to her girlfriend that her chronic consumption of alcohol is becoming a problem in their relationship. Per the terms and conditions of Help!INeedSomebody.com, a website that, for reasons still unclear to me, exists (I am the owner and operator, although Daisy is the dreamer-upper and concocter), I'm contractually obligated to deliver said recommendation within twenty-four hours or she gets her ten bucks back. Rose has been helpful with context, alerting me to the fact that her girlfriend has an alcoholic father, a thus far harmless but increasingly higher-stakes gambling addiction, and a temper to beat the band. She's quite a catch. Then again, who am I to throw stones at someone's inability to let go of things—humans included—that may not be good for them? I live in a big old glass house in the Not Letting Go neighborhood.

Daisy is eyeing me with impatience, like why haven't I solved car insurance.

"I don't know what to tell you," I say. "Stay in your lane? Signal before turning?"

Whereas I can forgo the expense of wheels, since my entire existence is lived within walking distance of itself and I don't have the time suck of family in the area, Daisy lacks the luxury of immobility. She has gigs to get to, relatives in absurd multitudes in and around Philly. She has what they call "a life."

Daisy's tirade ends, as it always does, with a funds transfer in the amount of an ever-escalating monthly premium, and she turns her attention to the sound system. Elton is rudely silenced. Yo-Yo Ma's jaunty cello fills the store.

"Does this have to happen?" I ask. It sounds like we're between segments on NPR.

I have nothing against classical music. It's just that I can't imagine it does our enterprise any favors. I'm not saying we need to be playing Stone Temple Pilots or The Flying Burrito Brothers. It can be Twenty One Pilots or The Flying Jonas Brothers. It can be some hip-hop artist with an intentionally misspelled name. (Sub out the *s*, sub in a *z*.) It can be some testiculess Coldplay ballad that makes me want to smack Chris Martin but also drop down next to him on a sofa and tell him my problems. I just think that in the unlikely event of a customer, it's better for all parties concerned if we're playing something edgier than Elgar's Cello Concerto in E Minor. The problem is, Yo-Yo is Daisy's homework.

Daisy is a classically trained and breathlessly booked cellist, with seats saved for her in chamber orchestras and string quartets all over town. She is also one of the most captivating performers I have ever witnessed—and I've seen Ozzy. Whenever I'm free, and I'm always free, I follow her to whatever theater, concert hall, church, coffeehouse, tearoom, or outdoor amphitheater, and I sit next to her boyfriend, a towering mountain of a creature called Chili, and I soak up her playing in true helpless awe. I stare at her in that black dress she always wears, her hair fluttering over her face, that diamond nose ring twinkling in the spotlight, and I marvel at the sounds she conjures by the mere act of scraping bow hair against string. Sometimes she plays her cello so mournfully smooth, so rich with melancholy, that I feel terribly alone in the world, and it's all I can do not to heave myself into Chili's lap and beg him to hold me. Other times, her playing is so tense, so bracingly choppy, that I become frantic to rush out and accomplish all the goals and dreams I've ever set for myself and seem well on my way to abandoning. *I could be a writer!* is what I tell myself in those moments. *A novelist! A war correspondent! An essayist on the human condition! I am all of those things, I just have to prove it!* Like doing it—actually writing something—is the easy part.

I'm a little jealous of Daisy. I don't necessarily wish I played the cello, but I do wish I played the proverbial cello. I guess I never felt strongly enough about being a writer, or a teacher, or anything else. I took a couple of writing classes as an undergrad, dabbled in a workshop or two, but always felt insincere, like I was filling the page with someone else's thoughts, telling someone else's stories, perhaps because I was fearful of exploring my own. Sometimes I ask myself about that proverbial cello: *What, Rowan Darling, do you feel strongly about, other than a woman you cannot have and a store you should not have?* Metaphysical Graffiti, this deserted museum, this shrine to a finished period in history when music retail was a thing, is all I've got. I love this place, but it's stupid.

I also have that website, but that's stupid too.

"I met my sister for lunch, btw," Daisy volunteers. "Please don't make a thing out of it." (She says "btw," by the way; I'm not abbreviating for her.)

"Which sister?" I ask. It's a reasonable question. She has, like, eight.

"Victoria."

I stare at her a beat. "I see."

The "thing" I'm not supposed to make a thing out of is that this particular sibling is on a ruthless crusade to poach Daisy from me, lure her away to more stable employment. Victoria (who, btw, is a self-centered, insufferable mess, literally the worst Pham out there) is some sort of manager at some sort of tech company out in some sort of suburb, and rare is the week when she doesn't remind Daisy that a desk and a paycheck are hers for the taking out there. It's obnoxious, intrusive, and patronizing, but to be absolutely clear, I wish my brother had done that for me. Had Holden tried just once to bail me out of here and into one of the rye distilleries or payment processing start-ups or youth sports organizations he noodled around in, I'd have given Daisy my notice on the spot.

"Did she offer you a job again?" I ask.

Daisy sighs three-dimensionally. "I can't go through this with you every time I get a burrito with my sister."

I cock my head. "But you brought it up."

She looks at me from the Yo-Yo Ma sheet music she's following along with but already knows by heart, then gazes about the store in that pensive, slightly restless way that comes upon her after every meal with Victoria. Her eyes land on me, probing me as though she's wondering why I'm not homeless, and although it's demeaning to be sized up that way, it's not an unfair thing for her to be pondering. I am, after all, probably pre-homeless. I'm not like Daisy, who has marketable abilities and talent in spades, or Greg, our one employee (part-time at that), who has a mélange of gigs through which he scrapes together hand-to-mouth solvency. The Graffiti is it for me, the soggy basket that bears all my eggs.

"You know, Daisy, I'm doing my best here."

"You know, Rowan, I certainly hope not. Because you're really not doing much of anything. Except waiting. You're waiting for unlimited, instantaneous online availability of every song ever to simply fall out of favor, like leg warmers or mood rings. And it won't. And it shouldn't."

"I get it. You don't think we're too big to fail," I joke.

"We're precisely the right size to fail. We might actually be too small to succeed."

Daisy isn't smiling, not even maliciously, which would be comforting. Unsettlingly absent is the playfulness upon which her words ride whenever we trash our own enterprise.

"What are you saying? You want to fold up shop?" I ask.

"I'm saying our lease is up next summer, and we need to make some hard decisions." She sighs. "Look, I love record stores too. My dad used to take me with him to buy his jazz albums at this tiny hole-in-the-wall in West Philly. It was gritty and grimy, and they were always playing something thrilling and alive. *A Love Supreme*, *Bitches Brew*, *Head Hunters*. The store isn't there anymore, which isn't even my point. My point is that it was a special experience for me, and I wanted to re-create that, here, with you. I knew we weren't going to get rich, but being rich is one of the last things I want to be. I just figured it would be fun to work in a record store. Which it has been. More or less. And I figured it would be fun to work with one of my best friends. Which it has been. More or less."

I clear my throat. "A deeply touching story, really, but in future tellings, kindly include the part about how I'm the one busting his ass around here. I'm not saying you do nothing, but I do everything. I'm the one constantly updating our social media outlets with 'news.' I'm the one who came up with Vintage Vinyl Fridays, Midnight Madness, Rowan Serves Soup Day, Shop Naked Day—which I'm still waiting for you to come around to. I'm the one trying to bring in the Wright Brothers, a real live band with real live fans who will pack this place with monied youngsters. And I'm doing all of this despite the mounds of shit I get from Greg for selling out, for aspiring to be something other than an impoverished purist. Which is ironic, because I'm the only one around here who's actually impoverished."

Daisy sighs. "Rowan—I'm not saying you're not open to new ideas. I'm just saying they don't work."

I honestly don't know what I would do if we shuttered this store. I lack—what's the right word?—skills. I couldn't get a desk job; I hate desks. I hate action items and elephants in the room. I even hate footnotes. Once upon a time, I could see myself in a classroom, pontificating about Melville and the Brontës (that is, after a necessary refresher period), but I don't know where that classroom is anymore. Closing Metaphysical Graffiti would be like being cast out of Eden all over again, and how many times must one man endure that? Yes, I jumped at the chance to open this joint because it was Daisy who was asking. But it was also a music store, and just like Gravedancer Records, where I worked as a teenager back in Maybee, the sleepy Illinois whistle-stop where I grew up, it's what makes home feel like home. That's why I'm always dreaming up cute little pet names for this place. Noise "R" Us. The Vinyl Frontier. No, We Don't Have That Records. Bed Bath & Beyoncé.

"Look," I say to Daisy, "our business is like licorice."

"Oh, good Christ on a bike. I can't listen to the licorice thing again."

"Hear me out. I hate black licorice, you hate black licorice, everybody hates black licorice. Except for the tiny segment of the population that doesn't. And they buy the shit out of licorice."

"But, you see, they wouldn't if they had an all-you-can-eat licorice plan, and they could have any flavor of licorice whenever they wanted, and they could eat brand-new licorice by their favorite licorice maker as soon as it came out, and they could eat old licorice, the kind they ate in high school, or the licorice that reminds them of the road trip they took when they were twenty or of that week they were snowed in with their boyfriend. If they had every variety of licorice on their phones and tablets and computers all the time, they wouldn't buy any licorice. Ever." She pauses for air. "That's why it's not like licorice. Your licorice thing is stupid."

"Music isn't the licorice, Daisy. The experience of going to a store and buying music—that's the licorice."

"I don't have the bandwidth for this. I can't listen—for the gajillionth time—about pimply nimrods who go gaga over album jackets, liner notes, and limited editions, who fork over an entire paycheck for some crappy demo from 1977 by a band with an umlaut in its name. If these nimrods exist, they aren't forking over jack dick in this store."

Daisy knows she's breaking my heart. This is not the breakup talk, but it is the talk people have a month or two before the breakup talk and then look back on and go, *I should've seen this coming.*

And that gets me thinking about Chili and how I know he's planning to ask Daisy to marry him, and how when he does—tomorrow, next week, next month—Daisy is at least as likely as not to accept. So yes, change, in all its surly forms, is finally on the wind. And if you see something coming, you can't later say, *I should've seen this coming.*

Daisy does that thing where she juts out her lower lip and puffs a stream of air that blows up her bangs. "Look. It's not that I don't see you sulking like a brat. I just really need to go home and get ready for my show. You know that's tonight, right? The South Street thing."

"Yes."

"Are you're coming?"

"I don't know," I say, putting my fingers to my face and wearily disarranging the flesh around my eyes. "I don't think so."

Daisy fixes a stern look on me. "I'm going to ask you one more time."

"Fine. I'll be there." I look at her, already missing what I have not yet lost. "You know, Daisy, it's not my fault I don't play the cello."

"Well." She shrugs. "Whose fault is it?" And on her way out the door, she slaps me hard on the ass to show we're still friends.

I now know what to tell Rose.

It is a peculiar phenomenon that lures people to Help!INeedSomebody.com, people who have never met me and have no reason to enlist my judgment, much less act upon it, much less spend their hard-earned cash on it, so that I might supply them with a few spot-on words to get them through their most awkward, painful, cringe-inducing, high-stakes conversations. But not the least peculiar part of it is that even if I am rarely able to utter those spot-on words when such situations arise in my own life, rarely do I not know what those words should be. So—

Hi, Rose,

Thanks for your inquiry. I suggest saying this to your girlfriend: "The first thing I want you to know is that I'm not going to leave you. I will stand beside you. But you have to continue to be worthy of that. I'm worried about you, and I can't be worried about you without being worried about us."

Say that. Then suggest a twelve-step program.

I hope I Help!ed. (If I did, please Yelp!)

Rowan D.

Chili saves me a seat at the play. No one asked him to. He just assumes I'm coming and places his program on the chair next to him, an entirely unnecessary move, since no one would dare take a seat within Chili's wingspan without his express permission. At six two, with a shaved head and alpine delts, he resembles one of those adrenaline junkies who flies off to New Zealand with his bros to get their BMX on with GoPros strapped to their foreheads. Should Chili ever suspect that occasionally I have sex with his girlfriend, he could drop gloves on me something ugly.

It doesn't happen often, sex with Daisy. Quarterly, I would say. As long as I've known her, she has had a significant other who is not me—these past few years it's been Chili; before him, Peter; and before him, two stints with Joshua separated by one stint with Serena—yet through it all, Daisy takes the occasional leap over the gerrymandered fault line in our relationship that evidently abides a physical interlude. I can't be expected to decline sex with someone so good at it.

By the time the house lights go down, nearly every seat in the cramped, creaky South Street theater is filled. The audience demographic is basically me and better-educated me. Black-rimmed-frames me. Ibsen-reading me. Grad students on group dates, young professionals home for Rosh Hashanah and antsy to get away from their mothers for a couple of hours.

The curtain rises, and immediately I can tell we're in the world of a shoestring budget. The set is minimalist to the point of being abstract, and the score is supplied by one lone instrument. Like a character in the play, Daisy sits astride her cello, off to the side of the stage, her elegant strings a steady presence throughout, at turns winsome, at turns wistful.

The play is called *Goners*, and it tells the story of a recently widowed professor and his son, a college sophomore. As they struggle to cope with the death of the woman of the house, the professor decides they could both use a change of scenery, so he arranges to teach at a university in Scotland for a semester and brings along his grieving child. The son exhausts a preponderance of his stage time petulantly griping about missing New York—that is, until he starts receiving the affections of a beautiful Glaswegian redhead. Then his whining miraculously abates. (The redhead's attempt at a Scottish accent was one of the play's distractions, unless it was an acting choice to sound like an old woman from Alabama gargling salt.) As the semester draws to a close and the son faces another loss—having to leave behind this fire-haired lass with whom he is utterly smitten—he falls to pieces in front of his old man outside the university bookstore.

"I love her, Dad," the poor lad sobs.

"I see," says the father, looking surprised. He was unaware it had come to this. "I suppose that changes things, doesn't it? Maybe we should stick around another semester, you and I."

The boy looks up, his face dripping. "You'd do that for me?"

"Of course, son. How could you think I wouldn't?"

Daisy's sweetly bowed strings rise in a climactic swell, and all at once, it seems as though the entire audience has come down with a cold. Quiet sniffling sweeps through the aisles, hands wipe at damp eyes, and in the seat next to me, Chili is a blubbering puddle.

As for me, I just don't know where to begin on that front, so I don't. Families are murky, impenetrable ponds. I never met my own father. He departed this world at the precise moment I was screaming my way into it. Patti was in labor with her second child when her husband, George, a CPA with a dauntingly well-documented family history of unwelcome cardiac events, suffered a massive heart attack out in the waiting room where he was standing guard over my five-year-old brother, Holden. Minutes later, on an operating table just down the hall, my dad's thirty-three-year-old heart thumped its final beat. The catastrophic blow cost Patti a husband, but as compensation it rewarded her with a brassy quip she has trotted out on innumerable occasions: "George died in childbirth." No one ever laughs.

The show ends. Everyone turns on their phones to see what they've missed over the past two hours, and Chili stands and holds up a bouquet of red roses. "I'm going to go find her backstage," he tells me. "Meet us outside. We'll go for a drink."

"Nah. You two go."

He looks surprised that I have declined, as I so rarely do.

"It's her night. Go celebrate it," I tell him.

"She was pretty amazing, wasn't she?"

"Yes," I say. "She is."

Among the herd of theatergoers I move, spilling out with them onto the sidewalk where the ambivalent air of a September night cools my lungs. On the walk home I invent a version of my father and stand him up against the father in the play. I would like to believe that George

Darling was the kind of man who would've held over in a foreign country, who would've stayed if leaving would've caused his son a broken heart. I can pretend that my dad would've stood behind me, that he would've believed in me and I in him, and in that way made me more sure-footed in this world. But it would really come in handy if I knew for sure.

CHAPTER 3

The next morning, Patti calls to tell me about my brother.

It's an odd time for her to call, as she should be in class, but when I answer and don't hear her voice all echoey in the blunt linoleum and cinder block of the public school, I know she's home. I can taste the bad news on the back of my tongue.

"Rowan, I'm calling about Holden."

That's all she needs to say to get every muscle in my body clenching. My heart rattles into a gallop before she has even said it. It is as though I already know.

"There was an accident," she says, unnervingly even. "He's gone, honey."

A moment drips by, slow, thick like tree sap. "No," I say.

"It was a boating accident."

I can't feel my feet. They've fallen away, down some dark well, miles below my legs now. So I grope for questions, because answers will root me.

"Where?"

"Colombia."

"South Carolina?"

"South America."

"South America?" For some reason, nailing down the geography is key. "Drugs?"

"No, Rowan. Just an accident."

I don't quite know how to process what I'm hearing. Standing at the counter of my store in downtown Philadelphia, a world away from my mother, three times that distance from my brother, I can't picture Holden's drowned body floating in the waters of South America. I see only the kid who used to sleep in the next room. I can't picture that boy as a dead man.

"Are you sure?" I ask.

"Yes."

"Are they sure?"

"They're sure."

Another moment passes, flies off, never to be seen again.

"Rowan, honey? Are you okay?"

"Well," I begin. "Are you okay?"

"Yes, I am okay," she answers, sounding eerily composed. You never know what's going to rile up my mom, but I certainly would've thought this would do it. Then again, after all the brushback pitches life has thrown at her, perhaps she's decided she'll react however she damn well pleases, thank you very much. Sadness has sunk as deep as it can go into her pores. Piss her off, and she might throw a shoe at you. She might also walk away in silence.

I ask how she learned the news. (I literally don't know a soul who populates Holden's life, so I can't fathom who might've sent word.) She tells me that she got a call from a friend of his, a girlfriend possibly, who was with him in Cartagena where it happened. "Layla or Lulu or Lala—something bohemian and ridiculous," she says, like the frivolousness of the name of Holden's final companion is yet another symptom of his capricious and fugitive lifestyle.

"You're going to come home, aren't you?" she asks me.

"Of course, Mom."

The stilted, sterile air on this phone line is beginning to freak me out. Somebody should be hysterical. I feel close to hysterical; I can smell it, I can hear it rattling the fence, but at the same time, I feel safe from it, like the fence is high.

"Do you want me to call anyone?" I ask.

"No. Just book your flight. I spoke with the US consulate. It could be a day or so before they release him."

"When did you speak with the consulate?"

"Last night."

"Last night?"

"Yes. Right after I got the call from that woman. Kiki, Koko, whatever the hell."

"Wait. You knew last night and didn't call me?"

"It was late, Rowan."

"It was late?"

"Why are you repeating everything I say in question form and louder?"

"Because you found out my brother died, and instead of calling me, you called around to the various branches of government; then you slept on it, woke up, made yourself some tea, and finally decided to loop me in. All of that happened. In sequence."

"I'm sorry," Patti says. "People came over as soon as they heard. I got a little distracted, and by then it was late."

"Well, I certainly wouldn't want you to neglect your guests," I shoot back. "Call your son when the cocktail party peters out."

"Rowan."

It infuriates me that I'm an afterthought in my own family tragedy, that I've dropped so low on the call sheet, and a mad impulse to heave my phone seizes me. A messy clump of concert T-shirts awaiting hangers presents itself as a safe landing spot. I wind up and pitch. It's a fastball, a strike right down the middle. It hits the shirts with a dull puff. I cannot ascertain whether or not I feel any better.

From across the room, my mother's voice, mouselike through the tinny speaker: "Hello? Rowan? Are you there? Hello!"

I stomp over and pluck the device from the nest of black cotton. "Yes. I'm here."

"What just happened?"

"I threw the phone."

"What? Why did you throw the phone?"

"No reason."

We both sigh in unison. Hers reminds me of my childhood. I heard that sigh a lot after Holden left, both because he was gone and because I was still there.

It is decided I'll fly out tomorrow. Patti hasn't called the funeral home yet—at least I rank above the undertaker—but she knows it'll take a couple of days to transport Holden home. It'll be good to have me around when the body arrives, she tells me, and to help out with the funeral arrangements.

It is when she refers to her son as "the body" that her voice catches, and she finally starts to sound like a woman who has lost her child. It is a surreal moment I am spinning through right now, as my mother has never really cried before and my brother has never died before, and I feel like the world's worst son for not knowing that this day was coming and moving home to sit and wait for it by my mother's side.

"Do you remember when he tried to hang your bikes in the garage?" Patti says, a non sequitur, if there is such a thing in moments like these, because right now it feels like everything is apropos of everything.

"What?"

"He got it into his head that bikes should be up on the wall," she recalls. "He hammered in a couple of nails, then went up on a ladder and hung your bikes. You don't remember this?"

I remember all of Holden's weekend capers. "Of course I do. They fell."

"They fell on my head!" Patti hoots.

I am laughing now, ambivalent about this moment being suitable for laughter but so relieved to hear that sound bouncing between us on the line. "You were so mad."

"Well, sure, I was mad. It was my head, for god's sake." She laughs a little, though not hard and desperate sounding like I do. Then, softly, resignedly, I hear her say, "This hurts way more."

"It's going to be okay, Mom," I tell her. "I'll be there soon. We're going to get through this together."

I wait for her to hang up, but she doesn't.

"Are you still there?" she asks.

"I'm still here."

"Ro?"

"Yeah?"

"Do you think your father knows?"

Patti has never been one for the religious. It's not an anger or resentment thing; she's not annoyed at God for the seemingly arbitrary cruelties she's endured. She's just always been more enamored with the philosophical than the spiritual, philosophy being something that could be found in books that one could open and shut at one's pleasure. But in the most traumatic moment of her life, if my mother wants to have a whirlwind romance with the separability of the soul from the physical body, far be it from me to piss all over it—even if my first instinct is to tell her that I don't think my father has known anything in thirty-three years.

"I think he probably does," I say.

"Do you really?"

"Yes."

She sniffs. "I'll see you tomorrow, honey," and we hang up.

The store feels emptier now without my mother's voice in it, and farther away from home than it's ever seemed. A sudden panic rises up inside me. I crave Daisy's presence. I want to call one of my friends and make plans to meet up. I want Larry Levin to materialize in those flip-flops and that pink tracksuit that makes him look like a wad of Bubble Yum and ask me to partake. Stronger than anything, though, is a surprise impulse, swooping in from somewhere in the deep, hollow past, that makes me want to call Skid.

Skidmore Hall Jr.: my best friend since I first had friends. A constant, unshakable companion, my witness to everything. He was always there, walking home with me after football practice, coming inside to play video games and charm Patti into helping him with his English homework, then staying for dinner, emptying his plate, and accepting seconds. When Friday night arrived, he would sleep over and often still be there come Sunday, even though he had a bed of his own and a perfectly good pair of parents right down the street. Patti was always happy to have him around, even more poignantly vocal about it after Holden left, for she was grateful, as I was, to have another noisemaker in the house to take my brother's place. The years drop away now in this outrageous, unaccountable moment that Patti has just sprung upon me, and I am dangerously close to letting go of everything, forgiving Skid his crimes and betrayals, his theft of the woman I loved, his occupation of the town I called home, just so I can hear his voice. But Skid married the girl I was supposed to marry. Which is why I haven't called him in fifteen years. And why I won't call him today.

A middle-aged man has somehow made it through the door and all the way to the counter without my noticing. When I finally do, I can practically feel my irises constrict with focus upon him.

"Hey, man," he says. When a thinning-haired forty-year-old enters a record store, dollar to a dime, he's going to call me "man" or "dude" or, regrettably for both of us, "bro."

"Crazy question: I've got this old Goo Goo Dolls song stuck in my head. It was a huge hit back when I was in school. I can't seem to find it."

"How does it go?" I ask.

He proceeds to sing. It is a professional hazard that people sing to me all the time. Not that I'm one to be a critic (I sound like a girl when I sing, and no, I don't mean a woman), but until I started working at a record store, I never appreciated how much of the gen pop suffers from stage-four tone deafness, an incurable condition readily diagnosable in this particular gentleman as he stares awkwardly into my eyes and delivers a tentative, mumbly, monotone rendition of a song that is not by the Goo Goo Dolls.

"That's the Spin Doctors," I tell him. "'Two Princes.'"

"No shit."

"None whatsoever," I say. I love how people just believe me, like I have a degree or something.

He goes "Huh" and smiles fondly as though he's just been yanked back into some debauched memory. "I could've sworn it was the Dolls."

It's not, I want to tell him. *And nobody calls them "the Dolls," so kindly refrain from doing so in my store.*

"Spin Doctors," he says. "Now that's a criminally underrated band."

Okay, one, that's just not true, and two, why is everything that's underrated *criminally* underrated? Can't some things just be plain old underrated?

In the middle of this conversation—perhaps because this conversation wouldn't be happening if it weren't for Holden, my love of music having been born in my brother's bedroom—I'm whacked upside the head by the realization that Holden has exited this world. The world should have more room in it now, and yet it feels stiflingly smaller for all the love he takes with him. His love of people, of things. They are all less wanted now. He leaves all his favorite songs in the care of other ears who won't prize them in quite the same way. It's now my job to love "Psycho Killer" a little harder, to love "Once in a Lifetime" and "Sugar Mountain" and "Comes a Time" and all those other Talking Heads and Neil Young songs.

"It's on *Pocket Full of Kryptonite*," I tell the man. "Pretty sure we've got a copy."

He nods. "Cool. Good to know. Thanks, bro."

I can still remember how Holden would crank up "Rockin' in the Free World," come bursting into my room, wailing on his air guitar, howling the chorus. I'd join in, and he'd yell "You suck!" so I'd yell "Get out!" but he'd know I didn't mean it, and we'd keep singing, and sometimes Patti would come marching down the hall and tell us to keep the racket down, but she didn't mean it either, because this kind of racket was welcome here, this was the plan. If only George were there to see it.

The customer, moseying toward the door, does not care whether or not we have a copy of that Spin Doctors album. Most days, the brazenness really irritates me, how unabashedly these people waltz in here with no intention of dropping a penny, treat me like I'm some outdated search engine, then waltz out to go stream, download, or otherwise steal the song. But today I'm just relieved to see him go.

In the renewed silence, I am unable to shake my mother's question. *Do I think my father knows about Holden?* George spent five fewer years on the planet than Holden did. He's been dead for precisely the number of days I've been alive. I told her I believed my dad did know, and I think she knew I was lying, but was I? Maybe word of his son's passing has somehow reached him, wherever he is. Maybe my dad has been watching over all of us and was on that boat in Cartagena and watched the end come for his elder son. Perhaps my father has aged in death and is a sixty-eight-year-old ghost, or maybe he hasn't and is stuck in time, and thirty-three-year-old George Darling is at this very moment taking his thirty-eight-year-old freshly dead boy by the hand and saying, *Everything's going to be all right. Walk with me, kiddo. I'll show you.*

None of that would make any sense, at least not to me, but since when has this world shown the slightest interest in making sense to its tiny, myopic inhabitants? It would certainly make no sense for Holden to be outside my store right now, but that is exactly what I believe. He is out there. I feel it. Strutting past the Graffiti in his Harley-Davidson leather jacket with the badass eagle on the back. *Remember that jacket, Holden? You'd never ridden a motorcycle in your life, which you freely admitted to anyone who asked, you fearless motherfucker. And still you pulled it off.* The window of seconds in which I could storm out, catch the miracle of him, and debunk these exaggerated reports of his demise has collapsed, and I missed it.

I don't care how little sense any of that makes. I can choose to believe all of it. That my brother really did just walk by, and my dad was with him, and they're headed off somewhere, and one day they'll be back for my mom, and then one day for me.

CHAPTER 4

Daisy flies in around lunchtime. The sight of her, her hair in tight antennae-like pigtails as if she's being remote-controlled, brings a flush of gratitude to my cheeks for the burst of life she brings. She stows her bag behind the counter while dispensing a mild chiding at me for disappearing after the show last night. I mumble a vague excuse about having been tired, although last night feels like a century ago, and I cannot relate to any state of mind I might've had in that bygone era of history before The Call.

Daisy takes a greedy gulp of water from her S'well bottle and wipes her lips with the back of her hand. She asks me what I thought of the play, and I lower my eyes to the blue ballpoint pen that my fingers are absently capping and uncapping, because I can't put my mind on a play in which sons bare their naked, aching souls to their fathers, and fathers change everything on a dime, saying, *Yes, of course, I'll help, I'm right here.* So instead, I look Daisy in the face, and in an almost apologetic tone—like I feel bad ruining her day—I say: "Get this: my brother died."

She freezes. "What?"

"Yeah. My mom just called."

"'Get this'? Are you joking?"

"No," I say. "Yeah, no, I'm not joking."

Her eyes bulge out. "Fuck, Rowan." There's a moment of frail stillness in the room, after which she lurches toward me and wraps her arms bear-tight around my torso. "Oh my god." She pulls back to gape at me like maybe she doesn't believe it. "This is for real?"

"Yeah."

And then she's back to hugging me. "Fuck. Are you okay?"

"I think so."

"I'm so sorry, baby." Daisy has never called me "baby" before, and the shelter that that word implies, coupled with the fixedness with which she is holding me, feels wonderfully unsinkable. I am okay.

Then come the questions. Lots of them. Daisy needs to know every detail. Okay, it happened in Colombia, but *where* in Colombia? What kind of boat was it? Was it dark out? What was the weather like? And it dawns on me that this investigative line of questioning is not really about Holden; it's about the hypothetical death of Victoria or one of those other non-Victoria sisters, a sibling with whom she has spent countless hours and had scores of screaming matches, birthday parties, and gossip sessions: a life lived together. She thinks that's what I'm experiencing, and although it's what I want to be experiencing, it's not. The death of my brother is very nearly the death of a close friend who had a lead role a long time ago in my youth, before other projects or perhaps a contract dispute with the studio boss relegated him to bit-part or special-appearance status.

After Daisy has run out of questions and I've told her all I know, she asks, "Do you want to talk?"

I thought that's what we'd been doing. I was kind of hoping that part was over.

"Do you want to get out of here and go make phone calls? Walk around and process?"

"No," I say to all of it. What I want is to stay right here and immerse myself in business as usual, reckon with that unsightly volcano of concert shirts on the floor, wait for Greg to clock in and strike up one of our pretentious, depressingly clichéd conversations. Like when "Third Stone from the Sun" comes on and Greg says he wishes he were Jimi Hendrix, and though I try to resist, I have no choice but to tell him he's ridiculous for wishing he were someone who died at the age of twenty-seven, and he says it's ridiculous *not* to wish you were Jimi Hendrix, and I point out (in vain) that you don't have to be Jimi Hendrix to enjoy Jimi Hendrix. I mean, think of it, Greg, you have been able to groove on *Are You Experienced* for much longer than Jimi himself ever did, so who cares if you didn't actually make it? And then Greg gives me one of his condescending smirks and tells me I just don't understand the soul of a poet, and I very nearly slug him, but instead I suggest that if he really wants to change places with a rock star, he should go be Ringo Starr, because not only did Ringo not die at twenty-seven, he was a Beatle, and he married the hottest Bond girl ever and thus wins at being a human being, and at last Greg offers me a smile of concession and says something like, "Well, you got me there," but then he adds, "I now see why they pay you the big bucks," and because he knows I get paid almost no bucks, I am back to wanting to slug him. Every day I'm drawn into miserable shit like that, and I always hate myself for it, but on a day like today, when the world coils itself like a cobra and fangs me in the face, at least there's here, this place, where I understand everything.

"I want to stay here," I tell Daisy. "I might roll out a little early to pack, but this is where I want to be." I stare off through the window at the blunt light of the outside world, my view obstructed by taped-up rock posters and album-release one sheets. "Where else would I go?"

"I can come with you, you know," she says.

"Thanks. You don't have to help me pack."

"No. To Illinois."

I stare at her. "You want to be my plus-one at my brother's funeral?"

The unflinching look on her face tells me her offer is sincere. She would really do it despite all the inconveniences: the airfare, the flight, the crashing in the guest room, the staying up late to keep my mom company, the sipping of weak kitchen coffee in the clothes we slept in and with our uncombed hair. Daisy has revealed herself to be the fictional English professor from that play and me the son, because I very nearly say to her, *You'd do that for me?* And if I did, I am certain she would reply, *How could you think I wouldn't?*

So I kiss her.

I grab her face in my hands and kiss her with such greed, such yearning and voraciousness that she's probably thinking I skipped lunch and have mistaken her for a meal. Despite the flicker of hesitation I read on her (traditionally, she is the one who initiates; I am the one who waits around for her to initiate), we are soon groping our way back to the storage room.

Not much is stored in the storage room. It's an airless, musty cave that smells of cardboard and sawdust and is marginally illuminated by a sixty-watt bulb on the end of a pull string. Ratty blue carpeting with prehistoric stains covers most of the cement floor, and an old vinyl beanbag lies slumped like a raisin against the wall. (The beanbag was my brilliant idea, acquired at a consignment shop one day when I suddenly fancied beanbags at our listening stations. It seemed so inspired at the time, a gimmick of retro comfort sure to attract bodies. But Daisy immediately deemed it unworkable and tossed the sad old lima bean back here, where it has remained ever since.) At long last, the beanbag finds its usefulness. Daisy guides me down onto it, stands over me such that I am eye level with the hem of her skirt, and proceeds to slide her baby-blue cotton underwear down her thighs. She kicks the garment over her suede boots, straddles me, and says, her voice dripping with sweet, consoling tenderness: "Can you be fast? We didn't lock up."

Like most guys, I can bang out sex like I'm double-parked. Typically, Daisy prefers things to be involved—acrobatics, minor stunts, superficial wounds, dirty talk, sometimes shockingly dirty talk (sometimes, frankly, excessively dirty talk)—but today she's scaling it back, keeping an eye on the time. She's being gentle with me, believing, I suppose, that the circumstances warrant it. What the circumstances warrant is the opposite: a complete unlocking of Daisy Pham unto me, full access to the deliciousness of the whole of her, this wacky pigtail-sporting girl for whom I'd do anything. She and she alone has the power to slingshot me into the echo and erase my mind, however briefly, of today's towering miseries.

But we're on a tight schedule. So it's pretty by the book. And then it ends.

—

"Are you okay?" Daisy asks.

"I'm uninjured, if that's what you mean."

"No, that's not what I mean."

We are lying there in the greenhouse effect of our exertion, the faux leather of the beanbag clinging to our backs.

"Why do you think we do this?" I ask her.

"Do we have to have the same reasons?" she says.

"Wouldn't it help?"

"Help what?"

I feel her eyes on the side of my face.

"Never mind," I say.

Surely our reasons are not the same. Hers are a mystery to me, given that her boyfriends are always better looking or better built than I am, and if they're not, they're more dazzlingly sophisticated or charmingly bookish. My body type is Target: a feast of unexceptionalism and reliability, everything in all the right places, nothing fancy or particularly memorable. Whereas Daisy has a dense, athletic build (ironic, as she can't throw, catch, or kick to save her life), I am the opposite: a solid athlete trapped in a form that has been called "slender," "spindly," and once—I hate this one, I really do—"slight." My reasons have nothing to do with Daisy's body type. I don't even think they're still connected to her physical appearance at all.

Daisy is cute; that's how most people would describe her, and that was my initial assessment upon meeting her during our junior year at Temple. She'd just plowed her mother's Lexus into a parking meter and was standing on the sidewalk, cupping her mouth in obvious agony, the impact having snapped her head down so hard, she chipped her tooth on the steering wheel. It was a cold Tuesday night, and my roommate Colin and I, walking back to our apartment, each of us swinging a foot-long hoagie in a plastic bag, stopped and asked the accident victim if she needed any help. Daisy lamented that she hadn't seen the parking meter, and I said something snarky like, "I guess that's better than seeing it and hitting it anyway," and she fake laughed and said, "That's helpful, asshole." I felt bad for her. She was alone in the cold and in need of first aid. Colin did not, so he went home with the hoagies while I escorted Daisy to the campus infirmary. The attending "professional" examined her tooth, diagnosed her as having "done something to it," and recommended that she see a dentist in the morning. He then handed her a pair of Percocet tablets, which she immediately popped into her mouth.

"Want me to walk you back to your apartment?" I asked.

"Okay. But don't get any ideas. Unless I tell you to."

I chuckled. "Understood."

The escort truly was safety-related, as her boyfriend was in Washington for some conference for future world diplomats, and both her roommates slept at their significant others'.

She lived on the fifth floor of a walk-up a few blocks from campus. We trudged all the way up the frigid staircase, and she opened the door onto a living room strewn with collegiate detritus: half-consumed water bottles, textbooks, three-ring binders, and random articles of clothing. Daisy shed her army-green coat, her boots, and her glasses, instantly rendering the cluttered common area four items more cluttered.

"You play the cello?" I asked, spying a large black case that looked to house a hefty string instrument.

"Mm-hmm," she replied. "Want to hear me play?"

"Sure."

"Well, you're not gonna."

I eyed her curiously. "That's a real letdown. I was so looking forward to it these past two and a half seconds."

She laughed without breaking eye contact and said, "You're funny. Still a bit of an asshole, but there's funny."

"There's funny?" I repeated. Either the pain meds were kicking in or she was always a little loopy, and even though I would later discover that it was the latter, I didn't know that at the time, so I bade her good night.

"Wait," she said. "I thought you wanted to hear me play."

Flummoxed but not unamused, I sat down on her couch and waited for her to take out her cello, although I figured there was just as good a chance that she'd ask me what I was still doing there. She joined me on the sofa, folded her legs under her body, stretched her arm out across the pillow behind my head, and proceeded to subject my face to a rigorous appraisal.

"I have a boyfriend," she said.

"You already told me that," I countered. "I think you have the wrong idea." That last part may not have been entirely true.

"I know what you're thinking. You're thinking I'm all effed up by the meds."

"That's certainly some of what I'm thinking."

"Well, I'm not," she said, and she stood up and gave herself a sobriety test. She marched the length of that overheated room in her black loose-fitting jeans and maroon sweatshirt, one careful step after another, eyes closed, taking turns touching her nose with alternating index fingers. She passed, clapped for herself, and hopped back onto the sofa cushion. "Happy?" she said.

I laughed. "I haven't said a word."

"Or have you?" she said, eyebrows all mysterious like a television detective. She slid closer to me.

After a few minutes of kissing, during which I snagged my tongue more than once on that serrated half tooth she'd recently acquired, I withdrew. "I think maybe I should go. You should probably get some sleep."

She ignored me and reached for my belt buckle. "It's fine," she said. "I'm completely sober. Didn't you just see?"

So I helped her out of her jeans and liberated her sweatshirt over her raised arms, and soon we were going at it on her sofa, she buck naked except for her socks and I fully clothed with an unzipped fly.

It was weird. Not the kind of sex I could handle every night. She did a lot of giggling, her fingernails nearly drew blood from my shoulder blades (that was with my shirt on), and in the throes of it she moaned, "Oh man, oh man," which I had to hear two or three times before I realized—with relief—she wasn't saying "Amen, amen," which would've been even weirder.

The next day, after having her tooth bonded, Daisy called to thank me for devoting my evening to the aid of a stranger in need (it was difficult for me to consider it charity, given how the night had gone), and reassured me she'd been in full command of her faculties all evening. When I asked if she wanted to get together again, she said, "Hmm. Let's not, okay? You seem really nice and all, but I'm kind of into my boyfriend."

"I'm nice? I thought I was an asshole."

"Those things aren't mutually exclusive," she said. "But I don't have time to draw you a Venn diagram."

I was only partially surprised when she called again later that same day.

"You know how you've always wanted to hear me play the cello?"

"It has been a dream of mine," I said.

"My chamber orchestra is playing tonight at a church on Broad Street. Are you okay with churches? Some people aren't."

I didn't have sufficient church experience to know whether I was one of those not-okay-with-churches people, so I figured I'd go and find out. I didn't recognize a single piece the quintet played during the hour-and-fifteen-minute performance, but I'd never in my life been so transfixed by an artistic event. It was like when I heard *Hollywood Town Hall* by The Jayhawks for the first time and I was like, *Hold on a second. This can happen? Music can sound like this?*

"Did you like it?" Daisy asked afterward as she packed up her instrument.

"Put me on the mailing list," I answered.

"Cool." She smiled approvingly. "I didn't know if this was going to be your kind of thing."

"Trust me. It's everybody's kind of thing."

Then she parked her hands on her hips and studied me in that mystified way she had when we were on her couch the previous night. "Who do you hang out with?"

I laughed. "Are you asking if I have friends?"

"Well, you're awfully available," she observed. "You seem like the type to have a lot of friends who don't know you very well."

I did have a lot of friends, and they knew me fine. We all knew each other well enough, which is sometimes how it is with friends. My friends went to dive bars and fraternity parties, not symphonies and cathedrals. They listened to music from the 1960s, not the 1760s. They were the puddle-deep, B-student, slept-through-the-nine-o'clock-class, pick-up-basketball-game, Rolling-Rock-in-the-mini-fridge crowd. The type of friends I'd expected to make in college. The ones I came looking for when I bailed out of the Midwest, no parachute. They pulled all-nighters for papers they should've been working on all semester. They ate every meal like it was *Monday Night Football*. (Wings, pizza, cheese fries.) They were mainstream. I was mainstream too. I just didn't feel like it.

It didn't take long for me to realize that Daisy was not my type, although in fairness, I'd never meaningfully explored what my type was. I'd always had Margot; hence, I'd never needed a type. I liked that Daisy had laser-focused moods where she was as productive as a bee and as blunt as a rolling pin, but that she could also sit for hours around a bar table without checking the time, laughing her high, silly laugh. I liked the style quirks that popped up out of nowhere. Pigtails. A little yellow Pac-Man nose ring. Overalls and a cowboy hat when—trust me on this—there's nothing remotely farmerish about her. She was very different from what I was used to, and I was clearly not *her* type. I didn't quite know what I was feeling for her. Was it the exhilaration of exploring my other possible selves?

One day early on in our friendship, I was walking through campus when she called out to me from a bench where she was sitting with her backpack and a mocha. I joined her, and she looked at me analytically, then pushed her glasses (which she did not need; 20/20 vision) up the bridge of her nose and said, "What's going on here? Do you dig me?"

"I don't know," I replied, deeming it a question best ducked, though I'd answered it honestly.

She thought a moment, then said, "Yeah, you're probably right."

In retrospect, that might've been my chance. Did I miss it, or was I just not ready to take it?

"What am I right about?" I asked.

"Let's just keep doing what we're doing."

"You sound like my boss. *Keep up the good work, Rowan!*"

"You don't have a boss," she said.

"Not really my point." Then, "Why? Do you dig me?"

She sighed. "Well. I've got the Joshua thing going on." Joshua was a worldly, politically active, exhausting Ghanaian law student.

"Yeah, I suppose you do."

"Does that bother you?" she asked.

I shook my head, maybe because *bother* was such an inapt word.

Daisy sat there nodding intensely, the way I used to nod when pretending to understand my trigonometry tutor.

"Do you want it to bother me?" I asked her.

Then *she* shook *her* head, and I nodded intensely, because I understood what was going on here about as well as I understood trig.

"Then let's just keep doing what we're doing," I suggested. "Keep up the good work, Daisy."

And we did. I caught most of her gigs, we checked out indie bands together on Sunday nights, and we shared a table at Starbucks to do schoolwork. Then Joshua broke up with her. (This was the second time, for good, not the first time, when she ditched him for Serena, a flautist, whom she dated for a month before going back to Joshua.) He told her he was returning immediately to Ghana to join the legal fight against a neighboring dictator whose seizure of trade at the border was both unfriendly and a violation of a treaty. The young lawyer, brimming over with fire, idealism, and no practical legal experience whatsoever, would be damned if he was going to miss out, so he split—leaving Daisy available. But by that time, I was dating Hannah, whom I'd met at one of Daisy's performances. That was a difficult stretch. Hannah ran hot and cold (redheads, am I right?), she drank at least seven nights a week, listened only to danceable pop, and sometimes just screamed at me for literally no reason. Hannah was bad for me, but someone being bad for you isn't really a thing in your early twenties.

I don't spend time thinking about what it would be like to date Daisy anymore. It's like my mother says: "It's like Pearl Buck says, 'Many people lose the small joys in the hope for the big happiness.'" I don't think I'm in it for the big happiness anymore. I'm not even sure I'd know the big happiness if it walked into my apartment open-kimono and said, *Hi! I'm the big fucking happiness!*

—

Sheathed once again in the articles of clothing we so hungrily shed only minutes before, Daisy and I head back onto the floor. As I follow behind her, I see a figure, some large customer lurking by the counter. The man spies Daisy and calls out, “Yoo-hoo! Anybody home?”

Chili’s voice is like a hand on my throat. Daisy’s too, apparently, as it nearly stops her midstride.

“Hey, stranger,” she chirps through the quake of artificial calm.

Chili gazes curiously at her. “I’ve been standing here for, like, five minutes. Is there nothing in here worth guarding?”

It’s too late for me to slink back into the storage room. “Rowan?” Chili calls, sounding even more perplexed now. I’ve been made.

“Chili dog,” I call back to him. (I’ve never called him that before. We’re not on a nickname basis.)

He looks at me, looks at Daisy, and the air goes thick. “You guys getting down back there?” he asks, making a joke but not smiling.

Daisy snorts. “‘Getting down’?” She must think that if she mocks his nomenclature, he won’t notice our heavy breathing, our state of dishevelment, or the guilty look that I know is plastered across my face.

“Yes, that’s how we spend most shifts—getting down,” I join in.

“We were moving some stuff around in the storage room,” Daisy says. “Frickin’ disaster back there.” She is retying her pigtails, which gives her hands something to do but at the same time draws attention to the fact that her hair needed redoing.

“Huh,” says Chili. He is scrutinizing us with such cold unreadability that I begin to worry that poor old Patti Darling might lose her second child in as many days, a high-probability outcome narrowly averted by Daisy’s tasteless, uncouth, downright offensive but ideally timed act of misdirection:

“So, Chili. Rowan just got some awful news. He lost his brother.”

She plays the grief card. My grief card. It rescues us, but it also reminds me that I have, very much indeed, lost my brother. I'd forgotten about all that for a few minutes.

Chili looks at me. "Lost? What do you mean? Like, died?"

I nod with due somberness.

The big dude's features darken. His mouth drops open. He looks earnestly wounded. "Are you serious?"

Good old Holden. He had to give his life to do it, but he may have just saved mine.

Then Chili hugs me, which means that within minutes of having been wrapped up in his girlfriend, I am wrapped up in him, and the tinge of comfort I experience in his thick, vein-strewn arms, as sturdy and immovable as Mount Rushmore's Roosevelt, only compounds my guilt.

"I'm so sorry, man," he says. "What happened?"

"Boating accident," I reply, which seems to be the phrase I'm going with, though it only gets me so close to the meat of it. What actually did happen? Collision with a jetty? Whale attack? Slow leak?

"Jesus," Chili says. "Are you okay?"

"He's in shock," Daisy answers, and although she's a cellist, not a mental-health professional, she knows that shock gives me and therefore us a bit of a free pass.

Chili is shaking his head. "I hate it when bad shit happens to good dudes."

That just makes it worse. Bad shit *is* happening to a good dude, but he's the good dude and I'm the one doing him wrong. Instead of co-grieving for my estranged sibling lost in a Caribbean capsizing, he should be stomping my rib cage with the heel of his boot. But he won't do it because Chili is not a badass. He is, in fact, a good-ass. He's actually kind of a nervous-ass, the imposing Rambo physique cloaking—sometimes even highlighting—a Rick Moranis temperament. When you talk to Chili, you see those furtive eyes, how he seems to second-guess everything that comes out of his mouth, even hello, especially hello, and you feel a weird warmth toward him, an odd streak of protectiveness. You want to grab his hand before he crosses the street. You want to make sure he doesn't leave the house without a jacket. At a minimum, you want to stop having sex with his girlfriend because, man, if he finds out, that'll really hurt his feelings.

Which is precisely what I promise myself right then and there. I'm not going to do that anymore. It was done to me, and it was a bitch of a thing to get over. If I'm even over it yet.

Chili has stopped by to see if Daisy wants to grab something to eat before her performance tonight, but now that he's heard my tragic news, he doesn't think I should be left alone. He invites me to join them, which is heartbreakingly thoughtful, but I can't think of a more uncomfortable dinner party under the circumstances, so I decline.

"Is there anything I can do?" he asks.

"No. I appreciate it, though."

He has let me live, which is more than I deserve.

"Home is Iowa, right?" he says.

"Illinois."

Iowa sounds great. I don't know a soul in Iowa. Illinois is always the last place I want to go. But it's not the dead people out there who so terrify me. It's the living ones.

CHAPTER 5

Greg and I are manning the store until close. I clue him in on the Darling family unpleasantness only because I need him to pick up extra shifts while I'm gone. As I tell him about Holden, I don't know what majestic misadventure Greg is mentally salivating over—surely some epic combination of *The Perfect Storm*, "The Wreck of the Edmund Fitzgerald," and *Jaws*—but when I finish talking, he stares hollow holes through me and says, "That is so fucking Promethean."

It makes me want to smack him, but it's just easier to agree: "Yup. Promethean. That's the word that popped into my head too."

Greg seems less shocked by my brother's death than by my brother's existence in the first place, but instead of prompting questions and displays of empathy, obligatory though they might be, all these cool new facts about me send him scribbling in that yellow legal pad of his.

Greg spends most shifts writing. Novels, articles, manifestos, limericks—you name it. For him, that is what working at Metaphysical Graffiti is all about: doing other things. He comes here to gather material, all of us just another teat on the milk-flowing bosom that nourishes his "art." I used to give him a hard time about it, even loaded him down with busywork. A part of me was probably jealous, as I figured that if anyone around here deserved to be dubbed on the shoulders with the scepter of inspiration, it should be me, the guy who writes the rent check. But then I got to thinking that maybe one day Greg will produce a great masterpiece, and we'll be the place where it all started. It's a long shot, but who knows?

Maybe it was the rare comment I'd made about my own dormant writing aspirations, or maybe he'd mistaken my politeness about his work as interest in it, but once, Greg looked at me with a sort of brothers-in-arms twinkle and said, "I've got my writers' workshop tonight. You should join us."

I laughed, then saw that he wasn't joking. "Thanks. I'm not really the workshop type."

"And the workshop type is what exactly?"

I'd been to a workshop before. A few years back, a woman I was dating who loved to bake dragged me to a baking class where I was given three hours to produce a trifle. Three hours later, I hadn't produced a trifle. I was instead standing before a pile of flour I'd barely touched and looking at everyone else's confections, finally learning what a trifle was.

"It just seems like a lot of sharing," I answered.

Greg shook his head and grinned like he was onto me in some way I didn't realize. "Have it your way."

As penance, he made me read his latest manuscript, titled, with no small amount of preciousness, *Nonfiction: A Novel*—although a more apt title might've been *Nonpublished: A Disaster*. It was set in a Cincinnati snow globe; had no discernible narrative (even less dialogue); the main character was an alpaca or an emu, some sort of farm animal; and Greg claimed to have written the entire thing in seven days. (I'm not sure how he spent six of them.) He asked for my honest feedback, which of course I withheld, and instead I told him I thought there was a really interesting book in there somewhere. Which he took as a Pulitzer-level endorsement:

"See, that's the caliber of art we churn out at my workshop."

"Duly noted," I said, and went off to a less irritating section of the store.

In addition to his shifts here, Greg Isquith has part-time employment at Market Street Meats and two locations of Enterprise Rent-A-Car. He's an aspiring writer and an amateur artist currently laboring over his third graphic novel. But the guy never misses work or calls in sick, his pride in the Graffiti far exceeds mine, and he loves music with almost monastic righteousness. (Use the term *guilty pleasure* in front of him and brace for the rebuke: *That's someone's art you're talking about. Taking pleasure in music should never make anyone feel guilty.*) He's a pill, but I kind of love him for that.

Greg goes back to pretending he's Hemingway, and I compose an email to Rob Wright. Rob is half of the Wright Brothers (his twin brother, Rich, is the other half), and together they comprise a local acoustic duo I'm trying to convince to hold a record release party here at the store. Rob and Rich are good, laid-back, unassuming guys, rootsy front-porch twang jockeys with the bona fides of woolly beards and hippie wives. I've known them for years. They shop here. But ever since one of their songs appeared in an episode of *Vicky of Venice Beach*, a popular TV show targeted at people a fraction of my age, they don't stop by as often, and they forget to reply to my messages. No hard feelings. I say good for them.

"How did I not know you're from Illinois?" Greg is suddenly wondering. "I mean, it makes perfect sense."

"Doesn't it, though?" I say.

He and I have logged hundreds, if not thousands, of hours together, almost all of them uninterrupted by customers, and I know all kinds of shit about him. Basic human wire-pulling would have me reciprocate, let him in a little, and I miss that part of me, the part that didn't hold back. I must've left that part back in my midwestern cradle, where my relationships were big and sumptuous and abided no borders. Skid, for instance: there was nothing he didn't know about me. He probably knew I was puppy-loving on Margot before I did. He was always around; we were always in each other's business. But Skid was the last of that breed for me. I'm more heedful now. My friendships bloom lopsidedly, like a houseplant only half exposed to the sun.

"You don't go back there very often. Illinois," Greg says.

"I do not," I reply.

His eyes sit fixed and unblinking upon me. "Why do you think that is?"

"Because I don't like anybody there. That's why I think that is."

He chuckles. "So in other words, a bad breakup."

"Yes, Greg." I sigh. "A bad breakup."

It happened so long ago, it's basically a story about children, and yet, to their credit, Margot and Skid behaved like adults. They came to my house, both of them—an illogical, paradoxical united front—and looked me in the eye, wanting me to hear it from them and not through the grapevine. They knocked on my door, stood on my porch, and told me what I could plainly see: they were together. So I left. I put half a continent between them and me and, in all the years since, have managed only the most fleeting blink of a return, stealing into that old house for a holiday or a flash visit, barely unpacking, then jetting out before the locals catch wind of me.

My tale of woe puts a certain look of skepticism on Greg's face. He says, "Huh," which means he thinks I've overreacted.

"Did you really need to move away?" he asks in his serious voice, the one where he drops an octave and overenunciates like he's hosting *Inside the Actors Studio*. Simply being on my side was too much to expect of Greg.

"Yes, I did," I answer. "I really needed to move away."

"Yeah, but teenagers sleeping with teenagers should never shock anyone. You have to admit that."

My jaw is tightening, my hand squeezing into a fist. "I don't accept that premise, no."

"But you could've lived here without running away from there," he suggests. "You didn't really need to flee. That was a bit much, wasn't it? Both places could've been home. You could've been, you know, bicoastal."

Yeah, or noncoastal, since neither place is actually on a coast.

"Maybe just worry about those shifts while I'm gone, Greg," I tell him.

I think he's missed the point. Although when it comes to my childhood and the people who populated it, I'm sure I've missed plenty of points myself.

Here's something else about Greg: his name is not actually Greg. It's Craig. I misheard him when he came in to apply for the job, then continued to mishear him until it was too late in the relationship to change course. He must think it's a dialect thing, like we pronounce our *cr*'s a little weak where I'm from, which means that every now and again, I go out of my way to keep up the charade. "Give him a store gredit," I'll throw out, or, "What are you doing for Gristmas?"

A new email has arrived from Rob Wright. Our email chain so far has been a call-and-response of sycophantic promises: if they launch their new album here, we'll promo the hell out of the event on all our platforms (all two of them), we'll let them play an unplugged set, we'll transform the store into such a Wright Brothers shrine that it'll be Kitty Hawk in here. In return, I get Rob's spirited declaration of commitment: "I don't know, man. Let me get back to you on that."

I tell Greg that I need him to keep on top of the Wrights while I'm gone, shore up the gig, since I'll be distracted. Naturally, Greg bristles.

"Just because they get a song on a TV show, we have to surrender our soul?"

"Precisely," I reply. "But if it makes it easier for you, think of it as my soul."

"I hope you've thought this through."

"There's really nothing to think about, Greg. This is life-and-death."

"Well, it's certainly death, I'll give you that."

Greg is always disagreeing with me about things I want him to do, and once in a while, I make him do them anyway. He thinks record stores should sell records, and anything else that happens here—band appearances, free beer tastings by local microbreweries—is gimmicky. But a gimmick, according to *Merriam-Webster*, is a device or conceit designed to attract attention or publicity. So I say bring on the gimmicks.

—

Later, just a few minutes before close, a man walks in, early fifties, pinstripe suit, the crease in his shirt and the red shine in his complexion implying a recent steak dinner with clients. He's in from Dallas, he tells me, and just happened to pass by on his way back to the hotel.

"Is this your place?" he asks with a look I could mistake for envy.

"Yeah," I answer. "My friend and I own it."

"Man, I wish my son were with me," the guy says. "I don't think he's ever been in a record store."

"How old is he?" I ask.

"Seventeen."

"Yeah. I'm sure he hasn't."

Standing by the counter, the man stares lovingly out at the racks of CDs and records with a glowing ray of a smile powerful enough to reach Greg, who is sitting in the back but doesn't notice the man, of course, because he's busy composing the next great work of American literature.

"When I was a kid, we had a store like this in town," the man says. "Friday nights, my dad would drive me down there to kill an hour. At first he had to talk me into it. 'Come on, Freddie. Cut your old man a break. I'll buy you that Springsteen guy you like.' And he did. He bought me *Born to Run*. So the next week, I played hard to get again, and the week after that, and after a month of Friday night bribes, I owned *Darkness on the Edge of Town*; *The Wild, the Innocent & the E Street Shuffle*; *The River*; and *Greetings from Asbury Park*."

"You're a crafty one," I say.

Freddie smiles. "My old man knew what I was doing. I'll bet you have a similar story. That's why you work here."

It's funny. I met Springsteen once. I was a high school kid pulling an afternoon shift at Gravedancer Records, Eloise Emerson's store on Main Street in "downtown" Maybee, and in he walked. It was such a surreal experience, mostly because it was so ordinary. He just kind of came in and hung out, shot the breeze with Eloise and me, bought some albums, behaved like any other customer. I was a teenage music geek, and I had a half hour in the company of the Boss, but as this kindly Texan tells me how he duped his dad into buying him the Springsteen catalog, all I can think is, *Yeah, I sure do have a story, but I wish I had yours.*

Off into the racks he goes with a slow, browsing amble.

Patti never talked much about my dad's musical tastes. I asked, especially when I got that part-time job at Gravedancer and started seeing dads, like this Freddie fellow tonight, strolling around, picking up albums by artists I didn't know. My mom was always vague about it, leaving me with the impression that music wasn't one of my dad's passions. But then one day in the car, "Babe" by Styx came on the radio, and Patti cranked it up—which was highly unusual, as everything was always too loud for her—and started singing along at the top of her lungs. Horrified, I looked at her and saw her face was alight. "Your father loved this song. My god, he loved this song." And as she sat there behind the wheel, belting out one of Styx's cheesier ballads, a wave of sadness crested over me. Collecting songs was something couples seemed to do as they moved through life together, and Patti and George were done with that. They would have no more favorite songs together. The very next day, I used my employee discount to buy her the Styx album that had "Babe" on it. When I presented it to her, I think she felt a little sad for me, like she thought that I thought she was missing something, and therefore maybe I was missing something too. Something about her expression made me feel like I'd given that song more significance than it actually had for her. She put the CD on and skipped to "Babe," which she played a few times that night, but I don't remember her ever listening to it again.

Based upon photographic evidence, my dad was a red-faced, wide-eyed devotee of sweatshirts and baggy jeans. His rude departure did things to my brother that I wish he'd opened up to me about. Holden always seemed to be searching for the guy in the games he and I would play when I was little. "I'll be the dad," he'd say as he meticulously twisted one of George's old ties around his neck and swam into one of the man's sport coats. "I'm off to the office to drink coffee. You stay here with Mommy." I was never allowed to be the dad. I didn't know how.

I've spent my life trying to see my father in every father presented to me on TV and movie screens, every dad who saunters breezily into my store. For me, George will always be defined by his sudden exit, which I have come to see as a harbinger of further vanishings to come. First, my brother, off to wherever-the-hell just as quickly as he could get there; then Skid, only technically not another son to my mother, who didn't leave but abandoned me just the same; then, finally, me. I graduated high school, drank the dark rum of summer, and said goodbye. I guess we Darling boys tend to leave. Like Daisy's play. We too are goners.

Freddie returns with an armload of Springsteen vinyl and drops it all on the counter. "When I get home, I'm buying that kid a turntable, and he's going to listen. He's going to listen *good*," he says. As I run his credit card and bag his purchases, he adds, "I mean, why the hell else do you have kids, right?"

Alone in my apartment, the first thing I do is scurry around turning on lights. It's a studio, so one would do the trick, but I flick them all on, even that useless night-light thing above the stove. I need brightness.

I have a notification on my phone from Help!INeedSomebody.com. A message from Rose, the New Englander who sought my assistance vis-à-vis her boozehound girlfriend. Apparently, she's grateful, and concerned, and a lot of other things, for the message is nothing but a strain of emojis implying a schizophrenic squall of feelings: a wink, a scared face, a face flushed with embarrassment, and finally an emoji who is either sweaty or not yet dried off from instructional swim. Another satisfied customer. Or a goner.

I sling selections of my autumn wardrobe into a suitcase, the knot in my stomach tightening the closer I get to my flight time. The one suit I own is hunched like a scarecrow at the dark end of the closet. Simple, charcoal, on the verge of unfashionable. Aptly funereal.

I have received condolence emails and texts from Daisy's parents and roughly half of her sisters, even Victoria, who set aside her self-preoccupation long enough to bang out a heartfelt "Sorry about your sister [*sic*], Rowen [*sic*]." The very second my plane is wheels-up, I know Victoria will pounce. She'll offer poor, underemployed Daisy a breathtaking cubicle in a scenic corporate campus in King of Prussia.

It is after ten when Daisy texts me that the play is over and she wants to stop by to keep me company. I want to say yes, as Daisy is an agent of comfort in my life. But I am beginning to see that maybe it is an unhealthy comfort, that we are held together by things destined to fall apart. Our joint venture is a joint failure, a dead flower upon which we continue to pour water, and our friendship is starting to fester with some of the properties of the worst types of friendships, like guilt and shifting contours and sex when a marriage proposal from a third party is imminent. None of this is Daisy's fault. She's just trying to be my friend at a time when people tend to need friends. That's why there's a good shot she'll drop by tonight whether or not I invite her. Daisy wants me to do what she wants me to do, when she wants me to do it. But that's not me. I don't want to do what anybody wants me to do, least of all when they want me to do it.

I'm really wiped, I text her back.

So be wiped, she writes. *I'll just hang with you. We don't even have to talk.*

But knowing you, I'll still have to listen.

Rude. Come on. I can be there in ten.

I type, *Ok,* because that's what I would normally do, but I don't feel normal about anything tonight, not even about Daisy. I delete the two letters and type, *I'm good. Have a good night.* "Send."

My final thought of the day is that maybe burying my brother will give me the courage to bury the Graffiti. It seems both are a thing of the past.

CHAPTER 6

Daisy does show up, but she waits until morning.

"So you're just going to leave town without talking to me?" she huffs. "When people are worried about you, it isn't fair to go dark on them."

"I didn't go dark. You invited yourself over, and I declined your invitation."

"We had an argument, and you went to bed," she says. Which sounds like something you tell the police. *We had an argument, and he went to bed. But he was very much alive when he went to bed.* "You don't think that's rude?"

"Daisy, you can't just barge in here and start yelling at me."

"Barge? You buzzed me in."

"And what are you doing here again?"

"I'm driving you to the airport."

"Oh." I don't know if this is something we discussed or simply another one of Daisy's unilateral decisions, but either way, I could use a ride.

The sound of the zipper climbing the side of my duffel bag feels fateful. It seems I'm really going.

"Did I do something wrong?" Daisy asks. She is standing at the door with her arms folded, a bouncer in reverse, refusing to let me leave.

"No."

Her aspect softens. "Do you want to talk to me about Holden? Because you never do."

"No, thank you."

"You can, Rowan. That's what friends are for."

I stare at her a moment. "So, about that: I think we should make some changes when I get back."

"What does that mean?"

"I don't know."

She eyes me with worry. She who just the other day was change's biggest champion.

I sling my duffel bag over my back like some bourgeois hobo wannabe, and we shuffle down the two flights of stairs and out the front door. It's noticeably cooler today, as if the morning has brought with it a whole new season. The newness on the air scrapes at my nerves because now it feels like I'm not only heading off to an unfamiliar town but leaving one too.

As I toss my bag into the trunk of Daisy's Mazda, she peels the parking ticket off her windshield and notices the fire hydrant, close enough to kiss the passenger door. "For fuckity fuck's sake," she mutters, no ire left in the tank for her anthological collection of traffic violations.

With an abrupt Formula 1–style acceleration, the car leaps onto the road.

"Please say something," she implores.

"I spoke to Greg. He's fine with the extra shifts, so your life won't really be impacted."

"That's not what I meant." Out of the corner of my eye, I see her frowning at me. "I feel really bad about this. I should be at the funeral. This is your brother."

There is a part of me that would love to have her there. Maybe the whole part. But it doesn't feel like an option right now. It feels like it would be dragging one complicated situation halfway across the country and introducing it to another complicated situation. Would they combust or would they cancel themselves out?

"I can't keep doing to Chili what I've been doing," I say. "He doesn't deserve it. You shouldn't be doing it either, since, you know, he could be your husband soon."

A few weeks ago, Chili stopped into the store. Daisy happened to be out for coffee, and he seemed relieved to have a few minutes alone with me.

"I think I'm going to ask her to marry me." He said it like he was pitching a highly dubious idea. "She'd marry me, right?"

I was scared; I was sad; I was scared he was going to see that I was scared and sad. Without looking up from the list of upcoming releases I was fake perusing on our distributor's website, I forced myself to say, "Sure." Then I managed to hoist my eyes to meet his. "That's great news, Chili. You guys are a terrific couple."

Not two days later, Daisy zoomed through the front door, folded her arms on the counter in front of me, and lowered her face onto her wrist. "I think Chili's going to propose."

"Yeah, I do too."

"You do?" She suddenly looked helpless. "What should I do?"

"Are you serious?"

"Assume I am."

"Daisy. Do you want to marry him?"

"Most days," she said with reflection. "Yeah. I think so. You never really know, though, right?"

"If this were an arranged marriage, I would understand the uncertainty. But I think you're supposed to know whether or not you want to marry your longtime boyfriend." Then I strode off, pretending I needed something from the storage room, although what I needed was not to be part of a conversation about Daisy moving on. Ever since then, I've been living my life in a crash position, bracing for impact. Which, incidentally, is my natural state when I'm in a car with her, as I am now.

Daisy drives in silence, and I stare through the cracked window, feeling the autumn sun warming the right hemisphere of my face.

"No, you're right," Daisy says after a while. "We shouldn't be doing what we're doing. It's not fair to any of us."

As we approach the airport exit, the hot whine of a jet engine erupts overhead, and an airliner descends low over the interstate. I watch the giant winged thing lumber onto a runway with an unnatural, improbable grace. Daisy steers toward the departures terminal, stops in front of my airline, and pops the trunk.

It's windier down by the airport, and Daisy stands on the curb hugging herself over her lightweight sweater, which is the precise blue of a police strobe light.

"Thanks for the lift," I say. "I'll check in in a day or two."

"That's it?" she says. "That's all I get?"

I shrug. "You also get this: keep an eye out for those guys on our street, the ones working down the block."

"The construction guys? They're sweethearts."

"Just be careful, okay?"

"I'm touched by your concern, but I've been chatting with them for weeks. We're basically friends."

"Well, sometimes friends rape each other."

"That's racist."

"Racist? They're white. They're from South Philly."

"See, this is what I'm talking about."

"Goodbye, Daisy."

"Rowan."

"What?"

Daisy hates when things are unresolved. She must talk her way through to an ending. I, on the other hand, am accustomed to the cacophony of unsettled affairs.

"Everything happens for a reason, you know," she says.

She is lucky to feel this way, as the opposite has always seemed so much closer to the truth. Nothing happens for a reason. Everything happens for no reason.

"Call me if you need me," she says.

"Sure."

"Will you?"

I suddenly have the urge to tell her that I need her right now, that everything would be so much easier if I could just bring her with me on that plane, hold her in front of me like a shield as I walk through my hometown. Daisy Pham is one of the things that works best about my life, one of the things that makes the most sense, and she doesn't even belong to me. It wouldn't be the worst thing in the world if we just gave up that lease after all.

"It's fine. I won't need you," I say to her. "Thanks again for the ride."

I shuffle off toward the automatic doors, and out of nowhere, the twitchy images of last night's dream snap into focus. The dream was about Holden. He showed up at the Graffiti, which never actually happened in real life, and told me he had borrowed a kayak and I should come down to the river with him. I couldn't picture water, so I asked, *Which river?* And he replied, *The one behind our house.* I asked, *Which house?* and he laughed like I was joking and said, *So are you coming?* I told him no, there was a storm in the forecast, and we should all stay out of the water. He made a quizzical face, current conditions being perfectly mild, and asked, *Who told you about a storm?* And I said, *Dad.* He stared at me a moment, almost like he was trying to remember what Dad looked like, or maybe he remembered all too well. Then he told me to meet him behind the house. He opened the door and a rush of wind blew back his hair. *I'm scared, Holden,* I said to him, or tried to say, but he wasn't listening. He just smiled into the spiraling wind and said, *There's never been a better time to fly.*

PART TWO

THEY SAW ME SEE THEM (NOW I HAVE TO SAY HELLO)

CHAPTER 7

A mechanical issue delays my departure out of Philly by one, then two, then four hours, so a quick three-state straddle becomes a full day of travel. The crunch of my middle seat is yet another exclamation point on my abiding resolution to make this journey as infrequently as possible, a pledge nobody could ever accuse me of treating lightly.

With the sun boring through the curved square of the plane's window, the memory of that day crawls back into my head as though on the paws of a jackal. I remember how the glint of that early-spring morning made my eyeballs contract when I opened my front door.

Knocking should've been my first warning. Neither Margot nor Skid had knocked in years; they just entered. It was a Saturday morning, and I was awake, lounging in bed, easing into the day with America's *Greatest Hits* (Eloise, my boss at Gravedancer and musical guru, was teaching me to appreciate 1970s soft rock; Bread was on deck, Ambrosia after that) when Patti appeared at my bedroom door looking concerned. I removed my headphones.

"Skid and Margot are here," she said.

We both just kind of looked at each other, as it was strange that my girlfriend and my best friend had shown up on a weekend morning, together. Stranger still that they were waiting outside. If they were here, why weren't they *here*, in my room, crawling onto my bed and disordering my shit like usual?

Slinking down the stairs in boxers and a T-shirt, I found them on the porch. Because they looked grim and because what they were about to divulge was the furthest thing from my imagination, my first thought was that they'd come to tell me about some horrific tragedy that had befallen one of our classmates. Maybe Joe Brody's notorious drunk driving had caught up with him. Maybe Tracy Rogers had finally Menendez'ed her parents, which we all knew was just a matter of time.

"We need to tell you something," Margot began.

They kept glancing at each other, and I suddenly felt something significant about the dividing line separating me, inside, from them, outside. I'm sure that's when I knew.

"What do you need to tell me?" I said.

Margot looked down and shook her head.

"Is somebody going to speak?" I asked.

"It just happened," Margot said. "I'm sorry." And she started to cry.

"What just happened?" I asked, icing over, pulling back into myself.

"We didn't plan this," said Skid. "Honest to god."

I glared at him. "I don't even know what the fuck you're talking about."

I watched his tongue push out his cheek, which he did when called on in class and didn't know the answer. It was his tell, a rarely needed SOS.

"Margot and I," he said quietly. "We . . . we have feelings for each other."

I gaped at him, then at her. "Are you guys for real?"

Margot couldn't look at me, but Skid wouldn't look away, wouldn't deny me something to grab on to in this terrible moment. I could tell he hadn't expected it to be this hard, and it was insult upon injury to see my best friend looking so adrift and diminished.

"These feelings just came," Margot said, her voice warbly through tears. "We didn't want to hurt you."

I was trembling. My legs quivered. The air smelled different. A metallic taste of fear bubbled up in my throat, and suddenly the only thing that mattered was being somewhere else.

"I hate that this happened, Ro," Skid said. "You know you're like a brother to me."

"You guys can get off my porch," I said, trying to appear disdainful and pitying, like they were too pathetic to waste my time on, like I'd probably forget their names by lunchtime. "Seriously. Get out of here. Go do your thing."

But I knew that the two of them were all I had, separately and together.

I slammed the door and stood there quaking in the foyer. Patti peeked out from the kitchen, and I bolted up to my room, slammed that door too.

I stared in the mirror. A look of true, horrible surprise swelled across my face. "Did this really just happen?" I asked my reflection, out loud, with an amazed chortle. Then my features mangled as though straining to hold back some monstrous storm, and I dove onto my bed and bawled into my pillow like a wounded dog.

I stopped when I felt my mother's hand rubbing my back. I looked up and saw her sitting beside me on the bed, the pink line of her mouth sagging like a telephone wire. "I'm so sorry, honey," she said.

I needed my friends. I needed my brother. Where had everyone gone?

I jumped up, yanked a pair of jeans from my closet, and slid them over my boxers.

"You're going to be okay, you know," my mother said.

My head burst through the neck of a sweatshirt. "I'm done with this place. As soon as I graduate, I'm out of here, and I promise you, I'm never coming back."

I sprinted to the garage, hopped onto my bike, and pedaled ferociously down the streets like I was trying to outrun the town, outrun myself. I rode for miles and miles, past the water tower and the chemical plant, out into the tumbling breeze of farmland where the low rows of corn eked slowly upward, testing the air to see if it was safe yet to stand tall. I sat against the trunk of a flowering oak tree and tried to imagine Margot and Skid together, really *being together*: the parting kisses before class, the rides home, the family dinners at each other's houses, the wordless, knowing smiles. How could I coexist in a town where that was happening?

I thought of the moment I'd realized I was in love with Margot. There truly was a precise moment. We'd sat next to each other in eighth grade social studies. Our teacher, Ms. Schaffer, had a horrible lisp, which I used to make fun of for Margot's amusement. (Our unit on the Civil War was an embarrassment of riches—*Jefferthon Davith*, *Thtonewall Jackthon*, *Ulytheth Eth Grant*.) One Friday, Margot had an early dismissal for a tennis tournament. She was quietly stowing her books and pencils in her backpack, trying not to disrupt the class, and just before standing up to go, she leaned over and kissed me on the cheek. She'd never done that before. It was completely innocent, entirely offhanded, maybe even mistaken, but it awakened something in me. A light went on, and I thought to myself, *Oh. I'm in love with Margot Beckett, a girl I've known since I was six.*

She wasn't an obvious choice. She was a jock, and while I got along with the jocks, she was also kind of a brainiac, and I generally avoided that herd. I couldn't stand around with those smarty-pants and talk about the periodic table and the square root of things. But one kiss to the cheek changed it all, and I knew exactly where I belonged. Where she went, I would follow. *Of course I'm in love with Margot Beckett. What took me so long?*

Wiping my eyes, I lifted myself off the roots of the oak tree, climbed back onto my bike, and continued on the road out of town.

Hours later, I was gliding back into the garage, toeing out the kickstand, and hanging my helmet on the handlebar. Patti, waiting in the kitchen, looked relieved I was home.

"Let's get something fun for dinner," she said. "Whatever you want."

"I'm not hungry," I told her, and I went up to my room and tried calling Holden. I say "tried" because that's just how it was. Some people you call, other people you try to call. He was living in Vail with college friends and working in a restaurant to support his ski addiction. I wasn't looking for advice; I just needed my brother's voice. Nothing got the best of Holden, so maybe a little of that unconquerability would conduct over the sound waves, make me just a little more like him.

He didn't pick up, so I went back down to the kitchen.

"How about tacos?" I said to my mom.

She winked. "My specialty."

She gave me a hug and went to work.

I spent the balance of the school year channeling my internal misery into an outward air of age-appropriate standoffishness. I ramped up my shifts at the record store and attended only the social gatherings I knew would be unattended by the two Judases. I let some of my football teammates get me drunk. I let Gwendolyn Jordan introduce me to weed. Gwendolyn, who was president of both the Student Government Association and the Black Student Union, had always been a friend, but suddenly she was also my date for the prom I'd been planning to skip. (One day in the middle of biochemistry, she got out of her seat and walked over to me. "Hey. You want to go to prom?" Me: "Really?" Her: "Yeah. Why not?" Me: "Yeah. Why not?" Her: "Cool." Ms. Ellerbe: "You couldn't conduct this transaction after class, Gwendolyn?") Margot's desk was directly behind mine, and she clearly overheard the entire exchange. I sat there not thinking about my prom date, but instead wondering how Margot felt about it.

Despite their complicity in a high-profile scandal, Skid remained the most well-liked person in school, and Margot's reputation absorbed only an evanescent hit. Everybody seemed to be on my side, even though I didn't want anyone on my side. I just wanted to be on the outside.

I deprived Margot and Skid of eye contact in school and all other forms of communication, including the cathartic satisfaction of a dustup, as I was determined that my last words to them would be those delivered on my front porch on that Saturday morning. *Let them live with that* was how I looked at it.

As the school year wound down, Skid made one last-ditch attempt. He tried to corner me at the record store.

"Come on, Rowan," he said, slinging his backpack off his slumped shoulder and onto the floor. "I can't tell you how sorry I am."

It wasn't clear to me what he was apologizing for. He and Margot were a legit couple by that time, so certainly there was no regret. Anyway, I was beyond the point of forgiveness. I didn't need anyone to be sorry.

"You're really never going to speak to me again?" he asked as I continued filing newly released CDs, pretending Skid wasn't there.

Finally, I looked at him. "What do you want me to say?"

"I don't care," he answered. "I just want you to talk to me."

We stared at each other for one weighty moment, during which I came close to unloading on him all my anger and disappointment, calling him out for acting like a second brother to me and a third son to Patti all these years, for treating my house like it was his house, and then simply burning it down one day. Fortunately, before I said any of those things, he said:

"It was my fault."

My eyes narrowed on him.

"I initiated it, Ro. The night of Dov's party. Remember how you were too buzzed to drive Margot home, so I did?" He swallowed visibly. "I kissed her. It just happened."

It just happened. Doesn't everything?

"I'm so sorry, man. I didn't mean to do it, and I sure didn't know where it would lead."

"Just get out of here," I said.

"So this is it?" He stared at me, a little incredulous. "This is how you and I are going to leave things as we go off to college? This is how it ends for us?"

"Yes, Skid. This is how it ends."

He hoisted his bag off the floor and swung it over his shoulder. "You know, Rowan, one day you'll wake up, and your anger will be gone. I know you. That's just how you are. One day you'll come home, and we'll be friends again. And whenever that day comes, I'll be ready. The worst of this for me is knowing how alone you feel. I wish I could make you understand that you're not."

At that moment, I thought of Holden, of Margot, even of my father, the whole treacherous lot of them, and I laughed in Skid's face. "This isn't my home. This is just the place I live until I don't have to anymore."

Four years later, I paid my pain forward when I told my mother I was staying in Philadelphia after college and not coming back to Maybee. Surely, I broke whatever corner of her heart had not already been broken.

"I think I'm going to stay, Mom," I said to her over dinner the night before graduation. We were at an Italian bistro not far from the future site of Metaphysical Graffiti. "Daisy and I are going to give that record store a go."

I watched my mother struggle with the impulse to saddle her twenty-one-year-old son with guilt over his eminently predictable decision not to move back to his one-horse hometown.

"And here I was thinking you liked me," she said, forcing half a smile.

"What gave you that impression?" I gibed back.

Patti cast a sad gaze upon the meal we both knew would now go unfinished. "Well, you're a Darling man," she said wearily. "Why wouldn't you leave me?"

I leaned forward over my heaping plate of linguini. "It's not like that, Mom. I just want to give this business a shot. But don't worry. It's me. I'll be crawling home broke and in debt within six months."

"Not even grad school?" she said.

"I don't think I have the grades for grad school."

"You have the grades for *a* grad school. What about writing? What about teaching? What happened to that?" She smiled. "Do you know how good it made me feel that you wanted to be an English teacher?"

That was once the dream. I'd be some sort of writer—of what, I couldn't say, since I'd never really written anything except a few inanities for the *Maybee High Dispatch*, whose only journalistic standard was that the piece arrived by deadline. (I put almost zero effort or craft into ginning up "Study Tips from the Nerd Table," "The Overlooked Benefits of Peer Pressure," "Five Things We Didn't Know About Vice Principal Sullivan," and so on.) I'd be married to Margot and teaching at the high school, where Skid would coach the football team, and together we'd be the cool teachers, perennially youthful, reluctant authority figures. We'd whip chalk at kids when they got answers wrong. We'd forever be on the principal's shit list on account of our boisterous classrooms disrupting education up and down the hall. Our names would come up on Friday nights when our students played Fuck, Marry, or Kill. It was a modest, eminently achievable dream, and in the end, Skid and Margot achieved it. Sometimes I wonder if it was easy for Skid to kick me over the cliff and take Margot for himself, if it ever bothered him to become the person he became by doing what he did.

"You know, there's a nice new apartment building right off Ogden Street," Patti said to me that night. "A lot of young people are moving in. Will you at least think about it?"

"I'll certainly give it the reflection it deserves."—i.e., none.

"I'm not trying to make you feel guilty, Rowan. I'm just saying it'd be nice to have you around. Since your brother seems to have forgotten I exist."

"Well, thank you for not making me feel guilty," I said.

My mother wasn't the only one Holden had abandoned. Growing up fatherless, I'd always looked to my older brother for everything, and he'd always delivered, imparting to me the wisdom every boy should be armed with when striking out into the world. That the sight of a Volkswagen earned you the right to plant your fist in your buddy's triceps. That "no trade backs" was the law of the land when it came to baseball cards. That if you really wanted to get a girl's attention, you had to withhold your own. The fact that he hadn't even made it out to my graduation was too devastating to complain about.

Patti sat there and watched me fish around in my pasta for the last remaining shrimp. "You shouldn't let anyone elbow you out of your own hometown, Rowan."

"Mom."

"It's childish."

"Patricia."

"Okay." She held up her hands. "I've said my piece."

My mom did not deserve to be the collateral damage of my self-imposed exile, but how many other people's wrongs was it my job to right?

The Maybee toward which I'm now flying is a place where every street, every structure, every patch of grass genuflects in grace at the indulgent benevolence and ostentatious love of Margot Beckett and Skid Hall. Having stayed together all through college, gotten married, and had a child, they have proved themselves neither fling nor fluke, and indeed have gone on to become the town's celebrated king and queen: Skid the beloved high school football coach he was destined to be, Margot the part-time tennis instructor and full-time MILF, serving on every local committee that works for the public good, organizing the annual Stella Ash Memorial 5K Run/Walk in honor of their neighbor's daughter who died of a heroin overdose, the proceeds donated to addiction treatment facilities all over the country, which is a wonderful thing to do, and yet I hate them for doing it because it's gloating. As is their ever-present look of zealous happiness in all those pictures, and not just happiness, which is moment to moment, but contentment, which is a permanent state of being and a perpetual slap in my face. Was all their good fortune and spectacular fulfillment absolutely necessary?

I never wanted to be a thirty-three-year-old man hung up on a teen romance. But the weeks slipped into years, then decades, and somehow the hurt still feels unanswered. My crushed dream clung to my side and became an old habit I never worked hard enough to kick.

CHAPTER 8

It is already late afternoon when the plane touches down at O'Hare, and I emerge from the terminal with trail-mix bloat in my stomach and oil from a refrigerated wrap glistening my pores. Patti gets out of her Taurus to greet me, and the grave look she wears assures me that Holden is still dead. It wasn't all some big misunderstanding.

Amid the swirl of rendezvousing travelers and cops blowing whistles at everyone for everything, my mother and I hug, and she tells me she's happy I'm here. I hear her sniffling into my collar. I assume my arrival has made everything more real. Maybe it's just been a long, lonely, horrid couple of days and she is finally letting it all out.

"It's okay, Mom," I say, holding her tightly.

Turns out she's sniffing, not sniffling. "Boy, does someone need a shower."

The cheap shot strangely warms me. I'm home.

It's an hour north to Maybee, and the receding skyline of Chicago shimmers like a hubcap in my side mirror.

"How are you holding up?" I ask as she drives.

"Oh, who knows?"

"You didn't need to come all this way," I tell her. "I would've been fine with the bus."

She glances over at me and can't help a big maternal smile at the oddity of my presence. I am Bigfoot. I am Halley's Comet.

Every time I see my mother, I'm jarred by the progressive whiteness of her hair. She's been this way for years, looking like there's a dandelion sprouting out of her neck, yet somehow I'm always surprised when she isn't forty.

She's planning to go to LaRocca's, the friendly neighborhood funeral parlor, first thing tomorrow. I have no reason not to join her, other than the fact that it is the physical manifestation of my most vivid childhood nightmares. LaRocca's (which has a weird SINCE 1947 on its sign like some family restaurant) was a forbidding marker of my youth, a macabre edifice that all kids eyed with morbid fascination, thanks to those reported sightings of corpses staggering around inside the building after dark and the scratching sounds that were no doubt the clawing of prematurely coffined children.

"You don't have to come," Patti says. "It is, I suppose, a mother's job."

I grimace. "Is it?"

I ask if she's heard anything further about what happened on that boat. For some reason, the details of Holden's exit matter to me, like the way he went out will tell me something about him that I didn't know or confirm everything I suspected.

"I got a call from the US embassy in Bogotá," my mother reports, then pauses to shudder at the image of her son's final moments. "It was apparently a diving accident. It looks like he hit his head jumping into the water."

"'Apparently'?" I repeat. "So they're not sure?"

I feel a warped sense of relief. When the black sheep of the family dies in South America in the company of a woman none of us has ever met, you're just waiting for someone to say *overdose* or *cartel throat-slitting*. Even with the consulate's report, Holden's death still feels distant and unresolved.

"I feel like we'll never know what really happened," I muse.

"What?" My mother makes the face that puts her students on high alert, the one where her features scrunch together into a knot of incredulity, like she's wringing the water out of them. "There's no great mystery here, Rowan. This isn't the Kennedy assassination, and Colombia is not some third-world country with no telephone lines and donkeys wandering the streets. We know exactly what happened. And I don't know what difference it makes anyway."

I exhale a tiny tract of fog onto my window, thinking how wrong my mother is deliberately being, how she knows, as I do, that it makes all the difference in the world.

The next few miles are a silent rush of highway exits hiding in shadows at the end of off-ramps. We follow, and eventually pass, a little old lady insulated in the wide berth of a Cutlass. She is peering optimistically over the wheel but seeing who knows how much of the oncoming road. Having passed a half dozen exits with her turn signal on, she is apparently alerting all other vehicles to the possibility that she may, at some point in the future, turn right, so be ready. This is when I know we're getting close. The unhurried pace of the nowhere-near-anywhere American middle.

"Did you talk to that woman again?" I ask my mom.

"What woman?"

"That woman who called."

She scoffs. "I've already tried to call her back. No answer—surprise, surprise. I certainly don't expect to be hearing from her again." My mother sighs. "Your brother never lacked for companionship. They kind of came and went."

"You make him sound like Jack Nicholson," I say, defensive on Holden's behalf and remembering him counseling me toward kindness and respect in the dating life that back then I could only dream about. "He was nice to women. He was nice to everybody."

Patti throws me a tight, commiserating glance. "Almost everybody."

She announces she's making tacos for dinner, my favorite of her home-cooked fare since I was a kid, and I almost make a wisecrack about the tacos being in honor of Colombia, but I worry she'll think I actually believe tacos are Colombian. I also recognize it's way too soon to start making jokes. But in a strange way, it's also way too late.

By the time we glide up the exit ramp, the sky has deepened into a red wine stain. A hunter's moon is on the rise. I watch from the safe remove of the sedan as we wind along the familiar streets and through the town, past the stalwarts like Antonio's Market, Gravedancer Records, and the hair salon, and the incrementally changing crop of bistros and coffee shops, then the lazy overgrowth that has risen up to make a secret of the withering creek. Farms beckon to hayriders, pumpkin pickers, and cider drinkers, and lonely baseball diamonds sit abandoned for the winter, already anxious for the stir of spring to bring out the Little Leaguers. For good or for ill, Maybee seems mulishly committed to its essential small-town Americana: cordial, though congenitally insular, chronically middle class, unto itself and at the same time a launching pad for commuters who scoot out for Chicago at dawn with their to-go mugs and their podcasts.

The high school where I graduated and where Patti has commanded a classroom going on thirty years is set back from the road on an expanse of heartland, a stark flagpole poised before it. Farther back on the tennis courts, I can just make out two figures darting and dashing, swatting at a yellow speck. Margot used to reign on these courts. How many weekends did I fritter away, following her to tournaments in the farthest reaches of the state, watching the flush build in her cheeks as the day progressed and her name advanced across the brackets? I was always there with her, nibbling at protein bars and Pop-Tarts in 7-Eleven parking lots, receiving her high-fives, her silent sulking spells, her tantrums.

This is the time of year that whispers to me most loudly of Margot. When the afternoons are brushed with autumn's browns and oranges, I think of her sitting in the bleachers after tennis practice, shaking out her ponytail and waiting for the football coach, Coach Zimmer, to release us for the day. Maybe all along she was watching Skid, the showboating star quarterback, instead of me, the journeyman running back. I know he was watching her, biding his time, working up the nerve to decide that I, his oldest friend, was worth the trade.

We were all so different back then. The world looked so different, so vast yet so conquerable. The sight of these tennis courts reminds me of the time Margot, in the midst of a key tournament, allowed herself to be more teenager than tennis player, stealing off with me into the woods between matches. She'd just bested her opponent in the quarterfinals and was told she had twenty minutes to rest before her next match. I accompanied her to the vending machine inside the building to get a fruit punch Gatorade, and after a greedy swallow, her lips popped so red, I couldn't help but kiss them. Seconds later, we were hustling through those heavy metal doors and out into the trees behind the school. With her back against the trunk of a white oak, I slid my hand under her tennis skirt and down the front of her underwear, making her slither against the tree and bringing soft whimpering noises from her open mouth, the smack of tennis balls not fifty yards off. Afterward, she quickly caught her breath, then sprinted back for the semis, and although she returned rosier and more depleted of energy than when she came off, she won.

This town is brimming with memories like that one. It's one of the reasons I stay away.

—

It's dusk on Campsite Lane, and all down the street, lights glow butter-yellow behind window curtains. Idling in front of our old split-level, Patti reaches up to the sun visor to press the garage door remote. As the panel rises in a labor of clanks and squeaks, like an old reflex, I begin to sing: "We're here because we're here because we're here because we're heeeeeere!"

When Holden and I were kids, Patti belted out that song every single time we pulled into the driveway. Her stately, soldierly delivery, perhaps initially sincere, became ironic, for it never failed to prompt groans from her boys. Eventually, the groans became the point. But this evening, instead of joining in, my mother stares ahead into the garage at the beach chairs, bikes, and bags of potting soil held in the headlight beams like caught burglars. She won't sing a note tonight.

Inside, we part company. Patti makes for the kitchen to ignite burners and fix fixings, and I haul my bag upstairs.

My bedroom sits unmolested by the flow of time, looking and smelling exactly as it always has since the day I left for college. It is a museum intended to preserve someone I guess I must have been. Yet as I stare down my Kurt Cobain poster, my Carmen Electra pinup, my framed Walter Payton jersey (I got it at the mall for thirty bucks, so the UV-protective glass might be overkill), the Tolkien books slanting across the shelf, and the Pringles tins still heavy with change, I wonder if the kid who lived here still swims in my bloodstream.

Before going back downstairs, I flick the light switch and peek into my brother's old room. This one was long ago bulldozed into an office, scarcely a trace of him remaining. Distance sunders people, but absence renders them truly separate, and for the past two decades, Holden has been absent, not distant. The words of his high school commencement speaker were still on the wind when he started packing for the University of Colorado. I spent a lot of time in his room that summer, suffering from premature separation anxiety, trying to fathom what our house would be like without him.

"You're going to be okay, buddy," he tried to assure me. I was thirteen, sprawled out on his bed, and he was addressing me as though he were a father going off to war. "You're the man of the house now."

"Whatever," I moped, and walked my bare feet up his wall. "It's going to be quiet as shit around here." I used to curse a lot around Holden. I thought it might make him forget our age gap.

"Well, I guess it's now your job to raise a ruckus," he countered.

"Yeah, but you're better at it than I am."

"Stop sulking."

He snagged a football from his shelf, threw it at me, and we started passing it back and forth across the room.

"You're going to be in high school soon," he said. "You'll have the run of this place. You can bring that bodacious babe around, the one you're crushing on so hard."

"I'm not crushing on anyone," I replied.

"What's her name? That little cutie pie you're always on the phone with. Margot, right?"

"No."

He grinned like a smoking gun. "That's a middle school *yes* if I ever heard one." And he composed and performed an inane song just to get my goat: *"Let's go, Margot, out to my bungalow."*

"Shut up."

"Hey ho, Margot, come to my bungalow."

"I'm actually glad you're leaving."

"Have you kissed her yet? You should kiss her. But always ask first. Nobody likes a handsy man."

"It's not like that."

"What's going on in the breast department? Does she even have them yet?"

"Sort of."

"Aha! Interesting how you know so much about those teeny little breast buds when you're not interested in her. Verrrry interesting."

"Dick." I heaved the ball at him extra hard. He caught it, dove across the room, and sat on me. Parking his ass on my chest, he depressed me down into the mattress springs.

After a while, I said, "How do I get her to like me?"

"Who? Bungalow Margot?" From under his weight, I watched him shrug. "I'm guessing she already does."

"She definitely does not," I said. Then: "How do you know?"

"Little man, I am not an educated fellow. I know almost nothing about everything. However, there are three things about which I am one hundred percent certain. One, the Cubs will never win the World Series in our lifetime. It just ain't happenin'. Get used to it. Two, 'This Must Be the Place' by the Talking Heads is the greatest song in the history of music—all the 'Stairway to Heaven' and 'Bohemian Rhapsody' fans can bite me. And three, you, little man, are unquestionably, incontrovertibly, outrageously, almost maddeningly awesome."

"Bullshit," I said.

"Never call bullshit on a man who's sitting on you. Besides, do you think I want to tell you this? Do you think it makes me happy that you're an improved version of me? A Holden 2.0, if you will? No, sir. No older brother ever wants to acknowledge his younger brother's superiority." He sighed dramatically. "But alas, it is my obligation as a gentleman."

I stared up at him. His heft was beginning to affect my breathing, but I didn't care.

"You'll come back a lot, right?" I said.

"All the time, buddy," he answered. "It's just college."

But college was in Boulder, and Boulder, with its abundance of ski slopes and hiking trails and fresh mountain air, was reason enough to spend his breaks somewhere other than home. Four years later, he graduated and still didn't come back. I liked to think that he was kicking around the country then, an itinerant bon vivant, striking up friendships, taking on lovers, living a smoke-ringed, nomadic life on his own terms. *My brother is a free spirit. My brother is at large.* I needed that romantic notion. It cooled the wound burned into me when he started being a no-show (at best, a sporadic-show) at holidays. That was easier to stomach than, *My brother forgot we were buddies. He doesn't need us—him and me—anymore.* When you spend your first dozen years on Earth with someone, when you share a house with them and a foil you both call Mom, when this person is always around, borrowing your shit without asking, doing his homework in the next room, hogging the shower, looking just as bored as you are on visits to those hick town–dwelling grandparents at their creaky farmhouse that you wish were haunted because at least that might liven things up a bit, you can't picture not knowing that person. But now all my memories of Holden are like my earliest dreams of childhood: I know they happened, they shaped me, but they exist in some unreachable cavern of the past. They are small moments I work hard to remember and keep alive. How many times have I wished he were around just to authenticate history, to say, *Yes, Rowan, I was there. That happened. I remember it just as you do. We went through that together.*

Patti used to remind us of that old Boy Scout rule about the campsite, since the name of our street lent itself to the axiom. "Leave the Campsite better than you found it," she liked to say. I guess Holden heard only the first part. He left the campsite.

I'm home, Holden, I think to myself now as I stare into his old room. *I'm home for your funeral.*

I flick off the light. Some bulbs just make a room darker.

CHAPTER 9

The kitchen table is congested with diced vegetables, two flavors of salsa, three hues of shredded cheese, and plates heaping with assorted bean and meat bounties. All of it sits under low light, as my mother is still enamored with that goddamn dimmer switch. She installed it ages ago but was never able to solve the high-pitched ringing it emits whenever the light is dimmed, so for decades we've eaten to a faint, relentless whine, and for decades the stubborn matriarch has pretended not to hear it.

Patti and I sit next to each other at the square farmhouse table that, unlike many things in this house, has aged gracefully, its nicks and stains allowing it to pass itself off as distressed wood. Assuming the same seats we've always occupied, we heave ourselves at the food as though the crunch and crumble of our taco shells might drown out the cheerlessness hovering over the roof and threatening to seep into the walls. I find myself wondering what Daisy's family dinner table would look like on a night like this, how it would sound as they all gathered around to grieve the one empty chair. No doubt it would be noisy there, which is why I have often coveted membership in the Pham family, that overpopulated cauldron of incivility, preciously guarded grudges, and raucous love. They're all loud and mean—even though, oddly enough, no one's ever drinking. Except Daisy's father. He's always drinking. And small wonder, with that gaggle of daughters he has sired and must surely regret. The first time I was invited over, I waded into the zoo of squawking children and arguing adults and was immediately intercepted by Mr. Pham, who led me into the seclusion of his office. "Wow. How many children do you have?" I asked as he produced a bottle of whiskey and two glasses from his desk drawer. He shook his head, like the battle had long ago been lost. "Several," he said. That's the last thing I remember about that night.

I shake a spoonful of guacamole into the tight lips of a taco shell and ask, "What was Holden doing in Colombia?"

"Vacation, it sounds like," my mother answers.

"He wasn't living down there, was he?"

"He was living in Miami, Rowan." She sounds annoyed that I don't know this, like Holden didn't pack up his few worldly possessions and U-Haul them over the state line with such frequency that when you called him, the place you pictured him answering was always a town or two out of date. "He knew where you lived," my mother adds sharply.

"I've lived in the same apartment since college."

"Consider the stunted evolution implied by that statistic," she says with a low chuckle.

"Or the stability," I rejoin. "He always knew where to find me. He just never looked."

"Oh, Rowan. You and your well of melancholies. Will it never run dry?"

I start to laugh. "You say stuff like that, Patti, and the part of me that wants to flick salsa at you bows to the part that's impressed by your literary whimsy. B-plus."

Instead of going for an A, my mother softens, suddenly regarding her dinner like a chore. "I'm sorry," she says, forking lifelessly at a mound of spiced meat. "I don't know why I'm barking at you. I'm the one who could've done better."

I soften too. "It's not your fault Holden left," I say.

She looks unconvinced.

"Done better how?" I ask.

"I parented you boys differently," she says. "You, I always called on the carpet. Remember when you and Skid drank my peach schnapps? I woke you up in the middle of the night to give you hell about that. You must've been, what, fourteen?"

"I learned my lesson. That stuff's disgusting. Haven't touched it since."

"And that time you said you were sleeping at Skid's, but I found out you were at Margot's, so I called you just so you knew that I knew you'd lied?"

"I did that probably thirty times. You busted me once. Let's call it even."

"I wasn't like that with Holden," she says, looking now like what was to be a leisurely hike has brought her to a thicket of uncomfortable memories. "I never gave him any flak when I heard an unapproved overnight guest sneaking out at dawn or when the vodka I hadn't yet opened was magically unsealed and half-full. I knew he was taking the car without my permission—and before that without the state's permission because he didn't have a license—but I never came down hard on him. I was tolerant, and that might've made him think I didn't care what he did or who he did it with. Or if he came home. So he didn't."

Something resembling awareness begins to darken Patti's features, awareness that this horrible ache she feels tonight will stalk her for the balance of her years, hiding in the pockets of her clothes, in the shoes lined up in her closet. It will be her final thought when she is lying on her deathbed.

"He should've been better to you," I say.

"It's okay."

"And he should've been better to me."

"He was a good boy."

"I know. That's my point."

I never learned. I never grew thicker skin, never turned the page the way I did with Skid and Margot, deciding I didn't need or want a replacement for either of them. From the day Holden left home, I cemented myself in the drying concrete of "the little brother"—calling his name, asking if he was ready to play with me, wondering how things became different between us, how he could have ever let them.

Some years back, when he was living in New Orleans, I was treated to a rare and thrilling period in which he and I texted constantly and spoke on the phone every few weeks. He knew what was going on with the record store, and I knew all about the rum distributorship where he was working. It was like we were kids again. My phone would illuminate with his incoming number, as opposed to my number illuminating his, which was the usual way. I didn't have to send out four communiqués in order to get just one back. We made plans for me to fly down for a visit. Calendars were consulted, dates blocked off, and I allowed myself, first, to look forward to it and then, eventually, to get truly excited about it. The Darling boys, reunited in the Big Easy over crawfish and gumbo.

I called him just as I was about to book the flights, and he said:

"So I got some news. I'm changing jobs. My company is downsizing."

"Whoa. That's a bummer." A job change for Holden was never more serious than a bummer. It happened too frequently to be a calamity.

"As luck would have it, though, my boss hooked me up with a job with a distributor in Louisville," he said. "So get this: I'm moving to Louisville. Like, tomorrow! Out of hand, right?"

"Yeah," I said.

"So let me get settled up there; then you'll come down. Deal?"

It was eight months before we spoke again. I remember being happy it wasn't a year and eight months.

"He missed you," my mother offers, as if reading my thoughts.

"Yeah. So he told me."

"He really did. He always did."

"Not exactly a thirst he felt compelled to quench, though, was it?"

"Keep in mind, honey, things weren't as easy for him."

"Are you kidding? Everything was easy for him."

"You were better at school, you were better at sports."

"He was better at girls, he was better at being liked," I argue back.

"He may have *made* everything look easy," my mother suggests. "But I'm not talking about that stuff. I'm talking about how he lost his father when he was five years old. That was really hard on him. Your dad wasn't some remote figure. He was the kind of guy who got down on the floor and played with the toys. Remember the Darling Family Olympics that we used to do, seeing who could run all the way around our house the fastest? Who could carry the most plastic cups down the hall without dropping them? Your dad started that. Remember how if it was supposed to snow but didn't, Holden would set up the sleds in the living room and you guys would pretend to go sledding? He got that from your father. Think about that. One moment, Holden's buddy was there, the next he was gone."

I'd really never thought about it in those terms: Holden as a kid whose earliest years were wrecked by a father's goodbye-less goodbye, who, like me, may have had his reasons for leaving, some stone in the pit of his gut that only distance could purge.

"I know he was larger than life to you, Rowan, but it's not fair to him to think of him that way."

"He was never larger than life to me," I say. "He didn't need to be. He was precisely the size of life. Anyway, I don't think it explains why he started skipping holidays."

"Don't you?" She angles her head knowingly. "What did you do when you suddenly lost your buddies?"

Her frankness lands like the back of her hand. "Fighting dirty in your old age. Good for you."

"My point is, you're not exactly a regular around here either."

"I usually make it back for the holidays."

"Well, bless your heart. I'm so very grateful for the three days a year you sneak into the house and hide under a blanket."

"Look, Mom—I'm sorry you feel like you didn't know your older son very well. I truly am. I'm right there with you."

"I know you are. But what you really should be sorry about is that I don't know my younger son very well either."

"Don't worry. You're not missing anything."

She lays a gentle hand on my arm. "I disagree." Then a grin appears. "Although sometimes I see your point."

For so long, Patti Darling's family has behaved like each member is an overseas subsidiary of some parent company. I call her regularly, once or twice a week, mostly to make sure she's still alive, but sometimes I just miss her and want to hear her voice. Still: how well do we Darlings really know each other? You can text, you can videoconference, you can show yourself off in pictures, but in the end, those are stages and screens, with set camera angles, tweaked lighting, and rehearsed dialogue. There's no sharing of the air when you communicate through technology, no living in the thick of it the way the Phams do. It's in the pulses of conversation and the interludes of silence, the notes that are played and the notes that go unplayed—that's where the knowing happens. And my brother, whether he realized it or not—and I pray he didn't—opted out. You miss enough birthdays, Thanksgivings, and

Christmases, they stop setting down a plate for you. There's no longer an emptiness to the photographs you're not in.

The abundance of Mexican food now reduced to carnage, we clear the table. As my mother rinses the plates and arranges them in the dishwasher, I toy with the dimmer switch, still vainly trying to find that point on the rotation of the knob that will silence the whine.

Patti carries over a plate of cookies, the seasonally festive supermarket variety, some caked over with orange icing to resemble a pumpkin, others apple red. I take a bite of an apple, and the layer of icing is so cloying, it hurts my molars.

"Tell me something," my mother says, dropping into her chair, the wild of her ivory head making her resemble a thirsty hibiscus. "Did I screw up somewhere along the line?"

"Absolutely. Almost everywhere along the line."

"Be honest, Rowan."

"I just was. You're a pain in the ass. Lean into it."

She is a pain in the ass, and not always in that lovable batty-old-bag sort of way. Although often in that way. Patti Darling has a bindle full of faults and foibles she hauls around just like the rest of us, an often prickly temperament, a history of throwing shoes at her children, and an alarming, highly specific case of dementia that manifests itself in her insistence that for a short period of time when I was growing up, we had a dog. (We absolutely did not; I would know if I had a fucking dog.) But she knows why I left, and it wasn't because of her. She knows how the closest confederates I had in the entire world pulled me down into the plunging neckline of a scandal, crushed me, balled me up, and flicked me out the window. After that, I couldn't bear the sight or sound or smell of any of this, couldn't survive the gray clouds and minor chords of one more Sunday morning here, couldn't get through the cricket-click and droning sunshine of another summer afternoon. I needed a new everything on every point on the panorama.

"Mom. It gives me no pleasure to say this, but you were an excellent mother. I did not move away from you specifically, and neither did Holden."

She smiles down at the flat, unbitten mini pumpkin pinched between her fingers. "I know they hurt you, honey, but did you really let them take your home away from you? They're not so bad, you know. Margot and Skid."

"I really don't want to talk about this."

"They're ordinary adults now. Just like you and me. Well, no, not like you."

"Mom. Please."

She takes a bite of her cookie, and tiny orange flecks tumble into her lap.

"Wouldn't it be wonderful if there were someone we could take our grievances to?" she says, heaving a sigh. "All the pain and injustice in the world can make you want to throw bricks at the temple. But there are no bricks, and not even temples to throw them at."

I cast a skeptical eye on her. "You didn't make that up."

"No, Stephen Crane did. But I agree with it."

And now I'm thinking about that copy of *The Red Badge of Courage* upstairs on my bookshelf. Long ago, I'd spied it in my grandmother's house, trapped between a Louis L'Amour paperback and *Everything You Need to Know About Your Overactive Bladder*, and decided to liberate it. My dad's mother was an animated little butterball who was always baking pecan pies and yelling at us to be careful around her porcelain figurines, relentlessly cheerful despite having already buried her husband by the time she lost her son. (Her husband at least waited until he was fifty-seven to have his heart attack, Methuselah compared to her kid.) Grandma is gone. She's someone else I'll never see again, not for the rest of time. She isn't even around to commiserate with Patti about the singularity of putting your own child in the ground. On the bright side, she's probably not coming for her book.

Crumbs cling to Patti's sweater, and I watch her ridged, pre-arthritic fingers gather every grain and morsel and deposit them on her napkin. There's a solace in this quiet grief. A nourishment.

"I can't believe he's really gone," she says.

"He's always been gone, Mom," I say. "It's just that this time we know for sure he's not coming back."

CHAPTER 10

My initial sensation upon waking is that I am outsize. How do I still fit here, in this bed, in this room? How have the laws of physics allowed for the maintenance of these proportions? One of us, the room or me, should be different.

I regard my phone and see a notification from my website. A new inquiry is waiting, this one from Mikaela. And although my website is a welcome reminder that my life is now lived in Philadelphia, far away from here, Mikaela's message has the distinct ring of this world, the world I have awakened in three states to the west:

> A guy I used to date just lost a family member. We broke up years ago, and I wasn't very cool about it, but I want to reach out to him. I worry that there are still hard feelings and it might be selfish of me to try to be there for him, or it could even cause him more hurt. But I really want to let him know I'm sorry for his loss. What do I say? How much is too much?
>
> Thanks,
> Mikaela

There are occasions when a customer (client? patient?) comes to me with an issue that hits so close to home that I convince myself that someone I know is surreptitiously reaching out to me through the one-way mirror of this website. With today's inquiry, the parallels are too seductive to ignore. Mikaela is obviously Margot. Any fool could see that. Margot is testing the waters to see how receptive I'd be to a condolence call. This is the consistently vexing come-on of my enterprise: reading about a universal problem but seeing only a page from my own diary.

It's all Daisy's fault. About a year ago, I helped her out of three separate jams over the span of a single afternoon. First, I suggested a tactful way of declining an unworthy cello gig offered by a former mentor. Next, I drafted a let's-be-friends-again email to a college friend she'd been close with, then neglected, then outright dropped when Daisy got caught up with one of her boyfriends. Finally, I helped her break the news to one of her sisters that Daisy had dented the BMW she had borrowed from her.

"You're good at this," Daisy noted. "You could do this for a living."

"A professional busybody?" I said. "Is there a lot of money in meddling in people's affairs?"

"I'm serious. It's like renting a friend for five minutes, but a friend whose advice you actually trust. I really think people would pay you for this."

As she and I stood in our record store with nothing but our flourishing inventory, it was not unreasonable for me to wonder how much Daisy actually knew about what people would and would not spend their money on.

"It's fascinating," she marveled. "As inept as you are at expressing your own feelings—and I could not overstate the depth of your gracelessness there—you're weirdly good at tapping into other people's."

When she started looking like she was serious, I reminded her that people generally don't tell strangers their problems, and she reminded me that there was an entire industry that revolved around people telling strangers their problems (they called it therapy), whereupon I pointed out that I did not go to therapy school, so there'd be no reason for anyone to trust my judgment, and so she pointed out that all I would need is a website and people would trust my judgment because if you weren't legit, you wouldn't have a website now, would you, and I laughed in her face but stopped laughing when she pried open her laptop and I saw her tongue stick out the way it does when Daisy is being calculating.

"If you build it, they will come," she said.

"If you build it, I will be stuck with a domain name and web-hosting fees."

"If this were 2002, yes. But here in the future, we can do it for free. I know HTML and JavaScript."

Before I could do anything about it, into the virtual world was birthed a service that no one had been waiting for and even fewer people needed.

"There. I went with Help!INeedSomebody.com," Daisy said, beaming with so much misplaced pride. "You get the Beatles reference?"

"Yes, I do."

"Write it down so you remember."

It seemed like something I could safely forget.

"You are coming to the rescue of the flat of tongue, the poor tactless masses who have something terribly important and awkward to say to someone but lack the social smoothness to do so," Daisy declared. "Congratulations. You're a hero."

"Excellent," I said. "I'm glad you're having fun. Now make it go away."

"This is the beginning of something big," she said.

"I want it to be the end of something small."

But it was the middle of something embarrassing.

It "launched," and like a whisper on the tundra, registered not a sound.

Daisy then plugged it on all her social media outlets, and because her natural inclination to make friends, join things, and overall maximize her global participation footprint has netted her a staggeringly grand social network, almost instantaneously my website pinged with more hits than I could've ever imagined: four. Certifiably viral when matched against my expectations.

My inaugural customer: a timpanist in one of Daisy's bands progressively haunted by the fact that in a low moment seven years earlier, he'd lifted sixty dollars from his mother's wallet. His internal torment had risen to such a level that he deemed it a fair bargain to invest a ten-spot in a rando such as myself to offer objectivity about what he should do.

I read the inquiry and looked at Daisy, who said, "Don't look at me. You're the expert."

For a fast ten bucks, could I not at least pretend to be an expert?

So—I instructed the thieving musician to go and confess his crime, tell his mother he'd been losing sleep over it. Hand her an envelope with whatever he could afford to pay back. Tell her Momma didn't raise no criminal. Do it in person. (If I know nothing else, I know that mothers prefer everything in person.) All would be forgiven.

And it was. And the timpanist, instead of asking for a refund, was overjoyed. So overjoyed, in fact, that he mentioned me to a friend who had a friend who had a sister who hosted a successful podcast that profiled unconventional businesses. (In my imagination, that podcast was called *So, I Know This Lunatic . . .* but that couldn't be right.) The following month, Help!INeedSomebody.com was the featured business on the podcast and I her guest, and though I had literally nothing to say, and for most of the twenty-minute interview the two of us ganged up on my silly little venture and ridiculed both it and me, there's no such thing as bad press. Within days, some lost souls came trickling into my den. One guy needed the right words to say to the father he thought was dead but had discovered was very much alive and in Fresno. A woman wanted help with a eulogy for someone she barely knew and had never much cared for.

The existence of my website is joke enough, but the bigger joke is that it actually brings in money. Not a lot, but some, and when you're me, some is a lot. Worse, I have to admit that I get an occasional flurry of satisfaction from all this. Not from solving strangers' problems but from the corroboration of my hope that everyone else out there has problems that seem just as crushing to the bearer as they are trivial to the observer.

I reread Mikaela's inquiry, then reply:

> Send him a note or email. If you really hurt him, it's probably better to stay out of his face and offer condolences from a distance. If it's water under the bridge, he'll let you know.
>
> I hope I Help!ed. (If I did, please Yelp!)
>
> Rowan D.

If Mikaela truly is Margot, heads up: it's not water under the bridge. To the contrary, the river seems to have carried it all the way back.

My first thought upon stepping into LaRocca's is that Holden may have hooked up with the undertaker.

I don't know if she's technically the undertaker—customer service agent? hostess? maître d'?—but whatever she is, she's the first body that greets us (a live one, praise the Lord), and I immediately recognize her as the fast-moving she-wolf a grade or two ahead of me in high school who, I'm pretty sure, had a dirty little spell of "hanging out" with my brother.

She introduces herself as Becca Fitzpatrick as she shakes our hands, already knows our first names, and administers some off-the-rack sincerity—consoling smiles, supportive slouches, an apology for our loss. She says she's been expecting us (not the kind of thing you want to hear when you enter a funeral home) and throws me a glance like she's trying to figure out if she remembers me or not.

"Did I have you?" Patti asks her.

Weird that my mother and my brother could ask Becca the same question.

"You did," replies the voluptuous mortician. "I fell hard for the existentialists that year. Sartre, Camus, Nietzsche. Boy, did I drink that depressing Kool-Aid."

"Apparently so," Patti remarks dryly, and everybody laughs except me, not because I don't get it but because this seems like neither the time nor the place for literary repartee.

As Becca leads us back to the "parlor" and I brace for cobwebs, candelabras, and the distant howl of wolves, Patti whispers to me, "She's nice, isn't she?"

Becca Fitzpatrick was a lot of things back in the day, but nice she was not. She was scary, mysterious, and dauntingly sexual at an early age. She carried herself with a formidable air of worldly experience attained through means that the rest of us could not imagine and probably could not handle. While we were mere boys and girls, Becca was a woman, with woman parts and a nasty gleam in her eye that implied expertise in using them. I used to watch in awe whenever Skid chatted her up, his status as varsity quarterback admitting him unto the realm of Becca and her sneering confederates. Unlike my best friend, I shared neither the language nor even an alphabet with those curvaceous terrors who drank coffee in class, smoked Newports in the parking lot while blasting *Led Zeppelin IV*, and casually threw around exotic weekend terms like *grain alcohol* and *ribbed rubbers*.

That Becca has moved away; the one who has replaced her doesn't frighten me so much (even if she is the town crypt keeper). This Becca is easy to smile. She wears her dirty-blonde hair in a ponytail, and is understatedly attractive in muted makeup and cat-eye glasses.

As we file along through the corridor, she looks at me. "It's good to see you again."

High School Becca never would've said that to anyone, much less me.

"Your brother was a neat guy," she continues. "Very cool. Really sweet too."

"Yeah, he had it going on."

"You were friends with Skid Hall and that crowd, right?"

"I was."

"I love Skid," she says. "Patti, you must see him all the time."

"I have the pleasure of crossing paths with Skidmore almost daily," my mother answers. "Live long enough and your students become your colleagues."

Becca smiles at me. "By the way, Eloise sends her love."

"Emerson?"

She nods. "You should stop in."

"I will. It's been two or three years since I visited the store," I say, although I know it's closer to five.

"Just beware: she'll probably try to hire you back."

The parlor is a bright, creamy, strenuously un-tomb-like sitting room with downy sofas and chairs and a mini fridge stocked with what is either bottled water or Evian embalming fluid. Patti explains to Becca that we don't yet have a body for her to bury, that Holden is being shipped home (postage prepaid by the Bureau of Consular Affairs), with delivery expected in a few days. As my mother imparts all these details and all her expectations, I find myself wondering if this is weird for

Becca, if seeing the name Holden Darling this morning on her calendar inspired a sad flood of memories about this person with whom she was once briefly but intimately entangled, if she'd gazed out the window and thought of how that dead boy used to feel and smell and taste when he was alive and so many years from the end.

"I want him buried next to his father," Patti says.

"Of course," Becca assures her. "I don't think I knew you lost your husband. I'm so sorry."

"It was a long time ago," my mother says. "George died in childbirth."

As Becca tries not to look confused, I chime in to say, "Forgive my mother. That's just something she says."

My dad is buried in the cemetery. It's just "the cemetery," the only boneyard around for miles. If you walked under the Maybee sun and slept under the Maybee moon, it's where you're bound. You could do worse. It's a vast, quiet, gently sloping field outside of town with an arching wrought iron gate at the entrance. In November, the trees go red and gold with such intensity that from the road, it looks like a wildfire. It chills me to realize that when we all drive out there to set my brother down, he'll be joining another Darling man who didn't make it out of his thirties.

"I don't want a long, drawn-out thing," Patti tells Becca. "I'm an old shoe in this town, so I suspect there will likely be a few geezers wanting to pay their respects, if only out of sheer boredom, but they can do it at my house afterward. I want a snappy funeral. Few people around here really know Holden anymore, and I don't want a parade of phonies getting up and telling stories just to hear themselves talk."

I regard my mother warily. "Try not to be this sentimental when you bury me."

"Don't worry," she shoots back. Then she clasps her hands together with such force that it approaches applause and says to our host: "I guess I have some casket shopping to do."

—

It's even more unpleasant than I imagined, shopping for the box that they'll stuff Holden into, hammer shut, and drop into the dirt. And while I sit there on the sofa and pretend to participate as Becca swipes through coffin options on a sleek silver tablet like we're all perusing beach rentals for the summer, mostly I look away.

"What do you think of this one?" Patti says, tapping my knee.

"It's perfect," I reply. "Go with that one."

"You're not even looking."

"Of course I'm not looking."

But there's a decision to be made here, a choice among mahogany, pine, walnut, cherry, oak, stainless steel, fiberglass, all the way down to laminate.

"Why would someone pick a metal coffin over hardwood?" Patti asks, choosing now to become a shrewd comparison shopper. "Do these things have, I don't know, features?"

"It's really just personal preference. And cost," Becca explains. "Metal is more durable."

"Durable?" Patti looks horrified. "What does that mean?"

"Do you really want to know?" Becca asks.

"No, she doesn't," I answer.

"Yes, I do," my mother says.

"Bronze and copper don't rust," Becca says. "They oxidize, but they tend to last the longest."

It's Patti's complexion that's oxidizing now.

"Just pick something, Mom," I urge. The breakfast I couldn't bring myself to eat is somehow surging in my stomach.

Becca reads the room and swipes briskly to the inventory she suspects will be a winner.

"Ooh. That's a nice one," Patti chirps, suddenly reengaged. "Rowan, what do you think?"

I steal a glance at the image of a stately wooden vessel open to a cradle of linens. "He'll love it," I say quickly. "Sold."

Becca makes a note and says, "Shall we select the interior fabric?"

"Surprise us," I tell her. "Can we please be done?"

Becca looks at me with sympathy. "I know this is hard, Rowan. Can I get you some water?"

Adds Patti: "Yeah, what's with you?"

I gape at my mother. "Are you serious?"

If Holden were here—and he soon will be—he'd be cracking up, teasing me, making this experience far worse and therefore making it better. He'd cackle like the Count on *Sesame Street*. ("Ah, ah, ah!") He'd show fangs and bulge out his eyes like Nosferatu. He'd pretend to see ghosts. ("Dad's sitting right next to you. He says you need a haircut.") And I see that what my mother said last night is absolutely right: Holden did make everything look easy.

Our meeting concludes, and Becca leads us back down the corridor, the soothing fragrances of rose and hyacinth suggesting a stroll through a flower garden or a candle shop, although I know they merely mask the stench of decomposing corpses.

When we pass the chapel, my mother pauses to peer through the little square window in the door. "You know what? Can I have a minute?" she asks.

"You're not serious," I say. We were almost out of here.

We Darlings are not a churchgoing people. Patti has always practiced a sort of flippant agnosticism intermingled with the occasional moment of respect for the possibility of a deity. But I don't suppose I can deny her an eleventh-hour purchase of church, especially since we just happen to be standing in front of one.

"Just the two of us," she says.

"Of course," says Becca. "Take your time. I'll wait for you both out here."

"No, I meant me and Him," Patti responds. "Or Her. Or Them. Not Rowan."

I roll my eyes, then groan in case anyone missed my eye roll, and Patti strides in, the door gliding closed behind her.

I suppose at times like these, there are no rules. I can't even be certain that Holden himself would protest a little religion mixed into his bon voyage. A few Christmases ago, when he and I sneaked out into the frigid garage to share a much-needed joint, he'd told me how the woman he was dating celebrated Kwanzaa and how much he enjoyed being exposed to it—the singing, the dancing, the candles. "Dude, I think I'm just down with all of it," he said, inhaling. He was referring to spirituality in all forms, whether practiced by the Buddhists, the Hindus, the Jewish mystics. "If it's got chants and meditation and shit, save me a seat."

Inside the chapel, my mother sits motionless in the pew. As I watch the desolate sag of her shoulders, something deep within me stirs, a feeling of boundless, eternal lonesome, a ravenous need to save her. Maybe because I couldn't save Holden.

Becca's voice draws me back:

"Did you know your brother sent me a postcard from Las Vegas?"

I look over at her.

"We were friends, you know. Kind of," she says. She doesn't wink, but a wink is implied. "I once told him that my dream was to live in Vegas. God knows why. I'd never been there before, but it seemed like my kind of town. All the glitz, the shows, the nightlife. Holden and I weren't anything serious. He was all about having fun, so I figured once he graduated and left town, I'd be long forgotten. But a year or so after he moved away, a postcard of the Vegas strip showed up at my house, completely out of the blue. He wrote something like, 'Vegas could never handle the likes of you.'" Becca allows herself a moment of reverie. "I've always remembered that."

I smile. "You must've made quite an impression."

And Becca has always been one to make an impression. I once had this dream about her, one of those dreams from youth that are so intense, so lifelike, that we never forget them, they become like memories. I dreamed I was at a party, and out of nowhere, Becca was there. She simply materialized, and in the anarchy of a dream, I wasn't even struck by the oddity of the two of us being at the same party. I walked up to her, took her hand, and pulled her into a closet. "Excuse me?" she said with a condescending laugh, like who did I think I was? But all of the sudden we were kissing, her warm tongue whipping at mine, my fingertips daring to explore the smooth skin of her lower back under her shirt. It was like making out with a movie star, which is how that dream feels when I revisit it now, a decade and a half later—vivid, unreachable, like an experience in another world. That dream has stayed with me, and though it was only a dream, the memory of it makes it difficult for me to stare for too long into Becca Fitzpatrick's eyes.

Inside the chapel, Patti is standing now, facing the altar. I don't know what she's saying to the poor guy hanging there on that cross, but I'd bet the store she's telling him he's got a lot to account for. Yanking her husband out of the world. Chasing both her sons out of town, then drowning one of them. Who does he think he is?

"Your mother's wrong, by the way," Becca says to me. "Plenty of us remember your brother. And I, for one, am really sad about losing him."

Before I know it, I'm giving Becca a hug. Because she looked like she could use one.

"By the way," I say, "I don't know if you ever got out there, but Vegas sucks. You're not missing a thing."

"Oh my god, totally," she agrees. "I took an early flight home."

Patti lasts about ten minutes in the chapel, then emerges looking even more defeated than when she went in.

"You okay?" I ask.

"I certainly didn't get any answers."

Of course she didn't. None of this will ever make sense to her, nor to me. Time will not bring understanding. Time will only allow us to grow accustomed to not understanding. Nevertheless, I say:

"The answers are going to take time, Mom."

She hangs her sad eyes on me. "Wait for the common sense of the morning, huh?"

"I think so," I say back.

It's a slow amble for us out to the parking lot where the Taurus, that indigenous beast of Middle America, awaits, solemn and tight-lipped as though it too were a mourner. I should stay by my mother's side, drive home with her, keep her company as she steeps her tea, sputter with her through a wordless lunch. But Gravedancer, the antidote to my gloom so many years ago, is blinking at me from across the street.

"I was going to walk over and see Eloise," I say.

Patti nods.

"I don't have to," I add. "If you don't want to be alone."

She grunts at me over the hood of the car as she clicks the button to open her door. "Boy, am I in the wrong place if I don't want to be alone."

CHAPTER 11

Gravedancer Records sits squarely in the withering heart of town. It is a deep rectangular space crammed with bins of every era's signature media. Halfway down the right-hand wall is situated a counter, behind which is generally situated the owner, Eloise Emerson, and that is where I find her today, perched behind the register, not even looking up from her newspaper (the citizenry of Maybee still reads actual newspapers) when I walk in.

"Excuse me," I call out over Mavis Staples's sweaty growl. "Would you happen to have Paris Hilton's *Greatest Hits Volume Two*? I'm just so sick of *Volume One*."

Eloise peers sharply over her Leisure and Arts section, sees the offender, then scoots off her stool and comes rushing out to the floor.

"Darling Rowan! Is it really you?" she coos, cupping my cheeks lovingly in her hands, massaging my face like clay, as if to mold my features back into the boy I used to be. When she throws her arms around me, I smell incense and weird organic oils, bohemian aromas that cling permanently to her clothes and hair. She pulls back, takes me in, and her eyes go sad. "Holden. Beautiful Holden. I'm so sorry, my love."

Eloise's hair is still long and light, her fingers still clunky with topaz and moonstone. She still glides across the floor on the sweep of billowy pants and the fringes of leather boots.

"You're home," she says, and whether or not she means this store, I think she knows that her enduring little mart is the only place around here I never felt any urge to flee.

Once upon a time, I was a middle school kid with a musical IQ derived mainly from the formulaic rotations of Chicago's pop radio. I knew there was a world of better music out there, more thrilling and dangerous, more raw and motley. I'd gotten glancing peeks into that nebula when driving around with Holden and his friends or when they sequestered themselves away in his room with the stereo too loud. Knowing I'd forever remain a child, never deserve my own respect or, perhaps more important, my brother's, if I didn't summon the gumption to strike out from the safe confines of Top 40 and risk getting dirty, into Gravedancer I hazarded.

A used CD by Insane Clown Posse caught my eye for no other reason than it had a parental advisory sticker on it. It was something that the grown-ups didn't want us to hear. So I added it to my stack of discs and carried them all to the listening station. Nothing I heard that day blew the lid off me, but the experience of disappearing into a twelve-disc changer and a bulky set of headphones turned out to be an addictive one. I came back the next day, and the day after that, and on the third day, the owner of the store started pushing me around.

"You dig Green Day, do you?" Eloise said. "Okay, tough guy. Let's see if you can handle The Clash." And she slapped *London Calling* down on top of *Dookie*.

A few days later: "I know you think you're cool and all because you're listening to *The Joshua Tree*, but *The Joshua Tree* is not U2. This is U2." And she handed me *Boy*.

A few days after that: "I'm trying to decide if you're emotionally strong enough for this collection of Nina Simone ballads. You don't have suicidal tendencies, do you?" Me: "Who's Nina Simone?" Eloise: "How dare you speak to me that way!"

The day I was old enough to collect a paycheck without making noses twitch at the Department of Labor, she hired me. Now, whenever I wasn't in school or at football practice or asleep, I was here, in the company of an exotic hippie lady who every day tied my wrist to another balloon and pulled me up into the heights of some new eye-popping musical asteroid belt. Unwittingly, she was grooming me for Metaphysical Graffiti. Or wittingly. Who's to say?

Eventually, I had to quit on account of college. "College?" Eloise said, looking thoroughly surprised when I told her. "But you were learning so much from me."

It soothes my soul to be back inside this place, but I can't help but notice that someone's been fiddling with the layout. A coffee kiosk sits along the left-hand wall near Country & Western, with two rickety wooden tables adjacent to it. Also, there's art on the wall. Not album art but paintings of birds, photographs of meadows. There are still a few concert posters and album one-sheets up there, but I get the sense Eloise is reaching for a different audience. The posters aren't of the sexy, sexualized pop stars of the moment but of bands fronted by men with gray in their beards and newsboy caps on their receding hairlines, women seasoned and self-assured enough to smile and not smolder on their album covers.

"What gives?" I say, hitching a thumb at all the changes.

"Reality—that's what gives," Eloise replies. "The twenty-first century. Streaming, downloading, everyone having every song all the time now." She cocks her head. "Shouldn't you know this?"

"I might've read an article," I answer darkly.

"That doesn't bode well for Rowan Records."

Pointing around the room, she tells me about the coffee stand she got someone to open up here, the performance space set up in the rear for budding musicians, the watercolors, pencil sketches, and pop-art collages she has plundered from local studios and classrooms and are now for sale.

"What you have here is a collective," I note, not hiding my disdain.

"What I have, my child, are customers," she says. "Thanks to the garage bands that deign to play here, and the fresh brew, and the maple muffins."

"My childhood in ruins." I shake my head. "Maple muffins?"

"Fresh from the oven every day."

I grunt despairingly. "I'll bet they're gluten-free too."

"Do you not eat gluten?" she asks.

"I only eat gluten."

As if to prove Eloise's point, the door swings open and in shuffles a customer. The paradigmatic customer, in fact, the one who inhabits the wet dreams of us shopkeepers: a young, moody-postured teenager, dressed for angst in a cinched hoodie.

Eloise regards the youth, then raises an eyebrow with self-satisfaction. "The vox rebel," she says to me.

Despite all the changes, it's soul-soothing to stand here again, especially since I'm surrounded by those ancient Halloween ornaments that Eloise will never upgrade, the kindergarten primitiveness of them being rather the point of the holiday. Hence the cardboard pumpkins, plastic ghosts, and rubber-faced witches that Eloise has been Scotch taping to the walls and windows since time out of mind. The paper skeletons are actually decaying. The fake spiderwebs have actual spiderwebs on them. Then my eye catches something jarringly edgier, a hideous thing with a face white as ash, eyes and mouth wide open as though screaming or gasping for air. It's just a rubber mask on a Styrofoam ball, but it makes me look away. This town is Halloween all year round for me. It's the place where I feel as dark as a burned-out jack-o'-lantern, where I walk around in costume, where I could swear there's something stalking me in the shadows.

"You seem good," I say to her.

It's been three years since colon cancer took Eloise's husband of thirty years, Edward, the town pediatrician. Both her daughters are grown and living in Chicago. But she is not lonely.

"I am good," she says. "I'm dating too. Really setting myself free. Going buck wild while there's still time, helping myself to men and women of all ages, shapes, and body-hair densities."

"That's great," I say uncomfortably. "And I didn't need to hear most of that."

Eloise's eyes suddenly narrow; something behind me has grabbed her attention. "What do you think you're doing?" she snaps.

I spin around just in time to see the customer, that be-hooded teen boy, slide something into his sweatshirt pocket.

"Freeze!" Eloise commands, like she's both Cagney and Lacey.

The kid breaks into a wild scramble for the exit, and although Eloise gives chase through the labyrinth of display racks, youth beats youthful every time, and before she can get a bejeweled finger on him, the hooligan is out the door with a pillage of CDs whose value can't possibly exceed twenty bucks.

This is the second shoplifting perpetrated under my nose in barely a week, and I'm beginning to take it personally.

"Oh no," I say. "Not this time!"

Out the door I bolt, screaming down Main Street in hot pursuit of that little punk. That surprisingly speedy and agile little punk.

CHAPTER 12

Maybe it's being back in the vicinity of the gridirons of my youth, but the high school running back in me is roused, and down the sidewalk I dash, high-stepping over, around, and sometimes on top of the oblivious pedestrians, wobbly toddlers, and reckless bikers blotting the pavement in my path. At the end of the block, I see him break right, around the corner, and out of view, so I kick it into high gear, eating up sidewalk squares and hearing 1970s chase-scene movie music in my head. It's thrilling, but I'm not loving my chances of catching this kid.

As I zoom around the corner at top speed, what lies before me brings me to a screeching halt: an accident, fresh and smoking. Two humans and one mountain bike, all three upturned, scraped, and dented. My fugitive is on his back, grimacing in agony and clutching his leg, while the other party, a woman somewhere between seventy-five and two hundred years old, is slowly getting to her feet. She's beyond elderly but evidently hardy. And mad as a hornet. Straddling the bike, she grips the handlebars and pulls the vehicle to a standing position, then bores into the teenager with an evil eye.

"Fuck nut!" the old lady barks.

The fuck nut is busy testing the soundness of his pain receptors, carefully touching various spots in his knee region, then wincing. I loom over the wreckage and ask if everyone is okay, although I'm particularly concerned about the lady, as she just seems too damn old to walk away from a collision without an EMT's blessing. At the same time, it's not lost on me that she and her Huffy finished the job I could not.

She dusts off her red windbreaker and dispenses a parting scowl to the leveled youngster. "Watch where you're going! Fuck nut." Then she thumbs her kiddie bell, which emits a silvery, innocent chime that rather nullifies her rage, and pedals off.

I stand over the teen and fold my arms triumphantly, though I myself accomplished nothing. "So. You ripped off a hippie, then got your bell rung by Betty White. Aren't you a stud."

He continues to explore his wounds.

"Your leg okay?" I ask.

"I'm fine," he sulks.

"How about those discs?"

He produces four CDs from inside his sweatshirt pocket, all of which appear to be intact, despite some cracked plastic, which may have been a preexisting condition, coming from the Used rack. I stare at the petty criminal. His is not the face of a rebel, but it is, I begin to realize, a face I've seen before.

"You look familiar," I say.

He shrugs.

"What's your name?"

"Alex."

Inexplicably, snapshots of this kid's life materialize before me. I don't know why or how, but I can picture him on vacation at a mountain lodge in the Rockies. I can envision him digging into a slice of birthday cake at a zoo picnic table. I see his face pasted into a crowded family photograph of three generations splayed out around a Christmas tree. It is when some of the other faces in those pictures take form that I realize where I've seen him, and that's when the horror sets in.

"Alex what?" I ask.

"Hall-Beckett?"

Of course. I know this boy because I have seen every frame of his life documented in his mother's social media feed.

"You're Margot and Skid's kid," I say.

"You know my parents?"

"I used to," I say, staring down at the little spawn of duplicity, wishing it had been me who'd ridden over him with my bike.

Mistaking me for some sort of authority figure, he pleads: "This wasn't my idea. I didn't want to do this. Honest."

Honest, says the thief.

"Let me see the discs," I say.

Alex places the CDs in my extended hand, and immediately I see that as little regard as he has shown for the law, the greater crime is his taste in music. The four albums he almost made off with are *Awake* by Godsmack, *Memories . . . Do Not Open* by The Chainsmokers, *Storm Front* by Billy Joel, and *True Stories* by Talking Heads.

"You risked a stint in juvie for 'We Didn't Start the Fire'? Eloise probably won't even want these back. Except for the Talking Heads."

The kid looks straight-up pathetic down there on the sidewalk, with his bruised knee, bruised ego, and malnourished artistic palate.

"Why are you ripping off CDs anyway?" I ask. "Do you not have an internet connection?"

He doesn't say anything, so again I extend my hand, this time to help him up. He flinches at the pressure on his right leg.

"Can you walk?" I ask.

He attempts to but can only manage to limp about in a lagging circle. I ask him where he lives, and he nods in the direction of the wooded neighborhood of old fixer-uppers just down the road, a ten-minute walk or twenty-minute hobble away.

"I'll help you home," I tell him. "You need to get ice on that."

"What are you going to tell my parents?" he asks.

"Nothing—if you go back to that store tomorrow, return these discs, and apologize." I slap the CDs against his chest. "The owner is a very good friend of mine. If she tells me you haven't shown up to make amends, you're finished in this town."

That last part just came out, an absurd threat. I have no idea what it means. But as we head toward the home of the very people who caused me to leave, I realize that, in fact, I know exactly what it means to be finished in this town.

CHAPTER 13

Alex's pained gait improves as we slowly cover ground. Being in his presence fascinates me, and I find myself stealing glances at this kid whose entire existence is owed to, and has been spent in the company of, a marriage that still doesn't compute. He limps along, wholly oblivious to what he represents to the stranger next to him.

On a densely shady street, he lifts his chin at an old Victorian looming before us. "That's me."

The house is a vintage wooden structure, well-kept and almost entirely bearded by ivy and other breeds of overgrowth. It sits directly beside what used to be the house of one of my grade school classmates, a boy named Ted who, because he was an albino, we called Ted the Albino. I know now, as I did then, that that wasn't nice, that Ted didn't want to be an albino, and even if he did, I'm sure he didn't want to be teased about it.

Thirty yards from the driveway is close enough for me, so I tell Alex he's got it from here.

"Thanks," he says. It only now occurs to him that I haven't been properly introduced. "Who are you, by the way?"

I either hate or love that my old friends will find out I escorted their injured son home. "My name's Rowan."

I examine his features for a hint of recognition. I think I want my name to register, but I can't begin to imagine how it might have been invoked except in the most deliberately vague of terms. *He's someone your dad and I used to know. We went to school together.* I warn him not to forget about our little agreement and watch as he mopes up the driveway.

The experience of being introduced to the Hall-Beckett home is just as entrancing as meeting the Hall-Beckett child. From the seclusion of Ted the Albino's old mailbox, I stare at the ivy-carpeted house as though at an alien spaceship crash site: it just doesn't make sense to me. They live there. *They. Right there.* Steeped in all the ordinary joys and tedium of a marriage well into its second decade. Dustbusting after dinner. Negotiating the movie selection. Knowing each other's toothpaste brand of choice. Tipsy sex when they get home on Saturday nights. It is all too much to see—or even imagine—at close range, so I turn and make my egress down the street.

A moment later:

"Rowan!"

The woman's voice that calls to me stings with familiarity. Everything about it—its midrange clarity with a breathy finish, its hint of a second-guess—inflicts upon me a visceral clenching of every muscle in my body. I turn and see Margot jogging toward me.

There's a curious sensation of inevitability now, of knowing that this moment would come. I must have wanted it to come, didn't I? I all but came whistling through her front door.

"Rowan?" She slows to a trot and stops five feet from where I stand. "I can't believe it's you."

"It's me," I say lamely. I can't believe it's me either, and I can't believe she and I are standing here looking at each other. A strange shyness comes over me.

"Wow. Rowan," she says, gaping, smiling. Then her head cocks. "Did you just walk my son home?"

"I didn't know he was yours," I feel compelled to make clear. "He was in a scrape with a biker. He's okay, though."

"Thank you," she says, still staring at me with a big, confused smile. "That's so nice of you. And so random."

All the times I've pictured her over the years, rehearsed my lines for this moment when we finally came face-to-face, and I don't know what to say. I'm just immensely disoriented by the experience of laying eyes upon this woman I haven't seen in fifteen years but who has really never strayed far from my thoughts.

And she's beautiful, damn her: fetchingly sheathed in a gray velour tracksuit whose color and comfort bring to mind a snow day; those blonde locks still lustrous; her compact, athletic frame still bouncing sprightly like a teenager queuing up for a Justin Timberlake concert; and I still see that eighteen-year-old I left behind. She's not that girl anymore, but the pickaxes of time have only improved her. Her eyes, mouth, and cheeks, shed of her wide-eyed cherubic gloss, seem more naturally fixed on her face, as if they have settled in for the long ride through adulthood. I look at her and, after everything, what I mostly feel is sadness. I am sad that I haven't seen her in nearly half my life; that is greater cause for sadness than the circumstances that made it so.

"I heard about Holden," she says. "I'm so sorry, Rowan."

"Thanks."

"I was actually going to call you."

"Oh, that's okay."

She moves toward me, as the circumstances require the dispensation of a hug, and the ache of having her in my arms again is overpowering. Touching her, it turns out, is different from simply looking at her, and instead of mere sorrow, a kaleidoscope of emotions—bitterness, longing, anger, regret, homesickness, everything raw and unwelcome—bubbles up.

I always imagined that when I finally ran into Margot, I would act cool and detached. I'd be over this provincial town, above the tininess and insignificance of the place and everyone in it. I'd pretend to flub her name. ("Hey, Margaret. Shit. Sorry. It's not Margaret. I know it's Marjorie.") But now I am deserted by everything I practiced, everything I expected, and I am left here to flounder, feeling quite tiny and insignificant myself.

"How are you holding up?" she asks.

"I'm okay, I guess."

"Are you?"

"Yeah. I guess."

"He was a good guy," she says.

"Yeah."

I'm being weird; I know this, and she knows this. The unfortunate thing is, I'm honestly not trying to be. My mental state is not entirely under my control at the moment.

"Do you want to come in for a minute?" she asks. "I could throw on some coffee. We could talk."

Her invitation affords me two distinct reasons to hate myself. First, for being tempted to accept, to surrender to the lure of her company because, after everything, being with her feels good, it feels natural and right. Awful too, of course, but really good. Second, I hate myself for resisting that temptation and being too small to rise above everything. Why is it that when we come across someone who brought us such happiness, we see only the way it ended? When I look at Margot now, a little part of me sees all those Friday nights slurping cheap beer together at the end of her driveway, and the afternoons lying around on her bedroom floor with unfinished chemistry homework, and our simultaneous virginity loss at that lakeside cabin owned by—I want to say her grandparents? Her uncle maybe? But most of me sees the day I found out about her and Skid.

"I really need to get back," I say.

"Okay." She squints up at me with that staring-into-the-sun smile. "Do you think we could catch up at some point while you're back?"

How could Margot and I possibly "catch up"? What does that even mean? Does she want to hear how work is going? Does she want to wax wistful with me about how fast her kid is growing up? (*Can you believe he's already in high school? It seems like only yesterday he was ripping off dollar bills from lemonade stands, and now he's shoplifting from boutiques. Where does the time go?*)

"Sure," I answer.

"Yeah?" She smiles and looks relieved. "To be honest, Rowan, I was going to stay out of your face. I thought that after everything that happened between us, you might not want to see me at all."

Stay out of your face. Aren't these the very words I proposed to "Mikaela," that visitor to my website who didn't know what to say to the grieving ex-boyfriend she'd dicked over long ago? I almost ask, but better judgment prevails. What would be gained from knowing?

"You might want to ice up your son's knee," I tell her. "It looked like a nasty spill."

"I will," she says. "He's trouble, that one."

I'm thinking she doesn't know the half of it.

"Well. Bye, Margot."

"Yeah," she says, something distantly sad tugging at her lips. "See you around, Rowan."

I begin my retreat down the wooded lane, feeling some form of relief at having made it through this encounter, when I hear her calling to me again. I turn back to her.

"Hey, Rowan? I'm sorry," she says. "I really am."

And I stand there stupidly, my eyes dropping anchor on her, waiting for more. *What are you sorry about, Margot? Are you sorry about Holden? Are you sorry that your kid inconvenienced me this afternoon? Or are you sorry that things turned out the way they did? Sorry about what you did to me all those years ago. How you deleted me from your life. How you married my best friend and robbed me of him, knowing how desperately I needed to have him in my house.*

"Thanks," is all I say, and though it feels meager and insufficient, like there was more I should've said, it is a modest reward that Margot too seems left cold by that response.

I wind my way back to Campsite Lane, the leaves sprinkling down around me as though I were walking in a cartoon. And it occurs to me that although I don't know what Margot meant about being sorry, and that even the things she should be sorry about happened so long ago that they're just not anyone's fault anymore, the statute of limitations has long run, there is still a part of me that's gratified by Margot's apology and replays it over and over. It's the part of me that's been waiting to hear it for precisely as long as I've been afraid to come back.

CHAPTER 14

My mother is already awake, dressed, and flooding her teakettle under the faucet by the time I shuffle into the kitchen the next morning, bleary-eyed and yawning.

"What are you doing up so early?" I croak.

"It's eight thirty," she replies, believing she's refuting my point. But I know she isn't sleeping. When I asked her yesterday if she'd gotten any winks at all since hearing the news, she clucked and said, "Who sleeps anymore anyway?" Like slumber is some fad that the species temporarily embraced, like cronuts or sudoku. Strangely, I slept fine—except for the dreams. My head was the all-night TV station broadcasting surreal, practically Dalí-esque clips from almost my life: Holden with a kayak at the doorway to the Graffiti, Margot swaggering down her driveway not with welcome but with an imperious finger pointed at the road to shoo me away from her and her family, a hysterical Daisy screaming and crying at me at the airport drop-off circle, though I can see only her wildly moving mouth for the rush of jet engines in ascent.

Patti glances at me over her shoulder. "You know Skidmore had leukemia."

My eyes zing to the back of her head. "What? Are you serious?"

She turns. "Last year. I assumed you knew."

The news knocks me into a chair, where I sit trying to picture Skid sick. I just can't do it. "Is he okay?"

"As far as I know," my mother says. "He's been back at school for a while now, teaching and coaching. He looks good. Are you sure I didn't tell you?"

"Quite sure. That would've registered."

Did I miss this post on Margot's social media? Or is it possible that Margot, who posts everything—the view from her deck at sunrise, the praying mantis that lands on her yoga mat—didn't post about this? Maybe she only tells us the things we don't actually need to know. Or maybe she was too frightened to type those words.

"You would have called him," Patti is saying-slash-asking.

"I don't know. Maybe."

She drops a look of disapproval. "Rowan."

"What?"

"I would like to think I raised a son who would put differences aside at a time like that."

Differences. Like we broke up over the recording of *Let It Be*.

"Skid and I don't have any differences, Mom."

"You know what I mean."

"Patricia. It's too early for this. We have all day."

"Haven't you worn that victim coat long enough?" she presses. "It's frayed and threadbare, and in case you haven't noticed, it protects you from nothing."

I nod at her with approval. "A somewhat obvious metaphor, but rather exquisitely developed. A-minus."

With one hand on her hip and the other on the checkered countertop so out of date that, chances are, soon it won't be, she eyes me with frustration, wondering perhaps why her son can't just rise above and walk on the way she has. "Just let the past be the past, Rowan. Not for Skid's sake or Margot's or anyone else's, but for yours."

"What about him?" I say. "Our family has had a pretty eventful week, hasn't it? I must've missed Skid's condolence call."

"You're right. He should reach out to you," Patti agrees, daintily dunking a bag of herbal tea into one of her fine porcelain cups. "He did call me."

"You're coworkers. How could he not? Plus, you practically raised him."

What does this crazy lady want me to do? Show up at Skid's driveway and start shooting hoops and fisting Cheetos with him like the past fifteen years never happened? Yes, it still catches me off guard sometimes that he and I are not the answers to each other's security prompts. *What was the name of your best friend in high school?* But where else did he think pawing my drunk girlfriend would lead?

"I'm just saying the guy had leukemia," my mother says. "Call him. It's not that hard."

"I'm not doing that."

"You'll feel good about yourself."

"I assure you that's not possible."

She emits one of her please-be-reasonable sighs. "He grew up, Rowan. They all did. Why can't you?"

Now I'm angry. I shouldn't have to listen to this—this being, most likely, the truth. "Are you fucking kidding me right now?"

"No, I'm not fucking kidding you right now."

"Well, you better be fucking kidding me right now."

"Well, I'm not."

"Don't tell me what to do," I say. "If you want to hang out with Skid, feel free. You can take my bike. As for me, I'm going to lie low, bury that deserting dirtbag brother of mine, and get the fuck out of here as fast as I can."

In a blur of motion, Patti reaches down to the end of her bent leg, pries off her shoe, and flings it across the room. Her aim is true, and before I can duck out of the way, I am pelted in the shoulder by a brown moccasin. The old girl has lost nothing on her fastball.

"Ow!" I yell. "You—squat little jerk!"

"Squat? How dare you!"

"How dare *me*?"

"Oh, please. It's a slipper."

I rub my shoulder blade and look down at the projectile. "It's Lands' End. It's hearty."

"It's faux fur," she says. The thing sits on the floor like a harmless kitty. "Be a man." Gripping my arm for support, she slides the moccasin back onto her stubby pink foot. "Now. Would you like me to make you some coffee?"

I stand, grip her shoulders, and guide her into my chair. "No. I'll make the damn coffee. You just—stay here."

It is still 1987 in my mother's pantry. There are tin cans of Dole pineapples, boxes of Jell-O mix and Lipton soup packets, a bag of O'Boisies potato chips, and a can of coffee that's not even Folgers or Maxwell House but some dodgy brand called Guaranteed Value. I peer into this menagerie of artifacts like I've just unearthed the Well of Souls. "Indy . . . why does the floor move?" I intone.

"What?" says Patti.

"Nothing."

As I spoon dried grounds out of the rust-eaten canister and into the filter, my mother warns me that visitors have been stopping by unannounced, so I should either throw some clothes on and drag some bristles across my teeth or be prepared to greet the townspeople in my current "state." I don't see why hiding in my room and avoiding everyone altogether isn't also an option, but upstairs I go to brush the night off my breath and out of my hair.

I'm the first to admit that I've wished bad things upon Skid Hall. No one would blame me for dreaming up dire, if fundamentally cartoonish, miseries for the guy. A nasty case of rectal itch. An unfortunate

Steinway plunging from the sky onto his spot of sidewalk. *Deus ex piano.* But leukemia. I've wanted to kill Skid, but I've never wanted him to die. I wonder if Margot would've reached out to me had the end really been nigh for her husband. That would've probably been my very first thought had I answered my phone and heard her voice. You don't reach out across fifteen years to share news of a curable disease. *I know things ended ugly between us, but—are you sitting down?—Skid's got a pretty bad case of strep throat. They're giving him antibiotics, which should knock it out in a day or two, but I thought you'd want to know.*

True to my mother's prediction, the doorbell rings while I'm upstairs making myself presentable. I hear the shuffle of Patti's shoes (they're really not slippers), the opening of the front door, then the kind, vaguely familiar, voice of an older gentleman. As with the B-list celebrity voice-over one hears on a car commercial, I listen in, trying to place it. Why, I begin to wonder, do I want this hoarse old-man rasp to utter the word *mitosis*? Why am I expecting him to say *endoplasmic reticulum*? The reason, I soon realize, is that the voice belongs to Mr. Garfinkle, my ninth grade biology teacher.

Mr. Garfinkle was one of my favorite teachers, not because I was some kind of biology buff but because unlike so many other teachers, who were either cranky, aloof, or just plain weird, Garfinkle was a gray-headed, red-nosed, incongruously muscular senior citizen who showed up every single day in a tracksuit (did he jog to work?) looking like he couldn't believe his good fortune. *Here we are,* his expression used to imply, *together in a classroom, embarking on another fifty-minute adventure into prokaryotes, Punnett squares, and DNA sequences. What could be better?*

I dress quickly, but by the time I trample back downstairs, the visitor is gone, and Patti is back in the kitchen, setting breakfast plates on the table.

"Was that Mr. Garfinkle?" I ask, shocked that he was actually in my house and not dead of spectacularly old age.

"It was," my mother answers. "I told you we'd get some VIPs."

"He's still alive?"

"Evidently so."

"How?"

"Rowan. He's only a few years older than I am." She gestures to the plastic shopping bag I only now notice on the table. "He dropped off bagels. Sit down and help yourself."

I open the bag, and the aroma of warm, oniony bread wafts forth. I snag a pumpernickel, slice it, and slather clumps of chive cream cheese all over it.

"I'm glad you remember Simon," Patti says. "He's a dear. Everyone at school has been wonderfully supportive."

I freeze, my cheek protruding with thick dough. "Did you just call him Simon?"

"Should I not have?"

"The man's name is Simon Garfinkle?"

"Yes, Rowan. That's his name."

I release a hoot up toward the ceiling. "Why was I not told of this twenty years ago? Do you know how much fun I missed out on?"

"Get over yourself," Patti says. "He was given that name before anybody sang 'The Sound of Silence.'"

Garfinkle may be younger than I would've thought, but he's still old. Doesn't anybody retire anymore? Patti too is three decades in and showing no signs of surrender. The pension would easily bankroll her modest lifestyle, but much to the chagrin of her students, and surely the principal as well, she is having none of it. When old Mrs. Darling finally goes to her great reward, it will likely be in front of twenty-five tenth graders, in the middle of a grammatically immaculate sentence about Bertolt Brecht or gerunds.

Soon, there's another knock on the door, and my mother asks me to get this one. I head to the foyer thinking maybe it's Ms. Carvalho from twelfth grade social studies, swinging by to pick up our discussion about the Navigation Acts of 1651.

It is not a teacher on our welcome mat but a student: Alex. That child of people I don't like.

"Oh. It's you," I say.

"Yeah," he says, seemingly just as disappointed in my observation as I am.

"How's the leg?"

He looks down at it, then shrugs. "It's okay. A little sore."

"Well, there you go. Crime doesn't pay."

He is skulking uneasily in his olive-green army jacket, the first person rendered less physically imposing by paratrooper gear.

"If you're here to rob me, come on in," I say. "My mom's jewelry is upstairs."

"No." He answers earnestly, like I was genuinely asking.

I sort of nod at him, and he sort of nods back.

"Do you want to come in?" I ask.

"Oh, that's okay," he answers.

More abject nodding ensues.

Alex Hall-Beckett, skinny with darting eyes, impatiently waiting on one last growth spurt, has knocked on my door, and yet I still have to do all the work.

"Help me out here, man," I say.

"I was thinking about what you said yesterday," he begins. "Remember how you said I should go and apologize to that lady at the record store?"

"You mean that thing you promised to do?"

"Yeah. Well, since you know her . . ." He is finding something fascinating about the laces of his black Converse. "I was wondering if maybe you could . . . I don't know, maybe come down there with me?"

The invitation takes me by surprise, given who he is, who I am, and the deep, dirty connections between us that obviously elude him. Is this interaction even allowed? Doesn't he need a permission slip to be here?

"How will this be a growth experience for you if I hold your hand?" I ask him.

Horror seizes him. "Oh, I don't want you to hold my hand."

I laugh, and he doesn't seem to know why.

"Okay. I'll take a walk with you," I tell him. "You got the loot?"

He gives his jacket pocket a pat to confirm that the four CDs are on his person. I invite him in while I throw on some shoes, but that too brings a look of trepidation.

"Your mom is Mrs. Darling, right?" he asks.

"Yeah."

"Maybe I'll just wait out here."

Who am I to argue, when I stay out of the house as much as possible too?

CHAPTER 15

Alex apologizes the same way he does everything else: inaudibly. After escorting him into Gravedancer Records and practically hip-checking him into its fierce bohemian proprietor, I witness a display of contrition that sounds more like the mumble of woe prompted by an early wake-up call.

It falls to me to interpret. "What Alex means is that he's very sorry he stole from you," I say to Eloise.

The kid nods his agreement, barely looking up.

"And it will never happen again," I emphasize. "Isn't that right?"

"No," Alex says.

"No, it's not right?"

"No, it won't happen again. E-ever," he stammers.

As Eloise stands there, imposingly postured with knuckles on hips, and Alex sways before her like a toddler in time-out, I feel as though I'm brokering a treaty between a world power and a fledgling banana republic.

"Why did you steal from me?" Eloise demands.

He shrugs. "I don't know."

"You don't know?"

"No."

"And you think that's good enough?"

"No."

"No?"

"No."

This whole exchange reflects poorly upon us as a species.

The kid appears terrified because Eloise looks pissed, both at the crime to which he is pleading guilty and at his shitty excuse for an apology. But what Alex doesn't appreciate is that Eloise is a hippie, and hippies get indignant, not angry. Indignation is the righteous strand of anger, and it manifests itself in outrage. Outrage is not personal. The whole point of outrage is targeting an injustice. Hippies just love justice. It's their favorite thing (aside from hash, Country Joe and the Fish, and finding a little time each day to hate the Vietnam War), and this is why, for all of Ms. Emerson's glowering, Alex really has very little to fear, because if there's one thing hippies hate more than injustice, it's authority. Which means the last thing Eloise is going to do is call the cops. Instead, she's going to try to make him a better citizen. He'll wish she'd called the cops.

"Is there something you want to give to Eloise?" I say to him.

He shoots me a look. "You mean like a hug?"

"No, I don't mean like a hug. I mean like your plunder."

"A plunger?"

"Holy shit, man. Are you for real? The loot. Give her back her discs."

"Oh. Right."

The CDs are placed in their rightful owner's palm, and Eloise lifts the burgundy-framed specs that dangle over her neckline and slides them onto the bridge of her nose. Riffling through the stack, she passes judgment, with inscrutable grunts and eyebrow twitches, upon the Talking Heads, Billy Joel, Godsmack, and Chainsmokers albums for which he felt compelled to risk handcuffs only yesterday.

"Why these?" she asks, her tongue thoughtfully exploring the inside of her cheek.

Naturally, Alex shrugs.

"Well, are you a fan of the Talking Heads? Or Billy Joel? Or these other two assemblages of genius?"

"I guess so."

"Do you like music, young man?"

"Sure."

"Who do you listen to?"

"Different stuff."

"A revelatory response," she says.

Alex's face contorts with pained pondering. "My dad listens to a lot of folk music. He's always playing it on his guitar."

"Okay, good." Eloise nods, looking mildly encouraged. "Now we're getting somewhere. You like folk music, then?"

"Not me. My dad."

"Ah. So we're back to getting nowhere."

I'd forgotten about Skid's flirtation with the guitar, which he took up the year he fell hard for AC/DC. He abandoned the instrument, though, when he learned that being Angus Young required not just volume but actual talent too.

Eloise taps her bejeweled fingers on the square plastic cases. *Click, click, click*. Alex, incarcerated in the straitjacket of her gaze, asks, "You're not going to call my dad, are you? Or the cops?"

"Darlin', I am the cops," she says, suddenly dropping her *g*'s like a child of Nashville. "I'm the judge and jury too, and I find you guilty, and I hereby sentence you—"

"This wasn't my idea. I swear," Alex protests.

Eloise clears her throat. "As I was saying: I find you guilty, and I hereby sentence you to the Talking Heads. Now follow me."

The airy sail of the shopkeeper's Aztec-print pants leads the way down the aisle, and Alex, all blank looks, follows cluelessly after.

Left alone, I pull the Talking Heads disc from the pile of Alex's stolen goods and feed it into the disc player behind the counter. The album is *True Stories*, and I forward through the tracks to the song "Dream Operator" and hop onto the counter to listen.

Holden was a delirious Talking Heads fan, and this song, particularly its extended intro—an arpeggio piano over three descending chords repeated—transports me back to that time when this music emanated through my brother's bedroom walls on endless repeat. He listened at peak volume. He mimicked David Byrne's unrefined, office-oddball, pencil-neck-geek yawp. He showed no regard for the homework or sleep habits of his younger brother. But instead of resenting Holden's discourteousness, his monopolization of the air in the house, I listened and learned. I forced myself to delight in this band until I no longer needed to be forced, and it became a mutually loved thing. When the Talking Heads concert film from the '80s screened at the art-house theater, he barged into my room and said, "*Stop Making Sense.* Friday at midnight at the Goodman. We're going." He didn't need to wait for my answer. As for me, we didn't even need to go. It was enough that he'd asked. But we did go, just the two of us. We sat in that crowded theater and watched the band up on that movie screen for two glorious hours, and when it was over, Holden looked like he'd seen the rapture. "That movie makes me want to take a balloon to the moon," he declared. He said those exact words to me a year later when the *True Stories* movie came through town.

I am humming along to the closing chorus of "Dream Operator" when the record merchant and the record thief return to the counter having collected three more Heads discs from the bins: *Fear of Music*, *Remain in Light*, and *Stop Making Sense*.

"Take these home and listen to them. Carefully," Eloise bids her new subject. "Then—and pay close attention to this part—bring them back."

Alex nods compliantly, if not enthusiastically. He's happy to avoid jail time but wasn't expecting homework.

"We're doing society a favor," Eloise rails on. "Shoplifting is immoral, not to mention illegal, but being musically clueless, although nonviolent, is a greater crime. An offense against public justice."

I eject *True Stories*, snap it into the CD case, and add it to the pile. "Take this one too—or should I say, take it again. But this time, listen to it."

Eloise clasps her hands together. "Now that justice has been served, who wants coffee?"

Alex declines; I, having a pot of Guaranteed Value waiting at home, take my chances with whatever is brewing at the in-store kiosk.

"Kind of sad, isn't it?" Eloise says as I follow her over and watch her duck behind the counter. "There's no such thing as lending someone an album anymore, which means kids will no longer grow up sharing music. It's gone out of style."

"And yet stealing it hasn't," I note.

Eloise pumps the lever on the coffee dispenser and fills a to-go cup for me. "Our official barista has a day job, but she taught me some tricks of the trade so I can serve when she's not around."

The name on the kiosk sign nabs my attention. BARISTA BECCA'S. First names often being uncoincidental in a small town, I say, "Barista Becca. That wouldn't happen to be Embalmer Becca, would it?"

"Dead on—forgive the pun," Eloise jokes before catching herself and wincing. "Shit. I'm sorry. That was the most insensitive thing I've ever said in my life."

"I've heard worse."

"You met her at the funeral home, didn't you?"

"I knew Becca growing up, but yeah, my mom and I were at LaRocca's yesterday. She was our—I don't know what to call it—hostess? Tour guide? Emcee?"

"She is a woman of many talents," Eloise declares.

Precisely what people used to say about her in high school too.

My former employer then proceeds to describe the Vienna roast she is about to serve me with the same soaring sense of enthrallment with which she used to describe her favorite songs. She tells me that this blend is a crossroads, a European checkpoint at which the light morning joes of the New World deepen into the bold, oily business of the Italian and French vintages before leaping into the complex, adventuresome blends of Kenya and Ethiopia. I listen, spellbound despite myself and reminded of the way Daisy looks when she bows the strings of her cello.

Eloise pushes the cup in front of me. "Sip."

I sip.

"And?"

I lick my lips. "Smoky. My tongue is bathing in something rich and velvety."

"Really?"

"Notes of burned sugar, maybe?" I squint. "Afternotes of bergamot? What comes after afternotes?"

"A finish. It's a wet finish, isn't it?"

"Sopping."

Eloise stops and folds her arms. "Oh, I get it. You're an asshole."

"I'm sorry." I laugh. "I just kind of taste coffee."

"Philistine."

"Wait. I take it back." I raise an expectant finger. "Here comes Vienna. I believe I hear opera! Yes, there it is! Ah, Mozart!"

"Get out of here and take your petty criminal with you."

"Are those the waters of the Danube I smell?"

"Unlikely, you little brat. The beans are grown in Nicaragua."

CHAPTER 16

Alex and I are kicking along together down Main Street, in my companion's hand the four-pack of Talking Heads albums awarded to him as a thank-you for stealing. He looks down at them, presumably so he doesn't have to look at me, and says, "I'm sorry about your brother, man."

At last, his awkwardness is endearing. "Thank you. Man."

I've been back in Maybee for not quite forty-eight hours and have spent most of that time in the company of the son of my ex-girlfriend and ex–best friend. There's something poignant about how in the dark he is. Not that he would, or should, care about such things that happened long before he was born.

"Don't you play football or something?" I ask him.

He laughs mirthlessly. "Why? Because my dad's the coach?"

"And it seems like a more productive extracurricular than burglary."

He rolls his eyes. "Gee, no one's ever suggested that before. Nobody has ever looked at the plaque in the school trophy case or the banner in the gym with my dad's single-season passing record and all-time touchdown record and said, *Hey, Alex, how come you don't play?*"

I show the kid a sympathetic smile. "Fair enough."

The thing about Skid is, to know what a dominant player he was, you'd have to hear it from someone else, or see that plaque for yourself, or stand under that banner. He was never the kind of guy to mention it. He was almost a reluctant jock, his prodigious athleticism a tool he brandished for the benefit of his teammates but nothing he felt entitled to brag about. Nor did his talent on the field define him (he was just as successful in the classroom and scored better on the SAT than most of his friends), which meant he didn't need to seek out other star athletes to pal around with. He could be best friends with the smallish kid who had an inconvenient habit of coughing up the football whenever an outsize linebacker so much as looked at him.

There was one game, junior or senior year, against Eastbrook High when Skid took a major pummeling. A defensive lineman—one of those teenagers who already looks like a grown man, with a full beard, thinning hairline, and dockworker delts—threw a seriously late hit on Skid that somehow the ref didn't see. Skid bounced right back up, but I'd never seen him go down so hard, and I became uncontrollably irate. Removing my helmet, I charged the giant and clubbed him with it as hard as I could. That, the ref saw. I was ejected, screamed at mightily by my coach, and threatened with being booted from the team. (Unlikely, since the coach was a good friend of my mother's.) As we filed out of the locker room after the game, Coach, still peeved, ordered Skid to do his job as captain and "tear [me] a new one."

"Ignore him," Skid said as we walked home. "Since when does Cro-Mag ever know what the hell he's talking about?"

We called him Coach Cro-Mag because he had a blunt skull and robust mandible, defining characteristics of Early Man.

"Dude—what were you thinking?" Skid went on. "That guy could've killed you. Like, actually killed you."

"I know," I said. "He almost actually killed you."

"There's no way that guy is in high school. I think he was just cut by the Bears." Skid stared at me with amazement. "I've never seen you so pissed before. Who knew you had a temper?" He yanked my neck down into a headlock. "Thanks, brother."

Alex and I advance in silence over sidewalk squares, the overhead sun warming the air, but blowing the occasional wind up against our sweatshirts.

"So you used to be friends with my parents?" he asks.

I nod. "Yup."

"And then?"

"And then I moved away."

I wonder now how much he knows, whether Skid or Margot said anything last night that made him curious, or said nothing at all, which made him curious.

"Why do you ask?" I say to him.

"Just a vibe, I guess," he answers. "My parents are just—you know, weird."

"All parents are weird," I say.

"I probably have you beat."

"Oh, yeah? My mother sings to our garage door."

Alex snorts. "My dad started a folk music society at school because he got leukemia. He doesn't have leukemia anymore, but he still thinks it's okay to sing 'This Land Is Your Land' in the auditorium."

I smile at that enjoyably absurd fact. "That's pretty good, but how's this: my mom thinks we had a dog when I was growing up."

"And you didn't?"

"Not unless it was an invisible dog. Top that."

"I can top that." He stops walking and stares at me. "My mom writes romance novels under a fake name."

This brings the contest to a thud.

"She what?"

He releases a long breath. "She secretly writes love stories and posts them on a website, and then people buy them."

"For real?"

"Who would make that up?"

"So you're telling me that Margot Beckett writes romance novels?"

"No, Portia Wentworth writes romance novels. And Portia Wentworth is Margot Beckett. You can look her up."

I laugh. "There is no chance I will do that." But there is no chance I won't, the revelations here being manifold and scrumptious.

"You can't tell her I told you."

"I won't."

"You have to forget I mentioned it."

I bite down on my smirk. "I won't do that either. Sorry."

Just then, an SUV slows to a stop beside us. The open passenger-side window frames a blond kid with a cocky smile. The youth looks at Alex and barks, "Hall-Beckett!" Alex turns to him. "What are you doing walking the streets? Shouldn't you be behind bars?"

"Oh. Hey, Gunnar," Alex says, smiling with something well shy of joy.

Gunnar lifts his chin at the CDs Alex is holding. "What did you do, go back for more?" And he laughs a loud, staccato machine-gun magazine of ha-ha-has.

I am thinking it strange that this Gunnar chap knows about Alex's attempted heist yesterday, as these two don't seem like buddies. (Gunnar looks a year or two older.) Also, why would Alex tell anyone, since the caper ended abysmally with his getting bulldozed by a Golden Girl?

Gunnar shifts his eyes to me and sneers. "Howdy, Uncle."

I almost say, "What? Fuck you," but instead I drop a look on Alex and ask, "And this fool is?"

"A friend," my companion answers, and at least he has the decency to look embarrassed it. Gunnar and the hairy-forearmed driver whose face I can't see aren't exactly cruising the avenue in Greased Lightning; it's a flimsy, home-assembled-looking Kia the color of unbrushed teeth. But then it occurs to me that I might be the source of Alex's embarrassment, being caught in broad daylight with an uncle-age person such as myself.

"Get over here," Gunnar says to Alex, and for whatever reason, Alex complies, and suddenly all I know is that I hate Gunnar and I want to punch him. The way he summons Alex over to the car, taunts him, flashes that switchblade grin, and chortles with a sort of Aryan superiority. Gunnar would've been Hitler Youth—you can just tell. He'd have marched and laughed—*Ha-ha-ha-ha!*—and dreamed of becoming a proud member of the Luftwaffe, flying his Messerschmitt over the skies of Poland, bombing nonmilitary targets like a dick. And why is Alex just standing there? Have some self-respect, man. You're the son of the football coach. It makes me want to punch him too. There's a lot of punching that should be going on that isn't.

Soon, Alex turns to me and tells me he's going to ride with these guys. I can't tell if he's looking for my permission or my approval on a purely social level, but I offer neither. What exactly is my responsibility here?

He climbs in, and Gunnar looks right at me with maniacally wide blue eyes. "We are the Dark, Uncle!" he yells. "We are the Dark!"

"You're the *what*, you idiot?" I mouth back.

Instead of zooming away in a rude plume of smoke, the mommy-mobile hums off politely, and I, left there on the sidewalk, feel a swell of gratitude. Gratitude that I'm not them anymore, that although I didn't emerge from childhood unscathed, I did emerge. People tend to forget that even the most comfortable childhood is something to survive. The memory of youth is often too clean, free of all shading and weight. It's when you witness it up close, all those molecular moments, blunt and floundering, that you're just relieved it's over.

CHAPTER 17

Two messages greet me when I walk in the front door. The first is Patti's yellow sticky note—a quaint medium of communication but very nearly her technological peak—which informs me that she has gone to Antonio's to stock up on groceries. Locals will be descending upon us in the coming days, and they'll want cheese and crackers.

The second is a notification from Help!INeedSomebody.com. I have a new customer, "Tom," another inarticulate staring headlong into some dicey situation through which only an expert such as myself can navigate him. I open the email and read:

> I think my girlfriend is cheating on me with her friend at work. I didn't catch them in the act exactly, but I recently showed up at their office and got the distinct impression that they'd been getting down. I was going to propose to her one of these days. And I can envision a scenario where I still would, assuming she loves me. That conversation I can handle.
>
> The hard part is what to say to him, the other man. He's a decent guy, we're sort of friends, and I don't

have a ton of friends. I feel like I'm supposed to punch him in the face. But I'd rather hang on to him, to both of them actually. I feel like if I play this right, I can do that, in some capacity or another.

Thanks,
Tom

Suddenly, all around me the house has gone humid. I stand there in its emptiness, convinced once again that my website is merely an apparatus through which people I already know communicate with me while pretending to be strangers. *Okay, Chili. Just punch me in the face and be done with it.*

Within seconds, Daisy's phone is buzzing somewhere back in Philly. When she picks up, I blurt out, "Is Chili's real name Tom?"

"Like, hello," she says. "You know—how are you?"

"Or Thomas?"

"Chili's real name is Chili. You know that."

"Fine, but is his middle name Thomas? Has he ever told you that he wishes his name were Tom? Or Tommy?"

"What's happening here?" Daisy asks.

"Remember when you said Chili was acting suspicious? Well, I don't think he's suspicious. I think he definitely knows about us. We're beyond suspiciousness."

She pauses to consider whether this is cause for concern. "Why do you say that?"

"I have a new customer on that stupid website you made me do. It's from quote-unquote 'Tom,' a guy who thinks his girlfriend is cheating on him with her business partner."

"So?" says Daisy.

"So. He says he's pretty sure he busted them at their quote-unquote 'office' recently."

Again: "So?"

"So. He considers his girlfriend's partner to be a friend, sort of, and he doesn't have many friends, so he'd prefer not to deck him."

"'Deck him'?" She laughs. "What decade are you calling from?"

I've taken myself out onto the front porch, as that's where the breathable air is. "Come on, Daisy. Doesn't this all sound a little too familiar?"

"Tranquilize yourself, will you?" she says. "Of course it sounds familiar. It happens everywhere, all the time. If you recall, it even happened in Maybee, Illinois, once upon a time. If you ask me, quote-unquote 'Tom' is just plain old Tom."

"Well, what if I were to tell you that Tom referred to sex as 'getting down'?"

Finally, Daisy goes quiet. "That's an interesting data point, I'll give you that."

"Not so flippant anymore, are we? Has he been acting strange since he busted us?"

"Not really. But he didn't bust us."

"He totally busted us. He's not stupid, Daisy, he just looks it."

"That he does," she allows, and I can hear her beginning to worry.

"Look. You love this guy, right?"

She pauses. "Go on."

"Daisy. Aren't you going to marry him?"

"I don't know. Why do you keep asking me that?"

"It just seems kind of pertinent."

"Why?" She sounds exasperated. "Rowan, aren't you in Illinois for your brother's funeral? Aren't you having the worst week of your life? In light of those facts, tell me why today of all days, it's *pertinent* to you how I feel about my boyfriend."

"Because, Daisy, it seems to be a tenet of my moral code that although it is perfectly acceptable to have sex with someone who is in a casual relationship, it is unacceptable to have sex with someone who is in a relationship that has a reasonable likelihood of becoming a marriage, even if that person is quite good at sex. That's my code. I make no apologies for it."

I bring myself to a stop; I tranquilize myself.

"Look. I'm just trying to do the right thing here. For all of us. Even me." Then it hits me like a slap square on the forehead. "Shit. I'm Skid."

"What?" says Daisy.

"I'm Skid. And you're Margot, and Chili is me."

"I thought Skid was the cool one."

"We were all cool," I say, a splinter of defensiveness sliding under my skin.

"You can't be Skid. Skid was the stud. I'm Skid because I'm sort of the seducer, and everybody's under my influence."

"You want to be Skid? Fine. Be Skid. Congratulations. You're a soulless, manipulative, duplicitous asshole."

"I've been called worse," she says.

I contemplate the lawn. Suddenly everything about the world seems to whisper of decline. Even the blades of grass, warmed by the indecisive September sun, look tired. The year has begun its slow plod toward the cold. Why is everything always so familiar? Why is it all so heartlessly repetitive?

Then Daisy asks, "Is that why you sleep with me? Because I'm good at sex?"

I don't have time for a question this loaded. "It's one of the better reasons. Let's leave it at that."

Now I know Daisy is smiling. I can practically hear her lips pulling up.

"Tell me how you're doing," she says, shifting topics. "How's your mom?"

A compact car moves mildly down the street, the first vehicle I've noticed since I sat down out here. It's a shiny red, a hue one sees only on rental cars and Ronald McDonald's hair. I watch as it slows to a stop and pulls to the curb across the street.

"We're okay, I guess," I answer.

"You haven't had the funeral yet."

"No. The guest of honor hasn't arrived."

She blows a stream of air into the speaker. "I can't believe you're going through this, Rowan. I can't believe this is happening to you."

"Yeah, I mean, it definitely sucks."

"I've been thinking about you constantly. At three o'clock this morning, I called each of my sisters and told them I loved them and that they'd better not die."

I laugh because that is a very Daisy thing to do, and I love that I know she did it exactly as described.

"Anything new back there?" I ask.

"Actually, yes. Guess who stopped in to the store."

"Uh, nobody whatsoever?"

"Good guess, but no. Joan from our Realtor's office."

"Did she buy anything?" I grumble.

"No, but she's clearly wondering if anyone else is. She hinted that there could be a hike in the rent if we renew our lease. She did that thing where she's like, 'I like you kids, but . . .'" Daisy trails off into an overtaxed sigh, a perfect impression of Joan.

"It's okay," I say with sudden, inexplicable confidence. "We've got an ace in the hole."

"What ace? What hole?"

"The Wright Brothers. We're going to land them. Greg is on it. It can't miss."

"Okay, but then what? They're nice guys, but they have day jobs and houses in the suburbs."

"And a song on a hit TV show," I point out.

"I'm not saying an event wouldn't be good buzz for us. I'm just saying that bailing out a store in an industry that doesn't exist anymore is asking a lot of your friends' band."

"If you look at it that way, we're too small to fail, aren't we?" I suggest.

"I don't think you understand business," she says.

"I don't think you understand music."

"Right. But I am an actual musician."

"We don't operate in the world of musicians. We operate in the world of rock."

"See, this is what I'm talking about."

And before we hang up, she offers to fly out here again, and although I decline, I realize that while phone conversations have always accentuated distance for me, reminded me that I was far away from someone or someone was far away from me, for the few minutes I was on the line with Daisy, she was here and I was also there.

I know what I have to tell "Tom," and I bang it out and send it before I have a chance to talk myself out of it:

> Dear Tom,
>
> If he's such a decent guy, why is he sleeping with your girlfriend? You seem like a decent guy too, but I don't see this friendship going anywhere. Not until she's done with both of you.
>
> I hope I Help!ed. (If I did, please Yelp!)
>
> Rowan D.

That red rental car is back in view, that ripe strawberry of a Ford Focus. I am aware of it again because there's a woman getting out of it at the curb in front of our house. She collects items from the back seat and makes her way down the driveway. She's young, midtwenties maybe; dark skin, long black hair in tight curls; and she's holding something against her chest, perhaps another delivery. Patti has been receiving lots of free food.

"Are you Rowan?" the woman asks as she reaches the porch. I see now that the package she is holding is not a fruit basket but a baby.

"Yeah," I answer.

"My name is Lulu," she says. "I'm your brother's fiancée. This is his son."

PART THREE

THIS MESS IS A PLACE

CHAPTER 18

Holden was bound to have one last trick up his sleeve. Or child up his jeans, with his genes.

As Lulu takes a seat on the sofa and tries to gently jostle her baby out of some mild fussing by inserting the nipple of a plastic bottle into his mouth, I sit there anticipating the scene that will ensue when my mother returns. How does one act toward people who, if they are to be believed, are both total strangers and the closest of family?

"I tried to call," Lulu says, something of an edge and weariness in her voice.

Reaching both hands behind her head to braid her hair—the better to keep it out of reach of wet, grabby infant fingers—she permits me full view of her face, which is both beautiful and dauntingly serious. Her skin is as smooth as a book jacket, unrutted, I am beginning to suspect, by frequent smiling. Her eyes are a pale green, the color of an evening sky just after a thunderstorm, which, against her deep-toned complexion, gives her a feline flourish. She can't be more than twenty-five, yet there is something seasoned about her.

"I'm sorry that my mother and I don't know about you," I offer.

She looks down at the child resting in her lap, seeming to find solace in the steady beat of sucking sounds from tiny pursed lips. "It's not your fault," she says.

No, it's the dead guy's fault.

She looks up at me. "But I am who I say I am."

"I know."

But I don't know. Holden may have been something of a severed limb vis-à-vis his mother and brother, but surely he would have mentioned *this*. I find myself hoping, in fact, that this woman is attempting a hoax because the notion that Holden went and made an entire family without telling us might be more painful than his dying.

By the same token, why would this woman lie? What possible game could she be playing? If she mistook an insouciant, sporadically solvent, albeit charming rolling stone like Holden Darling for an heir to aristocratic wealth, she's got bigger problems.

As though hearing my thoughts, Lulu offers evidence. She asks me to remove her phone from the side pocket of her bag and invites me to view the photo on the home screen.

And there's my brother. He sits cross-legged on a blanket on the sun-bleached sand, a baby in his lap—this baby. He looks like a man in this picture, not even a young man. He is approaching forty, an age he will never reach, and his features have hardened. There are lines and spots and badlands of scruff blooming unchecked on his chin and neck. He squints through a smile as the ocean shimmers like tinfoil behind him, and the infant reaches forward, his mouth open, surely babbling some nonword at his mother taking the photo. The day looks blown through with warm gusts of love, and the sight of it hits me hard, simultaneously warming my heart and breaking it. I am envious. I wish I had pictures like these, Holden and me together, looking happy and deeply engaged in the business of living. But we weren't in the same place at the same time often enough to be captured by the same lens.

I hand her back the phone. There is something aflame behind Lulu's green eyes as she takes in the room, absorbs the walls, the furniture, the air itself with a sense of mystery. "I feel him here," she decides.

Great. She's one of those. "Do you?" I say.

"His essence lives in this house."

Patti's going to love this.

"Well, that's good news," I say. Then I nod at the living thing in the crook of Lulu's arm. "What's his name?"

The question produces her first smile of the visit. Gazing down at her baby, she says, "Breeze-Brooklyn."

I nearly laugh, not at the child's name but at the look it is sure to inscribe on my mother's face.

"I was going to say he kind of looks like a Breeze-Brooklyn," I say.

Lulu eyes me like she isn't sure if I'm making a joke and, if I am, whether it's at her expense, or maybe she knows I am making a joke but finds all jokes in bad taste right now, since the Caribbean has just swallowed her fiancé.

Poor Patti. Poor oblivious Patti Darling is minding her own business; wending her way through the supermarket aisles on a diverting errand; grabbing a jar of this, a container of that; thinking about what her guests will want to eat, perhaps how Mr. Garfinkle will go to town on deviled eggs or her old friend Hillary Hoffman has a taste for eggplant dip. Then she will drag herself back into that car and drive home to the grim goings-on here in this house. Wait till she sees that there's a strange woman and a baby waiting for her. And the woman is her daughter-in-law-to-be. And the baby is her first grandchild.

And the baby's name is Breeze-Brooklyn.

As Holden's fiancée and not his spouse, Lulu had no legal rights. She did her best, but the consulate in Colombia would communicate only with Patti, the deceased's parent and next of kin. So Lulu took her son and flew back to Miami, where she again attempted to reach the woman who would've been her mother-in-law.

"Your mother didn't seem to want anything to do with me," Lulu explains. "I guess to her, I was just some stranger calling with bad news. In her defense, I wasn't terribly forthcoming. I didn't mention that we were engaged, I didn't mention Breeze. I suppose I didn't want to overwhelm her on one phone call—*your son is gone, but you've got a half-Cuban grandson in South Florida*."

"She would've understood," I say, and I believe it, or I want to. It certainly would have been safer for Patti not to get invested in the names and biographies of people she'd never get to meet, another of her son's vagabond relationships, drifting in, soon to drift out, but she never had a choice. It was Holden who held back. It saddened my mother how little she knew of her son's world, how he gave her only loose non-answers to her inquiries about his personal life. She used to ask him, and me, if he was seeing anyone, if he was in love. What she was really asking, because she did not know, was if he was happy.

Lulu decided she was entitled to a funeral. Holden's mother way off in Illinois could ignore as many of her phone calls as she liked, but that wouldn't change the fact that Lulu had a right to be there when the man she loved, the father of her child, was celebrated and then committed to the earth. Lulu also decided that Patti deserved to know she had a grandson, regardless of the reaction that revelation produced. So she packed a suitcase and the portable playpen and boarded a plane.

"I didn't want to just show up at your doorstep, but your mom gave me no choice," she tells me.

Breeze-Brooklyn starts to cry, and this time he's serious. His tiny lips arc downward, and the sputterings of a tired little pout ratchet up till his face is the angry red of a chili pepper, churning out repetitions of what literally sounds like the word *waah*.

"He needs a nap," Lulu states, getting to her feet and slinging the diaper bag over her shoulder. "I should take him. He slept maybe fifteen minutes on the ride up here and not a wink on the plane."

"Take him where?" I ask.

"The hotel."

"Where are you staying?"

"The La Quinta?" she guesses. "It's close. On Fayette Street, I think."

"Yeah. That place is pretty gross," I tell her, and I suggest we host the nap here, seeing as how the nap needs to be held immediately. Although Lulu puts up a convincing protest, I stand firm.

"Are you sure about this?" she asks.

I tell her I am, but she knows I'm not sure about anything happening here right now.

Soon, I'm dragging the Pack 'n Play out of the rental car and up to Holden's old room, which, having been repurposed as an office, may or may not be more comfortable than the La Quinta. I make an embarrassing attempt to erect the crib and do not even come close to producing anything structurally sound by the time Lulu jumps in and jerks the contraption into stability in less than a second.

Although well versed in adult napping (expert, I would argue), I have no idea what conditions are required for babies to safely sleep. Humidifier? Dehumidifier? Delicate chimes? But Lulu seems pleased with the arrangements. She surveys the air with a placid inquisitiveness, as though she doesn't hear the pissed-off creature in her arms who, at this very second, is displaying for us the full operatic vim of his lungs.

"This was his room?" she asks.

I nod and wonder if she's disappointed, since there is nothing of Holden here. Unlike my bedroom, where my seventeen-year-old self is remarkably well-preserved—right down to the musty, drool-crusted blanket—Patti steamrolled over my brother's dwelling space well before I'd even moved out, perhaps calculating that Holden was on pace to rack up no more than ten nights here the rest of his life. She took the hint and put the square footage to use: a no-frills desk that could've been lifted from a police interrogation room, a futon whose foam cushions are as soft and inviting as a graham cracker. I used to feel so at home in this room, when it was his. I moseyed in whenever I damn well pleased, flung myself onto his bed, and observed him doing older-brother things, like talking to girls or finishing overdue assignments.

Standing here now, a hollowness opens up inside me, and I miss him in a way I hadn't before. How brutal that we're all in here without him, his entire family, trying to sort out this great big mess he's handed us.

I leave Lulu to the wizardry of subduing her child and come down the stairs just in time to hear the rumble of the garage door. My mother is home. This is where things will get interesting.

I rush through the laundry room and out into the garage to cut her off at the pass.

"How'd it go?" I blurt out—already a false move, because since when do I care about the success of her grocery outings?

Patti pops the trunk, and I help deliver the bags to the kitchen counter but am shooed out of the way so my mother can unpack them in her customary manner.

It being only a matter of time before one of our guests makes their presence known, without further ado, I say:

"Mom, I've got something to tell you."

"What is it?" she says without looking up.

"It's kind of big."

Lifting a head of lettuce out of one of the bags, she exhales with beleaguerment. "Is it absolutely necessary that you tell me this now?"

"I would say so. Yes."

"Then tell me."

"It's about Holden."

The sight of my mother standing there, in one hand a two-liter bottle of tomato juice, in the other a tub of butter, actual butter (I can't believe it's not I Can't Believe It's Not Butter! God bless the Midwest), her features troubled and sleepless, waiting for yet another kick in the proverbial balls, I appreciate for the very first time in my life the hazards, the grave responsibility, of being the bearer of life-altering news.

"Remember the woman who called you from Colombia? Lulu?" I say.

"Yes." She rolls her eyes for some reason. "Did you hear from her again?"

"Uh, yes, I did."

Patti huffs. "What does she want?"

"I don't want anything," says a voice. Patti spins around. "Only to attend my fiancé's funeral."

For the first time in her life, my mother is speechless. That is to say, mute—not merely words failing her but any construct of reality that would lend meaning or context to the events unfolding in her kitchen. She stares utterly blankly at this foreign body in a billowy crewneck who has materialized by her dimmer switch.

Patti says: "Fiancé?"

Lulu perceives hurt, not anger, on my mother's visage. "I'm sorry you didn't know," she says. "Holden was going to tell you."

"Fiancé?" Patti repeats, louder this time. Homing in on the ring on Lulu's left hand, a white stone glinting from her finger, my mother laughs joylessly at my brother's old habit, still knifelike enough to draw blood after all these years, of holding out on us, keeping us beyond the gates. "My son gets engaged and doesn't bother to mention it. Why am I both shocked and completely unsurprised?" She looks at me. "How about you? Any marriages I don't know about?"

"Okay, Mom."

"I'm offering amnesty," she sings. "Speak now!"

Lulu tries to jump in: "Patti—"

"I'm just trying to marshal the facts," my mother continues. "In case anybody forgot to clue me in on, oh, I don't know, a marriage, a divorce, a tour of duty in a combat zone, the birth of a child. Let's get all the big-ticket items on the table."

"This is not Lulu's fault," I say. "She didn't fly all the way from Florida to watch you blow a gasket."

"It's okay, Rowan," Lulu says. "I understand. Your mother is entitled to her reaction."

Such magnanimity in the face of such inhospitality is impressive. I probably would've run out the door in tears, and although Lulu is not crying, someone else in the house is. In the quiet cease-fire that pervades, we can all hear a high-register wailing from a remote corner of the house.

Patti freezes. She doesn't even flirt with the fantasy that the noise she hears is coming from a stroller being pushed down the street outside or our TV. She gapes at Lulu. "Is that yours?"

And Lulu kind of smiles and says, "Actually, Patti, he's ours."

I'd always put the odds of Patti already being a grandmother at about fifty-fifty. It seemed eminently conceivable (no pun intended) that there were a handful of mini Holdens running amok and up to no good in Santa Monica or Vail or the Vegas strip (especially the Vegas strip), and it was just a matter of time before we learned of their existence via postcard or INTERPOL alert. How adorable that my mother evidently didn't see this coming.

We are all standing around the Pack 'n Play out of which Lulu has just hoisted her infant, thereby dousing his fiery tantrum like a bucket of ice, the only trace of it now being the rivulets of tears that have made it all the way down his otherwise stainless cheeks.

"This is Breezy," Lulu coos lovingly into the baby's face. "Breeze-Brooklyn Lopez-Darling."

It's almost a letdown how much of a nonevent the name reveal turns out to be, as my mother is obviously bewitched by weightier matters. "Are you telling me this is my grandson?"

Lulu holds him out to my mother, and for the first time in her life, Patricia Darling takes possession of the child of her child. She beholds him with the awe and curiosity of a prehistoric archeological find.

"My goodness, aren't you cute," she says. She says it with a frown, like his cuteness is only going to make things harder. "Six months is a long time to not know your grandmother."

"Holden was planning to tell you," Lulu reports.

My mother makes a clucking sound: skepticism.

"We were all going to come at Thanksgiving," Lulu says. "He thought it would be a nice surprise."

I don't know whether my mother believes that or not, whether she really thinks late November would've found this house, typically subdued at holiday time, noisy and congested. What matters to Patti right now is the small human she holds in her clutches. She combs for clues in his miniature features, pores over him for traces of her own boy, the one she will never again hold in her arms, and perhaps she is thinking that that is what makes this baby—all babies—a true relic: a thing that emerges from the ruins to document what was and enliven what is to come.

Maybe it's just me thinking those things, not my mother.

"Breeze-Brooklyn," Patti says, trying out the words. "Are you from New York?" she asks Lulu.

"Florida," the woman replies. "Mom and Dad were from Havana. Holden and I named Breezy after my favorite book, *A Tree Grows in Brooklyn*. I figured you'd appreciate that. Didn't you name Holden for *Catcher in the Rye*?"

Entranced as she may be with the baby, Patti still isn't sure what to make of Lulu, and she's keeping up her guard. "I think we just liked the name," she answers somewhat stiffly, although she's playfully tapping the bubble of Breeze's nose.

"Well, Holden Darling thought he was named after Holden Caulfield," Lulu informs her. "And he was proud of it. Thought it quite the gift."

Patti isn't giving herself over to a smile yet, but I can see in her eyes that this makes her happy. "Maybe we did, now that you mention it," she allows. "I think it was George's idea."

Lulu nods; she knows who George is. Another revelation that in most families would not rise to the level of one: Holden has spoken of us to her. His family was a part of him important enough to share.

This is not enough to rid my mother of her suspicions about our guests. When Lulu runs downstairs to retrieve the diaper bag, Patti scrunches up her face. "You really think this little guy is Holden's?" she whispers to me.

"Definitely not," I answer, straight-faced. "I don't think this woman even knew Holden. I think she doctored some photographs and falsified evidence of all of them playing family, then packed up her infant and traveled all the way from Miami to East Jesus, Illinois, to scam you out of a teacher's pension."

One of my mother's eyebrows climbs in reaction to all the inconvenient sense I'm making. She pivots. "Well, what kind of name is Breeze-Brooklyn anyway?"

"It's her kid. She can name him the Lorax if she wants to. Please behave, Patricia. You're doing so well so far."

Lulu returns with a clean diaper, a mini jar of yellow-green mush, and a bib. This forces my mother to confront the barrenness of her accommodations.

"I would've bought a high chair had I known," she says to no one in particular.

"It's okay," Lulu chirps. "We'll make do."

"I don't want to just *make do*." My mother pouts. "This is my grandchild. I don't even have any toys in the house."

Lulu smiles her down off the ledge. "It's really okay. We're fine. I promise."

The young woman puts a hand on my mother's arm. There's gratitude in that touch, a reaching out, the transference of the happiest part of Holden from one body to another. And Patti's reservations dissipate. She has surrendered them, at least for now. She looks at the child in her arms and, in the crux of this horrible week so full of loss, seems to discover the wonder of Holden's bequest.

"You were there when my son died?" she asks Lulu without taking her eyes off the baby.

"Yes, I was."

"Did he suffer?"

Lulu shakes her head. "I don't think so. I think he hit his head and never woke up."

For a second, I think my mother is going to cry, but in a strange way, I feel as though she might be past crying. What would be the point? It's like she said the other night: there are no bricks to heave at the temple, nor temples at which to heave them. There's no justice in the world except the kind we put in the stories we tell ourselves, so why should we expect any? For me, *that* is the point. I can't think of a better reason to cry than all that.

"We'll set you up nicely in here," Patti says. She casts her frown around the room. "I know it's like Communist Bloc accommodations now, but we'll do what we can to make it comfy."

"That's kind of you, but we'll be perfectly fine in a hotel," argues Lulu. "You've got enough to deal with."

Patti's mouth creases. "I think we all do." She smiles down at the baby. "Let's go downstairs and feed you your gruel, then find some nice cozy blankets for you and Mommy."

"Are you sure about this?" Lulu asks.

It's too soon to say if my mother has accepted these strangers as family—the indifference shown her by the universe hasn't made Patti quick to love—but she has accepted that they'll sleep here tonight.

"Don't fight it," I say. "My mother's a teacher. She's used to people doing what she says."

"It's a public school," Patti gripes, already chugging down the hallway. "Nobody does what I say."

CHAPTER 19

A pen name is a form of schizophrenia, if you think about it: the urge to reveal competes with the urge to conceal. I could only guess as to why Margot Beckett decided to publish her stories as Portia Wentworth, but surely that is no greater mystery than why she decided to publish her stories at all. If Margot was a writer back when I knew her, she was even more secretive about it than she is now.

It didn't take long to find Portia Wentworth's website, tucked away inconspicuously at PortiaWentworth.com. Her short stories are downloadable for the affordable price of three dollars per, or you can plop down an annual subscription of ten bucks and get access to the lot of them. And there are a lot of them.

I am lying on my bed with the lights low and the evening advancing, so while I may be noodling around in published works accessible to anyone in the world who wants to read them, there's a voyeuristic mood in the room. Why do I feel like I'm digging through someone's yard with a flashlight between my teeth? What am I looking for? Doesn't everyone want to know what jingles the bells in their ex's head?

I'm interrupted by Patti's soft knock. She pokes her head in to inform me that Lulu and Breeze have called it a night, so she supposes she'll do the same. She hesitates, then steps in and sits down on the bed. "Do you trust her?" she whispers.

"I've been given no reason not to," I answer.

"You don't think all of this is strange?"

"No, I very much do. I think all of this is strange."

Patti gives me a drained look, which she has certainly earned.

I shoot for lightness. "Want to hear something crazy? You're a grandma."

Her mouth twists with equivocation. How could she not be of two minds? As wonderful as it is to discover a secret grandchild, it's equally awful for a grandchild to be a discovered secret.

"Look, Mom—whatever doubts you have, how about we pretend that these people are who they claim to be? Even if it's not true, isn't that the better story?"

"This isn't a story, Rowan. This is our lives."

"Of course it's a story. And if we're wrong, if Lulu is a fake name and this is all an elaborate charade driven by some motivation whose plausibility you'll never convince me of, let's die believing it anyway."

My mother gives in to a smile. She's ready to believe too. For all her feisty opposition, she has lived by the creed that it is better in than out, that *we* are better in than out. My brother up and left, my father before him, but Patti was always here. Here for me. She made sure I had rides wherever I needed to go, she packed me a brown bag fat with grub five days a week, she required me to make check-in calls and dished out hell if I forgot. My world was never perfect, but it was always safe, thanks to Patti Darling.

My mother pats the topography of my legs under the covers. "You remember how you used to hide when you were little?"

I shake my head.

"I'd take you to the mall, and suddenly I'd turn around and you'd be gone. You'd disappear into a fitting room or under a rack of clothes, and not just for a few seconds either. Sometimes I'd be looking for you for five, ten minutes, which is a hell of a long time when you think you've lost your kid. I didn't believe you'd actually left the building or gotten kidnapped or anything, but sometimes you stayed hidden long enough to get me concerned. And that was always just when you came back. You'd hear a note of worry creep into my voice as I called out for you. The moment you sensed that your poor mother was truly anxious, you'd materialize. 'I'm here, Mommy! Don't worry! Here I am!' And you'd come running out with your arms wide, ready for a hug, and although what I really wanted to do was bop you on the head with my shoe and call you a miserable little bastard, I never did. I hugged you and told you you'd given me a fright, and don't do it again." She pauses to let her eyes drift around my room like she too hasn't been here in a while. "You always had my back, Rowan. You had your fun, but when push came to shove, you came out. You let yourself be found."

I lean back against the headboard and marvel at the wild dichotomy of my mother. One minute, she's gentle, the type of woman who might run a craft shop in a seaside town, Creations by Patricia, selling porcelain figurines and soap. The next minute, she's the city councilwoman who's had it up to here.

"I know I'm not the reason you moved away," she says. "But I think that's why your desertion stung me more than your brother's. Because you weren't born to leave me."

"I'll always come out when you call for me, Mom," I tell her. "Just like when I was little."

She leans in, puts a kiss on my hair. "And what about when I don't call?" she asks as she gets to her feet. "Will you be listening then?"

—

Wasn't it me, not Margot, who wanted to be a writer? Even if she has scant recollection of that (four hundred words on the senior production of *My Fair Lady* for the school paper isn't exactly a bibliography to boast about), this website feels like yet another example of Margot edging me out of my own dreams. I didn't expect to feel territorial, but that is one of the many sensations that comes on as I prepare to dive into her work. Part of me is saying, *I was the writer, not her.* The other part of me is saying, *Prove it, Rowan. All you did was take a few undergraduate composition classes, which you phoned in, and then an evening writing workshop with a highly regarded novelist whose books you read, loved, and were demoralized by when a real writer would have found inspiration in them.* Maybe I have nothing to say. Maybe I would have ended up in the same place as Margot: posting unedited short stories on a website under an alias. Even that is just something else I didn't do.

But I have come here to mock, not admire, to lie under my bed lamp with an unlimited subscription to the collected works of Portia Wentworth.

The design of Margot's website is a good place to start if derision is my game. The home page is a mess of treacly pastoral illustrations: meadows and horses, fish splashing about in streams, bees circling flowers. It's the stuff of boardwalk art, and if this is who Margot has become, I'm starting to think the last laugh will be mine.

My behavior over the ensuing hours is nothing to be proud of. I tear through her stories like a junkie, clicking on file after file until I've binge-read five of her pieces without so much as glancing at the clock. It's serial fiction, stand-alone stories, each fifteen to twenty-five pages long and portraying another adventure in the life of her heroine, Julianna Goodheart. (The "author" calls them "adventures," but at most I see flights of fancy, mild verbal altercations, the occasional shenanigans.) Julianna Goodheart is the town divorcée with a wild streak. She's also a heart surgeon. I suss this out early on, as the very first line of every story reads: "Julianna Goodheart is the town divorcée with a wild streak. She's also a heart surgeon."

Overlooking the eye-roller of having christened her heart surgeon "Goodheart"; that it's questionable whether small towns even have heart surgeons (aren't the highly trained specialists generally found in the hotbeds of medical ingenuity, like major metropolitan areas?); that

Julianna's husband left her for some innocent, bookish librarian (yup, she describes the librarian as "bookish"), even though no one in their right mind would leave Julianna, depicted as she is as sophisticated, moneyed, quick with a quip, and a hellcat in bed; the stories are really rather readable. The writing is neither awesome nor awful, the tales are diverting, and much to my chagrin, I am mildly, reluctantly, begrudgingly impressed. This is not the Margot I knew. Or the Portia.

I churn through her stories almost mechanically, forgoing sleep I probably wasn't going to get anyway, unsure of what compels me to read on, of what clues I might be looking for. I read a story called "The Soft Regret," in which Julianna reflects on the baby she gave up because she was very young and felt unprepared to raise a child. I know that story is beyond the realm of autobiography (the pregnancy she had at a relatively young age was the one that produced Alex), but it gets me thinking about Margot's regrets. Does she have others?

The sixth story, "Tournament by the Woods," finds Julianna at her country club preparing for a tennis tournament under the tutelage of the club's hunky Australian pro, Lon. The sexual tension between Julianna and Lon is palpable. (It's right there on page four: "The sexual tension between Julianna and Lon was palpable.") When Lon puts his hand on her arm to guide her through a swing, she bites her lip. When he stands behind her to demonstrate footwork, she looks over her shoulder at him with a slinky smirk. There is all manner of on-court innuendo involving words like *stamina*, *dominate*, and *playing hard*, and when I picture Alex happening upon these writings—erotica from his own mother's pen—I cringe for him and also applaud him for fighting off a psychotic break.

In the first match of the competition, Julianna faces Blair Berkshire, a reviled figure around the club for her sense of entitlement and her propensity to help herself to other members' husbands. After an achingly suspenseful tiebreaker—belabored with unnecessary but rigorously accurate technical detail (Margot showing off)—Julianna emerges victorious. She rushes off the court and into Lon's arms for, in this reader's opinion, an inappropriate courtside tongue kiss.

Informed by the tournament director that she has a half-hour rest before her next match, Julianna winks seductively at Lon and purrs, "I don't feel much like resting, do you?"

Off they trot into the woods, stopping at an old oak tree, where Julianna leans back against the trunk, and the dreamboat tennis pro proceeds to inch his fingers up our heroine's supple inner thigh, under her skirt, and down past the elastic of her Calvin Kleins. There is a hushed frenzy of gyration, a quickening of breath, and a rising birdsong of delicate moans, and just as it ends, the two of them upright in the shaded wood, Julianna hears her name being called for her second match. Which she races back for. And wins.

"You are magical," Lon tells her after her victory. To which Julianna says, "You are the love of my life, you know." To which Lon says, "I know. But I've decided to return to Australia to run the family shipping business." The story closes with Julianna standing on a beach many years hence, still carrying a torch for Lon, whom she pictures somewhere over the horizon, perched high on the mast of a rollicking vessel. A swell of violins and a slow fade-out are implied.

I'm going to give Margot the benefit of the doubt and assume the hokeyness is on purpose. She must know that an Australian tennis-pro-cum-shipping-magnate is unlikely to be found on the mast of a ship—unless he's Ferdinand Magellan or Vasco da Gama or some other turn-of-the-sixteenth-century maritime explorer. The story is campy and improbable, but it is also dead-to-rights true. I would know. I was there. This is not an author borrowing from her past. This is actual history, a diary transcribed word for word, proper nouns changed to protect the uncomfortable. To learn that I am still in there somewhere, a regret rattling around inside Margot, is a discovery as shimmering and glorious as anything that rose up to meet Amerigo Vespucci or Hernando de Soto. I don't need to be the lost thing that causes her to contemplate the horizon. It's enough that when she wrung out the sponge of her memory, this anecdote—an adventure that could happen only between two fresh-faced teenagers—landed on the page. I hope Margot does regret what she did to me, and I hope Skid read this and it led to an argument and everyone went to sleep mad.

I pull the blanket up to my chin. Darkness enfolds me here in my childhood bedroom, history swooping down around me like bats. I think of home, of Daisy, of the trusty mundanity of Metaphysical Graffiti. And then I think of Holden and allow myself to believe that sometimes, in those last moments of consciousness before sleep closed in on him, images of this house, of the bedroom next to this one, of me even, flashed before his eyes.

CHAPTER 20

That dream stalks me again. It ends before I learn what happens. Was there really a storm outside the Graffiti? Was Holden too reckless or I too cautious?

At two a.m., I venture out of my room for a drink of water, and the sound of soft humming draws me to Holden's room. Through the cracked door, I'm barely able to make out Lulu reclining against a pillow, Breeze lying next to her, the whites of his eyes incandescent in the dimness. Lulu's soft voice warbles a melody that I don't quite recognize but feels familiar, like a lullaby.

The singing cuts out, and Lulu whispers, loud enough for me to hear, "I think I see Uncle Rowan."

I have a new name. It ages me, sounding so next-generation, but rings bittersweetly of things lost and found. I nudge the ajar door wider.

"Come on in," Lulu beckons. "Nobody's sleeping in here."

I ask if she needs anything, and she pats the space on the futon next to Breeze in invitation. Though we've known each other for mere hours, I suppose we are overnight intimates now. I lower myself onto the foot of the futon and shift around to face them, all of us clad in pajamas.

I hear a sniff; then Lulu raises her arm and dabs the outside corners of her eyes with her sleeve. "Sorry. Nights are hard."

"I know," I say. I lean back, planting my palms on the blanket behind me. "I'm sorry that my mom is being a little prickly. She means well. Usually."

Through the darkness, I see Lulu bend sideways and press her nose against Breeze's cheek, drawing in the smell of him. "You're both very kind to welcome us in. This must've been a nice house for you and Holden to grow up in."

And yet we scattered. We became like members of a society that showed up reluctantly to the annual meeting. Sometimes we made the attendee list but didn't show up at all.

"I truly believe he was starting to change, Holden was," Lulu volunteers. Breeze pipes up with a noise that sounds part hiccup, part bubble pop; apparently, he too has something to say about his father. "The baby changed him. I changed him. I think he was ready to be someone different, someone who wanted to see more of his family."

"I really missed out," I hear myself say.

"He often spoke of you, and your mom."

I peer at her. "Really?"

"Oh, yeah." She nods, smiles. "That's why I feel like I know you."

I ask how she and Holden got started, and Lulu makes no bones about it: she'd gotten pregnant two weeks after they met. Holden was new in town, having recently moved to Miami for a job with a rum distributor, and one of his accounts was the South Beach Cuban restaurant where she was a manager. "What can I say? I was twenty-three and as fertile as the Nile."

At first, she wasn't sure she was going to keep the baby. She was barely out of college, barely knew the father, and was juggling both a job and a master's program in social work at the University of Miami. But in adherence to her strict Catholic upbringing that surprised even her, she put the degree on the back burner and chose the kid.

Her decision to have the baby didn't magically render the inseminator a fit coparent, and it didn't take a master's degree in anything to see Holden for what he was: charming, adventurous, sweet, possibly difficult to pin down. She continued to date him, but with caution, keeping the pregnancy a secret as long as she could. Nevertheless, the relationship got serious, fast. Holden was good to Lulu—sincere, committed, supportive of all she wanted to accomplish.

Then, a few months in, she noticed activity on his Tinder app and immediately broke things off.

"That was his out," she says. "And he didn't take it. He begged me to give him another chance. He told me he loved me, that this felt more real to him than anything he'd ever had, and he was in it for the long haul. So I told him about the baby. I figured that would be the litmus test. I'd know just how long of a haul he had in mind. But it didn't scare him off. He was ecstatic, and only grew more so when Breezy arrived."

As I listen, I find myself rooting for Holden like I root for a character in a book, the one who needs to get his act together and grow up in order to win the girl. That is the distance I feel. *I really missed out.*

Lulu was on the deck of that fishing boat with him, holding their six-month-old, when Holden dived off the stern into unexpectedly shallow bay waters. They'd been enjoying the peaceful sunset excursion, the cooler of watermelon juice, the captain's "famous" aguardiente recipe, the steel-drum yacht music. And she was standing right there when the captain and his first mate pulled his slack body out of the water, a dripping red gash smeared across his forehead.

I look across the mattress at my near-miss of a sister-in-law; I realize how much harder Lulu has been hit than Patti or I. Holden's death, much like his life, was in many ways an abstraction for us.

For Lulu, there's a freshly cold half of the bed. There's the memory of blood.

Suddenly, Lulu says, "I brought you something."

"Me?"

She holds Breeze out to me, then gets up to rummage around in her suitcase under the beam of her phone flashlight.

I look down at the baby. A wet babble begins to churn out of his mouth, and his limbs move in his onesie like he's running in place. I make soft shushing sounds and cup his head against me. Suddenly I'm laughing.

Lulu turns her head. "You okay?"

There's a lightweight sack of warmth gurgling against my chest. "Holy fucking shit," I say.

She smiles and sweeps back her long, snaky locks, wild in midnight disarray. "I know. He's yummy, right?"

The hunt through her luggage for god-knows-what continues. "This is actually the only souvenir I thought to bring. I plucked it off the wall literally on my way out the door to come here." Then, "Ah. Here we go."

She places an object in my free hand. It's smooth and flat, but I can't see what it is until she points the flashlight beam at it, carefully avoiding her son's eyes. It's a napkin in a picture frame. The napkin has writing, an autograph, scribbled across it in black marker.

I regard the illegible scrawl, then, carefully: "My brother's autograph? Very cool. Thank you."

She laughs. "It's not your brother. It's your hero. The guy from that band you love—Talking Heads. David Berg or something?"

I look again. "For real? This is David Byrne's autograph?"

"Byrne. Yeah, him. Holden ran into him in some restaurant years ago and got him to sign a napkin. I thought you'd want it. He said you were the one who got him hooked."

I gaze with reverence upon the keepsake. "This is incredible." An unimpressed Breeze-Brooklyn yawns into my clavicle. "Really. Thank you."

Lulu nods proudly. "I thought you'd like it."

An autograph from the Talking Heads front man would, under any circumstances, be a keepsake that reminded me of Holden; it's how I'd feel if I snagged one at a flea market. But the fact that Holden himself held the napkin, looked Byrne in the eye, thanked him, and probably shook his hand—it's almost too much. I nearly hand it back to her. *Why didn't he tell me?* The frustration I feel, the deluge of yearning for conversations I'll never get to have. *How could he not have* immediately *called me?* Had it been me, I would've been dialing before I walked away from Byrne's table. Why it did not occur to him that the vicarious thrill I surely would've felt would've made the experience a million times more thrilling for him?

I really missed out. You did too.

"Thank you," I say to her. "Truth be told, Holden was the real fan, the first fan. But yeah, I definitely caught the bug."

"Oh." Lulu seems surprised. "I thought he caught it from you. He used to joke that his obsession with that band was the best thing you ever gave him. He said you were constantly listening, way too loud, irritating him to no end, so he just surrendered and started loving them like you did."

I look up at her and meet her eyes in the soupy dark. "Did he really say that? I don't remember it that way."

"It was kind of a thing in our house," she says. "Wasn't there some Talking Heads movie you dragged him to? He remembered what you said about that movie. He said you got all amped up about it, the two of you went out and saw it together, and when it was over, you stood up and yelled to the entire theater that that movie made you want to take a balloon to the moon." She rocks back, laughing. "He loved that you said that. Balloon to the moon. That was actually kind of his catchphrase. That's how I first heard it. If he thought I looked pretty, he said I made him want to take a balloon to the moon. When I cooked him my *ropa vieja*? Balloon to the moon."

I laugh along with her, I tell her it was a pretty geeky thing to say. And it was. But I didn't say it. Holden did. Everything about this story gets the pronouns backward. But there's no need to set the record straight. I can just be happy. Happy that Holden remembered things the opposite of how they really were. Happy that, it turns out, I could influence my older brother, make him love what I loved simply because I loved it. I had no idea that this unaccountable teenager in the next room could learn anything from me worth carrying with him into the world. I had no idea he was out there using my catchphrase. (A catchphrase that was, I am positive, or maybe I'm only nearly positive, his own.)

"Do you mind sticking around for a few more minutes?" Lulu asks. "I was going to slip outside a sec."

"Outside?"

I notice the white stick between her fingers as her hand skirts furtively around her pajama leg. The autograph wasn't all she fished out of her suitcase.

She sees me trying not to look at her hand. "No, I don't smoke around Breezy."

She thinks she has read my thoughts. But I hadn't gotten that far. I was just surprised to see that cigarettes are still manufactured here in the twenty-first century.

As Lulu steals out of the room, I recline against the pillow and curl this baby into my arm. The child suddenly lifts his heavy head and stares at me straightaway as though he's got some critical information to divulge now that we're finally alone, but then he seems to think the better of it and drops back into the cradle of my chest. I'm soothed by his closeness and want to return the favor, puff out his incipient sadness like a birthday candle. It's an uncle's job, isn't it? *Sorry, little man. We Darling boys never get to know our fathers. Welcome to the family.*

He closes his eyes and his breathing steadies, and my own eyelids begin to droop. I'll sleep better now, possessing this framed autograph from my brother and a new truth about our favorite band. Sometimes the greatest thing in the world is to be completely wrong about something important.

CHAPTER 21

Bursts of daylight force my eyes open. It's half past ten, an unheard-of hour for me to awaken. I'm alone on the futon, alone in the room, in fact, the only evidence that Lulu ever returned from her cigarette break being Breeze's absence. Someone either snatched him out of my arms or he's crushed underneath me.

I lug myself through the silent house, down to the kitchen where, to my utter disorientation, I find Margot Beckett. Not her stories, but her. Seated at the table, engrossed with her phone, helping herself to my house so casually that she can only be an apparition. I am stunned speechless by the incongruous sight of her here, by the sight of her anywhere, in fact (I have already crossed paths with her since my arrival in town, but even that brief encounter now feels hallucinatory), and I'm terrified in advance by whatever catastrophic circumstances have deposited her body in our kitchen chair.

The apparition sees me. "Someone's a good sleeper." She turns sheepish. "Sorry I'm here. It is me. You're not dreaming."

I know I'm not dreaming. This isn't how I dream. Unless our breakup and the last fifteen years have been a dream and I have forgotten that we are married and took over the family home, in which case this is fine, perfectly natural that I'm standing in front of my ex in boxers and eye crust.

"Your mom and your sister-in-law went outside to take the baby for a stroll," Margot reports, explaining nothing.

"I feel like there should be more," I say.

She smiles. "I'm supposed to bring you to my house to help load some things into my van. Things for the baby." She nods at the Mr. Coffee on the counter. "They threw some coffee on for you before they left. And it's fiancée, isn't it? Sorry. I said 'sister-in-law.'"

I'm still pretty much speechless and feeling like I've slept a whole lot longer than one night. My brain can't seem to process the fact that Margot Beckett is in my house, lounging about while I was sleeping. It's like I've skipped two or three episodes of a TV show, and the plot has moved on without me.

Smiling shyly at me across the divide of vinyl flooring, sheets of fake tile that have never fooled anyone, Margot sets her phone down on the table and folds her arms. "For the record, this wasn't my idea."

"I still don't know what idea you're referring to," I say, lumbering over to the coffeepot while trying not to find her beautiful. I should concentrate on being affronted, on the fact that Margot's unceremonious occupation of this house is a trivialization of my feelings. One of us should leave. That's what I want. Isn't it?

"I came by to see your mom," she says. "I haven't seen her since Holden, and I just wanted to give her a hug. She introduced me to Lulu and the baby. Sidenote: Is his name really Breeze-Brooklyn?"

"Apparently."

"Like, with a hyphen?"

"I haven't seen it written out."

"Okay," she says. End of sidenote. "Your mom sort of implied that both of them were something of a surprise, so I said, 'You know, if you guys need any baby stuff, I've got plenty of it in my basement just collecting dust. I still have a crib, a high chair, and boxes of toys from when Alex was little.' And your mom was like, 'Actually, we have nothing.' So I said, 'I'll run right home and get it.' And she said, 'Great. I'll just wake up Rowan, and he'll help you lug everything over.' And I said, 'Let the poor guy sleep. He probably needs it'—am I a good friend or what?"

She winks at me, ironically I'm sure, as the second-to-last thing in the world she is to me is a friend, and the last thing in the world she is to me is a good friend.

"So they all went for a walk, I made myself comfortable, and here we are." She sits back in her chair and toys with the drawstring of her unzipped lightweight sweatshirt the color of an unripe peach. "And yes, I think your mom knew exactly how not on board with this you'd be, but no, she didn't seem to care."

I'm furious at my mother for allowing any of this to happen. I'm struggling to act normal in the presence of the person who produces in me the least normal feelings. I'm vehemently opposed to participating in this errand because it may well entail running into Skid, and the one person in the universe I want to see less than Margot is Skid. (I actually wasn't conscious of that ranking until just now.) And on top of everything, Margot's reason for showing up here feels weirdly like an excuse. She knew I was here. What does she want from me? For the last decade and a half, right up until last night, I would've said she wants absolutely nothing. But now I've read her stories (or Portia Wentworth's), and I know I'm in there somewhere, possibly something she's working to resolve, or maybe not, maybe just a featured player in some of her most colorful memories. And now she's here, in my house, and although I'm the only one of any of us who seems to know better, I'm also, as always, calling none of the shots.

I take a sip of the tin-can brew, then dump the whole mess into the sink. "I need to throw on some clothes."

"If you say so," says Margot.

And I leave her there in the kitchen, and all I can think about is when you see a bird in the mall, and everybody knows a bird isn't supposed to be in a mall, but nobody seems terribly concerned.

Except for the bird.

Which means I'm the bird.

Behind the wheel of her blue Dodge Caravan, Margot drives us along Campsite Lane like all of this is okay, and I sit in the passenger seat, largely mute and stiff, praying to God that Skid isn't home but daring not to ask.

"So your mom seems like she's doing okay. All things considered," Margot finally volunteers. "She's a grandma—I guess that helps?"

"She's rolling with it," I reply.

I sure hope I don't kick up nearly as much of an ordeal when it's my turn for the dirt nap. No surprise children, no shipping of corpses from the Southern Hemisphere. Simple. Understated. *Rowan Darling, 72, died at home after a brief illness. The body of Rowan Darling, 46, was discovered at the bottom of an elevator shaft. Whoever he is survived by, if anyone, could not be reached for comment.* Two gravediggers can grab my wrists and ankles and sling me like a sack of potatoes into an unmarked pit. That'll do just fine.

"We want to come to the memorial service, Skid and I," Margot ventures. "That's okay, right?"

That's an awful idea. Why would I want them there? "Yeah, sure."

I sense her eyes skirting over to the passenger seat, trying to attach to mine. "You know, Rowan," she begins, her voice flat and immediate in the confining air of the car interior, like she's lying next to me on the carpeted floor of her bedroom in the house she grew up in. "I know it was a million years ago, but I just want to say I'm sorry. It was a shitty thing Skid and I did."

"It's fine," is what I hear my numb self say.

"Well, it wasn't at the time," Margot says. "I know we hurt you. I've wanted to talk to you about it for a long time."

But I don't want to talk about it at all. Her apology, hideously overdue though it is, comes at me too suddenly, too anticlimactically. Is this what I've been waiting for? Is it even what I've wanted? Apology extended, apology accepted, and we're done? Hating her, hating them, clutching my victimhood: it runs so deep that it's part of my identity; it's how the world is organized. For so long, I've wished terrible—or at least moderately inconvenient—things on Margot, like that her car runs out of gas in a safe neighborhood or she gets stung by a bee but isn't allergic. But now she's right here, and she thinks of me with regret, and I still think of her as the grass stain on the knee of my jeans, the one that doesn't ruin the jeans but instead renders them irreplaceable.

Before I am forced to muster a reply, Margot's phone rings. She sees the caller, puts the phone to her ear, and says, "Hi."

"He *what*?" she exclaims. "Are you kidding me? You're kidding me."

Whoever's on the other end of the line is not, I suspect, kidding her. I'm hearing only half of this conversation, but the half I'm not hearing is not good news. I shift my head to the scenery as Margot agitates hotly about some unspecified person being "beyond stupid" and "a lost cause," and therefore, "What was he thinking? I'm going to kill him."

This is the way people talk about their kids. She can only be referring to Alex.

She heaves a long, loud sigh, one for the back row of the theater, and says, "I'm on my way." Then she adds, "By the way, just so you know, Rowan is with me."

She hangs up, and I am advised of a slight change of plans: Margot needs to swing by the high school to pick up her fine, upstanding son who has just been suspended for smoking pot in the bathroom. Since I'm in the car with her, I will be swinging by the high school as well. Margot asks if I mind the detour, which is polite of her but, I am beginning to understand, gratuitous. This was always a kidnapping. Who cares what the hostage wants?

Margot has gone angrily silent, or silently angry, which I find helpful because I don't think I could simultaneously concentrate on conversation with her and my imminent rendezvous with Skid. Countless are the times I played out in my head a reunion scene between Margot and me. Never once have I done so with Skid Hall. Why? Could I just not picture it?

Margot is still staring coldly through the windshield when we peel into the Maybee High parking lot like we're late for homeroom. First through the double doors is Alex, who I last saw about a day ago, and then comes his father, who I last saw about a lifetime ago. With that, I am overcome by a helpless claustrophobia, a visceral, imperative, instinctual need to tuck, duck, and roll out of this moving vehicle.

Margot pulls to a stop at the end of the long walkway that leads from the school entrance to the lot. She exits the van, and because I guess I'd feel even more stupid if I stayed inside the van, as though I were another one of her kids, I get out too.

I've guessed wrong. I feel just as stupid outside.

I take in the sight of him striding down the path. From the time I was old enough to have friends, Skid was my closest one. I was the George Harrison to his Paul McCartney, the Coke to his rum, the Ferb to his Phineas. He was the life of the party; I kept an eye on the time, made sure things didn't get too out of hand. I look at him now and see that kid who slept over at least once a week, who consumed more food from the Darling pantry than anybody actually named Darling, who was around so often that you couldn't really call him a guest because he was answering our door, answering our phone, even getting yelled at on occasion by my mother for spilling soda or moving furniture around for our WWF matches. I see the kid who calmly and very convincingly threatened an older and much larger kid when he threw an elbow that knocked the wind out of me during a pickup basketball game. I also see the guy who, on the night I was introduced to Jägermeister at Dov Halevi's party, drove Margot home and didn't return to retrieve me until noticeably later than that errand should've taken. I see the guy who, when paired with Margot for that American history project earlier that year, showed an inordinate level of interest in the spread of Communism and Soviet influence in the post–World War II era. I didn't think anything of it at the time. Why would I? Never in a million lifetimes could Skid Hall move in on the girl I loved. A million lifetimes have passed since, and like an emotionally stunted fool, I am still thinking about it.

He marches right up to me, his steps gathering speed. He says, "Rowan W. Darling," then bursts upon me, heaving his arms around my torso and compressing my upper body against his like he's trying to combine us. He used to do this all the time—after a victorious football game, when we met up at a party, in homeroom for absolutely no reason. (Once, he lost his balance and dropped me onto Lori McInerney's desk, which sent a pencil shooting up and pinging her in the eye. She had to go to the nurse, but Skid hooked up with her that weekend, so all was forgiven.) In the force of Skid's forced embrace, I feel myself go cold.

"I've missed you," he says into my ear.

You can go right on missing me, I think to myself, *because I'm not here. It just looks that way.*

Also: my middle name is George. Skid always thought *W* sounded better between my first and last name, so he unofficially changed my middle initial.

He releases me, steps back to take me in, then goes grave. "I'm sick about Holden. Sick about it." But he can't keep a smile from breaking like the day across his face. "I thought you'd lost your way home, Ro."

Margot clears her throat, a reminder to everyone present that there are other reasons we are all convened here. She wheels on her son. "Pot? At *school*? What kind of a fool are you?"

Alex starts to plead his case, but Margot shuts him down. "I don't want to hear it. We'll talk about this later."

Skid can't take his eyes off me. "It's really good to see you, man." And he's so convincing that I begin to wonder if the Great Betrayal is something I once upon a time invented, decided to believe, and eventually forgot was completely made up. Up close, I see the scars of battle on him: the ash-like dusting in his cropped hair, the slight sinking of his eyes, the noticeable if not dramatic weight loss. He wears his past sickness like a shadow. He is cured of his cancer, but reduced. Haunted at the edges.

"How many days is the suspension?" Margot is demanding.

"One. Just tomorrow," Alex replies.

"That's two," she snaps back.

"Let's split the difference," Skid jokes, his levity attracting a glare from his wife.

"You've met Alex, right?" Skid asks me.

I nod and do not say, *Yes, we were introduced at a previous crime.*

"We're going to have a long talk about this tonight," Margot says to the kid. "This and so many other things."

"He knows this was piss-poor judgment," Skid says. Then he glares at his son. "Right?"

Skid then regards his watch. He has a class to teach, he announces, and Margot shakes her head like she can't decide which member of her family is the greater source of ire.

"Just get in the car," she grunts at Alex.

As the delinquent slinks into the back seat of the van, Skid takes me in like he's afraid to say goodbye. "Are you okay?" he asks.

"Yeah. I'm fine."

"Can we pick this up later?"

"Sure," I say.

Brandishing that bulletproof grin, Skid lumbers back up the walkway. When he stops to interrogate a pair of shaggy hooligans coming down the walkway, looking like they've decided to knock off early for the day, I wonder if Skid is thinking about the times he accosted me in the hall, said, "I really don't feel like being here anymore. Shall we?" and instead of going to lunch, we walked out the front door. Is he the cool teacher he always dreamed of being, the one kids would level with, or did he become just another authority figure?

Margot guns it out of the lot while shooting daggers at Alex in the rearview mirror, and I momentarily forget how unnatural my presence is in this car, how unnatural Margot's presence was in my mother's kitchen. For one mind-bending chip in time, our participation in each other's catastrophes is unassailably logical, and I wonder if this is the way it's really been all this time, and we just needed the right catastrophe to come along and put us all on the deck of the same leaky boat.

CHAPTER 22

It's a silent ride back to the Hall-Beckett home. Margot is still fuming behind the wheel. Alex is back there, presumably contemplating the injustice of laws and the inconvenience of having parents who enforce them. And I'm sitting here, a little thrown by the awkward lack of awkwardness with Skid, and stealing glances at Margot, coming to the realization that there might actually be a throb of escapism behind her drive to write, her need for an alter ego. Maybe it's not all meadows and flowers and fish splashing in streams. Her life is not boardwalk art. I wish that brought me gratification. Maybe in time it will.

There was a story on Portia Wentworth's website that I deliberately avoided. The title, "The Lake Cabin," was enough to reroute me. I feared autobiographical content, a journal entry about that swampy little shack an hour's drive from here where Margot and I absconded one summer day to finally see what all the fuss was about with this whole sex thing. When I think about that day now, it's endless and halcyon: the smell of pine and honeysuckle, the eye-stabbing shimmer of the lake at sunset, the chink of beer cans that we drank on the moss-covered wooden planks, the lush quiet of the world. A coming-of-age movie collapsed into a single day.

There's a neglected-looking door in the back of the Hall-Beckett home that opens directly into the basement, and Margot pries it open and flicks on the light switch, illuminating a finished basement. It's your basic American family basement: a couch facing a wall-mounted TV, a foosball table, and an area of foam tile flooring with a treadmill, a weight bench, and a rack of dumbbells. Any of us could live here. But not all of us do.

Margot leads us across the room and into a mustier, unfinished part of the basement, where a furnace hums and the carcasses of outgrown toys and boxes of storage items dwell.

"You're going to help us carry this stuff up to the car; then you're going to your room," is Margot's stern command to Alex. "Without your phone."

The three of us then set about tackling a one-person job. It's just a folding crib, a high chair, and one box of toys, all of it very fourteen years ago and none of it so heavy that Breeze himself couldn't have hauled it out to the driveway. Once the behemoth is loaded up, Alex is dispatched to his room.

"We never got around to having a second kid, but I never threw any of this stuff away," Margot notes as she slides the van door shut. "I guess I'm sentimental. I don't know why. Kids kind of suck."

She stands in the asteroid-like shadow of her great Dodge, looking gorgeously aged to fine young motherhood. It's easier for me to acknowledge her gorgeousness because she just looks so woebegone. (Although when does motherhood not color a woman with just a tinge of misery?) So badly I want to ask her why she let him do it, why she let Skid wreck everything. In a reality that never was, we are standing in front of our own house; that's our son we just sent to his room.

"He's not a bad kid," I offer, generously and against all my experience so far.

Margot shakes her head. "I tried to get him into tennis. Skid tried to get him into football. He's falling in with the wrong crowd. I think even Alex sees that. What would be nice is if Skid put his foot down every now and again. That, I would appreciate."

She says "wrong crowd" like the Crips and the Bloods have opened Midwest offices out here, but from what I've seen, there's nothing more menacing than kids with driving permits taking the family car out for the afternoon and abiding by the speed limit.

As for Skid, I can see how it might be hard for him to get apoplectic over a little weed. He himself was involved in a drug offense on school grounds, and it didn't affect anyone's life. It barely affected their afternoon. Skid and I were sitting in the bleachers with Dov Halevi after lunch one day when the Israeli exchange student lit up a joint and offered us each a hit just as Coach Cro-Mag happened to walk by. (Between this incident and Dov's Jäger party where Skid and Margot hooked up, the Tel Aviv exchange program really did me no favors.) Because I was not a foreign student (those kids had some scholastic form of diplomatic immunity), nor was I Skid Hall (nobody was giving that guy a hard time), I and I alone got hauled into Principal Thomas's office. Principal Thomas was Eloise Emerson's brother, so he knew me from his visits to the store and kind of liked me. He sat me down and he said, "Listen, pal—I smoked more weed in one year of high school than you will in your entire life." (I'm not sure what his message was. I think he was just bragging.) He then agreed not to tell my mom, and we discussed Jim Morrison for an hour.

"Ted the Albino still live next door?" I ask Margot to lighten the mood.

"His parents do," she answers. "Ted himself graduated high school, got a job, and moved out. This is about fifteen years ago now."

We share a smile.

On the drive back to Campsite Lane, Margot says, "Your old buddy Skid has really changed. The cancer changed him. He's a different guy. Actually, you'd probably like him better now." She smirks. "I don't, but you might."

I know Margot doesn't expect an outpouring of sympathy from me, not for him or, for that matter, her. But she remembers me as someone who, no matter the past, would not be indifferent to an old friend's illness. And she's right. I've learned to live my life without Skid, but I've never dared imagine the world without him. I guess I've needed him out there, even at a distance. And with Holden being gone, perhaps now more than ever.

"That tends to happen, doesn't it?" I say. "A life-or-death situation can change what you think of as life-or-death."

"I don't think he thinks of anything as life-or-death anymore," she says.

"Except football."

"No. Especially football."

"He's still coaching, though," I ask.

"Well, he goes to the field," she says. "He shows up in person. Who knows if he's there in spirit?" She sighs at the road. "You haven't heard about his little folk group, have you?"

Alex did grouse about that in passing, but I play dumb.

"He started a folk music society at school. Folk music. Not only that, but it's mandatory for his football players. Now varsity and JV get together once a week to sit in a circle and sing 'This Little Light of Mine.' Sometimes they even perform. Meaning, in front of people." She shakes her head like she'll never believe this of her husband.

It's an absurd image, Skid Hall holding court at a hootenanny, but as with everything else, I can see him selling it.

"Maybe this is good for Alex," I suggest.

"A humiliating parent?"

"I was going to say diversification. Learning that life doesn't have to be about only one thing. You can change course midstream if you want." (Or, in my case, out of necessity, like when your one thing is teetering on bankruptcy and your partner has an escape hatch with no passenger seat for you.)

"I think what Alex is learning is that a side effect of leukemia is Pete Seeger," Margot quips.

I laugh, and she laughs with me. "That's clever. You should use that in one of your stories."

Suddenly, neither of us is laughing. Margot looks appalled and mortified. I do not want to discuss how I know about Portia, or what I've learned from Portia, or why there's a Portia to begin with. Fortunately, I do not have to bail out of a moving car, as we have just arrived at the house.

—

Infant furniture in hand, we come through the garage door and into the kitchen, where Patti is pressing little spoonfuls of porridge against Breeze's lips while Lulu supervises. The baby's indifference to his late-morning repast has created a blockage of congealed grossness that cascades down his chin until caught by Patti's spoon and shoveled back against the child's closed mouth. Both Lulu and Breeze are bundled up in layers, their thin equatorial blood expecting winter up here in the heartland, although it is autumn at its mildest and most welcoming.

Lulu and Patti regard the bounty of baby gear that Margot and I have transported, and although both make a show of gratitude, they might both be finally appreciating what they've gotten themselves into. These items are trappings of long-term dwelling, and like a spending spree at Raymour & Flanigan, they look awfully permanent. Both women might be wondering how long of a stay these articles commit them to.

Up in Holden's room, Margot unfolds the crib, kneels down to tug on the slats, then shimmies the structure a bit, testing its soundness.

"That looks a lot more comfortable than a Pack 'n Play," I note.

Margot nods, but now even she seems uneasy under these strange conditions, the two of us alone, upstairs in my mother's house. The air up here isn't breathable.

"I should go," she says.

"Yeah. Okay," I reply.

Out in the driveway, where I have for some reason followed her (the front door would've been a fine place to bid her goodbye, but no), she opens the driver's-side door of her van. "If there's anything you or your mom needs—help setting up the house, someone to watch Breeze while you're dealing with things."

"Thank you. But I know you've got your own drama to deal with."

"I'm just saying, I'm here," she says. "Try to think of me as a friend."

We are standing together in the shadow of my childhood home on a brilliant autumn day, like something that happened a million times before and seemed at one point destined to happen a million times more. I hate the part of me that still longs for that.

"Margot, I can't remember a single second in my entire life when I've wanted to be your friend."

Surprise flashes over her eyes; then she looks down and contemplates the washed-out brown of the grass, jingles her keys around her fingers.

"But," I continue, "If we are friends, then as a friend I should tell you that I know about your stories."

"Shit."

"Yeah. I feel the same way." I am smiling.

"I was trying to pretend that I didn't hear what you clearly said as we were pulling up." She curses again. "How did you find out?"

"Sorry. I'm sworn to secrecy."

Margot glares at me.

"Okay. It was Alex."

"*My* Alex?" I'm making things worse. "Oh god! How does *he* know?"

"I don't know how he knows. I just know he wishes he didn't."

Margot groans and sighs and curses under her breath.

"You have nothing to be ashamed of," I tell her. "I really like Julianna Goodheart, that divorced heart surgeon with a wild streak." I make sure she sees me wink.

Margot presses her palms to her face and hides behind them. "Please stop enjoying this."

"Sorry. Can't help you there."

"I have to move," she states. "I have no choice but to leave."

"Now, that's something *I* could write a book about," I say. "Look, it's really no big deal."

"No, it's a huge fucking deal, Rowan. You've read my stories. No kid wants to know anything about that compartment of his mother's head."

"He'll live. It's part of growing up."

"Imagine if you discovered that Patti had written dozens of stories about an English teacher who had wild affairs with everyone on the faculty. Do you really want to read about your mom doing the chem teacher in the lab?"

"What would you think of me if I said yes, desperately I do?"

"You want the graphic details of Patti Darling doing the gym teacher on the pommel horse?"

"Like she's spry enough. Her pommel-horse days are behind her."

Margot's lips curl into that specific type of smile born of absolute powerlessness. "My wayward son is gravitating toward the reprobates, he's smoking weed in the high school bathroom, getting caught like a pinhead, and to top it off, he's telling the world about the one secret his mother has, the one private thing. The only thing that's mine."

"To be fair—and I'm just playing devil's advocate here—you publish these stories. That's kind of the opposite of private."

Margot already looks gone, like she has resolved to leave town. Mentally, she's packing, deciding what to take, what she can live without.

"I didn't know you were a writer, Margot."

"I didn't either," she says.

On her way out of the yoga studio one day, her friend Billy confided that he'd written a novel and was hoping Margot might read it and offer some honest but discreet feedback. She agreed, and after reading the old-timey adventure piece about a barrel-chested swashbuckler sailing the Spanish Main in search of treasure—not gold, but love, the only true treasure—Margot had two overall reactions. The first, which she shared with Billy, was that all the escapism, fantasy, and steamy passion on parade in those two hundred pages boiled down to the fact that he had, like it or not, written a romance novel. Her second reaction, which she did not share with Billy, was that she could've done the same thing, probably just as well, possibly even better.

Though a brief flirtation with a career in journalism got her into some writing classes as an undergraduate, Margot had never seriously written before and harbored no illusions about *New York Times* best-seller lists. Fortunately, self-publishing was a thing. People did that. Writers of all varieties and talent levels churned out stories and put them up on websites, where readers found their way to them. People flocked to these marketplaces of trashy romance fiction starring trashy heroes and heroines with trashy names. So one afternoon, Margot invented Julianna Goodheart, MD, and banged out a fifteen pager in which Julianna's lover dies tragically, donates his organs, Julianna performs the heart transplant, and falls in love with the recipient of her lover's heart. It actually took less than a full afternoon. Too embarrassed (understandably, let's be honest) to use her real name, Margot invented a pen name, which, though she insists it was not her intent, sounds even trashier than anything in any of her stories. She posted the piece in a forum for enthusiasts of the genre, and, lo and behold, people bought it and wrote reviews in which they asked when the next one was coming. So she ginned up another, and people bought that one too. Egged on by "success," she paid a local art student a couple hundred bucks to design and launch PortiaWentworth.com, and just like that, she was legit.

"It's not exactly lucrative, so I haven't stopped doing the tennis lessons, but the fact that it brings in any money at all is hilarious." Margot says this with the same look of wonderment I must wear whenever I ponder Help!INeedSomebody.com. "I actually felt bad accepting money at first, like I was scamming people. But then it hit me: I enjoy writing these stories. I don't suffer over them. I sit down and slide away for a few hours into this alternate universe of my own creation, a place where I make the rules and everybody has to follow them. You, Rowan, of all people should get that."

"Why? Because I too went off and created my own universe?"

"No. Because you were a writer too."

I'm surprised she remembers. I myself barely remember.

"You were always writing really funny articles for the school paper. Our English teachers always asked you to read your compositions aloud to the class. You were good." She smiles teasingly. "Is it weird that instead of being inspired by Steinbeck or Salinger, I was inspired by Darling?"

"You have to aim high." I smile back.

We fall into a few quiet moments, and then, out of nowhere, I find my courage. "Can I ask you something?"

She looks worried.

"Am I Lon?" I ask.

"Seriously? The outrageously buff tennis pro?"

"Hear me out."

She is laughing. "Sorry, Rowan, but the thing you have most in common with Lon is being Australian, and you're not Australian."

"I'm not inquiring about nationalities and comparative bench-press prowess." My voice loses its muscle. "I guess I'm asking if you regret what happened."

She sighs. "Rowan. I told you I was sorry. I am sorry."

"I'm asking something different."

We stare at each other. She shakes her head with resignation. "You know me, Rowan."

"Do I?"

"Do I seem anything like Julianna Goodheart? Do I talk like those characters? Do I do the debauched things they do?"

"I wouldn't know."

"I think you would," she says. "And besides, I'm a married suburban mom. Do you know what passes for dirty talk in married suburban bedrooms? As we take off our clothes, we say, 'The roofer called me back. He's coming out Tuesday. Or, I didn't have a chance to shower, so I may not smell great.'"

She's making jokes, but we still shouldn't be talking like this. She's married—a married suburban mom—and I'm just an ex-boyfriend from high school, from way back before anything mattered, before anything real happened.

"I know you're not Julianna, Margot," I say. "But that doesn't mean part of you doesn't want to be. And forgive me for spotting real-life parallels in your literature, but you did write a story about a tennis player running off into the woods with her boyfriend in between tournament matches. And what about that story called 'The Lake Cabin'?"

Her gaze floats out down Campsite Lane. She looks wistful, uncertain, conflicted.

"How is that old cabin?" I ask.

"Still in the family," she says. "I haven't been back there."

Her uncle died a while ago, and her aunt has talked about getting rid of it. Margot wants to return, just once more before it's sold off. I don't ask her why, because I don't think I want her to tell me.

"It was a nice cabin," she says.

"It was a gross cabin," I counter.

"Rustic."

"Moldy."

"It had country charm," she says.

"It had mildew and rot, and I imagine it has a lot more of it now."

Margot looks defensive on the structure's behalf, or maybe on behalf of what happened there. But then she seems to remember to whom she's talking. "I guess I shouldn't be surprised that it's not all fond memories for you."

But I remember well that neglected little shack; the long, meandering gravel road that led to it; the rusted padlock on the front door that did not willingly admit a key; the musty camp-bunk smell of dewy wood; the slurping of oars paddling across the lake.

"I still think about that day sometimes," Margot volunteers. "Think about who we were back then. Do you remember that feeling? Nothing had happened yet. Everything was yet to come. Life was nothing but unforeclosed possibilities."

I do remember those possibilities, Margot. And I remember you foreclosing them.

"You know, that's what you'll always be to me, Rowan. You're like the memory of wide-open spaces."

I turn away from her, depriving her of my face. She doesn't deserve to see how this makes me feel, better or worse, or if it makes me feel anything at all. After everything, she doesn't deserve to matter. When I hazard a look back at her, I see she has turned away too. Then I see she's hiding tears.

"Margot."

She shakes her head. "I'm fine."

"I didn't know you were unhappy," I say. "Honestly, I never once imagined it."

"It's just been a rough time." She wipes her eyes and laughs, embarrassed, appreciating the absurdity. "You're the last person in the world who should have to listen to me about this. Literally the last."

Inside the house, a phone is ringing. Through the walls, I hear Breeze yapping at the noise.

"I'm sorry, Margot," I say. Amazingly, the illusion of an uncontainably happy Margot Beckett sits better with me than the lost version I'm looking at now. "Believe it or not, I really am sorry."

A moment later, the front door opens, and Patti ambles out. She arrives at the end of the driveway wearing a grim look.

"What's going on?" I ask.

"It's tomorrow," my mother announces.

"What's tomorrow?"

She trembles through a long exhale. "Your brother is coming home."

CHAPTER 23

The afternoon crawls. Not for Breeze. For him, it's a procession of feedings, snoozes, flurries of engagement with the new toys Margot has brought over. But the unease of tomorrow sits like a fog over the chilly house and the adults loping around inside it. At one point, while Lulu and Breeze are up in their room, Patti suggests we watch a movie together, but that idea falls apart. We all know concentration will be thin and fragile today. Plus, my mother and I can't watch movies together even under the best of circumstances. I like real movies with real actors, movies that cost money to make, while Patti prefers films no one has ever heard of. The last time I was in town, she made me sit through some documentary about a woman who found out at the age of thirty that she was half-Canadian. This inexplicably triggered an identity crisis, which inexplicably triggered a feature film. If my mother sat me down and told me I was Canadian, I'd be like, *Okay, fine, I'm Canadian, you're blocking the TV*. It would change nothing. Maybe I'd have a stronger interest in hockey. And Gordon Lightfoot.

Evening arrives, and as I lie on my bed, Lulu comes in, plunks her body down in my desk chair, then spins around to face me. In her hands, she cradles a mug. Lulu consumes more coffee than any person I've ever met. Every time my mother or I have offered, she has accepted, so now we're constantly offering and still feeling like we're not offering enough.

Lulu leans forward, forearms on her legs, the unbuttoned sleeves of her flannel shirt dangling over her knees. I realize then that she's not here to talk but to spy on the bath that my mother is administering to Breeze just across the hall. Lulu isn't sold on the old lady shepherding so perilous an activity. During the negotiations, she took pains to remind Patti that even an inch of water can pose a drowning hazard, so Patti reminded Lulu that she was bathing children long before Lulu was born, which didn't help Patti's cause so much as underscore how out of practice she was.

Lulu eavesdrops on Breeze's happy splashing with his new toy boats and rubber ducks and on Patti's mindless singing that filters through the muddled reverb of the tiled bathroom (off-the-cuff lyrics about tickling tummies and washing toes), and I find myself wondering if it's deeper waters that are really keeping Lulu so attentive. If she's thinking about South American tides that swallow up divers and spit back their lifeless bodies.

I ask her about her plan for when she gets back to Miami. It's clear she hasn't gotten that far. One adjustment at a time. She has plenty of friends, she tells me, but her father is dead and her mother is remarried and living in New York, so neither of her parents will be around to help.

"I guess Breezy and I will figure it out when we get home," she says, her outstretched legs crossed at the ankle, legs that are sheathed in my flannel pajama pants. There are Sundays in winter when I climb out of bed in those pants in the morning and climb back into it at night having never removed them.

Lulu sits forward and shouts into the hall. "How's it going in there?"

"We can't hear you because we're having such a good time," Patti sings back to her.

Lulu grins and sips her coffee. "And yet she answers."

I wish we had a cluster of family to offer her, but the Darling clan is just as scattered as Lulu's Lopezes. There was a brief spell during my elementary school years when my mother orchestrated a flurry of engagement with nearby relations. In a short-lived attempt to foment intrafamilial fondness, Patti thrust me into playdates with "Cousin Manny," a mean middle schooler who, at thirteen, already had the makings of a mustache and who responded to every single thing I said with, "You don't know shit." Were I to suggest that Spider-Man was awesome, he'd say, "You don't know shit." Were I to point out that the White Sox were in first place, he'd say, "Really? Well, you don't know shit." Were I to ask (as I suspect I started doing thirty seconds into the playdate) when my mother was coming to get me, I'd get, "See? You don't know shit." Then on the ride home, Patti would ask, "Is Cousin Manny nice?" And I'd reply, "No." And she'd say, "Well, he's your cousin." This was accurate (he dangled off some far-flung branch on my dad's side of the family tree), but unhelpful. I had no idea if Cousin Manny still lived around here. Which, I suppose, is my point.

Patti steps out of the bathroom clutching a swaddle of overlapping towels in which Breeze is presumably embedded. "Lotion time!" my mother cheerfully calls out, and whisks the child down the hall to her bedroom.

I'm grateful that Patti has a grandchild to distract her from tomorrow's looming trip to LaRocca's, but I am a little worried about how it will land on her. Like the cast of *Melrose Place*, she doesn't have great emotional range. Most ingredients in her fixings bar are kept back behind the sneeze guard. I was raised to believe in the fundamental conquerability of feelings, and it often seemed as though my mother was trying to dupe me into more palatable emotions simply by using different words to identify them. If I said *I'm nervous*, she'd pat my arm and say, *I think you're just excited*. Why did she feel the need to correct me? I knew what excitement felt like and I knew what nervousness felt like, and I was capable of telling one from the other. Was I not allowed to be nervous? Did she think she could cure my case of nerves simply by calling it something else? It took me years to realize that it was not a sign of weakness to feel something less blissful than bliss. And that's what has me worried. When the death of her son becomes more than a phone call from a stranger, more than a couple of houseguests whose identity she still sort of doubts, when her nose is rubbed in the grime of it, when she sees with her own eyes someone she loved who used to be alive but isn't now and won't ever be again, Patti Darling could freak the fuck out.

Lulu sets down her mug on my desk. "Where does your mom keep the photo albums?"

It's a good question. The underlying issue being, what photo albums?

"There really isn't much in the way of family pictures," I tell her.

"There has to be something. I'll look at your grandparents' wedding album if that's all you've got."

I lope down the hall into my mother's room and, sure enough, there's Breeze, plunked down on the bed in a onesie, my mother holding her phone and chirping for his attention, snapping enough photos to clog a hard drive. When I relay Lulu's request, Patti makes the same hesitating face I did. "Who knows?" she says. "You can try the hall closet. But it's slim pickings."

I suddenly see the logic, the poignancy, in her having buried all her old pictures. There are so few new ones that she doesn't want to be reminded of how seldom her children have been around of late to be caught by the camera's eye.

I find a couple of albums—old, heavy things—slumped like cat carcasses behind linens long out of rotation, and I carry them into my room and drop them onto my bed.

"Here," I say to Lulu.

"You're not going to look through them with me?"

"I'm good," I say. Then: "Do me a favor? Let me know if you find any pictures of a dog."

She blinks at me. "Why?"

"My mother is convinced we had a dog."

"Did you?"

"No."

She looks amused. "That's an odd thing to disagree about."

"Oh, we don't disagree. It's not a matter of opinion. No dog has ever lived in this house."

"But you still want me to look out for one."

I do, and don't really know why. "Just on the off chance," I say.

I'm almost through the door when she calls out to me. "Hey, Rowan?"

"Yeah?"

"Did Holden and your mom get along?"

The question catches me off guard. Or maybe it's just the fact that it's Lulu who's asking.

"Yeah," I answer. "I mean, they had their disagreements. Sometimes it seemed like he was biding his time, waiting to get out of here, which could bother my mother. But for the most part, yeah. They got along. Did he say otherwise?"

"No," Lulu says, like she's giving it thought. "It's just a feeling I got. Like maybe there was something between them."

I stare at her.

"He never said anything specifically. It's just that sometimes I got the impression he felt like . . ." Her voice trails off.

"Like what?"

"Like maybe your mother wanted him to leave just as much as he did."

"Nobody ever wanted Holden to leave," I say, my eyes dropping to the carpet line separating my room from the hall. "Holden was someone you wanted to stay."

"He had a happy childhood, Rowan. I'm just asking."

"The only person who wanted Holden to leave was Holden."

Leaving her there with the underwhelming anthology of Darling family photos, I head downstairs to snatch an IPA from the fridge, and decide to take it outside. I walk to the center of the backyard, a modest rectangle of well-tended grass ribboned by a thin palisade of pines. There is only solitude and darkness. The night bears down on me. There is nothing in the world that feels quite like the neighborhood you grew up in after nightfall.

Looking back at the lights in the windows, I think of the mess that awaits us tomorrow. Not that today wasn't its own dumpster fire. What happened to this place? What happened to the people in it? For so long, I'd thought of this town as a fixed solar system, distant but visible to my naked eye, when all along it's been just a shuffling gyre of planets daring me back into its gravitational pull. Still, here I am on the outside, still in the dark. I've been waiting years for the moment when everything between us—Skid, Margot, and me—changed, but I never asked myself the question that comes at the end of every revenge fantasy: Okay, now what?

I shouldn't have said no when Daisy invited herself out here, an act of friendship on her part I foolishly rebuffed all because I didn't know where I belonged in her life, so the notion of not being a part of it at all seemed to make the most sense. But it makes no sense. Do I really want Daisy's orbit to be yet another place where I don't belong? One more thing that deeply matters to me but from which I turn and run? I've got the leaving thing down. I've done lots of it. It's in my blood. When do I decide to stay?

I could use some of Daisy right now, her rocklike pragmatism, her constitutional inability to be dark, her lack of connectedness to everything out here. I pluck my phone from my back pocket and thumb a text to her. I should've let you come out here with me. I'm no match for this place.

Almost instantaneously, the thing rings. It's not Daisy. I don't recognize the number, but the area code is local.

"Hey," says a low voice. "It's Alex. Alex Hall-Beckett."

This family just won't leave me alone.

"Sorry to call so late," he says. His voice is tight with tension. "Are you, like, really busy right now?"

"Who wants to know?"

I hear a shaky breath. "I could use your help."

"Shouldn't you be busy being suspended?"

"I'm at my friend's house," he reports. A labored pause. "Something . . . happened."

"Anything in particular?"

"We did something."

"Alex. You have a real problem with specificity."

"My parents think I'm in my room, and I'm not. And they'll kill me if they find out."

"Wouldn't that save us both a lot of trouble?"

"So you can't, like, meet me?"

"Meet you? Yeah, I'm not going to do that."

He puffs out a breath, a man out of options. I look back at the soft light emanating through the blinds of the upstairs bedrooms. People who only a couple of days ago didn't exist for us are splayed out on our beds with photo albums, they're sloshing around in our tubs, mutating from outsiders to irreplaceables right before our eyes.

"What's so funny?" Alex asks. That's when I realize I'm laughing.

"It doesn't matter. Just shut up and text me the address."

CHAPTER 24

Nothing around here is very far—except civilization—so within ten minutes of receiving Alex's 911 call, I'm parking Patti's Taurus in an unfamiliar neighborhood and taking tentative steps up god-knows-whose driveway. This area, probably a cornfield back in my day, is now a crowded assemblage of ten- to fifteen-year-old cookie-cutter construction, houses not even grand enough to be McMansions. More like McCraftsmans.

A scrawny shadow belonging to Alex moves across the lawn. He thanks me for coming and says, with an unwitting flair for suspense, "It's around back."

We walk deeper into the yard, and I begin to detect the outline of a shed with two human shapes in front of it. I activate the flashlight on my phone, and the beam lands on a kid I instantly recognize as the arrogant Aryan from the SUV, one Gunnar. "Hey, dude," he says, as if a slick head bob and the use of the word *dude* will make me see something other than a weaselly punk who tormented Alex and called me "Uncle" like it was some kind of insult. (It is nothing of the sort, I have recently learned.)

A rustling to the left attracts my flashlight, and I find a thickset, moonfaced thing. This fine specimen has matted-down hair, a black eye, and a shirt with an iron-on of someone's head on fire. "And who's this Halloween costume?" I ask.

"That's Liam," Alex answers.

"I changed my mind. I couldn't care less," I say. "What am I doing here?"

Timidly, Alex begins to explain: "So. We sort of played a little prank. And now we don't know what to do."

"Did someone get hurt?" I ask.

"I got bit," this Liam kid volunteers, and he holds up a fleshy hand inscribed with a barely visible thin red line from which there is currently trickling or recently trickled at most one drop of blood.

"What about the shiner?" I say, pointing to his eye.

"Unrelated," says Liam.

I look at Alex. "Well, there'd better be more."

Suddenly, from behind the hapless youngsters, a grunting sound cuffs the night. My flashlight shoots to the side panel of the shed. It's your standard backyard wooden structure known to house lawn equipment—a mower perhaps, some rakes and shovels, a bag of mulch—and sometimes, as I'm beginning to suspect is the case here, a kidnapping victim.

"Who's in there?" I demand.

"Just chill a sec, dude," says Gunnar.

I reach for the door, but Alex leaps in front of me. "Wait! It's not a who. It's a what."

"What's a what?"

"The pig. There's a pig in there."

Some hardwired primordial reflex sends me dancing backward in retreat. I listen again. More muffled snorting, more groans of irritability. An impatient beast.

"My first question is, is there supposed to be a pig in the shed?" I ask this more calmly than anyone could reasonably expect.

"It was just a little prank," Gunnar says, deputizing himself as the leader and trying to sound like one. "Liam's sister works at the petting zoo, so we got him to snag her key. Then we let ourselves in tonight after it closed. We totally pulled it off too."

"Totally!" I echo.

"We got it into the car, then out of the car, then into the shed, all without anyone noticing." He has the gall to look accomplished. "It was quite a feat, if you think about it."

"Until it bit me!" Liam says.

I gape at the lot of them. "You knuckleheads really stole a pig?"

"Borrowed," Gunnar points out. "Only borrowed."

Liam is off and fretting. "Do you know how next-level pissed my parents are gonna be? My mom is on the town council!"

"Wow. The town council of Maybee, Illinois," scoffs Gunnar. "That's gonna make CNN."

"You think *my* parents are going to be thrilled?" Alex chimes in with his own domestic entanglements. "I got suspended today, thanks to you guys."

"Sounds like you gentlemen have a lot to sort out," I tell them all, turning on my heels. "Good luck. Do keep in touch."

"Wait. Where are you going?" Alex begs.

"Home."

"Dude, you've gotta help us," says Gunnar.

"No, *dude*, I don't."

"There's a pig in my shed, man!" Liam cries.

"Yeah, and you put him there." I suddenly feel philosophical. "What's interesting to me is that you guys have done something that comes impressively close to being, in mathematical terms, completely stupid. You're all exactly idiots. How about that? Okay. Night-night, kids."

Even in the dark, I can see desperation welling up from Alex's pores like sweat. "You're seriously not going to help us?"

"Put the pig back in the car, return it to the zoo, and Bob's your uncle. There. You're welcome."

Liam regards the shed. Another grunt issues through the wood slats, followed by the beating of small hooves on dirt. "We can't. It's too pissed off," he determines.

"I don't blame it," I say. "What do I look like to you guys, a zookeeper? I run a record store, and I'm not even good at that. I'm sure you'll think of something. Google 'how to care for your new pet pig.'"

"What about my hand?" Liam urges. "I got bit by that thing. Can you get rabies from pigs? Or the plague or something?"

"Oh, definitely something," I say agreeably. "What was the plan here anyway? Look at you guys. Huddled in the dark like a bunch of war criminals. Seriously—did this even have a point? And it's *bitten*, not *bit*. Stop saying you got *bit*. That makes this whole thing worse."

Alex exhales. "The plan," he begins, his tone confessional, "was for this to be an initiation of sorts."

"An initiation?" I say.

"Of sorts."

"Into what?" I look at each of them. "You three stooges aren't in a gang. That would just be too funny."

"It's a stupid little club," Alex says.

"The Dark is not stupid," says Gunnar stupidly.

"I don't want to be in it anymore," says Liam.

"You were never in," Gunnar retorts. He must be chair of the membership committee.

"Look, I don't really care about your secret order of morons. It's the saddest thing I've ever heard. Honestly. *The* saddest."

At this point, I'm just exhausted. I want to go home. The pig wants to go home. Everybody wants out.

"Here's what's going to happen. You—" I point to Gunnar. "Scram. You're out of here."

Gunnar starts to leave, pauses to ask me for a ride, sees the black-ops look in my eye, withdraws his request, and scampers off into the night.

"You—" I point to the stressed-out pudge ball. "Talk to me about your sister."

Liam is looking at me strangely, his blank stare growing progressively troubled. "I mean, I guess she's kind of cute? You might be a little old for her?"

"Oh, for fuck's sake. Tell me about her job, Mr. AP Course Load."

We soon discover an exploitable angle. Liam's elder sibling not only volunteers at the petting zoo, she also regularly hooks up with the petting zoo manager. Texts and calls are placed, and within a half hour, the sister and her zoologist boyfriend arrive on the scene, escort the animal down the Liam family driveway, and safely load it onto the petting zoo van. At long last, the pig is out of the care of feckless ninth graders and back in the care of people who know how to care for pigs.

"You're a lifesaver, Greta," Liam says to his sister.

"And you're a tool," Greta replies as she climbs into the van.

Liam says nothing. He knows he's a tool.

We are gliding along the sleeping streets, Alex a glum lump in the passenger seat. It's been another night of things not going his way, another hole punched in his transgressions card. I didn't know kids still shimmied out of bedroom windows after lights-out, and like nearly everything else around here, it strikes me as both quaint and uninspired. But Alex is a reluctant scoundrel. I think of his Gravedancer heist and his protestations afterward that it wasn't his idea.

"Talk to me about the record store, Alex," I say. "That was your initiation, wasn't it? Stealing CDs from a pillar of our community just to impress those buffoons."

Alex neither confirms nor denies the charge.

"Granted, I'm the last person to deliver a lecture about friendship, but you need all new friends," I tell him. "Just start over. That Gunnar kid is a bad seed."

Alex seems to ponder his own footing in that regard. "Doing bad things doesn't make you a bad person."

"Doesn't it? I mean, how else would the rest of us know? Why do you even want to be a part of that club?"

"I don't know," he sulks. "I guess because they asked me."

"Just because a club will take you doesn't mean you should join it. Think of the Manson Family. Or the Branch Davidians. Or Law Review." I puff a sigh onto my windshield. "Look, I don't know you, so I don't know if you're better than this. But you should definitely try to be."

Gunnar's airheaded rallying cry pops into my head. "We are the Dark!" Seriously? Sorry, Gunnar, but no. You and your whiny little friends are not the Dark. You're just a bunch of dopes who couldn't find your asses with two hands and a GPS. You want the Dark? Your parents are the Dark. Your teachers are the Dark. I am the Dark. You'll get there one day too. Dark as a sack of bad luck.

I flick on the radio, and because it's synced up to my phone, "Heaven" by the Talking Heads fills the car. Stirred by all this concentrated time in my old house and the pageantry of Holden-themed memories and dreams, I've been listening to this band every solitary moment I can find, soothing myself with its snug familiarity as I fall asleep at night.

Alex recognizes the song; he's already digested the albums Eloise force-fed him, he tells me, and has, in fact, gone back for more. At least one part of his life is on track.

"I like this one," Alex comments.

"Yeah," I say. "It was one of my brother's favorites."

We listen in silence for a while. I've always found something comforting about this song, the depiction of heaven as a place where nothing ever happens. A low-key afterlife must have appealed to a low-key kid like myself. Who says heaven has to overdo it?

Eventually, the lad looks over at me. "Does it help or hurt? Listening to his favorite songs."

I stare through the windshield at the wooded lane, dead quiet and tomb black. The engine churns out a low pant, and the headlight beams slice the night like the last stand against eternal darkness. If Alex had asked me this question a week ago, a month, or a year, I would've said it only hurt. Which is why I haven't listened to this band in so long.

"A little bit of both," I tell him. "Actually, quite a lot of both."

When the song ends, my playlist serves up "Early Late," a new tune by the Wright Brothers. A gorgeous, lazy-mountain-river of a song, like a lost outtake from *American Beauty*, it's on their soon-to-be-released record, an advance copy of which was sent to me, as an old friend and record-store owner, by Rob Wright. Or maybe it was Rich. I never really know.

"Tell me what you think of these guys," I say to my passenger, cranking up the volume. "They're friends of mine, and I'm trying to get them to play at my store. I know you're not a big music guy, but just tell me if this is something you'd come out to see."

His neck instantly swivels in my direction. "This is the Wright Brothers. You know these guys?"

I look back at him. "*You* know these guys?"

"For real?" he says. "You don't watch *Vicky of Venice Beach*?"

I don't, of course, because it's a cheesy teen drama whose most senior cast member looks like she was born during Obama's first term—and that's the woman who plays the mom.

"You should check it out," Alex advises.

"Well, I'm not going to do that, so why don't you tell me what I'm missing."

"The last season ends with Vicky breaking up with her boyfriend. It's a big emotional scene, and 'Golden Slipper' is playing the entire time." Alex is citing a song from the Wrights' first album, *Lines, Rows, Hills, and Villages*. "You really don't know about this?"

"I knew one of their songs made it onto that show," I say.

"It didn't just make it onto the show. That scene was all anyone talked about for weeks afterward. The clip is all over YouTube. *SNL* did a sketch about it."

I glance over at him. "Are you serious?"

"Are you serious that you don't know this?" he says back to me. "Do you live under a rock?"

"Yeah, but I get good cell service there."

Alex's eyes are wide with amazement. "I can't believe these guys are buddies of yours."

And belatedly, I can't believe it either.

We have arrived at the base of Alex's driveway, and I watch him regard the house with both trepidation and tactical calculation. "I guess I'm going back in through the window," he tells himself.

He releases a breath, which, if his parents are in there lying in wait, could be one of his very last.

"You may never see me again," he says.

"We can only hope."

Then he turns to me. "Thanks for tonight. You made a lot of sense. And I really needed someone to talk sense to me."

"No sweat," I say. "I can be very persuasive when I want to be." Which is a total lie. I've never convinced anyone of anything. In fact, I usually talk myself out of whatever it is I'm trying to talk the other person into.

Alex's parting words to me, issued through the open window after he's exited the car, are ones of admiration: "It's super cool, by the way, that you're in the music business."

Turns out I'm too charitable to laugh in his face, but I'm in the music business the way a volunteer museum docent is Paul Cézanne.

I'm dialing Greg Isquith before I even pull away. It's late-ish to call, but one, I don't care, this is an emergency, and two, I'm sure he's burning the midnight oil on some novella or epic poem.

"Mr. Darling," he intones grandly.

"Hey. Listen—the Wright Brothers absolutely have to play the Graffiti," I tell him. "Apparently these guys are pretty big. Bigger than I thought. People actually know them. Like, random kids from Random, Illinois."

"Dude, I'm the one who told you that," Greg says. "You don't remember me telling you about the *Venice Beach* soundtrack?"

He did, but I paid it little mind. Greg pulls from a bottomless well of fishy contentions and half-cocked theories, and frankly, it's usually an in-one-ear-out-the-other situation. We need to come up with a system where he lets me know when I should pay attention.

"While we're on the subject, I chatted with Rob," he reports.

"You're kidding." I'm always surprised when Greg does his job.

"It might've been Rich. Which one's really laid-back?"

"I wouldn't call either of them intense."

"Whoever it was, he loves me." An improbable brag. "I told him I heard echoes of Prince all over their new album, and he was like, 'Yes! Finally! Thank you!'"

Anyone who makes Greg feel like a visionary—musical, philosophical, commercial—has purchased a friend for life. Free kidneys, whatever you need. Greg is always telling himself how inspired he is, but I suppose it's even more gratifying when a non-him person recognizes it too.

"It's wonderful that he loves you, but have you picked a date?" I ask, like we're discussing a wedding.

"Getting there," he hedges. "He's a little noncommittal."

"I know he's noncommittal, Greg. Your job is to make him committal."

"I hear ya, man, but they're having a moment right now. They're blowing up. They might be going on tour with The Decemberists. How fucking Promethean is that?"

"It's very Promethean. But you know what would be even more Promethean? If they did an in-store at Metaphysical Graffiti."

I hear a majestic breath being taken. "Rowan. Listen. I was in a really activated and creative headspace when you called, and this conversation is rupturing it."

"Oh. Forgive me, Professor."

"I'm doing all I can to land the Wrights, but it's no small task. These guys are getting big, possibly too big to play a puny record store in Old City, Philadelphia."

"Please don't call my record store 'puny.' I know it's puny. I'm there every frickin' day, cooped up in its puniness, trying to come up with ways to make it a little less puny. If you could just for once not argue with me, if you could dial back the attitude and not make me feel like I'm an imposition on your time, especially since right now I happen to be paying for your time, puny though that pay may be, that would be so—well, it would be really Promethean, Greg."

I hear a deep sigh followed by a long, important pause. "Let's try to be aware of each other, okay, man?" he says.

Oh, for the love of god.

"Let's be really tuned in to each other, attuned to what each of us is looking to get out of this experience," he says. "Can we do that, you and I?"

Suddenly the line goes dead. I don't know how it happened. Someone must have been unable to suffer this conversation any longer and inadvertently disconnected on purpose.

I continue back to the house, wondering why I didn't just let Greg go, why I don't just let all of it go. Sometimes I wonder if there's even anything left to let go of at all.

—

By the time I get home, everyone has retired to their quarters for the evening. With nothing but a few sleepless hours separating me from a visit to the funeral home, and with the night air agreeably autumnal, I decide to resume my IPA consumption outdoors. I carry what is left of the six-pack—five perfectly worthy cans—up to the mailbox and drop down on the curb. I am drinking at the end of my driveway again. It's like the past fifteen years never happened.

The street is as dark and still as pond water. I crack open one of the beers. It fizzes. I chug.

As carbonation and hops pour down my throat, I feel my phone vibrating. It's my website telling me I have a new client. (Patron? Subject? Disciple?) Oh, good. More people nagging me for help. At least this one is shelling out ten bucks.

I maneuver into my notifications and read the message. It's from Sam. Sam wants to know how to put something.

> Hi. Sam here.
>
> I've known about this site for a while now, thanks to my wife. I never thought I'd use it, but here I am.
>
> It's like this: my family is kind of fraying. My son has become something of a troublemaker, and even though it's nothing too serious, my wife is losing her patience with him. She's also losing her patience with me because I'm "not taking things

seriously enough." She's not wrong. But I'm also going through something, changing, for the better I think. I'm becoming someone else, and I don't want to go back. I love my family, and I don't want to lose them. But I don't want to lose me either.

This is why I need your help. It sounds cruel and selfish, but how do I tell my wife, whom I deeply love, that right now, at what might be the most critical time in each of our lives, I can't help her?

Thanks,
Sam

Having read Sam's inquiry, I chug the rest of the beer (heartened that I still have four to go); then I reread it. I pocket my phone.

My preliminary thought is this: *Sam is an asshole.*

I drain the balance of the can. Three left now.

Does Skid really think I don't know he's Sam? He's not even really asking me anything. He's just venting, trying to dupe me into acting like his friend by pretending he's a stranger. It's a very Skid thing to do, and I sort of respect it.

But why is he trying to con me back into a friendship? Skid had friends in spades. Every kid in the school wanted to be his buddy. Did he betray and lose all of them too?

I pull out my phone again and read Sam's message for a third time.

"I love my family, and I don't want to lose them. But I don't want to lose me either."

I look up and see a cloud sweeping like a ghost across the sky. *It's okay, Skid,* I think to myself. *I've lost all those things. You learn to live with it.*

I snap open another can. The circular lid froths. I bring to my lips.

The next thing I know, I am opening my eyes. I am lying flat on the grass, shivering, and looking up at a sky pregnant with the gray of morning, no less than five empties encircling me in a ring the shape of a flat tire.

I stand, stagger, laugh (though nothing is funny), am brought to my knees by a pounding deep inside my skull, and have the presence of mind to appreciate that at least I'm not still drunk.

PART FOUR

WE ARE THE DARK

CHAPTER 25

Patti, Lulu, and Breeze are dressed, perfumed, and in the kitchen, ready to go, when I come downstairs to sniff around in the fridge for some juice. Larry Levin once told me that certain fruit juices can knock out a hangover, and even though Larry is as sketchy a source as they come (he is somewhat known for his Old City art gallery, but mostly known for being the neighborhood pothead who wears flip-flops in January), his advice on this point all the sketchier for its lack of specificity (which fruit juices exactly do the trick?), I can't afford to be picky. There's a miniature demon treating my brain like a mechanical bull, trying to claw its way out with a garden trowel. To add to the pain, there is shame: since when do I let a measly six-pack wreck me? And to add to the pain and shame, I am overdressed. Patti looks like she's ready to teach third period, clad in those loose-fitting middle-aged-woman pants and a smock-like shirt, while Lulu is dressed to rouse the corpses in a pair of thigh-hugging, buttock-boosting, crotch-demarcating jeans. It's just me all gussied up to meet the solemnity of the task.

My mother sees the sunglasses masking my eyes—indoors, where it is not sunny—and assumes I've had a long, red-eyed night of grief. "I know, honey," she says supportively, crossing the room to rub my back. "We'll get through it together."

I could take the credit, but it's the wrong day for dishonesty. "I'm not crying, Mom. The glasses are because I drank too much last night."

Her expression remains consoling. "And why do you think you did that?"

As Patti bundles up her grandson, I grab one of her store-bought smoothies, a greenish concoction boding of kale, wheatgrass, and flax seeds.

I look at Lulu. "You doing okay?" She stands calm and unreadably quiet.

"I am," she says. She touches my forearm. "It's going to be okay, Rowan."

She's strong, that one, but I would really appreciate it if both of us would lower our voices.

Patti is back from warming the car, which is something people still do out here, and now she's throwing eyes at us, making it known she is anxious to leave. "Is everyone ready?" she says to me. I am apparently everyone.

"One sec." I down as much of the bottle as I can in a single guzzle. The taste is atrocious, and I spit it all into the sink. "Blech! What flavor smoothie is this?"

She shakes her head. "Salad dressing."

It's a silent drive to LaRocca's; even Breeze holds his tongue. Each of us seems to be taking the measure of this crisp, beautiful morning and envying all the carefree souls we pass who have the good fortune not to be in this car, not to be part of our ugly mission. I sense tension emanating from my mother. It's understandable, to be sure, but as it thickens the nearer we get to our destination, the more worrisome it becomes.

Becca, funeral director and barista extraordinaire, barely gets a chance to welcome us before Patti jumps in. "Let's just get this over with." Then to me: "Take off your sunglasses, Rowan."

I remove my shades and pocket them in the sport coat I didn't need to wear, although if my hangover grows any more rambunctious, I just might climb into one of these caskets and pull down the lid. At least I'll be appropriately dressed for that.

I don't actually know what it is we're here to, as Patti so respectfully put it, "get over with," but Becca proceeds to explain that some family members like to have a few minutes with their loved one before the day of the funeral. "If any of you wants to go see him, now is a good time," she says.

It's a gruesome suggestion. "Do we have to?" I say to my mother, who shoots back a look that makes me expect a shoe.

"I'd like to see him," says Lulu.

Becca nods solicitously. "Okay." I swear she almost says *terrific*! "If you'd like to follow me."

As Lulu hands Breeze to my mother, Patti quietly huffs, "I guess that means I'm batting second." Fortunately, Lulu has already learned to ignore her.

Lulu and Becca exit the room, and I ponder the gumption required of a twenty-five-year-old to walk up to a casket and say goodbye forever to the person with whom she'd only just begun to scrawl her dreams across the sky.

"I like Lulu," I declare, primarily to Patti.

My mother shrugs. "I wouldn't get too attached." She is holding her grandson up to her cheek and making soothing little murmurs into the infant's ear.

"Look who's talking," I say.

"I'm not saying she doesn't seem nice," Patti concedes. "Just keep in mind we really don't know her from a bar of soap."

"She's lived with us for a few days now. We know a thing or two."

"Here's one thing we know: on her trip out here, she probably had to be reminded that it was a nonsmoking flight." Patti shakes her head like an old scold. "Did you know she smokes? In this day and age? And with a child in the house?"

Smoking is ill-advised and unhygienic, I'll grant her, but it's not a cocaine habit, so there's no need for my mother to be working herself up, certainly not right now.

"She doesn't smoke in front of Breeze," I say.

"How do you know?"

"She told me."

"Well, I'm so glad you've discussed it."

"Mom. Take it easy."

"I am taking it easy. I'm just pointing out that while Lulu may seem like a nice young woman, we just met her. There's a lot we don't know."

"What exactly do you think she's hiding?"

"Well, what about her family?" Patti wonders.

"It doesn't sound like she has much of one."

"You're probably jealous," my mother clucks.

"Why? What family do I have?" It's a harsh retort I instantly regret. "I'm sorry. I didn't mean that."

But the muscles in Patti's face are constricting, roiling under her skin. "Damn you, George," she says in a near-whisper.

I regard her with concern. "Did you just call me George?"

"I was talking to your father," she says. Even as she gazes down upon her grandson, a cloud of destituteness blankets her eyes. "I wish I could say I'm happy he didn't live to see his family in such a state, but he started the whole mess."

"Our family is not in any kind of *state*, Mom. We've suffered a tragedy, and we'll get through it. All of us. You, me, Lulu, Breeze."

She looks at me pointedly. "What about you?"

"What do you mean?"

"I mean—what are you doing with your life, Rowan?"

"Can we table this discussion?"

"You were such a smart boy. Inquisitive, creative, sharp as a whip. What do you see when you look in the mirror now?"

"A sport coat that never really fit right."

"You're thirty-three years old, you don't have a wife or a significant other of any kind—that I know of, anyway, though I seem to be the last to hear of such things—you spend all your time in a floundering record store that you opened in some tumbledown shack in Philadelphia. Is this it for you? Is this all you want? Where are your relationships? What happened to your dreams? Where's that English degree you wanted? You wanted to write, you wanted to teach. What happened?"

"Can I ask you a question?"

"Of course."

"You think they have a snack bar here?"

"I'm sorry, Rowan, but you need to hear the truth, and the truth is, every day that goes by is another day lost, another day that's never coming back. You need to hear that."

I can't fight back. Not here, not today, not at her. I would give anything to be back in my going-nowhere life right now, back in my tumbledown shack. I miss it, all of it. I miss my northeast liberals and their hatchback jalopies with NPR bumper stickers. I miss broccoli rabe and art cinemas swarming with urbanites. I miss the sound of Daisy Pham's cello. Doesn't anybody play the fucking cello out here?

I look at my mother. "I'm sorry you feel so helpless right now, Mom. I know that some really bad things have happened to you."

"We're not talking about me. I'll be fine, Rowan. It's you I'm worried about." She leans forward pleadingly. "I need to know if you're okay."

"Look, lady, I don't know what you want from me. Don't you see how hard it is for me to be here? Do you know what it's like to be so conflicted? I don't even hate it here anymore. It would be easier if I did, because then I would at least know I belong back home. Instead, it's all just mixed emotions—every step I take, every face I see, I don't know whether I'm in or I'm out. It's how I feel here, and it's how I feel in Philly these days too."

The click of the door handle brings it all to a halt. The door opens with a smooth sweep over the carpet, and Lulu enters, composed but emotionless, something brave in how she's holding herself up but also something defeated. Without a word or the slightest skim of eye contact, she walks over to Patti, gently reclaims Breeze, then carries him across the room to one of the black armchairs over by the window.

"Patti?" It's Becca's voice, joining the room from the doorway. "Would you like to go back?"

My mother doesn't seem to hear. She's watching Lulu, not with distrust now, or suspicion or spite, but with bare tenderness, and for the briefest of moments, I think she might go over and hold the younger woman so that together they could shoulder their braided sadness. But Patti simply rises onto her denim flats and follows Becca out. With her goes my chance to be a better son, to join her, to stand beside her, my hand on her shoulder while she says her last goodbyes. Would I have made it all the way down that hall? Could I stomach the sight of Holden, knowing he's not really there, knowing he's only flaunting his absence yet again?

On the far side of the room, Lulu considers the window in silence, the little green mints of her eyes looking adrift.

"Are you okay?" I ask. She nods, and I leave her be.

Not a full minute has passed when Patti bursts back into the room in a dither, Becca rushing after her.

"What's going on?" I ask.

"I'll tell you what's going on," my mother says. "It's not him."

"What?"

"That's not Holden."

"Patti, please," Becca says in the wary tones with which one handles the insane.

"Please nothing. That's not my son."

Lulu gets to her feet, the baby fixed to her shoulder like a koala. "Of course that's Holden," she softly offers.

"I know my child, and that's not my child!"

My mother is speaking with such authority that for a second, it seems preposterous for any of us to disagree with what is a plainly preposterous assertion. Has the sight of her dead child triggered a psychotic break? What if my mother has broken with reality and left me here all by myself?

"Patti, we are enormously careful here," Becca is saying. "The State Department is extremely careful."

"That's not his face. Holden has fuller cheeks. His jaw is—more angular." My mother's eyes nearly pop from their sockets. "It's not him!"

I look helplessly at Becca. This is her domain; she is in charge. She should have the words, the countenance, that will put this to rest. But then, incredibly, I realize that despite all the things I've yearned for in my life, all the truths I desperately wished weren't so, all the lost things whose return I have prayed for, I've never wanted anything so badly as for my mother to be right. What I wouldn't give to read some shadow of doubt on Becca's face, a microscopic twitch of hesitation.

"It's him," Lulu says. Somehow I am crushed by her certainty. I berate myself for indulging that little flare of hope.

"When was the last time you saw him, Patti?" Lulu asks.

My mother shoots daggers at the younger woman, and the air in the room changes. "Excuse me?"

"That wasn't an accusation," Lulu says.

"How dare you," Patti fumes.

"Easy, now," I say.

"You think I'm going to let some stranger tell me I don't recognize my own son?"

"That's not what I'm saying."

"Lulu's not a stranger, Mom."

"Of course she is. And in a couple of days, she'll go right back to being one. Just you watch. So forgive me, Ms. Lopez, if I don't allow you to waltz in here and claim membership in my family."

"But I'm already in," Lulu answers calmly, delicately. "And you're already in mine. That's just how it works, doesn't it? I brought you your grandson."

My mother's eyes fall on the baby. "A grandson I'll probably never get to know."

Lulu moves Breeze from one shoulder to the other. "You're right, Patti. You don't know me. You don't know yet how important it is to me that you're a part of Breeze's life, that he always has you and Rowan to connect him to his father. But I promise you that's how I feel. Without you, what will Holden be to him? A couple of photographs? Stories I tell him? As long as you and Rowan are in this world, I owe Breeze more than that. And so do you. The more people we lose, the more we need, and you've lost a lot, Patti. Rowan has lost a lot too."

I lift my eyes to Lulu. In this wild, disorienting moment, I no longer know who the parents are in this room and who are their children. I feel like Lulu is claiming me, claiming all of us.

"I don't need you to tell me what I need," Patti says. She won't soften, there's too much to let out. "What do you all think? That I'm some old library book to be borrowed and returned on a whim? I don't need anyone's charity visits or Christmas cards, I don't need to be your once-a-week phone call that makes you feel better, and I certainly don't need you standing beside me when I bury my son. Or whoever the hell that is back there."

"Can everyone just stop talking for a second?" I plead. I'm terrified that my mother will say something that sends Lulu and her child sailing out of here, never to be seen again.

Patti is shaking her head, her mouth tight as a suture. "I'm sorry. You're just my dead child."

"Mom!"

"That's all you'll ever be to me," she tells Lulu. "I'm sorry, but it's true."

"You don't mean that, Patti," Lulu says.

"I do." There is sincere regret on my mother's face. Heartbreak and bitterness. Her cruelty is incidental. "My dead son is the only thing I see when I look at you. It's the only thing I see when I look at your baby. I'm afraid it's the only thing I'll ever see."

"You need to stop talking," I tell her sharply.

"Don't you dare tell me to stop talking!" she barks. "And you—" To Lulu: "Don't you dare tell me what I do and do not mean!"

All at once, I'm standing and shouting. "Mom! I swear to god, if you don't shut your fucking mouth right now, I'm going to come over there and shut it for you!"

The room is shocked into frozen silence. Even tiny Breeze-Brooklyn holds his tongue. My mother and I hold each other in crazed glares, volcanos of madness burgeoning behind her eyes and mine. It feels as though the entire world waits in fear of whatever comes next.

Then a blur of motion: Patti snatches her left shoe with her right hand—her pitching arm—and with the speed and economy of her heyday, whips it at my head. It's high and outside and sails with an impotent *thud* into the sofa cushion.

A quake rumbles up from my planetary core and slices me in half, and as I peer down into the fault line, a bottomless canyon falling away, the sight of all of us being torn asunder, what rises up in my throat is a noise I have never produced in all my years: a howl. A long, piercing, openmouthed, feral showstopper of a scream. This is what it sounds like when everything ends.

Then, a precarious quiet. I have scared everyone mute except for Breeze, and it is almost a relief when the little baby begins to cry.

In my mother's eyes, worry has replaced anger. "Rowan," she says. She takes a step toward me, and I scramble out of the room, barreling down halls and through doors until the carpet turns to gravel and daylight gashes my eyeballs. I find myself at the rear of the building. Before me is a wall and within me a bellyful of foamy vomit begging to be splashed upon the brick. I oblige. Salad-dressing smoothie pours forth in a warm, putrid splatter.

And then come the tears. I cry like I haven't cried since childhood. I stand there, a bubbling, melting mess, my palms and forehead against the wall like I'm holding it up, weeping and weeping and weeping.

I reach inside my jacket pocket for my phone and dial the voice I need to hear, the one far away and untouched by any of this. I am so relieved when Daisy answers that I cry even harder.

"Rowan?"

I can't speak.

"Rowan?" More urgently. "Rowan! Are you okay?"

And then I bawl into the phone, heaving, gasping for air. "I would do anything," I utter over and over again. "I would do anything."

And she seems to understand. She slips inside it and swims along with me. "I know," she keeps saying. "I know."

That's the way it is for a few minutes, and when it's over, I raise the sleeve of my sport coat and wipe a tears-snot-and-barf soup from the center of my face.

"It was bound to hit you eventually," she says, her voice a bed of tenderness. "It's better this way."

I'm still far from words, but Daisy stays with me, neither of us speaking, a radio signal connecting her to me and no one else.

Eventually, after what feels like a long time, I ask, "How are you?"

"Better than you."

"How's the Graffiti?"

"Also better than you. But not by much."

I exhale a puff of putrid breath. "You know, I keep worrying that I'm going to come back there and find the store completely empty."

"I'm not packing this place up by myself," she says.

Between my mossy pallor and my bloodshot eyes still trying to adjust to daylight, I must look to passersby like a corpse making a run for it.

"I take it you don't think a Wright Brothers show would help us," I say. "They really are kind of famous."

"If they're famous, they're probably not going to come." She sighs. "And if they do, it's one show. What then? We book John Legend? Our hole-in-the-wall record store magics itself into The Fillmore?"

I want to put my faith in the Wrights. They're brothers, and I want to believe that brothers always come through in the end.

"So. About last night," Daisy says.

"What about it?"

"Your phone call? At two in the morning?"

"Did I call you?" I have no recollection of it. "Must've been a butt dial."

"Then it was a butt voice mail too, because you left me a long, largely incoherent message."

"Did I? Sorry about that. I was drinking." Then, because one worries what one says while drunk, I ask, "Any part of it not incoherent?"

She clicks her tongue. "You told me I should marry Chili."

"Oh."

"You said I should marry Chili, we should close the store, and all just move on."

"Oh."

"Yeah," she says direfully. "Not your warmest message, but you get a pass this week."

"I honestly don't remember saying any of that."

"It's okay." She pauses. "Rowan, do you really want those things? Do you want me to marry Chili?"

"I don't know, Daisy. If you want to, then yeah, sure."

"That's not what I asked. Why are you making what you want all about what I want?"

"Because I don't get a vote."

"But you're voting anyway. You're calling me at two in the morning to tell me to marry him."

"I can't explain things I don't remember saying."

This is a conversation we should have had way back when we first met and I wanted to spend all my time with her. This is a conversation we should have had before she got serious with Chili. And so maybe I really do want to lose her and my store. Maybe things would just be easier if there were nothing left for me back there.

"Your voice mail wasn't all petulance and insult. You also said you missed me."

"Like I said, I'd been drinking."

"Well, you know what they say about the drunk tongue—it speaketh the truth," she says, teasingly.

"I think that's a misnomer."

"I don't. I think it's a nomer."

The back door is pushed open, and Becca sticks her head out. She looks relieved to see me standing.

"I've got to go," I say to Daisy.

"I look forward to the next call you don't intend to make," she quips, and we hang up.

"You okay?" Becca asks.

"I'm not proud of my behavior."

She smiles. "I think you woke the dead."

If only.

"I'm sorry for freaking out," I say.

"I think you were just trying to keep up," Becca says.

I point to the bricks. "I also yakked on your wall."

She regards the green froth cascading toward the ground. "Gross."

She pushes the door wider. "It's safe to come back inside. Everyone's friends again. They're laughing in there now." She sees that this does not console me, and says, "That's good, isn't it?"

I stare at her. "It's him, isn't it? It is him back there."

She nods. "He's here with us, Rowan. I promise."

And I guess that's good news, or the best news I could hope for today, but I can't shake the awful thought that had I been called upon to cast the deciding vote about Holden, had it fallen to me to look into his cold, uninhabited face and say whether or not it was really him lying there, I don't know if I could have. With all the living we've each done without the other, I don't know if I would've been able to settle the bet.

—

I steer the Taurus into the driveway, and as I reach up and press the garage door clicker, my mother begins to sing. Peering into the rearview, I see her there, Breeze's little hand between both of hers, smiling into his face, teaching him what we do each time we make it home. "We're here because we're here because we're here because we're heeeere!" From behind the spiderweb of car-seat straps, Breeze stares at her with great interest, his eyes at full mast. Is there some part of him that hears the rich echo of years in his grandmother's tune? Maybe that comes through the way it can when you hear a song for the first time on the radio and you instantly know it's old, that it's been through a lot, and that it has made a lot of people happy for a long, long time.

Lulu takes Breeze upstairs to negotiate him into a nap, and I find Patti in the kitchen making herself a cup of tea.

"Well. I guess I owe you an apology," I say.

She spins around. "Apology accepted." And she pats my cheek. "It's over. Let's move on."

"Thank you," I say. "I hope you apologized to Lulu. If you didn't, she might be up there stuffing her suitcase."

"I did," she says. "Thank you for worrying about us."

"I do worry." I am surprised to realize it's true. "I worry about all of us."

"Oh, Rowan," she says, a shade of sadness moving over her smile. "Isn't it great that we're all here, that we can apologize and accept each other's apologies? Because I'd give anything in the world to be able to tell your brother I'm sorry. I'd give anything to hear that child forgive me."

"Forgive you? What for?"

Her shoulders roll with resignation. "For whatever I did that sent him packing."

I don't know what she means; I know only that, unlike me, Holden was not a man of grudges.

"He was the forgiving type, Mom," I say.

She smiles and pats my cheek again. "Thanks for being brave. Back at LaRocca's."

"Brave?" I laugh. "I'm the biggest chickenshit in the world."

"Fear is just fear," she says, returning to her tea. "Let's hope fear is the worst of it."

CHAPTER 26

The day improves from there. A pack of young men and women arrives to check in on Patti and pay respects. They look like high school seniors, but my mother insists they are teachers and introduces them to me as "the new guard," and what was surely intended as a quick stop-in turns into a rather spirited tea party that goes on for hours. Lulu, Breeze, and I run out to pick up paninis for an early dinner, and it's only a little after six when I hoof it into town to soak in the uplifting air of Gravedancer Records and her beatnik empress, Eloise Emerson.

A record store's last hour before closing time is its loosest, its wooziest, its most pub-like. The music veers off into genres unsuitable for the light of day or the faint of heart. Gypsy punk. Folktronica. Modern English songs that aren't "I Melt With You." The patrons, if patrons there be, laze over the counter while the staff tallies up the day's receipts and passes back and forth a bottle of spirits while bemoaning how no one makes music like they used to. This doesn't happen every night, but even on the nights when it doesn't, it feels like it's about to. And it will be one of the things I miss if we close the Graffiti.

But I find Gravedancer nowhere near closed. It is rowdier than ever, in fact, transformed into a concert venue. The house lights have been brought down a notch, and at the far end of the store, in the open space near the rear wall, a microphone is perched in a stand, with a teenage girl behind it. She has a streak of pink blistering through her pixie cut, and she chirps delicately while punishing her Stratocaster with brash, cacophonous strums.

Eloise comes gliding up next to me, everything on her person sparkling in the half-light—her rings, her necklace, even her smile—and welcomes me to open-mic night.

"Have you come to sing us a song, darling Rowan?"

"I've come to do what I do best: listen."

She stands next to me, rests her head on my shoulder, and together we admire the performer, who isn't sure if she wants to be Patti Smith, Tracy Chapman, or Joan Baez. She doesn't have to decide tonight, maybe not ever, but whoever she is, she's giving it her all for this rather unengaged crowd who lazes upon, around, and in some cases under the wooden tables near the coffee kiosk.

Behind the counter, house barista Becca tends to her cream-crested concoctions. It's a different Becca tonight. Having shed her funereal solemnity, her dirty-blonde tresses are down and blown out all messy, and she's clad in a burgundy shirt with white buttons bisecting her torso, neck to navel. This is the Becca I knew in school, the one we all found arousing and scary, best enjoyed from a safe distance, since we didn't have the game to enjoy her up close. This is the Becca of my dangerous dream, the one that takes place in that dark closet with a party thumping just beyond the door, her tongue viperous, my fingers prospecting all her contours. A dream so intense that it itself has become a fondly remembered experience.

She sees me seeing her from the back of the store and throws me a smile that implies we won't be discussing the ugly business that went down earlier at her day job. I guess she's hoping I've done all my barfing for the day.

"I forgot that the town mortician moonlights as your barista," I remark to Eloise.

"Here's a fun fact," Eloise says. "The barista also moonlights as my girlfriend."

I look at her. "You're dating Becca Fitzpatrick?"

She bites her grin like a schoolgirl.

"No way," I say. "There's no way you can handle that."

"Darling Rowan, I was married for a very long time, and Edward was the love of my life. But now I'm not married and I'm staring down sixty. I'm enjoying figuring out what it is I can and can't handle."

I extend a reverential nod. "I'm impressed. And frankly, a little jealous. Of you, not her—just so we're clear."

"You thought this town was so boring," she says, eyeing me rakishly. "But isn't it always the butter knife that calls everyone else dull?"

I've had my issues with this town, but never have I considered it uneventful. "You sound like my mom," I tell her. "Be warned."

I'm fascinated by how many budding rock stars Eloise has packed in here, huddled in the shadows with their guitar cases, waiting to test their mettle in front of an audience. I suppose this joint is now the county seat of musical culture, the runner-up being the King Street Opera House, a deteriorating theater that's not even on King Street, has never hosted an actual opera, and whose marquee currently advertises upcoming shows by such hot acts as Pink Lloyd (that's not a typo) and the Gin Blossoms: A Tribute. (Would it have been that much harder to get the actual Gin Blossoms?)

"Nice work with your shoplifter friend, by the way," I say. "He seems to be digging the Talking Heads. I applaud your offering him a musical miseducation instead of a life in the penal system."

"Maybe he'll finally have something in common with his father," Eloise speculates. "He seems to really want that. And it's not going to be sports."

"Yeah, I've heard about Skid's folk club," I say, snickering.

"Don't mock. You're supposed to be on the side of music."

"I'm not mocking the music. I'm mocking Skid."

"Well," she says, a cagey grin reshaping her lips. "You can tell me when it's over whether your mockery is justified."

"When what's over?"

She lifts her chin toward the back wall. "Skid's kids are up next."

I peer down at the performance floor and watch with shock and puzzlement as Skid Hall strides up to the mic stand, an absurd fedora on his head and an even more absurd acoustic guitar slung over his chest (and hanging a little high, like the early Beatles, if I'm picking nits). A baby-faced quintet joins him, draftees presumably from Skid's classes or the football squad, two of whom are also wearing guitars, one of whom sports a banjo.

Eloise looks at me with expectation, but words fail me.

"Ladies and gentlemen," Skid intones into the microphone, which registers its equivocation about this next act by issuing a screech of feedback. "Ladies and gentlemen, for those of you who don't know me, although I'm guessing you all do, my name is Skidmore Hall Jr., son of the late great Skidmore Hall Sr. I'm Mr. Hall to some of you, Coach Hall to others, Dad to my boy, and plain old Skid to my friends and relations. It is my distinct privilege to be up here tonight with these fine young musicians. We are the Free Consultations, and we have come all the way from Maybee High to dispatch love, to spread the word of eternal peace, and to revel in this wonderful little togetherness we are all fortunate to find ourselves in tonight. And let us say amen."

Only Eloise says amen. Everyone else says nothing. Why would anyone say amen?

"Margot did tell me he'd lost his mind," I whisper into Eloise's ear.

"Some might argue he's found it," she counters.

Skid steps back to stand with his players, and all at once, the trio of guitars falls into a bouncy, jangly strum; the girl with the banjo begins to pluck; and a few bars in, the lot of them begins to sing:

I'm gonna lay down my sword and shield,
Down by the riverside
Down by the riverside
Down by the riverside.
I'm gonna lay down my sword and shield,
Down by the riverside
I'm gonna study, study war no more.

I cannot overstate how difficult it is to process what I'm witnessing. The leader of the band is unrecognizable to me as a 1960s troubadour. Skid's father was a fan of folk music, and the tendency of the home stereo to ring out with Woody Guthrie, Bob Dylan, Richie Havens, and Peter, Paul, and Mary was one of the reasons Skid preferred my house over his. But he's all in now, making big, fat music with his students, which, though I struggle against it, renders me helpless to its message, its raucousness, its earnest, unrefined delivery. Skid sucks, but he sucks so good.

The band barrels joyfully through three or four verses and choruses and a man who earns his pay by scheming about blitzes and double coverage repeatedly declaring he ain't gonna study war no more. Then it's off to Scotland to pick wild mountain thyme in a slow-burning rendition of "Will Ye Go, Lassie, Go?" before returning to the States to conclude the set with the sweet longing of "Leaving on a Jet Plane." If it were anyone else up there performing—literally, anyone else in the world—I'd be loving it. But it's him. And it feels like he's singing to me directly.

When it's over, Skid beams with pride over the obligatory applause and gestures to the budding musicians flanking him in the spotlight. "Thank you! We are the Free Consultations!" he thunders. Then, more informationally: "We're always looking for more members. We have others, but they had tests to study for or ballet rehearsal, lesser matters than singing truth. So if you're out there tonight feeling like this is your bag, contact me or Sally Snodgrass." He looks down the line to the shy girl with the banjo. "Right, Sally?" Sally nods. "Okay. Have a good night, everyone. Get home safe."

I gape at Eloise. "What just happened here?"

She shrugs, winks, and floats off toward the coffee stand, suggesting with an air of danger that Becca has something hot with her name on it.

Before I can hide or duck out the door, I hear a voice mere inches away:

"So, what? You're one of my groupies now?" Skid has materialized in front of me. The fedora is gone but not the grand, sanctimonious smile.

"Bravo," I say, pointedly putting zero spunk behind it.

"What did you think?"

"Oh, I think a lot of things," I answer.

He's grinning. "Say more."

"I honestly don't know what to think."

"You've just contradicted yourself, but I know what you mean."

His fellow players file out past him. He bids them all good night, congratulates them on a great gig, and as soon as the last of them has gone, he nods at me. "You want to get a drink?"

"No."

"You don't want to get a drink or you don't want to get a drink with me?"

I always want a drink, even now as I cope with a hangover's parting shots. There is also a part of me that wants to go drink with Skid—the weak part, the part that can't help but be drawn in to his smile, his ridiculous but somehow passable performance, the way he asks like he's trying to erase my memory.

"I should get back home," I say.

"I'll walk you." It's not a suggestion. "It'll be good for you. And I'm not really supposed to drink, so you're kind of doing me a favor. The doc told me to steer clear of the stuff unless it's unavoidable."

Dubious medical advice. When would someone have no choice but to drink?

I don't want Skid to see me home. Even if the time has come for me to stop thinking of Skid as having ruined my life—and I'm not conceding that that time has come—I at least deserve to think of him as having ruined *something*. Don't I?

He's looking at me like he's trying to understand, like he almost does understand, like, *I know this is hard for you, Rowan, I honestly do, and I don't mean to trivialize your feelings, but I've already decided I'm walking you back, and you can't physically stop me.* This is what Skid does. He empties you of resolve. Everything he says receives a strange, begrudging welcome. In tenth grade, he claimed to have coined the phrase *just sayin'*. In eleventh grade, he doubled down and claimed to have coined the phrase *coin the phrase*. So now, here I am, not putting up much of a fight, about to be escorted home, nearly against my will, by the one guy I came here to avoid, and it's only nearly against my will because if I truly didn't want it to happen, it wouldn't. And that's the worst part of it. I must want to be around him. This must, as he so presumptuously put it, be good for me.

We cross over Main, veer right at the corner, and pass Ogden Street's eponymously named alehouse, a place where I am certain Skid is a regular, a place where I would have been a regular had I stayed. The floor is always sticky, there's a neon Molson Golden sign on the wall, a boxy wooden cigarette machine from the '70s *ka-chunking* out Kools and Virginia Slims, a vending machine with snack food that time forgot (Paydays and Dots, Certs and Chiclets), and there's a tomato soup special being served by a waitress who does not know and does not care whether it's cream or tomato based. I shouldn't be so judgmental. Bars have feelings too. But it has always helped to steel myself to everything about Maybee, its people and its places.

"You like living here?" I ask Skid as we stroll. "Do you ever wish you'd left?"

He seems to sniff at the cool night. Turning reflective, he says, "Well, if we walked into that bar, I would know or at least recognize everyone in it. I'm on a first-name basis with all the parents of all the kids I coach. I know how the mowed grass smells around here in August. I know how the weak winter sun looks on the roads in January." He sighs, somewhere between resignation and acceptance. "This is where I'm likely to die."

And now I'm thinking, *Like, when? You mean tomorrow? Do you have a time line?* Something drops inside me. Is Skid Hall another estranged brother who one day just won't be here anymore?

I stop walking and look at him. "Are you dying, Skid?"

"No." He stops walking too. "Are you?"

"Not in any physical way. I don't think."

"Good," he says, something upraising in the way he looks at me. "So there's still time for us, then."

There is, I suppose. But time to do what?

We start walking again.

"I guess you heard about my little leukemia battle," he says.

"I heard leukemia's side of the story, but if you want to tell me yours . . . ," I say. Are Skid and I bantering again? It is a notion that makes me bristle, then thaw.

It started on a lazy summer afternoon last year. Skid had nodded off in his easy chair, which he'd been doing with increasing regularity, and awoke to find Margot kneeling next to him, looking worried.

"What's up with you?" she asked.

"Not much. What's up with you?" he replied.

"Skid. You're not yourself," she said.

Skid scrunched up his face. "Just so we're clear, are you complaining or telling me to keep up the good work?"

But she was right: he was not himself. He'd lost weight, lost much of his appetite, and napped every day without feeling refreshed. There was an aching in his bones more deeply rooted than any of his countless football injuries.

"You're going to a doctor," said Margot.

"I'm not going to any doctor," scoffed Skid.

But Margot wasn't asking.

The doctor examined him, sent him to get his blood drawn, and his blood was found to be lacking in the necessary quantities of extremely necessary cells, both the reds and the whites. Skid made a wine joke when reporting this to Margot. Margot did not laugh.

When they sat down the following week, the doctor had a manila folder open on his desk. "You have acute myelogenous leukemia," said the doctor.

Anything with the word *leukemia* in it sounded to Skid like something best avoided. There's no such thing as, say, chocolate leukemia ice cream. None of the Hawaiian islands has a Leukemia Beach.

"That's not good, is it," asked Skid.

"It's not optimal," answered the doctor.

"I have a football team to coach, classes to teach," Skid told him.

"Well, you can either coach football this season or you can do things that might help you coach football for the next twenty seasons. Does that bring things into focus for you?"

Skid thought of Margot, of Alex, of youngsters in helmets running amok on the gridiron with no help from his well-meaning tenderfoot of an assistant coach. He thought of his uncle who'd died of leukemia at the age of fifty-seven. He thought of Monaco, where he'd never been. He thought of camping with his son under the stars of the Arizona desert, which he'd never done.

"I thought people my age don't get leukemia," Skid said.

"And since when do you, Skidmore, play by the rules?"

"Just so I fully understand what's going on here, this is a big deal, right?"

"To you, maybe," said the doctor with a shrug. "I'm just fine."

Skid eyed the man. "You're not very good at your job, are you?"

"Well, tough guy, you'd better start hoping I am."

Skid and the doctor were old friends.

Coach Hall spent a week in the hospital for a bone-marrow blast of death-metal proportions, which sucked; came home and felt like shit for a while, which also sucked; and had a standing appointment at the clinic for an intravenous tasing, which relieved him of his hair, his appetite, and sometimes even the food that managed to make it all the way down into his stomach. That too sucked. But he toughed it out, and everything that was supposed to happen happened, and now he was in remission.

"I remit!" he shouts gleefully into the night.

I tighten and untighten my lips. "That's scary, man," I say. And I wonder if he really was scared. Holden didn't have time for fear; he dove into the water and everything went black. But Skid, fearless in so many places, was not immune to the emotion. The original *Amityville Horror* cost him several nights of sleep, and he steered clear of roller coasters and skyscrapers. (On an escapade in Chicago one time, I talked him up to the observatory at the top of the John Hancock building. He wouldn't get anywhere near the windows. "This is *nuts*. Why would we take our lives into our hands, man?" he kept fretting, staying right behind me the entire time, his hands gripping my shoulders in terror. "Okay, Ro. Enough. You've seen it, now let's get out of here. Let's quit while we're ahead." It's all I remember about the Hancock tower. I recall nothing of the view.)

"It was scary," Skid admits. "But I just don't see myself dying of a blood disease. I don't know why. Watch me be wrong. I love a good surprise ending." He eyes me. "Have you ever had to go to a doctor for anything that actually matters? Have you ever gone to the hospital? It's kind of funny when you think about the people you entrust to keep you alive. I mean, they know a little bit more than you do, but not that much more. All they did was go to school for a few years." He shakes his head and laughs. "Nobody really knows anything. It's kind of crazy."

I've been to a doctor exactly once since my days in the care of the omniscient and omnipotent pediatrician Dr. Edward Emerson. While playing football with some friends a few years ago, I got tackled and landed hard on my shoulder. When the pain kept getting worse, I ended up in a rather scuzzy examining room with a rather scuzzy doctor who'd come highly recommended by my ten-second Google search. I could see the Van Halen tee under his lab coat, the one with the baby angel sneaking a cigarette. He sniffed around my upper arm for a few minutes, pressed down on a curious bony clump above my biceps, and said, "I think I can snap this back into place." He *thinks*? And I wanted to know what the "this" was in that sentence. (I at least wanted him to know.) When I asked if it was going to hurt, Dr. David Lee Roth burped up last night's Bud Light and said, "Quite a bit." Which was no lie: he jerked my shoulder, and I screeched like a monkey. The guy could've at least given me a stick to bite down on.

As our steps carry Skid and me deeper into the darkness, the air grows densely chilly, like a car in a garage in December. A waxing moon follows at our backs, and I'm following Skid, and maybe Skid is also following me, each of us knowing, or at least hoping, that we're headed somewhere we've been denying ourselves for almost half our lives now.

Skid knows everybody thinks being sick really got to him. He knows he's different now. But they're all wrong, he says. It was losing his father three years ago that started it all. When the old man died, there was this need to connect with the memory of Skidmore Sr., to keep him around through the music he listened to, the things he held important. Getting sick just moved all of that to the top of the priority list.

"You want to know something?" he says. "It wasn't until my dad died that I knew you and I were really over, Ro. I lost my father, and I didn't hear from you. I kept thinking I might, you know. I actually looked for you at the funeral, if you can believe that. I'm not saying it's your fault. I know it's mine. But that's when it hit me, all those years later, that you and I really weren't friends anymore."

Incredibly, I come close to apologizing. Patti had told me when Skid Sr. suffered a heart attack in his car, pulled over, and died quietly on the side of the road. It hadn't even occurred to me to call. My victimhood wouldn't allow it.

"You know, I almost left Margot after that," he says.

It is a strangely uprooting thing to hear, and it stops me cold. "You did not."

"I did." Skid has decided we're confidants again, or confidants still. "I thought I'd be doing her a favor. We were so young when she got pregnant, just a couple of stupid college kids. I was probably always destined to come back here, but Margot had plans, and suddenly she had to toss all of them out the window. She chose Alex—and me, I suppose."

"I always thought Margot wanted to stay here," I say. "I always thought *that* was her plan."

"I know you did," Skid says. "But nobody really knows what they want when they're in college. I mean, did you?"

I thought I knew what I wanted in high school. I wanted Margot. I wanted this. But he's right. I didn't really know. I don't even really know now. I guess all this time, I've been blaming Margot for not being sure of something she never could've been sure of, never should've been sure of.

"Margot had dreams," Skid goes on. "She was taking writing classes with the thought that maybe she'd go into journalism. She was also taking business classes, thinking that would help her run a tennis center. These things could've happened here or they could've happened somewhere else. But she was doing what you're supposed to do in college—discover who you are and leave who you aren't by the side of the road. I'm not saying Margot doesn't love me. But I don't think she gave much thought to the question of whether I was her happiness. I don't suppose I did either."

I have spent so much time hating Skid and Margot for being together. Their whole lives existed to insult me. But when I take myself out of the equation, they're just old friends who, in their fourth decade, have found themselves as unsteady in the world as I am.

"Look, I love my family. My kid is a boundary-pushing little cuss these days, and, being a teenager, he's perfectly entitled to be that way. I'm not wringing my hands over it the way Margot is. But I can love my wife and son and still wonder, can't I? Don't I get to do that? I used to think this was home, burn the ships and all that. And maybe it is. But stay or go, I want the freedom to change, to be someone other than the Skid Hall they all expected me to be, and who, for a long time, I was perfectly happy being. I've never forgotten what happened to my dad at the law firm and the lesson he learned from it, but when he died, I remembered it even more."

Skidmore Sr. was your proverbial country lawyer. Fresh out of law school, he got a job at a local firm called Schechter & Son, and there he stayed for a quarter century. It was a comfortable, family-friendly practice that allowed him to help the good people of Maybee with their wills and property disputes and the sale of their businesses. It also afforded him the flexibility to coach Skid Jr.'s rec league basketball teams and to be home every night for dinner. His bosses' families were part of his own extended family: they went to each other's weddings and funerals, he bought their wives their favorite scotch, he talked to their children about colleges. (One of them, to his great delight, even ended up attending his alma mater, Franklin & Marshall.)

But then something unexpected happened. At the end of the most successful year in the firm's history, old man Schechter called him into his office and told him they were making cuts, so, sorry, we won't have a job for you come January. That was it. Thank you for your twenty-five years of loyalty and friendship, but be out by the end of the month.

More money for them was evidently how they saw it. Skid's father suddenly saw these people for who they were, and was immensely disappointed. Not in them (a weasel has no choice but to be a weasel), but in himself for wasting so much of his precious time in the company of lowlifes who didn't deserve him. He should've seen it. He should've sought out better people.

"Be mindful of who you spend your time with, because it's *your* time, and it's all you're likely to get. That's the lesson my dad taught me after that," Skid says.

"And that's what led you to the Battle of the Bands with the Free Consultations?" I ask. "Whose parents are letting you practice in their basement?"

He laughs. "One of the ways I want to spend my time is singing the songs my dad loved with kids who want to sing them with me," Skid says. "Because when we're all sitting there in a big circle, strumming and singing and noising up that auditorium, Ro, I swear the old man is right there singing along with us. I can almost smell his aftershave."

I get Skid's impatience with how this town has typecast him as the benevolent loudmouth with the whistle around his neck, but at the same time, he sounds neglectful, irresponsible even. Who told him to go and have a family? Is he even aware that just the other night, while serving the double whammy of a parental grounding and a school suspension, Alex crept out his bedroom window to steal a pig? Does he know that he's left his wife alone to fight a multifront war against a glitchy husband and an aspiring degenerate of a son?

Then it occurs to me that he might.

"You didn't happen to send me a message," I say. "Under an alias?"

"What?"

After all Skid has confessed, there's no reason for me to hide. "Did you secretly write to me on my website? Did you call yourself Sam?"

Skid's features knot up in confusion. "Dude, what are you talking about? What website?"

I study the blank slate of his face. "Never mind." Our problems may seem singular, but they are universal, our antics dismally generic. "Sam," "Mikaela," and "Tom" are Sam, Mikaela, and Tom, not Skid, Margot, and Chili. They are not, and they are.

I wish I could let it all go, look upon everything that happened as mere childhood antics. At the time, antics are not antics at all but crusades, urgent and imperative. Maybe there's an age after which there are no more antics, just deeds and misdeeds to be inked indelibly onto your permanent record, or maybe it's the opposite and time reduces all we do to something harmless and erasable. I look at Skid now and see unrecoverable time. I can't make that right with Holden, it was never in my power to do so, but Skid is right here. Is it up to me to do the erasing? Is it my job to find those painful betrayals harmless? Is it my right?

"Can I ask you something?" I say. "How many girls dug you in high school?"

"Me? I don't know. All of them, I would imagine. Why?"

"I've just never understood why you did it. Why you went after Margot."

He sighs and sets down his guitar. "Ro, I didn't 'go after' Margot. And Margot didn't cheat on you. You weren't married. It was high school. Boyfriends and girlfriends."

"You were my brother, Skid."

He looks down at the pavement.

"I'm not saying I'm in love with your wife." As I utter those words, I am discovering that it's true: I'm not. Maybe it was never about that. "I'm just saying things would've been different for me."

"Are you sure about that?" he says. "How do you know? You remember that night a certain way, but are you sure that's exactly how it was? How convenient has it been to think Skid Hall just broke bad and stole your girlfriend?"

"I don't know what you're talking about," I say. "I just know I lost all my friends. I lost you."

"Yes, and I'm sorry," he says, wearily now. He raises his arms to the sky like a moonlit Moses and shouts all dramatic-like, "*I'm sorry!* There. Happy? Fifteen years on, that really ought to do it. We should all be laughing about this now. Time is short, Ro. Grow a sense of humor so we can all be friends again."

Despite myself, I'm smiling. It's just like him to make me feel needed, missed, and stupid all at the same time.

We are standing in the blush of the town's last streetlamp, cocooned by the limitless night. I look down at the concrete and shake my head. "There are so many things I've wanted to say to you."

"You can say them to me now," Skid offers.

"I don't know that I can."

"Well," he says. "Holden probably said everything anyway, and more."

I look up at him. "What does that mean?"

"You don't know?"

"Know what?"

He chuckles under his breath, kicks the sidewalk the same way I've watched his son do. "After everything went down between us, your brother came to my house and, shall we say, lit into me."

"What are you talking about?"

"It was Thanksgiving of our freshman year. We were all back home from college for the holiday, but you and I weren't speaking. Suddenly Holden Darling is knocking on my door. My mom answers, and I remember looking at him from the dining room like, what the hell? He was sweet as apple pie to my entire family, super friendly, waved to everybody, said the food looked delish, you know, did his Holden thing. And then he was like, "Uh, Skid. A word?" We went out onto the front porch, and that guy proceeded to give me some serious hell. He told me that you would never let on how much we'd hurt you, but he knew, and it broke his heart. He put the blame squarely on me too. What Margot did was wrong, he said, but I had different obligations. I'll never forget how he said I was like a brother to you. This is your actual brother saying this. Calling me his equal. He said what I'd done was unforgivable. *Unforgivable,* he said. I couldn't speak, I couldn't move. I just stood there feeling like whale shit."

As he says this, I am aware that I'm smiling. A shocked smile, like finding an old beloved toy in the attic.

"What did you say to him?" I ask.

"Nothing. I mean, there were things I could've said, but the fact is, he was right. I went back inside to my family and pretended like nothing happened. I remember sitting there at the table, and as low as I felt in that moment, I kept thinking how lucky you were. He came to our house during Thanksgiving dinner and put me in my place. I would've given anything to have a brother like him. And then I burst into tears. I started bawling like a newborn baby right there at that table in front of everyone. Because I realized that I did have that. Or I used to."

I gaze up into the black, dense panther's coat of night. The lights of a plane at cruising altitude wink across the sky in icy silence. I hope Holden isn't out there in that emptiness, drifting through the cosmos all alone. I wish I could've looked out for him the way he did for me.

"It's not unforgivable," I say, realizing it as the words come out. Deciding it.

"I know," Skid says. "Few things are, if you really think about it."

"I'm sorry I wasn't there for you when your dad died and when you got sick," I say. "I really wish I had been."

He smiles. "Me too."

Then he lifts his eyes and finds the same taillights I've been watching, and together we follow the airliner as it slinks through the night.

"This would be a good time for another round of 'Leaving on a Jet Plane,' wouldn't you say?"

Weirdly, yes. "No," I answer. "I wouldn't say that at all."

"My guitar's right here, and I know all the chords."

It sounds like a threat.

"We'd sound good together," he says.

I'm 95 percent sure he's kidding.

"Okay," he says, grinning at my silent refusal. "Rain check. There'll be other times."

"Maybe there will," I say, grinning back.

He reaches down and grabs the handle of his guitar case. "I was right, though, wasn't I?" he says. "This was good for you. You needed this."

"Oh, yeah? What makes you so sure?"

"Because I needed this," he says.

And off he heads down the noiseless lane toward home.

CHAPTER 27

I'm up early the next morning, roused, I suppose, by the unshakable foreboding of tomorrow. I head downstairs, knowing Patti will want my help preparing the place for whoever deigns to swing by after the burial to pay their respects and see what goodies we're serving.

I find Breeze alone in the living room, unattended and surely grateful for a rare moment of peace, which I am about to interrupt. On a safe expanse of carpet, he is surrounded by Margot's toys and seems interested only in the worst one, some generic male action figure in a business suit. (An IRS agent? The Undersecretary of the Interior?) Whoever he is, Breeze is gripping the poor guy, rattling him around, occasionally babbling heatedly at him, occasionally unaware that there's anything in his hand. I stretch out on the floor next to him and try to get him interested in a tugboat with a smiley face, and suddenly I'm thinking about Cartagena and remembering that dream. I had it again last night. Holden and the kayak and the ride down the river I was too scared to join him on, how I begged him to stay back with me, but he just stood there, the winds blowing into my store through the open door, an overmatched vessel under my brother's arm as he insisted that there had never been a better time to fly. *We should all be out of the water,*

I told him in the dream. *Let's stay together under this roof, where I can see you and you can see me.*

I hold the toy ship in front of Breeze and rock it easily on an imaginary tide. "There's never been a better time to fly," I whisper to him. The infant pauses to furrow his brow at my mouth, like he's lip-reading, but then goes right on shaking his. . . Comptroller of the Currency? Middle school vice principal?

Patti comes in from the kitchen and sees the two of us on the floor. "I didn't know you were up," she says. "So it's just the men in here, huh?"

Lulu helps me haul some folding chairs up from the basement, and my mother arranges them in the living room in an intimate formation that implies book club. She exhumes a party-size stainless-steel coffee urn from the depths of the pantry and sets it on the kitchen counter next to the canister of Guaranteed Value grounds. Mr. Garfinkle and some other Maybee High faculty fossils have pitched in for platters and trays, which Knuckle Sandwiches over on Stroeb Street will deliver tomorrow, and because Simon Garfinkle is "bound to overdo it," in the faux-irritated words of my mother, Lulu and I go out to the garage to fetch the card table.

"Do you expect a lot of people tomorrow?" Lulu asks me as I shimmy the ancient aluminum furnishing out from behind my old bike, which, for some reason, my mother won't give away but which has almost certainly been pedaled for the last time.

"My mom has taught everybody in this town between the ages of fourteen and forty, so yeah, maybe," I speculate. "She gives a lot of Cs, though, so that might thin the crowd."

Lulu grabs the other end of the table. "And the guy who ordered the food—that's the one she's seeing, right?"

"What?"

"Mr. Garfinkle. I think that's his name."

"No." I laugh. "They're old friends. Known each other since the Great War."

"Are you sure?"

"I'm sure." And then I realize I'm not. I would, in fact, have no way of knowing.

We set up the table along the living room wall and look to Patti for the next assignment. She assesses her surroundings, taking stock of everything, and declares party planning complete—or, put another way, time for her to meander from room to room, doing, undoing, then redoing our acts of preparation.

Lulu heads out for a walk while my mother proceeds to dispense, I suppose, brunch (my best guess, it being 11:10) to her grandson, who is penned in behind the high-chair tray and a bib bearing the illustration of a dog and the word *woof.* As she shovels what resembles mildewed paste into the baby's mouth, she seems happily distracted, humming and singing and echoing each noise Breeze makes as though they're having a conversation. In her chipper grandmotherly lilt, she asks, "Who wants to help Gram-Gram make lunch for Mommy and Uncle Rowan after this?"

"Who wants to help Gram-Gram pick another name?" I mutter from the kitchen chair where I'm sitting with a bag of Doritos.

"I always wanted a gram-gram," Patti reflects, adding in a stage whisper to Breeze-Brooklyn Lopez-Darling: "I'll change my name when Mommy changes yours."

Brown-green slush decorates the baby's cheeks. The only sound in the room is the effortful snapping of his lips. And, of course, the low complaint of the dimmed lighting.

"So. Have you booked your return flight yet?" my mother suddenly says, a little haltingly, like it's taken a few days to work up the nerve to ask.

"I don't know," I reply. I'm staring at the back of her, at her dense growth of white hair, the defiant but progressive hunch of her shoulders, the doggedly department-store sweater that makes it look like she's wearing Cookie Monster. And then, from some uncharted hollow deep within me, I say, "Do you think I should stay?"

She spins around to face me. "Stay?" She looks utterly surprised by the question, although no more so than I, who'd given it scarcely any serious thought. It was just the embryo of an idea, and I'd slipped it into the daylight to see what it looked like, how it sounded in the open air. "Are you really thinking about moving back here?"

"I don't know." What I'd thought about is that I could use a change. And change was coming anyway, so maybe get out in front of it?

"What happened to all the reasons you left?" Patti asks. "All the people you left?"

"I don't know," I say again. "Leaving didn't change me as much as I thought it would. It didn't change anyone else either. Plus, nobody has been around for you in a long time."

She smiles at me, but I can sense her reservations.

"To be honest, Mom, I'm just not sure where I belong anymore."

"You always belong here," she says.

For so long, I thought I'd relinquished my entitlement to Maybee, that when I exiled myself, life went on here, and the people I left behind filled up the space I once occupied, got too busy to care that I hated them. But maybe that's why it's safe to come back. I'm just like them now, and they're just like me, bearing the piling on of long days and brisk minutes, good years and bad, one after the other until we can't get out from under them, can never be who we once were and can never be someone completely different. We're all omelets now; you can't take the egg out of us.

Scraping the interior walls of the little jar so as to get the very last of the pureed green beans, Patti says, "Rowan, there have been billions of people since there started being people, and almost all of them have been forgotten. Think about that. There's Beethoven, Jesus, Galileo, a handful of others perhaps, and that's it. Everyone else: forgotten. Everyone is unremembered in the future."

"The point being . . ."

"The point being, make it easy on yourself. Let go of things that only cause you hurt. Except your children." She rolls her eyes. "Them, you have to hang on to no matter what."

She sets the miniature spoon down on the tray, then wipes Breeze's mouth with his bib. "One thing I don't want you to worry about is me. I've been fine, and I'll be fine."

Which I think is, on balance, true, but also the product of making the best of things. And it reminds me: "Hey, Mom? Are you and Mr. Garfinkle . . ."

"Are we what?"

"Are you—you know, hanging out?"

"You mean, dating?"

"Sure."

"Yes," she says.

I thrust forward in my chair. "Wait. Are you serious? Are you kidding?"

"Yes, I'm serious. No, I'm not kidding."

"You're dating Mr. Garfinkle."

"I suppose you could call it that."

"You've got to be kidding me."

"I just told you I'm not kidding you," she says.

"Why didn't you tell me?"

"Why didn't you ask?"

I stutter out the beginnings of many questions, all shouldering for primacy. "How long?"

"A while now," she says, guessing. "Four years, maybe five."

"Christ on a bike!"

"Okay, Rowan."

"All the times I've been out here and you've hidden this from me? For four years?"

"Maybe five," she says, smirking.

"How did this come about?"

"It's a long story."

"Tell me the short version."

She shrugs and casts her eyes out the window dreamily. "We have fun together."

"Unreal."

"A lot of fun."

"That's disgusting."

"You're disgusting," she shoots back. "What do you think I've been doing all these years? Waiting for your father to wake up, dust himself off, and walk back into town? You should be happy for me. You want your poor old mother hanging around singles bars at all hours, loitering at nightclubs just to find a little company?"

"Singles bars? Nightclubs? Okay, boomer."

"Sounds like I'm doing better than you, Mr. Big Shot," she says. "And don't condescend. Remember—I wiped your ass."

"Well, hang in there, Patti, and maybe one day I'll be wiping yours."

She cackles loud and pure, then lavishes me with a smile that conveys genuine affection, bracingly nonparental, like in this one slender reed of time, we're just two people connecting. Some people wait their whole lives for such countenances. So I tell her I'm ready to listen to the long version of her Garfinkle romance, and she asks me what I want for lunch.

Lulu fills the day with walks and drives. Noticeably edgier today, antsy and perhaps feeling caged in by this house and the people in it, she is surely eager to have tomorrow behind her. With all of Lulu's self-assuredness and parental poise, it's easy to forget that she's only a few years out of college. She sits in her jacket at the table on the back patio and makes phone calls to friends. She gives the coffee maker a full day's work. My mother and I offer to join her each time she announces she's heading out, but she politely declines, disappearing for fifteen or forty minutes and sloping back in through the garage door, smelling of cigarettes.

If Patti is experiencing any of the dread that Lulu so clearly is, she's not showing it, and seems, on the contrary, enlivened by all the time with her grandson. Maybe she's just doing her best not to think about tomorrow. For me, the waiting is at turns stressful and unbearable. It's like we're heading off to war in the morning—our gear is packed up at the door, and all that's left to do is wait for the bus.

When late afternoon befogs the sharp blue sky to a muted purple, we opt for an early dinner. I propose we order from an Indian place I saw in town, and the vote carries, so I make the call. I ask if they deliver, and Patti, standing two inches from the phone, shouts, "Of course they deliver. Nobody eats in there. It's vile," which the guy on the other end definitely hears, so in addition to our order, he's no doubt preparing the mother of all loogies to hock into our *saag paneer*.

The food arrives, it's meh, and other than me, no one has an appetite (except Breeze), and we all decide to go to bed early, although we agree that everyone's prospects for sleep are pretty dim (except Breeze's).

Then, at about nine, Margot calls, which is weird in the scheme of things but weirdly unweird in the context of this fantastically weird week. She's calling to see if I'm okay, and I say I suppose I am, I don't know, whatever. I ask if she and Skid are planning to come tomorrow, and she says, of course, they wouldn't miss it, and for some reason, I say, great! and then it feels like we're talking about an annual Fourth of July bash. I share with Margot that I'm dreading going to bed because I know either I'll have that damn kayak dream again or I won't sleep at all, and it's really stressful to lie there wide-awake all night. "So you'll be losing sleep over the fact that you're losing sleep," she points out, so I tell her I might end up requiring a Portia Wentworth story or two to keep me company, at which point she surprises me by volunteering her actual company, not that of her romance novelist alter ego. For some reason, she's offering to stop by, in person, right now. And for some reason, possibly having to do with the fact that this is Margot Beckett we're talking about, a woman who in so many ways is still that girl who kissed my cheek in eighth grade social studies, and is also a woman upon whom life has heaped a healthy helping of problems but who is still trying to be my friend because she suspects I need one, might even need her specifically, and I'm thinking she might need a friend too, maybe even me specifically, I accept.

Twenty minutes later, Margot and I are standing at the curb beside my mom's mailbox, in the spacious darkness beyond the ring of light cast upon the driveway and grass by the floods hanging off the house.

"I'm not going to stay long," she says. "Unless you want me to."

"I don't," I tell her. I'm smiling, so she sees I mean no offense, I mean only that it's complicated and that it's been a long day and tomorrow will be longer. "Honestly, it's bizarre that we're out here. But I'm glad you came."

She smiles back at me in her oversize yellow sweatshirt with the words BANANA SPLIT across her chest. "Thank you for letting us be your friends this week. It means a lot to me, and to Skid."

I'm not ready to be drawn into official certifications of bygones being bygones, but I can't deny that it's more of a comfort than a gash to be around these people again, Margot more than Skid. Her betrayal was the paler of the two. We might have ended up together and, I can now admit, we might not have; she has less to account for. Maybe she sees herself as another of Skid's victims.

"Are you going to go back to hating us after this?" Margot asks, smiling.

"I don't think so," I reply, not smiling back. "I don't want to."

"Because this is okay, isn't it?" she says. "Just standing here, you and me? Talking? This is good, right?"

Despite everything, it really is.

"Actually, Skid told me something I didn't know," I say. "Holden chewed him out after we broke up. He went to the Halls' on Thanksgiving Day and got all up in Skid's grill over what he did the night of Dov's party. I didn't know my brother had stood up for me like that."

"I knew," Margot says.

"I'm not trying to dredge up the past. It's got nothing to do with you or me or Skid. I'm just really glad he told me that. I needed to hear it. It's the thing I'll remember best about this whole visit."

Margot looks down and takes a breath. "I should go," she says. "I hope you sleep." She gives me a hug, she opens her van door, and I start up the driveway.

As I near the garage, I look back. Margot's door is swung open, but she hasn't climbed inside. She is staring at me, something unsettled hanging on her, detectable even in the murky floodlight glow. I head back down the driveway toward her.

"Margot?" I say when we're standing face-to-face again.

"You should probably know that I started it."

"Started what?"

"Of course, Holden was right to light into Skid. He's at fault too. But Skid told you he was the one who made the first move because that's what he wanted you to hear. That's not what happened. It was me."

I stare at her as history reshuffles. "What are you talking about?"

"We don't need to go into it," she continues. "You just need to know that I loved you, that I didn't want us to break up, certainly not that way, but I was also eighteen and unsure of what I wanted and curious. I'd never been with anyone else. You were the only guy I'd ever really kissed. I was drunk. You and I were both drunk that night, Rowan." She pauses, sighs, and folds her arms. "I was the one who initiated it. I kissed Skid."

For a while, I say nothing. I stand there trying to adjust to the reordered architecture of my fifteen-year pout. "Why are you telling me this?" I ask.

"I don't know," she says. "I guess for Skid."

"Is this supposed to change things?"

"Now? After a lifetime? I don't know. Should it?"

"He told me what he told me in order to protect you?" I ask.

"He thought it'd be easier."

"Easier for you if he was the asshole."

"Easier for *you* if he was the asshole," she says.

Once upon a time, this would have mattered, maybe even to the person who got off that plane in Chicago just a couple of days ago. That person savored his stacks of blame, guarded them preciously from the thin air of the mountain.

"It didn't make it easier," I tell her.

"I know," she says. "I think we all had to grow up a little in order to realize that."

This does make a difference. It means it wasn't all a lie, Skid and me. It redeems him a little, and so many years later, with so much water under the bridge, a little is a lot. I can reapportion my stacks of sand, move some of the grains from one pile to another. I could also just let the wind come and sweep it all away.

"Okay," I say to Margot.

"Okay?" she says.

"Okay."

She reaches out and gives my hand a squeeze. "Okay."

PART FIVE

WE SHOULD DO THIS LESS OFTEN

CHAPTER 28

"I really don't think this is going to be so bad."

That's my mother talking about the funeral for her son to which we are currently en route. The remark, delivered from the back seat with an almost psychotic chipperness, provokes an exchange of concerned glances between Lulu and me, in the passenger and driver seats, respectively, like we both see that Patti's starting the day way too high and she could go south real fast.

"I just have a feeling this will be fine," she says.

She's not actually being optimistic, she's just speaking optimistically, which is not the same thing. People often talk in hopeful terms precisely because they are concerned about all the things pessimists are certain will happen.

Patti declined the limo pickup because she was insistent that we bring Breeze along and we'd already moved the car seat from Lulu's rental to Patti's Taurus. I question the wisdom of dragging a baby to a funeral, but I don't know anything about funerals, even less about babies, and since we didn't have any alternatives, the poor tyke is strapped in back there next to Gram-Gram, his tiny hand clenched around her index finger, very possibly the only thing keeping my mother from spinning off into crazy.

I take the wheel; driving will give me something to do. The widow (or near widow) sits eerily calm in the passenger seat. Not even edgily calm like yesterday. Since everyone's being weird, I'm wishing we'd decided to open up this event to the public. A private service and a private burial seemed like a good idea a few days ago when I wanted nothing to do with everyone. But now I could use the friendly faces, even the unfriendly faces, strangers' faces.

"Can I just say something to both of you?" Lulu suddenly asks.

Her voice is dry and serious, expectant with some big reveal, and for a split second I fear that Patti's initial instinct about this woman, that she is an impostor, a fraud who has never met my brother, is about to be validated.

"I just wanted to tell you that Holden changed," Lulu says.

In the rearview, I see my mother staring with arched brow at the back of Lulu's head.

"Before Breeze was born, I already loved Holden, but I knew what he was. I didn't know if this kind of life—a child, a partner—would be for him. But it was. He set out to change my mind by changing himself, and he did. This was what he wanted, me and Breeze, and he took to it. I think you would've liked the man he was becoming, and I'm sorry you didn't get to see it." She takes a breath. "And in case you're wondering what I'm feeling now that I'm on the other end of the telescope and I'm here with this family and I can see you all up close, I want you to know that I feel love for you both. I love you, and I'm so happy I'm here. I know how weird that sounds. You don't have to say it back."

I can't say it back now, since she's told us we don't have to—and thank god, because no one says *I love you* more awkwardly than I do. (Not that the occasion has presented itself with any regularity.) But I like Lulu, I really like Lulu, and I want to be around her more so that I can feel love for her and her baby and not feel like I'm trivializing the emotion. Be that as it may, the pervading silence in the car right now demands some sort of reply, which Patti isn't offering—she's just gazing out the window, mute and inscrutable—so to Lulu's declaration of affection for all of us, I cough.

Game time is eleven, and we arrive at LaRocca's right on the nose. The first person I see, am surprised to see, but then actually happy to see, is Simon Garfinkle. He's standing by the main entrance waiting for us, all gussied up in a black suit that fits him far better than mine fits me, his silver hair radiant in the crisp autumn sun like his head is lighting the way. I park, and Mr. Garfinkle opens Patti's door and helps her to her feet. I watch as he pulls my mother close, kisses her on the hair, then looks down at Breeze, still in my mother's clutches, and pinches the baby's cheek.

"Hey, Mr. Garfinkle," I say, grateful for, and even reassured by, his presence.

He shakes my hand and, with a pitch-perfect blend of somberness and warmth, says, "Hey, kiddo."

They all file inside, but my attention is hooked by the sound of a car swerving wildly into the lot. I watch as a red economy barrels to a stop, the driver's side door is kicked open, and an Asian woman in a black dress gets out. For a brief disorienting moment of wishful thinking and, I suppose, racial profiling, I think it's Daisy.

And then I realize it is.

Stunned to the point of somnambulism, I begin to cross the expanse of asphalt, doubting my own eyes. "Daisy?"

She remains by her car, tentative, holding her features in a flinch, like she's not sure if this is okay. Like I might actually turn her away.

"You're here," I say.

"It would seem so," she answers.

"How did this happen?"

"You really want to know?"

I nod. Mostly I stare.

She folds her arms. "Well, it all started early this morning. Like, super early. I got on an airplane. It was big, with two wings and a

Rolls-Royce engine—which, by the way, is like the Rolls-Royce of engines—and it went up in the sky, and they gave me a Sprite and a little packet of cookies, and then it came down, and I was in Chicago, and the people at the rental car desk didn't have access to my driving record, so they gave me a car." She takes a breath and hugs me. "How are you?"

"Speechless," I manage to reply.

"I had to come, Rowan. I didn't like the way your voice sounded."

"How did it sound?"

"Farther away than it should have." She tilts her head. "You're not mad at me for coming, are you? You know you don't have to entertain me."

"Entertain you? With what, card tricks and a unicycle?" I gape at her, still dumbstruck to see the immense, glorious trespass of Daisy Pham in Maybee, Illinois.

She takes in the empty parking lot. "Am I early? Where is everybody?"

"Everybody is not here, because everybody is not invited," I tell her.

Her eyes go wide, and her hand shoots over her mouth. "No. I'm crashing your brother's funeral, aren't I?" Naturally, mortification quickly turns to accusation. "This is so unfair. You should've told me."

"I should've given you a head count for the funeral you weren't invited to halfway across the country?"

"See, this is what I'm talking about."

We meet up with the others in the chapel, and I immediately realize that Patti was dead wrong: this is not going to be fine. For starters, there's a casket. It's just sitting there at the end of the aisle, a cold wooden box containing the slack body of my brother. I don't know why that surprises me; it's what we came here for. Lulu is standing over it, weeping softly, her hand gently resting on the smooth, shiny surface. Patti stands back, eyeing her son's coffin and shaking her head as though she still can't believe that whoever's in charge has let this happen. (No bricks to throw at the temple, no temple, etc.) The floral aroma in the air is cloying. The silence sounds like Satan banging dark chords on his church organ. This whole place feels so—there's only one word for it: funereal. Which is to say, so much darker than death.

Becca has been standing next to us this whole time, present but out of the way here at the back of the chapel. She extends me one of those tight, sad-eyed smiles. "How are you holding up, Rowan?"

"I mean, you know," I reply. Then, "This is my friend Daisy."

They shake hands.

I lean into Daisy and point out the cast of characters. "That's my mom—you've met her. That's my brother's fiancée—we didn't know there was one of those. That's my brother's son—we weren't all that surprised there turned out to be one of those. And that guy over there—that's my ninth grade biology teacher."

Daisy nods, like it all makes total sense, or like she's used to families not making total sense, and we proceed down the aisle to join the crowd.

The sight of Daisy brings a sort of mournful smile to Patti's face, and she reaches out to stroke the younger woman's cheek. "Rowan didn't tell me you were coming," she says, to which I reply, "Rowan didn't know," and Daisy gives Patti a long, shoulder-rubbing hug and apologizes for her tragedy.

Then my mother looks at me and asks, "Do you want to see him?"

"Him who?" I say.

"Your brother."

"No."

"He looks very nice."

"That's great, but I don't want to see him. Like, at all."

"Are you sure?"

"Do I not sound sure?"

And Patti makes a face like, *Okay, but you're missing out.*

The next thing I know, we are all seated in the front row, Breeze on Patti's lap as her security blanket and Becca up at the—I want to say, podium? pulpit? stage?—formally welcoming us, offering her sympathies, and telling us the chapel is ours to share stories, express our feelings, or—and I guess she's professionally bound to say this—pray. That last part forces Daisy to notice that there's nobody here wearing a white collar.

"You didn't get a clergy," she whispers to me.

It only now occurs to me that we didn't. "I guess not."

She momentarily ponders my religious roots, or so I imagine. "What are you guys anyway?"

I shrug. "Open to suggestions."

The next thing I know, Lulu is up at the lectern, looking brave and composed as she relates the first time she and Holden met, at the Cuban restaurant where she worked. He came in and introduced himself as the new rep from the rum distributor, and the first thing she said was that she really liked the old rep, but he told her she was going to like the new one a lot better. He had a new spiced rum he wanted her to try, which she did and found disgusting, so she told him she already liked the old rep better. He confessed that he too found the spiced rum disagreeable, so she asked why he'd made her try it, and he said, "One, I'm contractually obligated, and two, I didn't make you do anything, we all have free will, and, besides, you hardly seem like the type to do anything you don't want to." Lulu imparts one more light anecdote about Breeze eating a penny, and then her voice begins to break as she says, addressing her remarks to this wooden box in front of her, how much she was looking forward to being married to him and how hard it is to accept that Breeze will never know his father. And as she says this, I feel the grip of a hand on my shoulder, and I turn and see that the hand is attached to Skid Hall. He is sitting directly behind me, tears in his eyes. And the last thing in the world I want to feel right now is the thing I feel right now, which is: *Fuck, am I glad Skid's here.*

The next thing I know, Lulu is down in her seat, and I'm the one up at the mic, no idea how I got here, no memory of agreeing to say a few words, and, worst of all, no material. Then I hear myself telling the small assembly that I've learned a thing or two about my brother in recent days, one of which is that in his strange, largely absent way, he had my back, he stood up for me when I wasn't around to see it. I look at Skid as I say this, and I can see the trace of a smile on his face, like that guilt trip Holden laid on him all those years ago was finally worth the haul. Then I say that another thing I learned about Holden is that some of the things I remember him loving were actually things he remembered me loving first, and I was happy to discover that my brother and I had, like I imagine most siblings do, a gray area where the things that kept us connected were community property, and we borrowed and stole from each other in equal measure, and I wish I'd known both of these things a long time ago, and soon I realize that I'm not speaking to the small assembly at all, but instead I'm speaking to Holden. *I really missed out. You missed out too. But not always. No, not always.*

Before I yield the floor, I hear myself saying something I hadn't consciously realized until just now: that the reason my mother didn't tell me about Holden the night she found out he'd died, and instead waited until the following morning, was because she couldn't. She knew that Holden was not just the brother I'd hoped to one day have back, but also the father I never had, and she just couldn't bear the thought of calling me up and telling me I'd lost them both forever.

The next thing I know, we're back in the car. Daisy is riding with us, stuffed in the back seat next to my mother, and a gorgeous fall day filled with bright oranges and deep reds is flinging itself past us. Patti tells Daisy she likes her shoes, and Daisy says thanks, they're Cole Haan, and Patti nods like maybe she'll order a pair after the burial.

Then we're standing on a gentle grassy slope pockmarked with gravestones, one of which is my father's, which I haven't visited in decades, but it's right there staring up at me, marking time too great to mark, and just as I'm thinking what a curiosity George Henry Darling's tombstone is, it dawns on me that George Henry Darling himself is no less a curiosity. He's a complete stranger and my nearest relative.

"Put me down right there," Patti is saying, I think to me, as she regards the patch of grass just before our feet. "I want to be here on this nice hill, with my husband and my son."

"Done," I say.

"Just do me the courtesy of waiting until I'm dead."

"No promises there."

I wonder if there's a spot for me here, if this is where I'll end up in five decades, or five years, or five months.

Right next to my father's grave is an open pit over which hovers Holden's casket, and I'm thinking about how much windier it is out here at the cemetery than it was back in town, so I glance over at Breeze to make sure he's well jacketed, which he is, he's even got his hood on, and then I turn to Daisy and see that she's staring at me, she looks, in fact, like she's been staring at me the whole time, a perfect blend of worry and sorry on her face, all just for me. I want to tell her it's okay, because that's what I typically do—I tell her things are okay. But it's not okay. And then that pulley system lets out an awful creak and begins to lower the casket down into the earth, and I'm thinking, *Hold on a second, is this for real? He's really going down there? For good? Like, until the end of time? We'll come back for him later, though, right?* And then I think my head is going to explode, but just before that happens, I feel that hand on my shoulder again, and even before I turn around and confirm that Skid has driven out here to be with us—still uninvited, unwelcome even, but who gives a fuck about that when you're Skid Hall?—I realize what a comfort it is that the best friend I've ever had, am likely ever to have, is right behind me.

Then there's Patti, shaking her head at the receding coffin, and with a deeper and more hollow hopelessness than I've ever witnessed, she utters, "Damn you, George." And everybody looks at her and seems to know exactly what she means, and just as I raise my arm to wrap around her and hold her close, Mr. Garfinkle beats me to the punch. Which, I discover, does not make me unhappy.

"I'm sorry, Holden," my mother is now saying. "I didn't mean it."

I stare at her. What didn't she mean? But she doesn't see me looking over. I can't imagine what she's seeing right now.

Then we're pulling back into our driveway after a silent ride home, plus a quick stop back at LaRocca's to let Daisy out to retrieve her rental, and as our garage door grinds open, for some reason my mother decides it would be a fitting tribute to belt out our coming-home song, and even though I'm sitting there behind the wheel thinking, *Please, lady. Why would you do this to yourself?*, Patti launches into a rather poignant, unwavering rendition of, "We're here because we're here because we're here because we're heeeeeere!" She makes it all the way through, and I wait till it's over before pulling forward into the garage, realizing for the first time how much that song resembles the bugle call of "Taps."

Daisy arrives right behind us (no fender bender, no moving violation) and accompanies me up to my room so I can shed my tie and jacket. My childhood bedroom seems to mystify and amuse her, and she moseys around it, taking in the schoolboy vestiges that my mom never took down. A smoldering Carmen Electra. A shaggy, unshorn Kurt Cobain. A poster of my high school football team senior year in which we're holding our helmets and giving the camera our most ferocious glower, bold block letters below spelling out YOU THINK YOU CAN BEAT US? NOW THAT'S FANTASY FOOTBALL! (Tough talk for a team that went 3–7.) Daisy finds me in the crowd, my young, cherubic cheeks and overgrown thicket of hair, and reaches up and touches my face.

Then we all huddle together in the kitchen as though there truly is strength in numbers. Patti is firing up the coffee maker and tearing plastic wrap off food trays, and Lulu is shaking a bottle of formula she has just warmed in the microwave. All day, Lulu has appeared composed as she fiercely weathered what I imagine has been the darkest day of her life, but now she just looks sad, a depleted woman with a baby and with a family she seems to want more than anything to call her own. She sits down, positions Breeze in her lap, then plugs the bottle into the bibbed infant's mouth. Daisy is next to them, slouching over the back of a chair, looking amused at this little human suckling going to work on a half carafe of the good stuff. At one point, she gently rubs Lulu's back, and Lulu looks up with a smile that conveys intense gratitude for the perfectly timed gift of Daisy's existence. At another point, Daisy grits her teeth at Breeze and says, "I'm going to eat you up. Every last bite of you. You're going to be delicious."

Lulu says to Daisy, "So I hear you and Rowan work together."

"Oh, it's so much fun, can you even call it work?" Daisy replies.

"Daisy should be back in Philly making sure our business doesn't go out of business," I volunteer.

"Better the friend we can see than the money we cannot," Patti chimes in as she marches in from the dining room.

"You didn't make that up," I say.

"No, the Greeks did, but I agree with it. Take Daisy's things to her room."

"Which room is that?" I ask, having lost track of our vacancy situation.

"Yours," Patti says.

Daisy immediately protests. "No, no, no. That's really kind of you, Mrs. Darling, but I'm all set. I reserved a room at the La Quinta."

"Well, cancel it."

"That's really not necessary."

"Do me a favor. Let me decide what's necessary today." She pats Daisy's face as she scoots by us, then wearily utters, "Welcome to the campsite, honey. 'Into the forest I go, to lose my mind and find my soul.'"

—

For a few precious minutes, the house is free of visitors, but merely acknowledging that fact and hoping it will remain that way jinxes it. Mr. Garfinkle knocks, and his arrival opens the floodgates, for within twenty minutes it's a madhouse, a gaggle of randos interspersed with older versions of people I used to know. A din of conversation befitting our times. "Yeah, the third season was definitely weaker than the first two." "I never use Uber or Lyft, not after hearing a podcast about those poor taxi drivers."

Some guy comes up to me, says, "You must be the brother," and proceeds to describe a Genghis Khan biography he is currently reading and insists I'd enjoy.

A second guy follows, says, "You must be the brother," and shows me snapshots of his tractor.

A third guy comes along, says, "You're the brother, right?" then proudly tells me that his son on Long Island has just paid off his mortgage. This third guy has a medical condition I suppose you'd call a "bad eye." The left one is looking at things the right one isn't, and it's quivering as though perpetually trying to wink. Still, I feel like it's working too hard to be called a lazy eye. That wouldn't be fair.

"You have to come for dinner," this third guy tells me.

Is that true? I have to? I don't even know who I'm talking to.

"That sounds great," I reply. "Count me in."

I would never go to this total stranger's home, even if he weren't a stranger, but I am oddly stirred by the fact that he's asking. It dawns on me that I've always been someone who prefers the invite to the party. Why am I like that? Why does the menu always beat the meal?

Patti approaches. She looks severe. "Can you at least pretend to be interested in these people?"

I thought I was pretending.

We then turn in unison to witness the grand arrival of Hillary Hoffman. Aunt Hillary, as I've always been commanded to call her, is one of my mother's closest friends but also, in my mother's words, "an ostentatious little peacock who represents everything that's wrong with new money." As Hillary makes her entrance, Patti gives her BFF a once-over and cattily remarks, "Will you look at that getup." The difference between an outfit and a getup I never could discern, but I'm pretty sure it has everything to do with the person wearing it. You take one of my mother's outfits and slide it onto Aunt Hillary, just like that you've got yourself a getup.

I look around for Lulu, as I suspect she could use an ally. I spy her on the other side of the room, cornered by a large fellow about my age with a long, thick, Civil War–general beard. He doesn't look like someone you talk to so much as get stuck talking to, and if it is not my obligation to rescue the poor woman, whose is it?

I sidle up next to them, and Lulu's face immediately brightens. "Rowan, you have the *nicest* family! Your cousin here is so sweet." She touches the bearded man's furry forearm. "It's Manuel, right?"

I begin to extend my hand to introduce myself to this purported "cousin," and the man smiles. "Rowan. It's me. Manny."

My jaw drops. "Cousin Manny?" It's him: that obnoxious fifth or sixth cousin on my dad's side who terrorized me during playdates, the one who only ever spoke to me to tell me I didn't know shit.

He hugs me powerfully, then shakes his head. "I'm so sorry, cousin."

"I didn't know you were still in town," I say.

"Nah, we're in Chicago."

"His wife is pregnant with their third," Lulu reports.

"Extremely pregnant," Manny confirms with a weary grin. "She stayed back, but I did bring the twins." He looks around, finds two blond children lurking guiltily by a tray of chocolate chip cookies and snickerdoodles. He calls them over. "This is Abby and Justin."

"So nice to meet you, Abby and Justin," Lulu says to them. "How old are you?"

"Seven," Abby reports. "I go by Abigail now."

"No you don't," says Justin.

"Yes I do. Shut up."

"Manuel's wife's parents live in Boca, so we're all going to get together the next time they come down for a visit," Lulu tells me, and if there's any subtext from her to the tune of *this will never happen, and if it does, kill me*, I'm not catching it.

"Breeze and our new one won't be too far apart age-wise," Manuel notes. "I'd love to see our kids really know each other."

It'd be so fun for me to jump in here and tell the cousin formerly known as Manny that, gee, I just don't know shit about Chicago, I don't know shit about Boca, and I certainly don't know shit about twins or pregnancy. But I resist. He's being so damn nice and seems so damn into being family with people he's just learned are family.

"I hear you own a record store," he says to me. "Is it awesome? Because it sounds awesome."

I really want to say yes. I want to validate his *High Fidelity* fantasy that we're all just hanging around like John Cusack and Jack Black, debating every absurd, unprovable hypothesis, like *"Tempted" by Squeeze was all wrong for* East Side Story *and would've worked so much better on the* Cool for Cats *album two years earlier*, or *Diana Ross didn't make a truly great record until the '90s*. I want to indulge the illusion that it's all just superior douchebaggery and doling out abuse to innocent eggheads who come in looking for a song by the "Doobie Boys" or asking about a good Bon Jovi "anthropology." The truth is less cinematic. The closest we get to the world of Nick Hornby is when some guy old enough to know better hears the cello on the stereo and asks if we're listening to "that violinist Yo Mama."

"Yeah," I say to Manuel. "It's pretty awesome."

And he smiles. Another satisfied customer.

I see Daisy and Eloise Emerson chatting in the corner, and I cross the room to join them.

"I've been talking to your mentor," Daisy says. "Sounds like she's really made things work out here. She's quite an innovator."

I regard them both dubiously. "Steve Jobs was an innovator. Eloise has live acts and coffee—things I've proposed and you've shot down."

Daisy shakes her head at Eloise. "He doesn't understand. I don't shoot his ideas down. The public does." Then to me: "I've been picking Eloise's brain about our, shall we say, situation."

"Our lease is ending, and you don't want to renew because you have other options," I say. "The only person dealing with any kind of 'situation' is me."

"Then what's your plan, Stan?" Eloise asks me.

I have no plans, only last resorts. "I don't know. Nothing's off the table. Who knows? If we end up closing down, I may just stay out here."

Eloise looks surprised, but not half as surprised as Daisy.

"Really?" Eloise says brightly.

"Really?" Daisy says, not at all brightly. She is taken aback, in fact. Like, *Thanks for the heads up, bro.*

When Eloise gets pulled away from us into a conversation with actual adults, I ask Daisy if she wants something stronger to drink.

"Okay," she says.

We duck into the laundry room to pour Jim Beam into our Cokes.

"You're really good with families," I tell her.

"I'm just used to them. And I like yours. It's small but nice." Which, today only, is apparently not sexual innuendo.

As thin, disjointed, and cobbled together as my family is, we've got a leg up on Chili's. The last time Daisy saw Chili's dad, he asked her if she still had family back in China. The time before that, he asked if she still had family in Japan. Daisy said yes both times.

She hands me her cup to hold while she tightens her ponytail. "Hey. Were you serious about moving back here?"

"I don't know," I say. "I just don't know what I'll have in Philly if we shut down."

"What do you have back here?"

I shrug. "A fresh start." The irony isn't lost on me: Maybee was the place I ran from; Philly was the fresh start. "I think I might be needed back here. My mom and all."

Daisy reclaims her cup, takes a swig, and licks her lips. Eyeing me tightly, she says, "You were right, by the way. About Chili and the marriage proposal thing."

"Oh." My heart shakes like an out-of-control motor. "He asked?" My voice is suddenly a rasp. "Daisy, are you engaged?"

"No." She waves her hand, showing me a ringless finger. "He sort of pre-asked."

"Pre-asked."

"It was like he was testing the waters."

"Is it a good sign that he feels like he needs to do that?" I ask.

She shrugs and looks down at her cup. "I don't know."

"So? Did you pre-answer?"

She locks eyes with me. I feel her looking for something in them. Does she want my approval? Does she want me to let her go? Release her from this shape-shifting, multiheaded beast our relationship has become? Or is she just gauging how badly she'll hurt me with the truth, today of all days?

"I told him I'd say yes," she says.

"Oh." I take a sip of my bourbon and Coke, but the sip keeps going until, wouldn't you know it? I've poured the whole thing down my throat. "Well. I guess pre-congratulations are in order."

Just then, I hear the front door shut and the sound of familiar voices. Skid, Margot, and Alex have arrived.

CHAPTER 29

I wade into the party—and it is definitely something of a party. It has kind of an office-holiday-party feel: refreshments, a lively but restrained noise level, people milling around in business casual, and even some of us examining our feelings about a coworker's quasi-betrothal. *This isn't news,* I remind myself. *This was always coming. You weren't going to have meaningless storage-room sex with Daisy forever.* Then, my internal self-retort: *Just what are you calling "meaningless"?*

Skid awards me a tight hug freighted with all the unspoken words, unlaughed hysterics, and uncried tears of which we have each deprived the other these last many years. Alex attempts a handshake but gets vetoed. "We're huggers in this family," his father counsels. "News to me," mumbles the boy, but he complies.

Margot has drifted over to Patti to assume that traditional supportive, sympathetic posture she wears so well, just like the black dress in which she is sheathed and the muted but noticeable application of lipstick. It is the first time since my arrival out here that I've seen her in something ill-suited for a spinning class. She looks beautiful, *is* beautiful, and I give myself permission to envy Skid for having her all this time.

"Mrs. D. hasn't done one damn thing with this room," Skid notes. "It's like an archeological dig site." He walks over to a wide, windowless expanse of wall, slides his fingers across it until he finds a dent, a small crater precisely the size of a rubber Super Ball. He turns to me, beaming. "It's still here!"

I smile. "I know."

He shakes his head. "She was so mad."

"She had just warned us that those things leave marks."

"And she was right," Skid says. "We ruined her wall."

"You ruined her wall."

"No, *you* ruined her wall. I just took the blame because we knew she'd go easier on me."

I stare at him with the ghost of a smile that says, *Now, why does that sound familiar?*

Skid turns to greet a pair of women, fellow faculty members is my guess, and leaves Alex and me standing there, looking at each other. He and I have stories, secrets I can't bring up around his parents, and our mutual appreciation of that confidence nearly brings both of us to nervous laughter.

"Just a heads up," I say to him. "You might come across a six-month-old with one of your old toys. If you do, try to be the bigger man."

Alex snickers. "If people are stealing my shit, I guess what goes around comes around."

I see his eyes settle on the framed photo of Holden that Patti has propped up front and center on a nearby table. It's a dusty one, his yearbook picture: perfectly centered head, immaculately brushed hair, royal blue backdrop. "I see a resemblance," Alex says. Maybe he's trying to be kind. It's just something people say.

"Do you?" I reply, staring into my brother's proud, restless eyes. "It's hard to do a side-by-side comparison, since there aren't many recent pictures of the two of us together."

"He wasn't around much?" Alex asks.

"Nope," I say, shaking my head at the photograph, sorry for Holden that he's all alone in that frame, sorry for me that I'm not in there with him, sorry for all of us that there aren't a mess of albums for Lulu and, one day, Breeze.

"It's weird," I say. "If I had any good pictures, I'd put them in a frame or keep them in a drawer. I'd know that they exist, which would mean that *we* existed. That's the whole point of family albums, isn't it? Something to remind yourself of where you fit in. But ours are always missing someone—him sometimes, me sometimes. There isn't much to prove we were ever a complete family. Mostly my history with my brother is hide-and-seek, me shouting 'Marco!' into the wind and waiting to hear 'Polo!'"

I have made Alex uncomfortable. "Sorry," I say. "Adult themes. Forgive the overshare. How's it going with you and Eloise?"

"Not bad," he says. "I asked her to help me out with some of that hippie music my dad is so obsessed with now. I figured you and Holden had all that Talking Heads stuff, so why not give it a shot with old Skidmore?"

"And?" I ask.

"She's starting me off with Bob Dylan."

"I can't quarrel with that. You like it?"

"No," he says. Then he smiles. "Maybe one day I will."

There's still time for Alex and Skid to fill the shelves with family albums, photos of each other in the same frame. I'll have to see Holden in music, to find him in that jittery extant cough of David Byrne. "Once in a Lifetime." "Heaven." "Psycho Killer." "Dream Operator." I trust those songs to safeguard my brother's survival more than any dead-eyed photograph.

My cup is empty, and I should probably hit the brakes on the hard stuff, so I head to the dining room table to assess the beverage options.

"Everything go okay at the cemetery?" It's Margot sidling up next to me.

I puff out a long breath. "Well, we left with one less person than we showed up with, so I suppose things went according to plan. Your husband crashed, you know."

"I know. The rules don't apply to him."

"It's okay," I say.

We stand there, each of us holding a crinkly plastic cup fizzing to the brim with Diet Coke.

"To Holden," Margot toasts.

"To Holden," I answer.

Together we sip.

"Want to hear something strange?" she asks. She is staring through the sliding double doors that open onto the backyard, our modest, well-manicured clearing with a lazy herd of oak trees leaning over it like giraffes. "I used to have a dream about this house. There was a party here. You attended, but you weren't the host. It was really crowded, all humid and sweaty, packed with people from all different pockets of my life—high school, college, extended family, mommy-and-me groups. And then everyone got sick and went home. One by one, they started looking pale or feverish, leaning against the walls, unable to hold themselves up. Gradually everyone staggered out until I looked across the room and saw that the only person left was you. We were both kind of amazed that everyone else was sick except us. You said you felt fine. I said I didn't but that I'd been sick for too long and was just flat-out tired of being sick."

She stops talking and continues to gaze out into the afternoon.

"What happens then?" I ask.

"I don't know."

"You wake up."

"I don't know if I wake up or not. All I know is that's where the dream ends."

"Sucks when that happens," I say.

"Depends on the dream." She looks down and jumbles her ice. "Rowan?"

"Yeah?"

"If it had occurred to me for one second that you'd leave town and stay away for good and I wouldn't know you anymore, I swear I wouldn't have done what I did."

I've had my fill of apologies; I only feel diminished by them now. It may sting a little to learn that Margot hadn't wanted me the way I wanted her, but she has redeemed Skid, even if only in small measure. It turns out it's not too late to feel better about him. It's far too late to feel worse about her.

"It's okay, Margot," I say.

"I made a mistake," she says.

"No, you didn't."

She swallows down another sip without detaching her eyes from mine. "Sometimes I feel like I did."

Just then, Daisy comes through, brushing past us on her way from the kitchen. She sees us and comes to a cold stop.

"Hey," I say to her. "I want you to meet somebody. This is Margot."

I watch something register with her. "Ah. Margot. I've heard quite a lot about you."

"Uh-oh," Margot says.

"Daisy and I run the store together," I say. "We're old college buddies." It is the first time I have ever described her that way, even thought of her that way, and I stop to wonder if I'm doing so on purpose.

"Oh, sure," says Margot. "You're from Philly. Really nice to meet you." One black-dressed woman to the other.

Daisy gives me a chummy swat on the arm. "If you'll excuse me, buddy, I think I'm going to go for a drive."

"A drive?" I say, but she's already at the door.

I look at Margot and offer her a shrug of ineptitude. "It seems I've done something wrong."

Consulting the contents of her cup, she says, "I'd be surprised if that were true."

—

I catch Daisy on the driveway. She's marching toward her rental car, pressing her finger down on the remote, but the door won't unlock.

"Daisy," I call to her.

"I need a few minutes alone," she says, sighing irritably. "Can you just give me that?"

"I don't understand."

"It's no biggie."

"Well, it seems like a big biggie, Daisy. Let's just talk."

She spins around with sharp, incising eyes. "'Margot, I want you to meet somebody. This is Daisy.'"

"What?"

"That's what you should've said."

I stand there, shaking my head at her ineffectual clicking, seeing her not noticing that with each press, the lights blink on another car farther down the curb.

"I don't know what you're so pissed off about," I say. "You've done nothing but reject me."

"Reject you? I'm standing on your fucking lawn, Rowan!"

I sigh grandly. "You're a terrific friend, Daisy, but you've always made it clear that that's all you've ever wanted to be. And don't you have a fiancé? Or pre-fiancé?"

"I just want to be alone for a little while," she begs. "Is it really too much to ask you to get out of my cheese?"

"Okay, okay." I show her my palms, and she continues her futile fidgeting with the electric key, pressing harder and harder, growling in frustration.

"Daisy—and I'm not trying to be in your cheese, but—that's the wrong car." I point to another red economy parked farther along the curb. "That's Lulu's rental you're trying to unlock."

She spots the other, virtually identical vehicle, says, "Oh," and heads over to it.

"Come on, Daisy. Let's just talk," I implore her. "I don't want you to go."

But she's carried off on screeching wheels and the stench of burned rubber, long out of earshot as I stand there repeating my plea: "I don't want you to go. Please don't leave."

—

As I charge back inside, making for the steps and the seclusion of my bedroom, Margot intercepts me at the door. "Is she okay?" she asks. "I can go and try to talk to her, if you want."

"You? No. Thank you. That's very sweet, but no, that's a terrible idea."

"Oh." She looks affronted. Why does everyone suddenly feel the need to have emotions? "Why is that such a bad idea?"

"Because, Margot," I say, and I nearly laugh with exasperation as I wave my hand before her like I'm presenting her to the queen. "Because you're Margot. Don't ask me to explain it. I'm going upstairs for a bit. I'll be back down later."

Then I hear Skid's voice calling out to me. "Rowan," he is saying.

The fascinating thing about his voice is that it's the only noise I hear, the lone sound in a house gone strangely quiet. When I turn and see him standing in the middle of the room, I learn that Skid has brought his acoustic guitar to our house, and I know this because it has been let out of its case and is now strapped across his chest.

"Oh, dear god," Margot utters.

Skid strums slowly through one dulcet chord. "This is for Holden," he announces to the silent room. "And for Patti and Lulu and Breeze-Brooklyn." He parks a meaningful gaze on me. "And for you, my brother."

"Skid?" Margot says with sheer alarm.

Another slow strum chimes from his strings. And then, very softly, Skid begins to croon, slow and ballad-like:

We are traveling in the footsteps
Of those who've gone before,
But we'll all be reunited
On a new and sunlit shore.

Margot gapes at me, abject with embarrassment. "I'm sorry?" It's kind of a question.

"This is something he does now, isn't it?" I ask her.

"I'm afraid it is," she answers.

Another broken chord with more plaintive vocalizing:

Some say this world of trouble
Is the only one we need,
But I'm waiting for that morning
When the new world is revealed.

The strumming begins to gather steam, chugging forward in one insistent, life-affirming major chord. Then Skid fairly shouts:

O when the saints go marchin' in!
O when the saints go marchin' in!
O Lord, I want to be in that number,
When the saints go marchin' in.

When one finds oneself in a crowd, and someone begins to sing a rousing spiritual or a popular sing-along, or really anything with an anthemic chorus, it is predictable, perhaps a feature of human nature, that, egged on by the power of assembly and the safety of anonymity, one joins in. And so, because, definitionally, predictable things happen all the time, the fifty-odd mourners in this room gradually become an audience; then, one by one, a participatory audience; and then, all at once, a choir.

And when the sun begins to shine,
And when the sun begins to shine,
O Lord, I want to be in that number,
When the saints go marchin' in.

It is a thing of grotesque beauty, I suppose: Skidmore Hall, not a single musical bone in his body, hovering like a preacher and stirring each of us into song—Lulu, Mr. Garfinkle, Cousin Manny, Alex, my Swedish hygienist (Finnish, now that I think about it; she once told me she was from Helsinki), the Genghis Khan guy, the man with the tractor pictures, the many townspeople of Maybee, Illinois, all of them initially reluctant but ultimately defenseless. Skid is here, Skid is trying, and as he sings his guts out—I repeat, not a musical bone in his body—he looks straight at me, defying me to resist him, daring me not to see that he's making this house his own again and thereby making it ours again, recognizable to me again, inviting me to surrender all my resentments and let everyone back in, including myself.

So I do. I heave myself in and sing. At the top of my lungs. With all I've got. And it feels like I'm taking a balloon to the moon.

The last chorus is a barn burner. It's like a Neil Diamond concert during an encore of "Sweet Caroline." And as we raise the roof with our united dreams of a new world being revealed and wanting oh so desperately to be in that number, I look at Patti and see her weeping, cleaved with grief, but still singing her heart out, her voice carrying all the forsakenness and wanton hope that a day like today stamps forever upon a mother's face, and I put my arm around her and hold her head to my chest, and we all stand together, a couple dozen throats warbling in unison. And this house on Campsite Lane has never felt more like an actual campsite.

CHAPTER 30

When "Skid Hall: Live & Unplugged at the Neighbor's Memorial Service" ends, I once again worm my way back to the laundry room to top myself off, my reasons for needing to spike my soft drink only multiplying.

I shoot Daisy a text: I think you've had enough time without me in your cheese. Please come back. If you can find your way.

No sooner do I spot Skid's guitar case reclining against the dryer, its slender black form resembling a runt Johnny Cash, than thc "musician" himself appears.

"Who let you backstage?" he wisecracks.

"I have an in with the owner—much to my chagrin," I answer. "You here to grab a quick smoke before going back out for the encore?"

I can tell from the posture of Skid's brow and the ethereal cool behind his eyes that he's proud of himself, that he believes he has helped me along the path, in some small or possibly monumental way, toward the restoration of my soul.

With an air of serenity, he says to me, "I'm happy you're here."

I shrug and smirk. "It's my house."

"Mine too, though, wouldn't you agree?"

My head rocks back and forth a bit because it's hard to disagree. If Skid Hall was once my mother's de facto third son, he's the only one who never left her.

"And the other Free Consultations?" I ask. "Aren't they going to be pissed at you for going solo?"

"I'm their teacher. If they kick me out of the band, zeroes for everyone! And they know I'd never go solo. Going solo is for pussies."

"Now you're picking a fight with Sting. George Michael, Gwen Stefani—"

"You," he says.

I smile, but it's his band, not mine, that seems closer to breaking up. Just ask every member of his family. I wonder if he knows how desperate Margot sounds. I wonder if he knows that I really would help if I could.

"I hope you guys are okay," I say to him. "You, Margot, Alex. You guys would make a nice family."

He chuckles. "We are okay, or we will be, whatever that ends up meaning." He posts a hand on the washing machine and leans on it as though steadying himself. "Margot is a little overwhelmed—you can see that. Alex is overwhelming. Shit, I've always been overwhelming. Maybe even having you back is a little overwhelming. She loves you, Ro. Maybe not the way she used to, but in a way that isn't going anywhere. Ditto for me. That's what happens. You grow up and realize you still care about the people you used to care about."

I suppose he's right. I showed up here and started acting like a friend to Margot and Skid. Then I realized I wasn't acting. I was being a friend, and I was doing it because it was the best way to even the score, to settle things with them and with myself. But having crossed the country and looked my nemeses in their eyes, I see now that there are no scores to settle, and I still care about the people I used to care about.

"Nothing's easy, is it," I say.

"Hell no," he agrees. "But one thing I've learned from getting sick and getting better is that everything worthwhile is sloppy. If you don't get messy, you weren't really there."

I stare at him, this skinnier, slightly smaller, but somehow stronger, more indestructible, more immediate rendering of my best friend. "Thank you for being at LaRocca's today, and at the cemetery."

He lowers his eyes. It's not all songs and marching saints; he's suffering our loss too. "I'd like to think I wouldn't have missed it."

"Seeing you there didn't make it any easier, but if you hadn't been there, it would've been a lot harder."

He puts his hand over his chest, a wordless, if excruciatingly folk singery, sign that he knows what I mean.

"And I'm really sorry I wasn't there for your dad's funeral."

He smirks. "You'll catch the next one. Just make sure you're around for it. Like they say, keep your friends close, keep your guardian angels closer."

At that, I laugh. "If I have a guardian angel, he's been passed out drunk in a ravine for the last ten years."

"They're only human," says Skid.

I look down and shake my head. "I sure wish Holden had had one of those."

"Didn't he? What about that tiger-eyed lady out there? Lulu."

"She didn't save him."

"You sure about that?" he says.

I contemplate the buckling, blemished faux-tile floor. I'm not sure at all. And what does it cost me to believe it? It's the better story.

"I'm happy you're here, Skid."

"It's my house," he replies, smiling.

I smile back. "Mine too, though, wouldn't you agree?"

Beyond the laundry room door, I hear my mother's voice and the sound of plastic wrap. She's sending people home with food.

"We're in good stead, Skid," I say. "This time around, I think you and I are both leaving the campsite better than we found it."

"You don't have to leave the campsite, Ro. You never did."

I wonder if I would have, had I known the truth about that night all those years ago, that it was Margot who'd gone after Skid, not the other way around. Skid lied to me for Margot's sake, believing it made her offense slightly less offensive. But he got it backward. He didn't know I needed him more. I suppose he's right: guardian angels are only human. Defective, occasionally warped of judgment, and murky of motive, but they come through in the end.

Out in the kitchen, a voice I don't recognize subs out, and one I do—belonging to Becca Fitzpatrick—subs in and chats easily with Patti. At the sound of our old schoolmate's voice, Skid's mien gets heavier, freighted by something he seems loath to speak of.

Then: "Just so you know, Rowan, what happened between Margot and me that night at Dov's party, it had nothing to do with what happened between you and Becca. Margot didn't know, and I didn't mention it."

My head cocks. "What are you talking about?"

Skid is holding me in a look. It's the way someone regards you when they know something they shouldn't know, something you've never discussed.

"Seriously, Skid. What are you talking about?"

"Rowan, I saw you."

"Saw me what?"

"It doesn't matter now, not in the least, but I saw you and Becca come out of that room together. Margot didn't see, and I never said a word to her. You should know that. What happened between Margot and me that night was not about that. She didn't know."

Skid is talking, but the words aren't connecting. It's like they're hanging over us, shifting around under the low laundry room ceiling, crowding up an already confining room. Then, amid these shapeless words, I stare at Skid, he stares back, and some horrible new piece of our history begins to crystallize.

"Fuck," I mutter. "It wasn't a dream."

Suddenly, my phone rings, a perfectly incongruous, jovial jangle. I pull the device from my pocket, see that it's Daisy, and when I answer and hear the tone of her voice, a finger of adrenaline floods my bloodstream. She delivers the news I am always half expecting to hear when she calls:

She's been in an accident.

"It wasn't my fault," Daisy swears. "I swear."

It will take some convincing. We'll discuss fault later.

"Just—are you okay?" I ask.

"I think so. Some idiot ran a stop sign," she says, which could end up being self-referential. "Rural Illinois drivers, am I right?"

"Where are you?"

"Do I sound woozy? I banged my head on the window."

"Tell me where you are, Daisy."

I can almost hear her squinting at road signs. "I'm at the intersection of Campsite and—does that really say *Deerpiss*?"

"Deerpath. You're really close."

"To what?"

"Me. I'll be there in five."

Skid hears the news and offers to sprint over there with me, but I tell him it's probably best I go alone. When Daisy left here, she was rather displeased with me, and something as routine in her world as a traffic accident is unlikely to jolt her out of her state of disgruntle. I'll go deal with the car wreck involving my friend; he should stick around and deal with the train wreck that is his family.

It's a short, three-minute sprint to Deerpath, a quiet, tree-clustered intersection of residential streets. As I approach, I see Daisy's rental angled on the shoulder, a police car behind it with flashers off and, suspiciously, no other vehicle. Daisy is flopped against the passenger side door, adjacent to a sizable but nonlethal dent and holding something to the side of her head. An officer stands over her with his hands on his hips. The way cops do.

I come rushing up in a pant. "You okay?"

"My hero," Daisy quips dryly, making a show of checking her watch, like maybe I stopped for a drink on the way.

I introduce myself to the cop. He's about my age, white hair and a startlingly pale complexion to match.

"I think she's just got a bump on the noggin," he reckons. "The impact jolted her head against the glass. I don't think she has a concussion, but if she starts to feel nauseous or disoriented, take her to the ER."

"But what if it's him who's making me nauseous?" she asks the patrolman while pointing at me.

I find my attention drawn more to this uniformed man than to my injured friend. "Do I know you?" I ask.

"Yes," he replies evenly. "It's me, Ted the Albino." Not a hint of irony.

A smile curls the edges of my mouth. "Huh. So it is. How are you, Ted?"

"Fine, Rowan. Now, then: the car is drivable, but I recommend your friend not drive for a while."

"I've been recommending that for years," I rejoin as Daisy sneers at me from behind her ice pack. "Please tell me there was another car."

Ted nods. "According to your friend, she got the driver's insurance information and then dismissed him, said she was fine."

"I *am* fine," Daisy insists. "And I didn't need police intervention."

"Is that like, *thank you, Officer*?" I say to her.

"I didn't like the look of the vehicle, and even with the wound being superficial, I thought she should call someone," Ted informs me.

"Thank you, Officer," I say.

"You can keep the ice pack, miss," Ted says. "You folks have a nice day."

His work here done, Officer Ted the Albino heads to his car.

"Good to see you, Ted," I call after him.

"Likewise, Rowan," he mutters without turning around, and I watch as the lawman's taillights recede down Deerpath.

"I grew up with that guy," I say.

"Yeah, he seemed thrilled to see you," Daisy remarks.

We are alone now, she and I, just the two of us in the hospitable quiet of suburbia. I take a second look at the crater in the body of the rental and emit a whistle. It is not a love tap. It's a frightful thought, Daisy being injured in her first car accident that she didn't cause.

"So some guy ran a stop sign?" I ask.

"It was like he didn't even see it. Then again, why would I take my turn at the four-way stop when he's the one with the Beamer?"

She removes the ice pack and explores the side of her cranium with her fingers. Finding a raised mass of skin, she winces at the tenderness. When I lean in to examine, she feints out of reach, then looks up at me with inconsolable eyes.

"Rowan, are you in love with your high school girlfriend, who you haven't spoken to in twenty years and who's married with a kid, so it would be really pathetic if you are?"

"I think that's what they call a 'leading question,'" I reply.

We slide down the side of the car and sit on the cool gravel, side by side, our knees bent and our backs against the car door, both of us showing the wear and tear of a long day.

Out of the blue, Daisy says, "I told you about my sister and Eve Guttman, didn't I?"

I'm about to ask which sister but realize it doesn't matter. I shake my head no.

"When my sister Gracie was at Michigan, she had a sorority sister named Eve Guttman. One semester, Eve developed a wicked flu, so she went home to Colorado, and she died a week later."

"Whoa," I say.

"Right," Daisy says, pinching a pebble between her fingers. "Gracie reacted to her friend's sudden, inexplicable death by—what's the best way to phrase this?—losing her shit. You know Gracie. She's the together one. But this threw her for a serious loop. She didn't sound like herself on the phone, she stopped going to class, stopped leaving her room, and my mom got so freaked out that she drove to Ann Arbor and brought Gracie home. It was pretty hideous. She basically locked herself away in her bedroom for weeks. Didn't talk to anybody. Every minute she was awake, she was either catatonic or crying hysterically. I was a freshman in college, and I called her almost daily during those weeks. My mom would hold the phone up to her ear, and I'd go, 'Gracie? It's going to be okay, Gracie.' Nothing. Eventually, my mother would say goodbye and hang up.

"And then one day, just like that, it was over. Gracie came downstairs, dressed and packed, ready to reenter society. And she did. My mom put her on a plane back to Michigan, and that was that. The thing is, Gracie and Eve weren't even that close, so I used to wonder what it was about Eve's death that pitched my sister into such paralyzing grief. And I decided that it was how mundanely death had arrived for a young person, how it had come unsuspectingly, clothed in a common cold. Eve Guttman went home sick from school and never came back. That's the scariest fucking thing in the world."

I sigh. "Daisy, what happened to Holden is very different from what happened to your sister's friend. It's really not like that at all."

"That's not what I'm saying. Holden isn't Eve. You're Eve. And I'm Gracie. You packed up and left, you had no plan to come back, and to be honest, it spooked me."

"So you've been catatonic this whole time because I flew out to a funeral?"

She shrugs with half a heart. "I didn't say it was a perfect analogy."

She flicks the pebble she's been holding. It skims across the road, makes it over the center line. "I'm not trying to make your brother's death all about me, Rowan. But there is a part of it that is about me. Something happened when I dropped you off at the airport. It was watching you walk into that terminal. I felt like I should be walking in there with you."

I look at her. "You're here. You came. I didn't even ask you."

"I didn't want you to ask me. I wanted you to expect me to come *without* asking." She does that thing again where she puffs a flow of air from her jutted-out lower lip and it lifts her bangs. "I wanted to walk into the airport with you. That's what I wanted. I wanted us to take our shoes off together in the security line. I wanted to buy snacks together for the plane. I wanted you to hold both of our boarding passes, hand them to the guy at the gate at the same time, have him scan them and wish us a good flight, but only say it once because we're together."

"Daisy—"

"Let me just get this out," she says. "I called Victoria after I dropped you off, and I told her everything I just told you, and she was like, oh, you love this guy, and I was like, really? How could I love Rowan Darling? And she was like, beats me, I don't know how anyone could love that drip, but apparently you do. But here's the thing, Rowan: I don't actually know if I love you or not, and I don't think we need to discuss that or decide that today." She stops to release a long, pent-up breath, her shoulders stooped, her head pitched downward in a sulk. Allowing a shy glance and a tentative smile, she adds, "But I wouldn't mind discussing it at some point."

I stare at Daisy's profile and try not to smile, to reveal the overwhelming throes of relief that tumble around inside me like clothes in a dryer. How long have I been waiting for the cycle of our relationship to return to the place where we could have that discussion again?

I take in her smell, which rises up from her neck. The aroma of Daisy up close—a fragrant batter of airplane, rental car, and Daisy—somehow fits here. Her presence in this town just makes sense, as much sense as mine or Skid's or even Patti's. People always tell Daisy upon meeting her that they feel like they already know her, and she always replies, "I'm familiar. That's my thing."

"Did you mean what you said about staying out here if we close the Graffiti?" she asks me.

"Did you mean what you said about saying yes to Chili?" I shoot back.

"No," she answers.

"Wait. No?"

"No."

"But you told him you'd marry him."

"No, I didn't."

"Yes, you did. I distinctly recall this conversation. It was less than an hour ago. He pre-asked you if you'd marry him, and you pre-answered yes."

Her pursed lips wrinkle like an overripe plum. "I told *you* I'd marry him. I told *him* I wouldn't."

I gape at her. "So you lied to me."

"That's correct."

I sit there, unsure of what information exactly is being conveyed, to say nothing of its reliability. "Why?"

"Because I wanted to hurt your feelings," she says, shrugging like it's the most obvious thing in the world. "You had just told me you were done with me. What did you expect me to do?"

"I didn't expect you to say something completely false just to make me jealous."

"Rowan, as long as I've known you, I've been in serious or semiserious relationships, and I've never gotten so much as a whiff of jealousy from you."

"Maybe I'm adept at hiding my emotions," I say.

"Maybe. Or maybe you're adept at not having them."

The sound of bemused laughter is sputtering out of me as I stand up. "I think it's time for us to go back to the dance."

I hold out my hand to her; she grabs it; I yank her to her feet, and suddenly her face is centimeters from mine, each of us looking hard at the other. "Don't lie to me anymore," I say. "You can make things up—I know Daisy Pham will always make shit up—but don't lie. Otherwise, I can't be your friend anymore."

"Oh, really?" She laughs and shakes her head. "Well, that's kind of the point of this whole conversation, dummy."

CHAPTER 31

I navigate Daisy's dented hunk of lightweight tin down the street and into my mom's driveway, where we are immediately swarmed by eager guests spilling out of the house as though they'd been watching for us by the window. Patti, rushing ahead of the pack, veritably plucks Daisy out of the passenger seat.

"Skid told me what happened. Are you hurt?" my mother asks. She sees the welt and clucks at it. "Let's get you inside."

And off they shuffle, my mother cursing the rise in congestion in this neighborhood (in fact, the roads are not one car more crowded than they were a quarter century ago) and Daisy a compliant recipient of Patti's TLC. Meanwhile, Lulu's ear is being bent by the tractor-photo guy, who is actively appreciating the cavity in the side of the car and comparing it to the damage recently inflicted upon his Bronco by a drunk neighbor wielding a two-by-four.

A trio of Hall-Becketts comes striding up to me to inquire about Daisy's welfare, even budding criminal Alex showing some concern for his fellow citizen. I tell them Daisy seems fine and that her car took most of the beating, which is generally the way these things go with her.

"Did you guys know Ted the Albino is a cop?" I ask.

"We did," Skid answers. "And did you know Ted the Albino knew you called him Ted the Albino and wasn't down with it?"

I don't remember being the one who invented that moniker, but since these guys have to live here, I don't blame them for pinning it on the boy who moved away.

Something strange is going on with Alex. I can't help noticing that he can't help noticing the crater in the side panel of the rental, his distress seeming unalleviated by the fact that the damage, both to the vehicle and the driver, is relatively minor. Then Margot and Skid notice me noticing Alex noticing the dent, and now everybody's looking at him.

"You okay?" Skid asks him.

Alex stands there looking small, a gray queasiness deadening his complexion.

"Alex? What's going on?" Skid presses.

Alex says nothing but swallows uncomfortably and visibly.

"Alex," Margot says, growing stern.

Then he blurts out: "I swear I had nothing to do with it." Kids always lead with the exculpations.

"Nothing to do with what?" Margot asks, confused and not happy about it.

The boy is already protesting. "I didn't think they were actually going to do it. I told them people could get hurt. Like, seriously hurt. I told them this was way over the line and that I'd go to the police if they didn't promise that they wouldn't."

"Promise what?" Margot says, overenunciating.

"Alex. None of us knows what you're talking about," Skid says. "Clarify things. And do it now."

The teen lobs a helpless look at his father, then at his mother, then, for good measure, at me, and says, "They stole a stop sign."

Margot's eyes constrict. "They *what*?"

"Who did?" asks Skid.

"Those moron friends of yours?" Margot says.

"They're not my friends," Alex insists. "It was supposed to be some new kid's initiation. He had to steal a stop sign for Gunnar to hang in his room. I told them they could kill someone."

With fascinating instantaneousness, Margot is unglued. She shakes. Her eyes and mouth pitch wide open. Her nostrils flare like they're ready to emit fire. "They could've killed someone!" she bellows.

"That's what I just said!" Alex yells back.

"Hold up," comes Skid. "You knew that someone was out there endangering people's lives, and you didn't tell anyone?"

"I told *them*," the kid pleads.

"That's telling no one," Skid counters.

"What is wrong with you?" Margot wants to know. "What kind of sociopath steals traffic signs for fun?"

"Not me," Alex tries to point out.

"What kind of sociopath is friends with sociopaths who steal traffic signs for fun?"

She's got him there.

"Everybody just take it easy a second," I say, finding myself in the marrow of yet another Hall-Beckett family squabble.

"These are the pot smokers, right?" Skid asks. "The pig thieves?"

Alex nods, then, "Wait—you know about the pig?"

"I know about everything."

"What pig thieves?" says Margot.

"The same guys who made you steal from Eloise?" Skid asks.

"Shit. You know about that too?"

"I just said I know about everything. And don't look at Rowan. He didn't rat you out."

I see now that I should have, for Margot is gaping at me like I've committed an unpardonable betrayal against her. (And she knows a thing or two about betrayal.) "You know about all this?"

I look at her feebly. "I'm sure there's plenty of stuff I don't know."

"So all of you are keeping secrets from me," Margot says, which seems to be her big takeaway.

Behind us, the festival of mourners, fearing that this front-lawn fracas could yield another body in need of burying, gingerly retreats into the house.

"Look. Everybody—" I begin.

"What other wanton acts of criminality am I not aware of?" Margot queries the group, and the question breathes a pregnant pause over all of us. It hovers there, seemingly without end, until Alex, finally and with great reluctance, says:

"I stole a box of condoms from the gas station. But I swear that's it."

"I didn't know about that one," I state for the record.

Skid snorts. "You should've at least swiped something you were going to use."

That's the tipping point for Margot. She's finished with us. She storms off in the direction of her Caravan, parked a few houses down in the unbroken line of cars flanking our driveway.

"Margot," Skid calls to his fleeing wife. "Where are you going?"

"Away," she answers. And we all watch as she traverses the lawn in a steady, resolute parade, not even stomping.

"Margot, wait," Skid pleads, and though he starts after her, he stops dead in his tracks when she turns back to us and shows us the tributaries of helpless tears spilling from her eyes.

"I can't fix this mess by myself, Skid," she cries. "I can't fix you, I can't fix him. I can't even fix me. I'm just done."

Of the three of us—Skid, Alex, me: a triumvirate of male disappointment and underperformance—I know I'm third on the depth chart to rightly chase after Margot and console her. I'd be jumping the line. And yet for the oddest reason, I sense that I'm the one who feels the strongest about consoling her, and I'm betting I'm the one Margot would be most willing to receive. Me—a relic of the past and a Johnny-come-lately.

"Dad! Stop her!" Alex is urging.

"It's okay. We need to give her some space," Skid counsels.

"But the stop sign!"

Skid lifts his eyes and squints down the road at the dust his wife's van has just kicked up. "Shit. You're right."

"Guys—it's okay," I cut in.

"No, it's fucking not okay," Alex puffs. "She's pissed, she's crying, she's not paying attention—"

"Calm down. She's going to be fine," I say. "There was no missing sign."

The Hall boys stare at me.

"Daisy's accident was at a four-way stop, and all four stop signs were there," I explain. "I saw them. The policeman saw them."

This possible stroke of good fortune seems difficult for Alex to digest. "You're absolutely sure?"

"Yes," I tell him. "Your friends had nothing to do with this."

The teen looks almost orgasmically relieved to imagine that he might have talked his cohorts out of their prank, that because of him, the Dark—the Dim, the Duds, whatever they call themselves—might not have put Daisy in harm's way, and thus did not put Margot in harm's way. The key word, though, is *might*. We don't actually know that Alex talked anyone out of anything, and that fact dawns on Skid the very moment it dawns on me.

"We're not out of the woods yet," Skid says to his son. "We don't know that there isn't some other intersection out there missing a stop sign."

"Shit," says Alex. "I didn't think about that."

"You're going to call those numb-nut limp dicks right now and tell them that if they took down anything anywhere, they'd better drop whatever Xbox, PlayStation, Nintendo bullshit they're doing and put that sign back *immediately*. Because if I find out that any sign is missing from any street anywhere in this town—I don't care if it's a stop sign, a slow-for-bump, or beware-of-moose—I'll be showing up at each of their houses, I'm bringing a cop, and I'm going to kick their asses while the cop watches."

Folk-singer Skid is gone, and the quarterback who governed the huddle has returned. I think Margot had been waiting for this parent to show up.

"Do it. Now," Skid commands, pointing at his son. "I know where the Dark lives."

CHAPTER 32

Evening comes and breathes the guests out of the house. People stayed late, thanks to the free food and live music, but now the dwindling autumn daylight chases them home, clusters of locals filing out and issuing empty promises to "check in on" my mother "soon." Even the house itself seems tired, the narcoleptic roof and siding ready to call it a day.

Mr. Garfinkle sticks around to help pack the leftovers into Tupperware and plastic wrap. Skid, Alex, and I lug trash bags out to the bins in the garage. Daisy and Lulu restore the furniture to the original indentations in the carpet, as Daisy takes questions about her cello career. Patti assesses the ring stains on the table and wonders what animals decided not to use the coasters she'd conspicuously positioned by the cups. Daisy hears the high-pitched mosquito-wing buzz of the dimmer switch and points into the air. "Does anyone else hear that?" she asks. "Of course," I reply. "Hear what?" says my mother.

When I walk into the living room, I see Alex making his call to Gunnar, or Liam, or some other member of that rotating, Menudo-like coterie of fools, as his father towers over him. I know it is Skid's job at the moment to loom, to teach his son that making this phone call is the right thing to do and that the right thing must always be done. But I can't help but feel sympathy for the child who twists in Skid's imposing shadow, and in the brief time I've known Alex, I have sensed in him the deep murmurs of flight, the urge to run from his parents and be somewhere else. I saw it in Holden, I saw it in myself. I can spot it a mile away.

I feel a hand on my arm. It belongs to Becca, who is still here, but not for long. She is buttoning and belting her trench coat, and I am watching her, seeing her differently now. My great dream of kissing Becca Fitzpatrick in a closet during a party has turned out not to be a dream at all. It is a dream I would've preferred not to have come true.

"So I guess this is it," I say. "I think we've run out of reasons to visit you at work."

"Well, I certainly hope so. Let me just say again, Rowan, how sorry I am."

"Look, I threw up on your building, and my mother accused you of sneaking a stand-in into my brother's casket, so I should be the one apologizing."

She smiles mildly. In her profession, only the grieving are entitled to make light.

I say, "Can I ask you something?"

"Sure."

I case the area for potential eavesdroppers. "It's not the most appropriate question for a house of mourning."

"I'm not easily offended," Becca assures me.

"So—I don't know how to ask this question without insulting at least one of us." Her eyes start to pinch with unease behind those cat-eye frames. "Did you and I ever, like, hook up?"

Her chin shifts. She needs to think about it. That's how memorable I am.

"Hmm. Maybe. I was a bit of a wild child." More reflecting. "Yeah, actually. I think we did," she decides. "Like, at a party or something? Does that sound right?"

"I don't know," I say. "It's okay if we didn't."

"No, we did." I am watching her remember. "Yeah. That happened. It was definitely at a party, because I remember saying to Deb Goetz the next day, 'Guess who kissed me last night.' And she was like, 'Who?' And I said, 'Rowan Darling.'"

"And Deb probably again said 'Who?'" I remark with a smile. "Or at least 'Why?'"

Becca laughs. "I'd forgotten all about that. We just kissed, though, right? In, like, a bathroom or something? It was no big deal."

"If you say so."

"I didn't mean it like that."

"It's okay," I say. "Maybe everything back then was no big deal."

Becca smiles. "If you say so."

I so want to be impressed with myself for having kissed Becca Fitzpatrick at an actual party, not at a party that took place in a dream, but I'm too disappointed to be impressed. This didn't need to have actually happened. Things were, in fact, much easier when it hadn't. How did I not know this? How drunk must I have been to not remember kissing Becca Fitzpatrick? How drunk must I have been to have kissed her in the first place, with Margot ten feet away?

She readjusts her bag on her shoulder and shakes her head wearily. "Do you ever think about how different you are from the person you used to be? Sometimes people who knew me growing up ask me out now, expecting to date the rambunctious teenager I haven't been in a long, long time. They want the girl who did five shots of tequila and went dancing until four, and I'm like, I'll do two glasses of wine and go dancing until nine thirty or ten? Will that work?"

I return her smile, but I'm just wondering how different I am from the kid I was when I graduated, and whether I'm the only one of us who didn't change.

"Take care of yourself," Becca says to me. "Don't be a stranger."

She leaves, I close the door behind her, and I stand there in the foyer, hating Skid for being right about that night but loving him for having never told a soul. Not even his wife, who was only getting me back by hooking up with my best friend that night. She just didn't know it.

Turns out, Alex's threat to tip off law enforcement to the Dark's plan to endanger public safety was sufficiently credible that the outfit tabled it. The intersections of Maybee have remained unmolested. Motorists are safe (at least while Daisy is off the roads for the night).

"I'm proud of you," Skid says to his son as I, ever the interloper, stand with them in the otherwise vacant and returned-to-order living room. "Now we go home."

"How?" Alex asks. "Mom took the car."

"Well, I'm getting a ride," Skid informs him. "Sy Garfinkle will drop me off. You, on the other hand? You're hoofing it."

"What?"

"I want you to walk home, and I want you to take that time to reflect," Skid says. "It's not a punishment. I really am proud of you for talking sense into those kids, but now you need to think about whether it's wise to continue hanging out with them. Who you spend your time with says a lot about who you are, Alex. You need to give some serious thought to what kind of person you want to be. Nobody's saying it's too late for you to change, but it ain't too early either."

"And I'm going to figure all that out on the twenty-minute walk home," Alex complains.

Skid delivers a light, good-natured slap to the side of the boy's head. "Take the long way." Then, as he consults his phone again, I watch the skin around his mouth tighten and his tongue protrude against his cheek.

"Still nothing?" I ask.

He shakes his head.

"She'll turn up," I assure him.

"Well, her Pilates machine and tennis racquets are in the house, so she's got to come back eventually," Skid jokes. Then to Alex: "I'm kidding, buddy." But he throws me a covert look like he's only half kidding, like there's a lot I don't know, even taking into account that there's a lot I do know that he doesn't know I know.

Suddenly I'm reminded of a fight Margot and I had the summer after junior year. She was working at her tennis club, as she did every summer, helping out with on-court instruction of the campers during the day, staffing the pro shop or the front desk in the evenings. One night after closing down Gravedancer, I walked over there, showed up unannounced, and I saw her with one of the pros. She was behind the front desk, and the pro, a midtwenties, fair-haired pretty boy with a British accent, was lazing over the counter. Margot was smiling up at him in a way that immediately put me off, but I might not have thought anything of it until I noticed how she instantly withdrew her smile and sat up straight the moment she saw me. She looked guilty. For the next several weeks, I was tortured by that incident and complained to Skid. My best friend thought I had nothing to worry about—that's called irony—but he enjoyed the fact that the pro was British so he could call him "the Englishman." ("You're still worried about the Englishman? Do you want me to go rough up the Englishman? I can get rid of the Englishman for you.") Now, here we are, all these years later, and I'm reassuring Skid about the rock-solidity of his relationship with Margot just as he did for me—with more confidence than accuracy, as it turned out—way back when. (Now that I think about it, maybe it's the dreamy Londoner and not me who inspired Lon from the Portia Wentworth story. He did have very toned calves.)

Skid heads off to hit Mr. Garfinkle up for that ride, so I escort Alex outside, where night has fallen in earnest. Day is gone, and with it the light wind. Now there's only darkness and still air. It's over. We did what I came here to do. We got Holden home, and he's here for good now. Knowing that brings me a strange kind of solace. I'll always know where he is.

"Your mom's going to be fine," I tell Alex as we trudge down the driveway. "She just needs to cool off."

He shakes his head. "Whatever."

"Look, man, adults get pissed off just like kids do. We get angry, we flip out, we say things we don't mean. And then we calm down."

"My mom isn't angry," he says. "I mean, yeah, she's angry, but that's not the whole deal. This wasn't just about today."

"What do you mean?"

"I mean"—he pauses for a sigh—"she was pissed about the stop sign—no doubt about that. She didn't know about the pig or the shoplifting, and when she sits me down for those details, she's not going to be particularly happy about any of it, that's for sure. But taking off like she did today? That's about my dad and his obsession with having leukemia and my grandfather dying, which suddenly made my dad want to be John Denver. I know my mom posts all sorts of happy shit on Facebook and Instagram, but I promise you, that's not her life. She's just trying to keep up with her friends. She isn't living the dream, even if you take me and my less-than-stellar behavior out of the equation."

"Nobody's taking you out of the equation," I say to him. "You're in the equation. Sorry. That's family."

I hear an under-the-breath snicker; then he stops walking and stuffs his hands in his pockets. "Did you ever end up reading my mom's secret stories? The ones I told you about?"

"Regrettably, yes."

"Did you happen to read one called 'The Soft Regret'?"

I recall the title, not the plot. "I don't know. Maybe."

"You should," he says, a bitter edge in his voice.

"Why are *you* reading these stories?" I ask. "I thought you were appalled by them. I thought you were appalled just knowing about them."

"Well, how would I know that if I didn't read them?" he argues. "I don't know why I read them. I just did."

I suppose the search for rational thought leads no one to a teenage boy.

"In 'The Soft Regret,' some girl gets knocked up. She's too young, so she gives up the baby."

"Yeah. I do remember that one." And I remember being freaked out by it too. I read Julianna Goodheart's wistful reflections about the child she felt she couldn't handle and decided not to, and I spent the rest of the evening worrying if I was someone's father.

And then I see it. It's all over Alex's moonlit face. Like me, he fears autobiographical content. He worries that he is the child.

"Dude," I say to him. "You're not serious."

"They were really young when they had me," he argues. "All my friends' parents are much older."

"So?"

"I was a mistake."

"You're being ridiculous."

"I was never the plan."

"Of course you were. You just showed up early. Accidents happen."

"This Julianna lady is walking along a beach thinking about how she was too young to have that kid, how that kid would've messed up all her plans, all her big dreams. You don't think that's my mom talking?"

"No, I don't," I say. "I know your mom. I grew up with her, and there is no way that Margot Beckett could ever feel that way about her own son. Whatever reservations she may have, you're not one of them. Your behavior? Maybe. Your existence? Not a chance."

"I just can't wait to get out of here," he says to the night. "I've got, like, four more years of this place; then I'm out."

"Aren't you missing the point of the story? She *regrets* giving him up. See? It's the soft *regret*. It doesn't sound like you read very carefully."

"They want their freedom back? They can have it. They can do whatever they want."

"Can you shut up for a second?"

"Fine."

"Listen—you don't know this yet, but you're extremely wrong about everything. Do you remember what I told you earlier today? I was all bummed out because there aren't a lot of pictures of my brother and me together. We lived a lot of years far away from each other, and we've got almost no proof that we were family. Or a lot less proof than we should have. You remember me saying that?"

"Yes."

"Well, is that what you want? Do you want to come back here one day and find the same thing in your house? Do you want your parents' picture frames to look like history just cut off when you turned eighteen? I am here to tell you that that is not what you want. You'd be punishing your parents, which I'm sure sounds delicious right now, but you'd be punishing yourself more. You can write that down because it's true and it's always going to be true. Where there aren't any photos, chances are there aren't any memories."

As Alex stands there, mulling the inky pavement below his sneakers, I am reminded once again—as if I ever needed reminding—that anyone who speaks fondly of the simplicity of youth suffers from self-induced amnesia. It's the great lie of adulthood that childhood was easy.

I smile at him. "Now, hit the road. You've got between here and home to figure out the kind of person you want to be, so you'd best get cracking."

I watch him slink off into the night, and as I turn to head back up the driveway, I hear his voice calling out to me. "Hey, Rowan? Am I going to see you again?"

I surprise myself at how quickly I reply and how sure I am of the answer. "Yes," I call back. "You will see me again."

CHAPTER 33

Lulu and Patti tackle Breeze's bedtime routine: a fresh diaper, a warm bottle, and a bouquet of baby powder (which I thought was a carcinogen, but Lulu also smokes, so maybe she just doesn't believe in cancer). I get Daisy situated in my room for the night, hauling up her suitcase and snapping fresh sheets onto the bed while she lies on my floor and pretends to be groggy from the accident.

A futuristic ripple from her phone announces a FaceTime caller. She regards it and groans.

"It's Greg. Should I answer? I guess I'll answer." Her back still flat against the floor, she extends her arm into the air and angles the screen down at her face. "Good evening, Craigory." (Daisy toys with mispronouncing our only employee's first name, for kicks and out of solidarity to me.)

"How's it going out there?" Greg asks.

She sighs rhapsodically. "Well, it was a funeral for a young person, so it wasn't exactly festive."

And yet, I am startled to realize, at times that's exactly what it was. The burial itself seems so long ago, eclipsed by so many intervening episodes. Life really does go on.

Greg doesn't really care. "I'm glad I caught you both, because I just got a call from Rob Wright. Or Rich Wright. One of the two."

"Lay it on us," Daisy says as I circumnavigate the bed, tucking in sheets and blankets.

"So, remember how I told you how he and I really hit it off?" Greg says of the man whose name he doesn't know. "How he totally flipped when I told him I thought Prince was a major influence on their new album?"

You told me that you complimented his work and he appreciated it, is what I want to say, but don't, as I know that for Greg, it's all about the pronouns, his favorites being the first-person singular and the second-person accusatory: *Here's what* I *did. Here's what* I *said.* You *did something different, and that's why things went to hell.*

"Yes, you told me," I say, abandoning the bed-making and lying down next to Daisy, scooting my face into the frame so that I can see Greg and his distorted nose-forward, gargoyle-green video-conference complexion.

To heighten the drama and his essentiality to it, his fundamental outstandingness in the withering rose that is Metaphysical Graffiti, Greg pauses to sip a drink of some sort. "So here's the deal. The Wrights want to do an event at the store. They want to play a show."

This is not news. "I know they want to, Greg. They've told me a bunch of times that they want to."

"Yeah, but now they're *going* to."

"Wait." I feel a flutter of hope. "They've committed? We have a date?"

"There's more." He grins. "A lot more. Not only do they want to do a show, they want to do a record release party. A *release party*, at our store! And on top of that, they want to record it. They're going to play a set, the label is going to film it, and then they're going to put it out, like a companion piece to the album. You know they're on Steel Wheel Records now, right? That's Glen Carlo's label. When he heard their song on that teenybopper show, he went after them and signed them right up. Carlo has a sick rep for breaking artists."

"Wait. Slow down," I tell him, still leashing my enthusiasm because it's Greg who's talking. "Please tell me that at least some of what you're saying is true."

"Oh, it's all true, bro. Glen actually came to our store! Can you believe that shit? He was here, like a week or two ago, scouting it out as a venue. I guess I wasn't around, because I totally would've recognized him. He still rocks the Rick Rubin beard, the Jeff Lynne shades, the Julian Casablancas leather jacket."

Daisy tilts her head toward me and whispers, "Do you understand the words coming out of his mouth?"

"Let the man talk," I tell her.

"The label totally digs the store, guys," Greg continues. "They think it fits the gritty, homespun vibe of the band, like the Wright Brothers and Metaphysical Graffiti both have the same origin story. They even want to use our name in the title of the video, like *The Wright Brothers: Live at Metaphysical Graffiti*, or something like that. They don't not love the Zeppelin reference."

I am sitting up now, giddy from even the speck of hope that we can pull this off.

Daisy looks at me. "We can do this, right?"

Greg answers for me: "Of course we can do this. I've got it covered."

"And it's worth it?" she asks me.

"Of course it's worth it," he answers again, this time scoffing. "Just bask in the cool, you guys."

"Did he just say 'bask in the cool'?" Daisy whispers.

He did. And there's nothing not cool about it. Forget the commercial potential, which is almost certainly a low ceiling. This is an in-store concert, recorded live by a legit kick-ass band. This is what animates the nightly dreams of every music geek who ever toiled in a record mart. And who would believe that in the end it would be Greg Isquith who would make that dream come true?

"Look, things are going to happen fast," Greg advises. "We weren't on Glen Carlo's radar until a few weeks ago, and the album comes out the week after next. So a lot has to happen in a short amount of time."

"Beautiful work, man," I say. "I didn't know you had it in you."

He laughs; he thinks I'm kidding.

"So do I reach out to them, or are they going to reach out to me?" I ask.

"Why don't you let me be the point person?" he suggests. "Since I've been dealing with Rich, Rob, whoever, and the folks from Steel Wheel. Sound like a plan, boss?"

"That's a terrible idea," Daisy whispers. "Tell him no. It's the road to failure."

"Sounds like a plan to me," I answer. "And let me say, Greg, that I'm extremely impressed with your work. I would go so far as to say that you're behaving in a very Promethean manner."

"Cute." He chuckles. "Now, sit back and let me work my brand of magic."

The call ends, and I stretch out again next to Daisy. We remain there awhile in silence, our backs against the carpet, our eyes staring upward, each of us in our own contemplative haze.

"What do you think?" she eventually asks.

"I think if we want the Graffiti to still be the Graffiti a year from now, as opposed to a branch of some regional bank, this is our best bet."

She turns her head to me. "And is that what you want? The Graffiti to still be the Graffiti a year from now?"

"I don't have a better offer yet," I answer.

Another few minutes of silence pass. Daisy's breathing shallows, and just when I think she's fallen asleep, she pipes up. "Do you exactly know what brand of magic Greg works?"

"I sure don't," I reply. "But I say we let him work it."

CHAPTER 34

It feels like three a.m. when I close my bedroom door, leaving Daisy—who says she might love me, says that, contrary to earlier reports (her own), she is not engaged to Chili, but has very possibly lied about both—to spend the night on the mattress and pillow that rested me for the first eighteen years of my life. It is, however, only a little past nine. A stream of light shines under Patti's door, and I hear Lulu's soft lullabies coming through the walls of my brother's room. Otherwise, a hard-won silence envelops the house.

Downstairs, I change into sweats and throw a blanket across the sofa, but before dropping onto the cushions, I am drawn to the dining room, to that senior yearbook photo of Holden. I stare at him awhile, that kid, frozen for all time in the brine of youth. Then I carry the frame over to the sofa, where I prop it up on the coffee table so I can see his face and he can see mine. The sleepover we never got around to having.

I crawl under the blanket and look at the photo. "What should I do?" I ask my brother. "What should I do about that woman upstairs?"

There are three women upstairs, he replies. *All of them want the same thing for you.*

"Which is?"

I wait and wait and hear only silence, a quiet house.

"If you were here for real, you would've answered me," I grumble.

No, I wouldn't have, he says.

I nest my earbuds in my ears and scroll through the Talking Heads playlist on my phone until I find "Dream Operator." The piano and drums kick in. I look at my brother's face. "Good night, Holden." And I'm out cold before the first verse.

Sometime later, I am stirred from sleep by a presence in the room, and I open my eyes and see my mother creeping through the house. She's making her final rounds of the night, monkeying with the thermostat, confirming all doors are locked, flicking off the last of the lights.

"Hey, Mom."

She peers over at me from the sliding glass door. "Did I wake you?"

I reach up, switch on the lamp, and yawn. "I know I'm supposed to say no, but let's not insult each other's intelligence."

I slide over to make room for her on the sofa so she can sit down next to where I'm sprawled out. She asks if Daisy is comfortable, and I report that she seemed more wiped than any of us.

"That's the mark of a good friend," my mother says.

"And the mark of a head injury," I note.

I tell my mother that Daisy is booked on a flight back to Philly tomorrow evening.

"And you?" my mother asks. "When are you heading back?"

"I don't know," I reply. "I was going to stick around another day or so, just to make sure you're okay." I look at her carefully. "Are you?"

"No." She laughs. "But I will be, honey. I won't be who I was before I lost my son. I don't think I'll ever be that person again. But I'll be okay. I promise you that."

I prop myself up against the arm of the sofa. "Mom, why did you apologize to Holden? Today, at the cemetery. You said you were sorry."

She shrugs and casts her eyes off into the unlit house. "We never know what we could've done differently, if we could've changed the path of things."

But I feel like there's more. It stuck with me when she said it, that there was something specific behind her repentance. So I offer her my silence in case she's ready to put some of it on me.

Patti stares at me, and for a long time says nothing. Then she posts her arms behind her and lists back on her hands. "You know, after your father died, I had a rough time. Here we were building a life together, making a family, and then in an instant, he was gone. He was gone, but I still had these two little kids to care for, and I didn't know if I could do it. Those first two years without him were very challenging for me. One night I was on the phone with Aunt Hillary, and I broke down. I was having a dark moment, and I said something terrible, and when I turned around, there was Holden. He'd heard the whole thing. He was probably five, maybe six, old enough to understand." Patti pauses, sighs deeply. "A better parent would've gone out of her way to show she hadn't meant it—which, of course I hadn't. I adored you boys. I was just clawing my way back. But instead of doing everything I could to show Holden how much I loved him and how lucky I felt to be his mom—which I was able to do by the time you'd remember—I just froze. I started wondering if I really was equipped to raise you kids on my own." She shakes her head at the memory of those days. "I started pushing more playdates on him, dropping him off at friends' houses, at Grandma and Grandpa's. I did the opposite of what I should've done: I taught him that I wasn't all in. And boy, did he learn it," she utters gravely.

She leans forward, cringing at the carpet as though seeing an old, familiar stain. "He may have forgotten about that awful phone call, but you don't have to remember something to internalize it, for it to become a part of you. I know it sounds crazy, but I truly believe that by the time that kid was seven years old, he was already destined to leave. To leave me."

I stare at the sad contour of Patti's face, wondering what that terrible thing was that she'd said in front of Holden. Then I look across the room, breathe in the air of this old house on Campsite Lane, and decide it doesn't matter.

"You want to know what I remember?" I say to her. "I remember you down on the floor doing Lincoln Logs with me. I remember you taking the training wheels off my bike and running down the street next to me. I remember you being a pushover every night at lights out when I begged you to read just one more book. I remember you refusing to call me Rowan D. when I was in fourth grade, even though I wanted you to because I was Rowan D. at school, since Rowan Kolman was also in my class, and I thought it sounded kind of cool, but you said, nope, I can't do that, you're the only Rowan in this house, the only Rowan for me. Mom—this was a great fucking house to grow up in. I don't know if Holden lived to appreciate it, but I know in my heart that if he didn't, he would have. 'Children begin by loving their parents; as they grow older they judge them; sometimes they forgive them.'"

She smiles at me sideways. "You didn't make that up. Oscar Wilde did."

"I know. You told me that once, and I agreed with both of you."

Finally looking content, Patti pats my blanket-covered leg. "There's something else I want to tell you," she says, turning her body square toward mine. "I know you think it might be your job to move back here and look out for me. So it might be useful for you to know that I've decided to leave."

I sit up. "What?"

"I'm moving."

"You're leaving Maybee?" It's so absurd, I nearly laugh. Patti Darling *is* Maybee. "Where do you think you're going?"

"I have a grandson in Miami now," she says.

"You're moving to Florida?"

"Why not? Lulu and I have been discussing it the last couple of days. I don't know if I'll be down there full-time, and I'm not selling this house quite yet. But I've decided to retire, and I know that one of the things I want to do with the years I have left is watch my grandson grow up. I want to be a part of his life."

I wonder for a moment if I'm still asleep, if this is all some vexing dream.

"When you said 'moving,' I thought you meant to an apartment. A place with an elevator so you don't fall down the steps."

But Patti is immune to my teasing. She wears the look of utter serenity that comes with being fully committed to a decision.

"You're really serious," I say.

She nods.

"And Lulu is on board?"

"Of course she's on board. Her father is gone, and her mother lives in New York. She has no family around. Frankly, I'm going whether she's on board or not. She can't stop me from buying a condo in Miami. And I don't intend to smother her. I'll have other things to do. Simon is coming with me."

"Mr. Garfinkle is moving to Florida with you?" It's all so mad now that it's past the realm of a dream.

"He said, 'Patti, I'm a Jewish guy in his sixties. I was going to move there eventually anyway.'" Her eyes settle peacefully on mine. "Simon and I make a good team, Rowan. I hope you get to see more of that."

An anxious feeling settles over the room, like this is my very last night in this house forever, like dawn will come and I'll awaken to the rumble of a moving van, everything packed up in boxes. My eyes wander the walls and the furniture, drinking it all in.

"You've lived in this town your whole life," I say.

"I've done my time. Everyone else left the campsite. Why can't I?" She stares ahead pacifically, like she's already picturing palm trees, poolside villas, evening strolls hand in hand with Breeze-Brooklyn. "I'm ready for a change, Rowan. Remember: 'The snake which cannot cast its skin has to die.' That's Nietzsche."

"Oh god, please don't throw Nietzsche at me."

She stands. "You can handle it."

I look at the image of Holden, his cluelessly youthful face beaming back at me from the oblivious safety of that picture frame. "Can you believe this?" I say to him. "Look at the shit you've pulled."

Patti regards him too, stricken less with grief now than with something approximating hope. Hope for those of us left, and those of us just getting started.

"He came back with a vengeance, didn't he?" she remarks.

PART SIX

NOBODY KNOWS THIS IS EVERYWHERE

CHAPTER 35

If the human body has the good fortune to live past thirty, it is no longer fit for improvisational sleeping arrangements. It can snooze, nap, or pass out drunk on a sofa or love seat, but those articles of furniture cannot stand in for a proper bed. So I am up early. Wide-awake in the living room, I stare up through the slats of the window blinds at the lonesome cold of night's closing hours. Stillness reigns in the house, all across the whole world in fact, as morning tiptoes in and drains the dark from the sky. City habitation has rendered me unaccustomed to this intensity of calm, and it seeps into my pores and mellows me in a way I haven't felt in a long time.

Before seven, I hear the palpitation of footsteps overhead; then silence returns. Lulu, I suspect, plucking Breeze from his crib and bringing him into the futon to hush a few more moments of tranquility out of him.

Restless, I consider walking out and getting breakfast for everyone. But you can't order food for Daisy. Every one of her meals is governed by a matrix of unique and unpredictable rules, inconsistent dietary restrictions, and arbitrary preferences that change with the direction of the wind. Daisy always enters a restaurant with an air of defeat. "I don't know if there's anything here I can get," she'll say as she glumly attempts to refashion the menu. "I guess I could get the shrimp appetizer as my main," or "If they can do the brussels sprouts without the bacon, I could get that." It's better to be me. I can walk into the swankiest bistro or the greasiest spoon in Cleveland, Bangkok, or Gdańsk, and I'm not walking out hungry.

Daisy Pham is upstairs in my bed. She's in my bed, and she's open to a conversation about us being together. I haven't given myself permission to want that in so long, it's as though I don't remember how. But I can relearn. It's not buried too far down.

I kill a few moments talking myself into and out of sending Skid a text to check in on his domestic situation. Primarily, I suppose, to make sure he still has one.

Things go okay when Margot got home last night? I write, figuring he'll see it when he awakens.

His reply is instantaneous. She never came home. Still haven't heard a word.

Now I'm a little worried about her. And about him. And I suppose about Alex too.

I call Skid. Like we're eleven years old again and seven isn't early.

He has called and eliminated every person he can think of with whom his wife might seek shelter for the night. He's wondering now if there might be such a person about whom he does not know.

"Don't make this about something else," I suggest. "She felt hurt, and this is her hurting you back."

He makes a grumbling noise in his throat, then says, "By the way, in the middle of the night, I remembered something: you owe me ten bucks."

"Do I?"

"Yeah. I want a refund."

"A refund?"

He lets a silence bloom between us, slick and knowing, and eventually, into that silence, understanding dawns. *Sam!* There was that visitor to my website. His child was unhappy, his wife was unhappy, while he himself had never been happier. I knew Skid was Sam. That's why I ignored the inquiry.

"You bastard," I say, laughing.

"No, *you* bastard," Skid retorts. "Your business is a scam."

Maybe it wasn't that I was ignoring him but that I didn't know how to help or if I even wanted to. That's when I know I have to deactivate the website. The conceit has been compromised; it shouldn't be a game of cat and mouse, me trying to figure out who's *really* out there writing to me, which friend or foe is playing at being anonymous. It's decided: I will close it down. Besides, I'm not helping anyone by spoon-feeding them answers to important questions. Let them make it on their own. Even if they screw it all up, they'll be better off.

"You want an answer to your inquiry?" I say to Skid. "I'll give you an answer. Two words: Portia Wentworth."

"What?"

"She's a writer. Look her up. Portia Wentworth."

"And why should I do that?" he asks.

"She's an author you should get to know."

Somebody brought over a bag of Barista Becca's brew yesterday, the embalmer's designer java, so I am not forced to subject my stomach acid to that antediluvian tin of grocery store grounds in the pantry. The luscious espresso blend upon my lips warms me in the otherwise chilled kitchen, and I find myself imagining the moment when Skid Hall meets Portia Wentworth. He'll discover his wife in those pages, and a rich supply of her secrets, and he'll be horrified and thrilled at all the revelations, and he'll ask himself what compels her to write stories like these, part fantasy, part memory, and hide them from him. And if I know Skid, he won't want her to stop. He'll just try harder to be someone she writes about.

As I stand there thinking about Portia Wentworth and her heroine, Julianna Goodheart, who is always on the lookout for another wild exploit (even while maintaining a busy cardiology practice), my mind catches on one exploit in particular. That story I couldn't bring myself to read on account of its title. I think of Margot and wonder about that tendency we all have to reach for the past when the present isn't enough.

I pick up my phone. It's a shot in the dark. I am not unmindful of the arrogance behind this.

Margot—are you at the lake cabin?

I see the typing bubbles, and my pulse bursts into a sprint.

She writes, Seriously? How did you know?

I've flown the whole mess over the cliff now. The vapors of a new day illuminate the blinds.

Go home, Margot, I write, because unless you can outrun yourself, you can only run so far.

I can't, she writes back.

But I can't leave her there. I may not be able to show her the right turn, but I can help her avoid the wrong one. She just needs to be found.

Margot?

Polo.

Stay there, I write. I'm on my way.

CHAPTER 36

Daisy is still asleep when I steal into the bedroom and swipe a cleanish sweatshirt and a pair of jeans from my dresser. When I see her there, twisted up in my sheets, her feathery strands fringed over her eyes and cheek, I almost change my mind. I could stay out of this. I could slide under the warm covers next to her unwitting shape. We'd wake up later, figure it all out, and go home.

I leave her a note under her phone: *I went out for a bit. There's something I have to deal with. I'll call you later.*

Not the love letter she might deserve to wake up to, but if I tell her where I'm headed, all she'll get is the wrong idea.

I leave one for my mother too: *I hope you don't need the car this morning.*

The cabin was near the town of Rock River. That helpful piece of information streaks back to me as I remember Margot and I joked about how ill-fitting a name that was for a tiny burg that, one, was situated by a lake, and two, did not in any way, shape, or form *rock*. That's all I've got to guide me. No address, no landmark, no geographical adjunct whatsoever. Just the reckless hope that I'll get close enough to intuit a route that feels familiar and end up on the banks of a great pond, at a spot I visited precisely once in my life, so long ago that I was little more than a child at the time.

Rock River is east, so I head east in this shivering Taurus, crossing the plains that link one exit to another, each one hemmed in by gas stations, fast-food chains, and shopping centers with superstores. The heart of the heartland. America in all its mundane and infinite familiarity. Eventually, the highway humbles into a two-lane road, and fifty minutes after pulling out of my driveway, I am passing a sign welcoming me to Rock River, Illinois. I spy a gas station up ahead just before a bend in the road, and I remember now that Margot and I stopped here that day to load up on snacks. It's still there, not older and decaying but bigger and shinier, renovated and corporate.

Almost immediately after the curve, I become enshrouded beneath a canopy of pines and red sunset maples, leaves blazing red and yellow bearing down on me from both sides as though lighting the way and at the same time sheltering a secret. I slow to meet an unpaved turnoff and begin a ramble along a winding stone road that leads into a deepening thicket, a path that feels like it could only lead to a place where dusty, dangerous memories are held captive.

I see the blue Caravan before I see the cabin or the lake; it is the only thing around here that isn't the color of nature. I'd forgotten how truly remote this house is. When I told Margot I was coming, I'd interpreted her nonresponse as assent or acquiescence, but now I see that maybe it was just the spotty cell service.

My sedan breathes, the tires crunch over twigs and branches, and the sounds draw Margot out the door and onto the wooden steps.

I get out of the car and step into the spotlight of Margot's stare. More than the sight of this place, it's the smell that takes me back to that day, the musty fragrance of damp wood and still water. The isolation here is so complete, so overwhelmingly *Blair Witch*.

"Well," I say, looking around, taking it all in. "No one will hear you scream."

I notice the baggy gold sweatshirt that blankets her, shoulders to thighs, the jeans and tennis shoes. Clothes she was not wearing when she drove off yesterday. "You stopped home for an overnight bag."

She looks down and regards the evidence.

"Does that mean you plan to stay?" I ask.

She says nothing.

"How long?" I ask.

"What are you doing here, Rowan?"

"That stop sign wasn't missing," I tell her.

She folds her arms and listens.

"Daisy got into a car accident because that's what Daisy does. She gets into car accidents. Nobody stole any signs. Alex talked them out of it."

"Alex is a delinquent," Margot states.

"Not yet," I say.

She lowers herself onto one of the splintery slats, and the way she drops her elbows onto her knees brings to mind a camper outside her bunk.

"Margot, your family has no idea where you are," I say. "I came here to bring you home."

"I don't know if I'm going home." Her head drops into her hands. She explores her hair with her fingertips. "I don't know if I can."

"Delinquent or not, Alex needs you."

"Skid can pick up the slack," she says, her voice sharp with spite. "I've picked up plenty of his."

"Look, I don't get a vote in your domestic matters, and I don't want a vote, but the thing is, Skid didn't write 'The Soft Regret.'"

Margot lifts her eyes. "What does that mean?"

"Alex read your story, and he thinks he's the regret. He thinks he's the ill-timed pregnancy for which his mother sacrificed all her dreams."

"That's not at all what that story is about."

"I said he's not a delinquent, I didn't say he's a genius," I say. "It's a misreading of your literature, but in his defense, not an entirely unfair interpretation."

Margot sits there wilting on the step, her limbs, neck, and back folded over, her entire body tucked into itself. I turn and let my eyes go out in search of the lake. In the all-consuming silence, I listen to the soft rippling, the water gently licking its shores just beyond the trees.

"I'm sorry," I say.

"About?"

"I don't know," I answer. "I don't know why I'm sorry. I just know that I am. I want you to be okay."

She laughs. "Did you ever, in a million years, imagine that you and I would find ourselves back here at this cabin, *you* saying sorry to *me*?"

"Well, why not?" I say. I walk over and sit down next to her on the step, knee to knee. Immediately, the seat of my jeans moistens against the dewy moss. "Since I've been back here, I have learned a lot of things that I did not know. I've learned I have a nephew. I've learned my brother had a fiancée. I've learned that even though Holden wasn't around much, he was a better brother to me than I thought." I look at her until she meets my eyes. "And I've learned, Margot, that I'm not the victim in the story of our relationship."

A question hangs on her.

"The night you hooked up with Skid, I hooked up with Becca Fitzpatrick. I was so drunk that I barely remember it, so drunk, in fact, that I've always thought it was something I dreamed. It turns out it wasn't a dream. Skid saw us come out of that bathroom or closet or whatever. He saw that before he took you home. He kept it a secret, but he knew. Margot, I swear I have no idea why I did that with Becca when I was so in love with you, other than that I was a kid and thought the stakes were low. If that's what I was thinking, then I was right. The stakes were low, Margot. Which is probably the reason you hooked up with Skid in the first place. This is all ancient history, and I know it doesn't matter now, not in the slightest, but here's why it actually does matter, and why it matters a lot: I would've been your friend all this time. Yours and Skid's. Eventually—not immediately. I've been blaming you guys all these years, and blame is a huge burden, much heavier for the person doing the blaming than the person being blamed. All of this is to say, Margot, that I wish I'd known, and had I known, I would've told you. And I would've grown up sooner."

Margot's unreadable expression settles into something that looks like wisdom. "I know," she says.

"What do you know?"

"All of it."

"All of what?"

"I know about Becca. Actually, I think it's kind of funny that you didn't."

"Skid said he didn't tell you."

"He didn't, not until recently," she explains. "Several months ago, Skid and I had a big blowup. We were finally coming out of the leukemia battle, and I thought he was doing better with all the issues stirred up by the death of his father. Then one night Alex stayed out late and didn't call, and I was really worried and angry and blowing up his phone with calls and texts. And in the middle of all that, Skid tells me he's not sure he wants to be a football coach anymore, that he felt called to do something else, something that would fulfill him in a different way. That something else, I was soon to learn, involved a guitar and my husband embarrassing himself in public with his father's favorite songs.

I think at any other time in our lives I would've said, okay, you're thirty-three years old, you can do what you want, let's figure it out together. But at that particular moment, *I* wasn't fulfilled. All I'd been dealing with were Skid's issues. I'm not saying they weren't worthy of all my mental energy, but I was at the end of my rope. And telling me this while I'm trying to locate our son?"

"What did you do?" I ask.

"I freaked out. I told him the only reason I stayed with him was because I got pregnant."

"Ouch."

"No, not ouch," she says, annoyed and dismissive. "He knew I didn't mean it, or ninety-five percent didn't mean it. But he hit back with something just as cruel. He said he never would've gotten together with me if he hadn't seen you and Becca come out of that room together. And I was like, uh, what in the actual fuck are you talking about? So he told me." Margot shakes her head and sucks in her lips. "I can't cry foul, since I didn't know about that when I kissed Skid that night. But hearing that you'd cheated on me? It shouldn't matter at all fifteen years, a husband, and a child later. But it did. It hurt." She gazes up at a towering pine, sharp lasers of sunlight slicing through the branches and causing her eyes to constrict. "It hurt a lot, and I've been trying to figure out why."

She reaches down between the steps and yanks a buttercup out of the grass. She stares at it as she twirls it between her thumb and index finger. "Things have been different between him and me ever since."

An insect lands on my forearm. We both look down at it and watch together as its black wings flutter to life and carry it off between the tree branches and out in the direction of the water. Now that I'm here, this place has come back to me so naturally, like it's lived inside me. I can picture the humid interior of the cabin, but I remember these woods too. I know that if I walked beyond our parked cars, where the pebble road becomes brush, I would meet an old trail, overgrown and nearly impassable with branches, and if I followed it for fifty yards or so, it would deposit me at the bank of the lake, and I would need to find a log to stand on to protect my shoes from the mud and the yawning reeds. But now I'm afraid of all of it. I'm afraid of whatever it is that sent Margot away from her husband and back here to this place, to *our* place. I'm afraid of the hurt she felt when learning of an intoxicated groping between Becca Fitzpatrick and me when I was eighteen years old.

"You think I'm still in love with you," she says. "That's why I ran away from Skid and came here, of all places."

"I don't think that."

"Yes, you do. How could you not?"

"Because I know that that's not the way things work."

"It's strange," she says, "to feel so unconnected to your own family, to the people who live in your house and sleep in your bed. I love them, but I don't know them these days. And then you came back, and I recognized traces of that same thing in you. You too felt misplaced, you too felt like you didn't belong anywhere. Rowan, since you've been back, I haven't thought about you in a nostalgic way. This has nothing to do with what we were. The connection I feel with you is only about now, it's only about the person I've come to know these last several days. I don't know what it is, and I don't know what to call it."

I turn to her abruptly. "Let's call it confusion," I say, and I put my arms around her. I hold her like it's over. Over, like we've come to the end. Over, like we've made it through and survived.

"I'll always love you, Margot," I tell her. "I'll always be there for you when you need a friend."

I release her. I stand and walk down off the steps.

"You should go home," I say. "Alex didn't almost kill anybody. Go home and celebrate that. It's something, right?"

She produces a smile. "I guess it's a start."

"Staying away will only make everything worse. You shouldn't kick yourself when you're down. You don't deserve that."

I walk to my mother's sedan and open the door. Before getting in, I look back. Margot is still sitting on the cabin steps, drying her eyes and cheeks with her fingers.

"Will I see you back in Maybee?" I call to her.

She gives me a shrug, one that from a distance seems to be trying so hard to be hopeful. "Maybe," she says.

CHAPTER 37

On the drive home, I'm desperate to speak to Daisy. I need to tell her that I've found my place here, and now that I have, I can be anywhere, and the place I want to be is with her. I keep calling her, but she's taking a page out of Margot's book and has gone dark. I'm almost home when she finally answers.

"Oh, it's you," she says with mock surprise. "To what do I owe this rare pleasure?"

"I'm really sorry, Daisy."

"No, it's totally fine. The whole point of my coming out here was to wake up with you inexplicably gone and spend half the day drinking tea with your mom while she empties the dishwasher and both of us wonder where the hell you are."

I fumble around for the right words, but baldly stating that I drove out to a secluded cabin with my married ex-girlfriend, with all the wildly inaccurate inferences such a statement would compel, doesn't seem fair to any of us.

"I had something to deal with."

"Whoa, whoa, whoa," Daisy says theatrically. "That's way more detail than I was looking for."

"I promise to explain. I'm minutes from the house."

"I'm not there," she reports. "I walked into town. I'm in front of . . . some restaurant called the Twisted Spoon."

"I'll be there in ten," I say.

"I'll hold my breath." And she hangs up.

But eight minutes later, she's still there, forgivably grouchy but amenable to a croissant that I buy for each of us at the gratingly hipster café before which she stands. The Twisted Spoon has been around a few years, and whenever I'm in town I am a reluctant customer. It's a statement as much as a restaurant, the statement being, *See? Young, edgy people can live here too.* It's owned by a steampunk fetishist with a shaved head and a handlebar mustache who has trained his staff to say, "Yeah, for sure, dude," when patrons order their acai bowls and soy chorizo omelets. It's a place that judges you for requesting ketchup because everyone knows ketchup is socially irresponsible.

"Did you go to see that girl?" Daisy asks me.

"It's not what you think."

"You went to see that girl."

"I had to."

"I don't want to talk about it," she decides.

"Fine," I say. "But it's still not what you think."

"Everything is what I think," she says.

Shards of flaky dough fall from our fingers as we bite into our pastries on the sidewalk.

"What brought you out here?" I ask her.

"I went to find you, if you must know," Daisy answers, still playing hurt.

"You went out looking for me?"

"Not physically, but in a manner of speaking," she says. "I went to see where it all started for you." She points a buttery finger across the street; I don't need to follow it to know it's directed at Gravedancer Records.

"What did you think?"

"I haven't gone in yet," she says.

So we go together.

Inside, we find Eloise reading the newspaper behind the counter. She comes out and hugs us, Daisy too. A five-minute conversation at a memorial service has sealed their friendship for life. It's just who they are, both of them.

Daisy takes in the store, every square foot of it, with what looks from the outside to be admiration and even a touch of envy. "Yeah, this is nothing like our joint," she concedes.

"It ain't much, but I call it home," Eloise drawls.

"Yeah, me too," I say, drinking the place in, giving it a parting look, as I've always done, since who knows if it'll still be here the next time I roll into town?

"So this is where it all started for you," Daisy says to me.

"I'll do you one better," Eloise says with a wise twinkle. "I can pinpoint the precise *moment* it started for him."

I stretch out over the counter, shaking my head. "You always get this story wrong."

Eloise looks at Daisy and explains. "It was just the two of us that afternoon, darling Rowan and myself. Then in walks this man. He's middle-aged, unaccompanied and unassuming, wearing blue jeans and a suede vest. I glanced at him, glanced at him again, and then I thought, *Oh, my stars and garters, that's Bruce Springsteen!*"

Daisy gasps. "No!"

"You see, the thing about Bruce Springsteen is that he really looks like Bruce Springsteen. I guess some people are so stratospherically famous, so self-evidently *them*, that they don't even bother to attempt a disguise. The Boss just waltzed in and began to browse. I didn't rush at him or anything. I gave him his space, respected his privacy." She pauses to hook a thumb at me. "This fella here couldn't move. He was so starstruck, he practically swooned. I smiled at Bruce, and Bruce smiled back with that slightly off-kilter, genetically working class, all-American smile. He meandered around, and eventually his meanderings brought him over to us at the counter, and I tell you, he was delightfully chatty." Eloise sees disbelief on Daisy's hooked-fish mouth. "I'm not lying. Am I lying, Rowan?"

I shake my head. "The lady speaks the truth."

"He was in between shows in Chicago," Eloise goes on. "He'd jumped in a car to get out of Dodge and have some alone time, maybe see some of the quieter parts of the state. He stayed and talked with us for quite a while, didn't he? And he even put some cash in the local economy. I don't remember exactly what he bought—"

"He bought a live recording of Odetta *At the Gate of Horn*, a Roy Orbison tribute album, The Smiths *The Smiths*, B.B. King *Live in Cook County Jail*, and Bonnie Raitt *Give It Up*, which he said he had on vinyl, but not on CD," I report. I regard each of the women. "Or thereabouts."

"I told him to keep his money," Eloise says to Daisy. "But he insisted on paying. And that—that was the day that sealed Rowan's fate as a lifer. He probably still hasn't washed the hand Bruce shook."

I grin. "You're right that the incident blew my mind. But you're wrong about the reason."

I remember the Boss's visit. Who could forget something like that? Bruce Springsteen, in the flesh, in our tiny store in our tiny town, with only Eloise and me to bear witness. Up close, he was a canvas of hard, plain features. He had the early stages of a goatee to which he may or may not have ultimately committed. He talked to us. He looked us in the eye. He spoke in a gravelly grumble. He laughed at Eloise's jokes.

"I wasn't starstruck," I say to Eloise and Daisy. "To the contrary, I was struck by how un-starlike he was. He was effortlessly *not* larger than life. He was, in fact, precisely the size of life. That's what floored me that day: the ordinariness of genius, the astounding relatability of the people whose art flavors our lives with meaning and emotion." I shrug at Daisy. "I've been a junkie ever since. Can't seem to kick it. I'm sorry, but I make no apologies for it."

I say my goodbyes and till-next-times to the eternally lovely Eloise Emerson, who holds me and hugs me and kisses both my cheeks and reminds me, as she always has, to flip the record from time to time, to hear what's on the other side.

Then Daisy and I are back outside in the brunt of the midday sunlight.

"I need to get back, Rowan," she says. "I want to make the six o'clock."

"I know," I say. "We'll make it."

I see her eyebrow twitch, her nose ring sparkle like a sequin. "We?"

"I'm coming with you, Daisy."

She folds her arms, assumes an oppositional stance. "Why? Because you need a ride?"

"This town is full of people who'd fight each other to drive me to the airport," I say. "But I want to travel with you. We're going to check our bags together. I'm going to put my shoes next to yours on the security belt. I'm going to buy us snacks for the plane. I'm going to hand both of our boarding passes to the agent when they call our zone."

She smiles, thinks maybe I'm making fun of her, and maybe I am, but only a little.

"Are you going to cheat and go before our zone is called?" she asks.

"Do you want me to?"

"No. Those people are assholes."

My head bobs equivocally. "We can debate that on the plane."

We walk back to the house through this day of dazzling light, an electricity in the air that makes me feel newly born, fully awakened, kicking myself to life. Daisy and I are talking about nothing in particular when she interrupts us both and stops walking.

"Let's just make everything work when we get home," she says, sounding simultaneously exhausted and energized. "Can't we just do that?"

"I don't know," I answer. "Can we?"

"If we decide to, yes. We can be junkies together, and make no apologies for it. Let's just decide right now that that's what we're going to do."

"Okay. It's decided," I say. "What are we talking about specifically?"

"We're talking about"—she breathes grandly—"being precisely the size of life. We'll be un-starlike, you and I. Our ordinariness will be our genius."

I stare at her, humming with every emotion I've ever felt about anything. "But what if you're not un-starlike to me, Daisy? What if you're not ordinary?"

She smiles. "Then that will be our little secret."

I smile back at her. "Want to hear something crazy? I think I know exactly what you mean by all of this."

"I hope so," she says. "Because you're the one who said it, like, five minutes ago."

"Hmm. Then I agree with me."

"Want to hear something even crazier?" Daisy asks.

"Definitely."

"You left your mom's car back in town."

"Shit."

CHAPTER 38

It's a brisk goodbye on Campsite Lane. We have a plane to catch.

"Go, go. I don't want you to have to rush." That's Patti as she ushers us out. With Daisy and me carrying our luggage, Patti shooing us down the driveway, and Lulu and Breeze following along, the infant bouncing in the crook of his mother's arm, we're an unlikely coalescence, some of us total strangers to the others just days ago. We are expediting the farewells not just on account of the time crunch but because, while my mother and I are both pretty adept at being apart—we have that down to a science—saying goodbye never feels right. Although this time, it's different. Maybe that's because we'll be together again in a few weeks for Thanksgiving.

When our bags have been heaved into the trunk, I pluck Breeze from Lulu and hold him directly in front of me. I stare deep into the baby's devouring eyes. "Boy, am I glad I met you. You showed up at just the right time," I say to him. "You and I are going to be buds. I promise."

He begins to cry. Okay, I get it. He needs to think about it. I kiss him and hand him back.

I take a one-armed embrace from Lulu. She and the baby are sticking around for another couple of days, then heading back to Florida, eventually to be joined, under a separate roof, by Gram-Gram.

"By the way, I love you too," I tell her. "That's what goes through me, now that I'm, as you put it, on the other end of the telescope. I love you, I love this kid, and I'm so happy you were here."

Daisy overhears and looks shocked, like she didn't think I knew those words. But I do. I just have to earn the right to use them, find the courage to say them out loud.

"I'm sorry I was such a mess," I say to Lulu. "I'm sorry I *am* such a mess."

"You're not a mess, Rowan," she says. "Look at it this way: You know how there's a before picture and an after picture? You're a during picture."

This makes me laugh. "What does that mean? I'm somewhere in the middle? I'm lost?"

"It means you're getting there."

And once again, it feels as though Lulu is claiming me, claiming us all.

As Daisy climbs into the passenger seat, Patti grips my shoulders and puts her face close to mine. My mother's face: the first thing I ever saw, the most familiar face in the world to me. She looks like she's on the verge of a smile, then she looks like she's on the verge of tears, and then it looks like she's about to speak, and I'm hoping she will, because one of us has to, but I wonder if words matter now the way they did all the other times I left. I know I'll see her again soon. This is not a big goodbye.

Then one of my mother's favorite expressions rushes into my head, the one about waiting for the common sense of the morning, and it occurs to me that after all the waiting I've done, this was the morning when common sense finally showed up. Patti might be thinking the same thing, about the irrelevance of words, because she lets her hands fall away without saying anything.

And that's that. That's just how we leave things. Daisy and I honk, wave, and drive off. There was nothing that needed to be said.

CHAPTER 39

A few weeks later, Philly has slid down the thermometer into November, the time of year when the day clocks out early and every night is a long story.

It's just me in the store tonight, waiting out the last hour before I can lock up and bike across town to catch Daisy's concert. Her chamber orchestra is performing every night this week at a jazz club off Broad Street. The theme is adagio, which is a fancy way of saying "depressing." And beautiful. Grievously beautiful, as I discovered last night when the featured composer was Debussy, and that melancholy slow dance between piano and cello had me wishing Chili was still attending these performances with me, sitting next to me just like old times, so I could jump into his arms, as I too often came mortifyingly close to doing.

But no. I'm glad Chili's out of the picture. I can handle all the beauty and power Daisy wants to throw my way. I'm just grateful she wants to, grateful I found the courage to make it known that that's what I want.

The Wright Brothers are coming. Greg, off-putting though he generally is, was apparently not off-putting enough to put off Steel Wheel Records. I stayed out of it, let him "work his brand of magic," and he inked a deal with the label reps, showing them courtesy, competence, even some business acumen (who knew he had any of those coupons in his wallet?), and now the good old Philly boys are going to record a live set here in this beloved little tumbledown shack of ours. Steel Wheel's social media reach is staggering. Even music mogul Glen Carlo, the mere mention of whose name brings Greg to giddy giggles, tweeted about the show on his personal account. Madonna follows Glen Carlo. Barack Obama follows Glen Carlo. The show is set for the Saturday night before Christmas, and if nobody comes, it won't be because half a million people didn't know about it.

We haven't decided what to do about the lease. I'm not naive enough to bank on a one-night engagement by one semi-hot band rescuing us from the inexorable death march of our own industry. A reunion of all four Beatles couldn't do that for us, and anyway, that's not the job or the point of any artist. I am doing this for the Wrights because I love their songs and I love that they are brothers. If Holden had ever invited me to strike up a band, I would've said yes and then run out and learned an instrument. We would've made some atrocious albums and gone through some highly publicized acrimonious splits and three or four reunion tours, and it would've all been worth it. Whatever happens to Metaphysical Graffiti, I will go on being a junkie. It's a feature of mine, not a glitch. Music is everywhere. I'm on a first-name basis with the Wright Brothers. I can hear Daisy's cello whenever I want, and it's like dawn in Eden every single time. Even Skid Hall wants to soothe my soul by showering me with folk songs. If I have to walk away from this store, I will, but the music will still be the clothes I wear, the specs on my eyes. It's got me surrounded, and it's coming in.

Not long after Daisy and I got back from Illinois, I turned to Greg during a shift and asked if his offer to join his writers' workshop was still open. He blushed with self-congratulation, like what took me so long? An overpowering sense of inadequacy and intimidation: that's what took me so long. I went that week and joined his group of roughly a dozen passionate men and women, most of them younger than I am, one or two a good bit older. The woman who runs it, an English teacher at Central High, assigns a theme or a form, and we have to show up the following week prepared to discuss and share the fruits of our creativity. My first assignment: pick someone you used to know, and write five pages about meeting that person for coffee. I chose Dov Halevi, the exchange student whose party radically altered the trajectory of my senior year, of some of my most important relationships, of the next fifteen years of my life. In the scene, Dov had no idea that any of those critical events had happened at his party, and when I told him, fictional Dov found it hilarious. He fell off his chair. When he climbed back on, he asked the server to top him off, then proceeded to tell me about his wife and kids in Tel Aviv. Why, I wondered, had I made him react that way? Why had that seemed the most natural thing for that character? That intrigued me, which is why I go back to the workshop every week with an itch to say more, to continue to shovel away into the sand and see what's crawling around down there. I understand now why Margot invented Julianna Goodheart—or why she invented Portia Wentworth, who invented Julianna Goodheart. I told her so:

I'm writing again, I texted her after starting up. I guess after all, YOU inspired ME.

We inspired each other, she wrote back. Isn't that what good writers do? And good friends?

I texted back a heart.

I still don't play the cello, but I'm learning to play the proverbial cello. Now, when Greg and I are alone in the store, he's not the only one at work on some feat of literature.

With fifteen minutes to go before close, I breeze through the nightly humiliation of reconciling the cash register to the receipts (the user manual for our point-of-sale system outlines a "process" for this, which, when applied to our venture, is both laughable and insulting; our process consists of peering into the drawer and muttering like a cranky grandpa), and just as I am about to shut down, a shiny new email graces my inbox. It's from Alex Hall-Beckett, from whom I have not heard since my exodus from Maybee. I texted him once, weeks ago, after I learned that his parents were separating. He didn't write back.

Margot stayed at that cabin for three more nights, then returned home and told Skid she wanted to get an apartment. They were too young to be working so hard to be happy, she said. It wasn't a terrific shock to Skid; he sounds okay. We've been speaking at least once a week. I'll check in on him when I walk out for lunch or when a song comes on in the store that reminds me of home. He calls me on the way to school or on Saturday mornings when he's waiting for Alex to wake up. I've texted a little with Margot too. I told her I was sorry, and she told me not to be, that now that she and Skid don't have to worry as much about each other, they can focus on Alex. I told her I meant what I said, that I'll always be here.

Alex's email is short, a couple of lines; he writes with the same economy with which he speaks. He apologizes for not texting me back weeks earlier and says he just didn't know what to say. But things are okay, he's adjusting, and both his parents seem to be on an upswing.

Alex also reports that his tutelage under Eloise is ongoing and has, in fact, progressed to the point where he is picking up shifts at her store, after school and on weekends. He jokes that he's following in the footsteps of another illustrious Gravedancer alum, which seems misguided to say the least, there being no future in it, but I would argue it's still a better use of one's time than stealing pigs with the neighborhood reprobates.

His email concludes with, I hope you don't mind that I did this, and then a link. I click it, and a video file launches onto my screen.

I hear the sound before I see the images. A stately piano and drum waltz: the opening measures of "Dream Operator," my brother's favorite Talking Heads song until it became mine, or my favorite Talking Heads song until it became his, which is the version of history that sits best with me. Then a photo fades in, and to my surprise, I am looking at Holden and me. We are standing in the kitchen on Campsite Lane, grinning for the camera, each of us with an arm slung over the other's winter sweater. I've never seen this before, this picture from the holidays that my mother must've taken no more than three or four years ago. I study Holden's features for hints of restlessness, some clue that he was with me in person but over the state line in spirit. That was what I always feared. But I don't see that now. I see him present. He's there.

A moment later, the shot dissolves and another blooms in its place. In this one I'm two or three, clad in overalls (overalls, Patti?) and dangling precariously on my brother's lap. He's got one hand on my waist, and I appear to be sliding, so chances are I was on the floor seconds after this picture was snapped.

Then that one's gone, and now I'm looking at two teenagers in my brother's bedroom. It's an action shot, and the story it tells is that of a headlock being thrust upon me the instant before the shutter contracted. Holden's features are distorted in wild laughter, and the part of my face visible from the restraint of his clenched arm looks pissed. I'm sure I punched him in the shoulder immediately afterward, and I'm sure he kept laughing.

Another fade-out and fade-in, and I'm seven or eight, Holden just cracking the teens. It's the dead of winter, and we're bundled up in coats, gloves, and ski hats in a foot of snow in our backyard. You can see the red in our cheeks and spots of blurriness where flecks of precipitation have smeared the lens.

They keep coming, one after another, lost relics excavated from god knows where, blushing and receding for the entirety of the song, a montage of a shared childhood that, it turns out, was more shared than I recalled. Most of the photos were taken when we were both young, but there are, thrillingly, some rarities from recent times, snapshots of documented moments I'd lost track of. But they happened. So many things happened, and now I have proof. Memories don't care if they're remembered or forgotten.

I am wondering how Alex pulled this off, and though I don't put breaking and entering past him, I will later learn that he came to my mother's house and requested access to her few family albums, to the plastic bags stuffed with loose snapshots, to the hard drive, to any place in which old photographs might be hiding. He told her how I'd lamented all the photo ops of Holden and me that never happened, that there was virtually nothing to mark our history since the day he left home, and now that he was gone, history was over. Alex asked her if there was anything in Patti's house that might prove me wrong, and she said she doubted it, but would be most grateful to be proven wrong herself.

It turns out there's more than I'd remembered. No jetting off to Vegas or Jazzfest, no baseball stadium road trips, but plenty of small moments, moments that came, hovered over us, drenched us, then moved on.

And there was a dog! After everything, my mother was right. A dog! All I have to do is see one photo of eight-year-old Rowan down on the rug on all fours, facing off with an inquisitive beagle, the two of us playfully barking into each other's faces, a frank exchange of views, and back comes that summer when our neighbors spent two months in Australia and left us their puppy. His name was Crickett, and I cried when they came for him on Labor Day weekend, and Holden cried, and Patti saw us and she cried too, so we begged her for a dog of our own, and she said forget it, it's out of the question. If a monumental make-out session with Becca Fitzpatrick can slip my mind, I suppose I can forget all about the affectionate hound who slept on my pillow and who licked the broccoli from my palm under the table so my mother couldn't see. Memories don't care if they're remembered or forgotten. There was a dog!

When the song ends and the screen goes black, my fingers hang over the keyboard as I consider how to thank the fourteen-year-old who did this. But I want to watch this montage again, sink into it, then try to find the words to tell Alex what it means to me. I glance up at the framed napkin, the one with David Byrne's signature, which used to hang in Holden's house and now hangs in my store. When Lulu handed it to me, I mistakenly thought it was Holden's signature. Had it been, I think I still would've posted it on the wall.

I shut the laptop, kill the lights, lock the door behind me.

I pedal through the wind and the traffic on Walnut Street, chain my bike to a parking sign, and am settled into a table in the sultry warmth of the club, whiskey and bitters in front of me, just as Daisy and the four other musicians onstage glide into their first adagio. She is wearing a black dress, and her mane glows in the spotlight with richness and dimension, like those velour shirts from the '70s I've seen in old photos of my father. The piece is slow and winding—I'll bet it's a *meditation*, or a *study*—more cozy than elegiac, although maybe that's just how it meets this particular listener's ear on this particular night. The music seems to move like some fabled winged creature from an ancient culture's mythology—graceful and balletic, an exquisite, delicate force that sweeps quietly through the streets when everyone is asleep, and then when it reaches the edge of the city, it lifts off into our dreams.

Dreams: I had the one about Holden again last night, the one where he comes to the Graffiti in the midst of a storm. It always keeps me awake for a long time after, staring up at the fuzzy black expanse of my ceiling, trying to record the images in my memory so that when the sun finally crests, the feel of it will still be deep in my gut, the taste of it still on the back of my tongue.

The dream comes all the time now; it is as though I'm summoning it. Holden shows up at the store, stands in the doorway toting a kayak or canoe, some ill-considered and overmatched vessel, and proceeds to beckon me down to the river.

Which river? I ask.

But I know which river.

The one behind our house, he says.

Which house? I ask.

I know which house.

Are you coming? he asks.

The forecast is the worst it's ever been. Gale-force winds, sheets of rain. It's a promise, not a threat, this storm; I've seen the sky, dark and full of motion, an ominous crackle of drumfire way up on high.

Are you coming? he asks again.

What about Dad? I say to him. *Dad says we need to stay home until he gets back.*

Let me worry about Dad, Holden says. Because he knew him.

I know Holden is going in, and I know I can't stop him. The best I can do is stay beside him.

You're scared, he says.

Yes. For both of us.

He smiles. *It's okay. The fear is the worst of it. Trust me.* Something in his eyes shifts. *Do you trust me?*

And so we go, and that's my answer.

We step out of the store, and everybody was wrong except Holden, because the skies are an incredible cloudless blue, and up into them we sail like we're riding a balloon to the moon, and I'm laughing and he's laughing, and we don't say a word because we can hear each other's thoughts. And this is what we're both thinking:

There has never been a better time to fly.

ACKNOWLEDGMENTS

I've had the privilege of working on this book with talented, committed, and good people, and I am immensely grateful for their sweat, support, and patience:

Caryn Karmatz Rudy of DeFiore and Company, my terrific agent, who has guided me and my books in all the right directions;

The insightful, enthusiastic, and outrageously kind Chris Werner and his incredible team of creatives at Lake Union;

Tiffany Yates Martin, whose developmental edits are truly inspiring, who is an absolute blast to work with, who just makes books better—a lot better—and who makes me want to write better, and who has a picture with Colin Hay;

David Small, one of my favorite authors, still showing me the way after nearly thirty years;

Some wonderfully supportive friends: Marc Greenberg, Michael and Jamie Cohen, Gregg Marsano, Andy and Kelly Goldenberg, Melissa April, Jonathan Palmatier, Amy Montemarano, Rich Coughlin, Kim Roosevelt, Philip Glahn, Nell McClister, and Omar and Gerlinde Harb;

Elliott Langbaum, my boundlessly kind and generous father-in-law;

Michelle and Jon, who have given me a deep well of rich, happy experiences to draw upon when I write about siblings (the bad stuff I had to make up)—I am so lucky to have you both, and I'm grateful that you both married so well (thank you, Mitch and Stacy);

My parents, Ferne and Les Abramowitz, whose bookshelves and record collection inspired me from my earliest days, and whose warmth and love and goodness have inspired me every day since;

Chloe and Chelsea—my beautiful "babies," always two-thirds of what matters most;

And, of course, the lovely and only-getting-lovelier Caryn, who knows how I feel.

AA

ABOUT THE AUTHOR

Photo © 2019 Jonathan Palmatier

Andy Abramowitz is the author of two previous novels, *A Beginner's Guide to Free Fall* and *Thank You, Goodnight*. A native of Baltimore, Andy lives with his wife, two daughters, and their dog, Rufus, in Philadelphia, where he enjoys classic rock, pitchers' duels, birthday cake, the sound of a Fender Rhodes piano, and the month of October. He is also a lawyer.